Stories for Men...
and Women with spirit

AZZARO
by Roger Pullen

A Trilogy – Part II

Includes Chapter 1 of **DIVIDEND,** part 3 of the trilogy

Published by Tigermoth

AZZARO

The right of Roger Pullen to be identified as the author
of this work has been asserted by him in accordance with the
Copyright, Designs and Patents Act 1988.

Copyright © Roger Pullen 2009

Azzaro first published 2009

Cover design by www.design-ig.co.uk

A CIP catalogue record for this book is available from the
British Library

ISBN: 978-0-9562714-1-9

Tigermoth is a division of Royalblue Ltd

www.tigermothbooks.com
tigermothinfo@me.com

ONE

Take-off had been five hours ago. A cluster of chilled, hunched figures had waved encouragingly from the lee side of the temporary control tower as the aircraft lined up in turn, facing down the slush-covered runway. Once airborne, they gathered, a small, tight flock of five, setting course eastwards as the pale, winter light extinguished behind them.

Nine hundred miles on, and nearing the point of no return, Michael Kelly looked around from the cockpit of his lead aircraft. The ruby-red pinpoints of navigation lights of two other machines held station in the darkness far below, way out on their starboard side. But where were the other two aircraft? The weather had not been kind, despite the Met man's promises. Hopefully the crews of the absent aircraft had remembered the detailed procedures he'd set out during their briefing and were safe, although not in touch.

He was concerned. Had he done and said everything he could to help? But they were all highly experienced and knew the risks of flying the route in an unforgiving northern winter. He also knew too well that any serious failure of man or machine would almost certainly lead to a solitary end in the heaving wastes below.

He'd spoken to Sarah, his new wife, briefly the previous afternoon over a crackly transatlantic telephone line that had taken almost three days to arrange. Her voice was tense at the prospect of his long flight at this time of year.

Since returning to London from Singapore in the final cold, grey and depressing days of November 1938 there had been many issues for Michael Kelly to resolve, not least of which was learning to walk again after the crude but vital emergency amputation of his lower right leg, following the enforced ditching of the Empress Airways flying boat Cornucopia in the storm-tossed Bay of Bengal. Sarah's divorce had finally come through from her husband, who was in the army in India, and she and Michael had married at Westminster's Caxton Hall in a civil ceremony, after Alistair's birth. He was a sturdy eight-and-a-half-pound boy, who had inherited his mother's classic looks – blue eyes and tufts of curly blond hair. Alistair was not Michael's but he loved him as he would his own. Michael was out of work and they were living off the remains of his final cheque of appreciation from Empress Airways. Trying not to plunder Sarah's fortune, they had moved from her comfortable apartment in a quiet part of Belgravia in West London to less extravagant accommodation: a Victorian farmhouse with a few acres of land, set in the rolling Hampshire countryside north of Winchester.

The phone call and the opportunity to fly again was a gift, and he volunteered immediately. To his surprise, he was accepted without qualms.

◆ ◆ ◆

Bitter, damp cold penetrated his bones. The draughty wooden hut barely kept the freezing wind at bay. With his back to an ancient cast-iron pot-bellied stove – a permanent cherry-red, day and night – he scanned the leaden skies. An uncontrolled shiver went through him at the prospect of nine or ten hours up there. The rotting windows rattled noisily as each blast struck their

grimy panes. The scene beyond was a bleak monochrome of grubby whiteness scattered with stark black hangars and wooden accommodation huts.

He thought himself lucky. Some of their flight and ground crews were really suffering; sleeping and eating in ancient unheated railway carriages brought in especially by the Newfoundland Railway Company while proper accommodation was hastily erected in the heavy earth under wet snow. But the priority had always been the airfield; far off to his left he could see dark outlines of monster bulldozers and trucks moving jerkily in the embryonic landscape and chugging palls of black smoke into the icy air.

Kelly remembered reading somewhere in a rare idle moment that construction had actually begun in 1936; a year later there were no less than nine hundred men working in this God-forsaken spot to build what would finally be four long paved runways. In one of the dilapidated wooden offices a simple placard celebrated the fact that in January 1938 Gander was officially opened for operations when a tiny de Havilland Fox Moth aircraft operated by Imperial Airways had landed there; an understated precursor of what was to come. Pulling his collar up and his heavy dark-blue uniform coat tightly around him, Michael Kelly yanked open the warped wooden door and stepped out into Gander's seasonal sub-zero temperatures.

Known until quite recently as Hattie's Camp and literally carved out of the raw muskeg, the new aerodrome had been rechristened Gander, taking its new name from a nearby lake. Now, apart from the growing runways, there were hard aircraft dispersals, taxiways and aprons well under way or completed. Lying on a remote

tract of once-heavily forested land in Newfoundland off Canada's eastern seaboard, the new Gander airport had become the final jumping-off point for aircraft bound for deprived and depraved wartime Europe. And a place of plenty, safety and temporary relaxation for tired crews battling from the east against prevailing weather systems, onward bound for Montreal and all points in luxurious North America.

Compacted stained snow and ice lay rutted on the well-trodden path that lay between his spartan quarters and the flight operations hangar six hundred yards away. It was an exposed and windswept route. They were the sort of conditions that he detested on the ground. His 'tinny' leg, as his five-year-old step-daughter Beth had christened it, had already proved to be a liability on such a surface – his rump and elbows bore recent and bruised testament to that.

A few flakes of new snow swirled around him as he faced into the cutting north-west wind. He briefly contrasted his new situation with the warmth and humidity of his previous position, based in Singapore, as a senior captain of a huge 'C' Class flying boat with Empress Airways. That was, until the unheralded storm and their forced ditching in enormous curling seas in the Bay of Bengal. It had caused the loss of passengers' lives – and his lower right leg – with, ultimately, no blame ascribed to him. His shortened limb had now been supplemented with a cleverly constructed aluminium prosthesis that under normal conditions was highly satisfactory, but his tinny leg was unreliable on these treacherous winter surfaces.

Out of a job after his employers, Empress Airways, had had all of their aircraft requisitioned by the Air Ministry just before

the outbreak of hostilities with Germany, Kelly had been invited by an old BOAC contact to join the crews that were flying vital military aircraft from America and Canada to England, so saving dangerous weeks at sea – and the need to reassemble and test machines that had been dismantled and crated for the ocean-crossing. Michael's contact explained the background: the Atlantic Ferry Organisation, quickly put together by Lord Beaverbrook, Churchill's Minister for Aircraft Production, had been rapidly created so that no time should be lost in delivering new machines to help fight the Nazi threat. This bold and dangerous venture was being led by ex-RAF and former Imperial Airways captain Don Bennett, who had been appointed as Flying Superintendent for the whole complex transatlantic ferry operation.

◆ ◆ ◆

Despite the fact that Australia was the land of their births, separated by just two years, Michael Kelly and Don Bennett had never met, though there were many parallels in their early-life experiences.

Both learned to fly with the RAAF at Point Cook, and both later sailed from Australia to England to fly with the RAF. Both had learnt to operate flying boats from Pembroke Dock in south-west Wales and later at Calshot in the protected waters of the Solent, between the Isle of Wight and Southampton. However, severely disillusioned with peacetime flying in the RAF, and the pedantic and short-sighted nature of some of its commanders, Michael Kelly left the service with some regrets in 1933.

Bennett followed, resigning his commission in 1935 but not before he had gained a sound reputation for his navigational skills and flying training expertise, largely on flying boats. He enjoyed some early fame in 1934 while still serving with the RAF through entering the MacRobertson Air Race, from England to Melbourne. Starting from Mildenhall in Suffolk on England's east coast in late October, Bennett and his navigator made good time as far as Aleppo in northern Syria, where their aircraft, a single-engine Lockheed Vega, overturned on landing while being flown by his co-pilot, Woods. Depressed, and after a trip back home to Australia, Bennett joined Imperial Airways flying their European, Middle East and South African routes.

Out of the RAF, and despite being keen to continue flying in his new civilian life, Michael Kelly spent time in various non-flying jobs, working for brief periods in shipping and in the oil industry – he found most of it, stuck at a viewless desk in central London, soul-destroying and was seriously contemplating a return to his native Perth in Western Australia. Lunch with some business colleagues of his managing director led, some days later, to an evening telephone call and an early-morning meeting with Sir Claude Vickers, chairman of the embryonic airline Empress Airways. The new airline were intending to take delivery of five new four-engined flying boats after Imperial Airways had received all of their order for twenty-eight type S.23 Empire Flying Boats, or 'C' Class boats, as they became known, from Short's, the builders, at their Rochester factory in north Kent, flying them finally off the River Medway. It was a calculated risk; competing with the State-supported Imperial Airways, but Sir Claude and the new Empress Board, including Michael Kelly, enjoyed and were prepared for a challenge. Joining as their senior pilot, Michael Kelly led the pioneering mail and passenger routes to Darwin for Empress, operating from a new flying-boat base at

Sandbanks, near Poole, in Dorset, on England's south coast.

Arriving intact, and slightly relieved, at the substantial wooden extension built onto the rear of one black hangar, he made his way gingerly towards the entrance door feeling cold but safe. Pushing the heavy door open, he was enveloped by a fug of tobacco, wood smoke and damp humanity as he climbed the three gritted steps into a large well-lit room. Inside were dozens of pilots, radio operators and navigators, all chattering noisily nineteen to the dozen: American, English, French, Poles and Czechs, and some of indeterminate nationality; all with a diverse mix of valuable, and sometimes hair-raising, flying experience.

Turning as the open door unleashed untainted blasts of arctic air through the gathering, they quietened momentarily. Some shouted greetings of recognition; others looked on, assessing the man now taking off his heavy coat and shaking the snow from it. Some were to be his men for the next twelve hours, and they were a truly mixed bunch.

Before his pioneering first flight of seven Lockheed Hudson bombers across the North Atlantic in November 1940, Don Bennett had established a set of routines and standard procedures for ferrying much-needed aircraft to the Royal Air Force and Royal Navy's Fleet Air Arm. The Hudson was a welcome and necessary replacement for the RAF's Avro Anson, which had eventually proved less than suitable for the hazardous wartime roles assigned to it, including patrolling the unforgiving seas around Britain as part of the RAF's Coastal Command.

Successfully developed as a military version of the Lockheed Company's twin-engine Super Electra passenger airliner, the Hudson had been flown briefly by Michael Kelly while he had been attached for three short weeks to the government's purchasing commission in Washington DC. He'd been impressed with its speed, equipment and handling.

Half a dozen of the men now watching Kelly had been on Don Bennett's inaugural flight; the first non-stop delivery across the Atlantic in early winter. Other successful crossings had been undertaken since, and now, three months later, Michael Kelly was going to lead a smaller but equally valuable formation into the coming night skies aiming to arrive on Prestwick's new tarmac runways on Scotland's Ayrshire coast in about nine or ten hours – if the meteorological people had got their forecast of tailwinds right – he'd spent some time with them and their spidery synoptic charts immediately before lunch.

Ensconced in a wooden box-like extension to the new control tower and huddled around a brightly glowing stove like a coven, the Met men's view, with all of their inevitable caveats, mumbo-jumbo and hieroglyphics, was that the weather now casting its depressing spell over Newfoundland would move swiftly off into the North Atlantic, leaving them almost-clear skies during the early evening and the first part of their transatlantic flight. Three days earlier, the initial leg of their long journey had begun at Dorval airport, just outside Montreal, where the Atlantic Ferry Organisation HQ was located; from there they had flown in safe company and clear, bright weather along the well-established Canadian airways following a regular series of radio navigation beacons; it had been a piece of cake, they all agreed. Beyond Newfoundland's eastern shores no navigation beacons existed to provide easy step-by-step guidance to far-off Europe; it was more akin to flying by Braille, as one of his captains had pointed out, looking concerned at the stark emptiness of the landless charts in front of them.

Michael Kelly moved carefully through the hubbub of mingling men, smiling, exchanging greetings and occasionally shaking hands or thumping someone on the back, before relaxing on a tall stool set against a wall supporting a huge map of the North Atlantic. Eastern Canada and Western Europe formed its extreme left and right margins. He began the briefing. He was going to lead five Hudsons in loose formation nearly two thousand miles across an empty, inhospitable, winter ocean. Empty, save for U-boats and their prey: vital convoys of deeply laden ships with their crucial supplies of military equipment, food and oil for an isolated but increasingly defiant Britain.

The next hour and forty-five minutes were spent briefing the crews: the route, what action to take if separated from the group, engine revolutions to maximise range, and the need to maintain radio silence except in an emergency, particularly as they came within range of enemy ships and aircraft approaching Europe. Kelly had opted for the classic great-circle route to Prestwick – the shortest distance across – instead of breaking the journey and calling at either Goose Bay in Labrador or the new American-built Bluie West 1 airfield on Greenland's south-eastern coast – at the end of a long and dangerously fog-prone fiord.

He knew that the airfields in Greenland and Iceland were popular, and they were often included by some crews in their flight plans, depending on their experience and the forecast weather, and also, crucially, their need for cheap and tax-free booze and nylons. But each of his five aircraft would have two highly experienced pilots on board, one of whom was fully qualified and licensed as a navigator able to take astro sightings of the stars and other heavenly bodies en route, to complement their dead-reckoning and radio navigation. The third member of each crew was the wireless operator/gunner, able to report their advancing position from radio bearings on distant navigation beacons, complementing the pilot navigator's sextant skills as they approached blacked-out Europe.

There were questions and some lengthy discussion about altitudes to be flown to avoid the sometimes-catastrophic results of airframe and engine icing. During winter in particular it was of real concern to his pilots, particularly as later that night the small formation would catch up with frozen air captive in the depression that was wending its way slowly across the Atlantic ahead of them. Finally satisfied, the five crews went to the mess for their last unrationed meal. Just over an hour later a battered and muddy American-built five-ton truck with a ripped and flapping canvas cover picked the airmen up from their various accommodations, transporting them out to their aircraft, which were standing remote and inert in wet snow and treacly, dark earth.

Arriving at their individual machines, they jumped from the battered truck carrying charts, bulky flying clothing and precious boxes of rations including Thermos flasks. They laughed and joked with forced bonhomie, wishing each other luck and the promise of haggis and beer in Scotland tomorrow. Most of them hadn't a clue what a haggis was. Michael Kelly's crew was the last to be dropped. It was just before two-thirty in the afternoon, and the daylight had almost run its course.

Their Hudson bomber sat lifeless, cold, its metal freezing the hands of those foolish enough to let them linger too long on its exposed camouflaged surfaces. The ground crews had been motivated by the cold to keep busy, warmed by sweeping wet snow off the wings and tailplanes and applying thick, sticky anti-icing paste to the machine's propellers and wing's leading edges. It was a time-consuming and laborious activity on the exposed airfield, some doubting its efficacy. Finally settled into the left-hand seat, Kelly commenced his pre-start checks for the twin-engined machine.

Sitting alongside him, his co-pilot, Paul Mossman, a Canadian, called the list of items. Kelly undertook the checks carefully; the machine had to be one hundred per cent for this long and potentially dangerous sortie. Mossman was a young man, late twenties, Kelly guessed. Paul had learned to fly with his father around the wastes of north-western Canada and Alaska and in doing so had acquired rare skills and an instinctive understanding of his chosen craft. He'd volunteered for Atlantic Ferry just after his father's death; his mother had died some years earlier, so now there was nothing tying him to the coastal town of Prince Rupert, north-west of Vancouver. He'd never been too far from Canada's beautifully rugged western seaboard; a chance to go east and to see England tickled his fancy and innate sense of adventure. Mossman didn't say much, but Kelly instinctively knew he was a man he could trust, both on the ground and in the air. Typical outback Canadian, he was tough, above average height, and well built, a reflection of one or two years spent logging instead of at university. He had a well-deserved reputation for being able to drink most men under the table, and with a wide, open smile below unkempt dark hair, was immediately loved by any woman that came within his orbit.

Three minutes later Kelly opened the side window to signal to the relieved ground crew that they were ready to start. Making a circular motion with a finger, he pushed the starter button, and the propeller on the port engine turned slowly, its oil, cold and viscous, making difficult work for the straining starter motor. Eventually, after some stuttering, the Wright Cyclone settled into a regular beat, followed by its identical twin on the starboard side. The machine was alive, vibrating; even beginning to warm slightly as limited hot air was ducted into the tight cockpit. Behind, in the empty fuselage, a temporary additional fuel tank had been fitted at the Lockheed factory in Burbank, California. They would need all the available fuel for their long ocean-crossing.

Looking around the crescent of parked aircraft, Kelly noted with satisfaction the shimmering discs of their spinning propellers in the harsh, white light from lamps placed around the remote aircraft dispersals. Behind their windscreens they watched, waiting for him to make his move. Thumbing the radio transmit button on the control wheel, he advised the air-traffic controller that they were ready. Waving 'chocks away' to the shivering and hunched ground crew, he released the brakes. Opening the throttles gently and taxiing clear of the dispersal, they turned left onto the slush-carpeted taxiway passing in front of Kelly's gently growling flock. The surface was unfinished in places, and he and Mossman watched carefully, avoiding areas where the machine might become bogged down.

Just short of the long runway Kelly carried out final checks on the health of the machine in general – its engines in particular – temperature one hundred and twenty degrees, oil pressure sixty-five pounds per square inch, all magnetos on, OK. With all other checks completed, Mossman confirmed, after twisting right around in his seat, that the rest of their small air fleet were behind them, lined up and waiting.

"Seems no problems during the taxi, Skipper." Kelly nodded and grunted an acknowledgement into his face-mike.

Their noisy rush down the runway was punctuated by sharp decelerations as the wheels cut through piles of slush or huge puddles of icy water that had failed to drain off the near-freezing concrete surfaces. Despite this, the main wheels lifted clear well before the runway's end and they drew away from the land with twenty-three hundred revolutions showing for both engines, and a speed of one hundred and twenty miles per hour.

Climbing steadily and turning the aircraft gently to the left, Kelly allowed the undercarriage to remain down for a few minutes, encouraging the speeding air to blow icy water off its streaming-wet mechanisms – it could freeze at altitude and give problems when they eventually selected 'down' for landing. Turning to look over his left shoulder, he could just see that the second aircraft was airborne behind them, the twin beams from its yellow wavering landing lamps like probing fingers piercing the dense, cold air; the third aircraft, he noticed, had now commenced its take-off roll. They made a wide orbit of the darkening airfield, allowing the remaining four Hudsons to climb and formate on them in a wide 'V' before setting an easterly course out over the black ocean. Minutes later the lights of Newtown and Wesleyville sparkled invitingly up at them as they left the coast over Cape Freels at one hundred and forty-five miles per hour and climbing slowly into clear, star-spangled indigo.

The depression that had inflicted so much cold and wet on Gander over the previous two days had departed North America to the east, as forecast by the Met men. What these same weather wizards had not fully predicted was that the depression would finally stall as it butted up against a newly developing area of high pressure drifting lazily south from the Arctic and Greenland's high frozen tundra. The widely spaced 'V' formation of five Hudsons soon reached the near-stationary weather system, plunging headlong into its heavy mass of dark, swirling stratus from behind. Instinctively, the pilots of the five aircraft separated further, the danger of collision uppermost in their minds as they entered the ragged, wet cloud. Every so often they emerged briefly from its folds as they continued east, eyes alert, each crew counting their fellow travellers and their relative positions before they plunged again into roiling grey vapour.

Then, for a while, they were able to fly with their special station-keeping lights clearly visible to each other, a formation spread wide in the clear, freezing air, sandwiched between two opaque layers of dark grey murk. Now and again there would be a clunk or bang from somewhere behind them as pieces of melting ice detached from wing or propeller. It had been quietly accumulating like some insidious disease in the dark as the machines had driven up through clouds of freezing moisture. The noise was felt as much as heard. Chunks struck the fuselage side or tailplane, shattering, then arcing down thousands of feet to the ocean.

After four and a half hours their sandwich of clear air was consumed, the two levels merging in the darkness into a single dense, unstable mass. They droned on, now and again the aircraft lurching unpredictably and violently in the system's turbulence.

Working quietly behind the two pilots, Peter Gaul, the radio operator, spent his time taking radio navigation bearings on any of the few available powerful radio beacons within range: Bermuda, way to the south, Bluie West 1, Largens in the Azores, and much later he would hear Prestwick itself. There had been no opportunity to use the sextant for star shots over the last hours, the sky above them completely obscured by hundreds, possibly thousands of feet of turbulent, icy water molecules.

Mossman was now in control. Michael Kelly had left his seat, stretching his legs and taking time to look at his charts and the radio plots gathered by their wireless operator/gunner, Peter Gaul. Together they studied the information, holding firmly onto the aircraft as it bounced and lurched unpredictably across the sky. Kelly's thoughts returned continually to his co-flyers, out there somewhere in the heaving darkness. The hot coffee from the Thermos was seriously welcome. Now, at nine thousand feet, the outside air was well below freezing and inside he doubted that the temperature inside was much above that. Their bulky, sometimes awkward Sidcot flying suits were fully vindicated in the conditions.

Mossman called Kelly back to the cockpit; he was experiencing difficulty in maintaining height, and the machine was handling sluggishly. The next two hours had them worried and fighting to keep the Hudson free of accumulating ice. They descended every so often to the marginally warmer air near the surface of the sea, where it might be persuaded to melt and break free. There was the ever-present risk of damage should large chunks strike some vital area such as the elevators, stuck out at the tail extremities of the aircraft.

On one occasion they flew so low in their desperate attempt to dump the weighing ice that as they fell out of the lowering cloud base they found themselves barely two hundred feet above the Atlantic's heaving, white-scored surface.

As they maintained a great-circle course to faraway Prestwick, the cloud base sank lower until it almost merged with the sea; forward visibility at times became nil in the cloud and near-darkness. This was highly dangerous instrument flying, with no real reference points to allow them to gauge their height accurately, so they were forced to rely on their two altimeters, whose sensitivity in indicating proximity to the sea was normally considered dubious at such low levels. Climbing the machine again, Kelly decided to look for clear air away from the maw of the ocean. The Hudson rocked and rolled violently as it clawed up through the increasingly turbulent mass, engines roaring solidly and comfortingly either side them.

Later, safe on the ground, coffee and cigarette in hand, they talked light-heartedly and with ill-disguised relief about those worrying couple of hours as they had sought the safety of clear air away from unpredictable turbulence and the freezing moisture quietly accumulating on their aircraft, weighing them down.

Eventually it was past; after a final bout of severe turbulence they had finally overtaken the intense weather system and were now cruising comfortably at five thousand feet in smoother, brighter air. Glancing around the horizon, Mossman saw them first; way off to the right and some way below. Two aircraft loosely formating on each other were heading in the same direction as themselves. They still had their navigation lights illuminated despite orders, two pinpoint red jewels dancing in the gloom. It had to be two of his flock; who else would be wandering about mid-ocean on a night like this, Kelly surmised with some relief. Peter Gaul focused the aircraft's powerful Aldis lamp on the two machines sending a short burst of white Morse to confirm their identity. A minute later both aircraft acknowledged – it was them.

He was tired. He'd managed to snatch a star shot of Betelgeuse with the sextant through the gunner's Perspex-covered turret as the upper layers of cloud had thinned and broken open for a few brief miles. Ten minutes later, after laborious calculations with a cold-dulled brain that seemed unable to engage fully with the problem, the outcome from his single star sighting was a general confirmation that they were roughly where he had anticipated they would be, with some six hundred miles still to run. With help from a strengthening tailwind and the two roaring Wright Cyclones, they should be settling onto Prestwick's new hard runway in just over three hours.

They kept looking, scanning the sky around every one of three hundred and sixty degrees. Where were the other two Hudsons? Pale shafts of daylight were beginning to penetrate the layers of cloud ahead, and despite his worries Kelly decided to doze, slumped uncomfortably in the cabin behind the radio operator's position. Soon he would need all his faculties about him as full daylight, hastened by their flight eastwards, brought increased dangers from lurking enemy aircraft.

The need to be alert and prepared for a landing at what would be a new airfield for them was vital. Fifty minutes passed before Paul Mossman's nasal Canadian twang cut in over the intercom. Kelly awoke with a start, uncomfortable and stiff; it was almost full daylight; the soft grey light cast a metallic sheen on the sea thousands of feet below. They were closing the west coast of the Irish Republic, he knew; occasional fishing boats began to appear plunging south-east on their way home in an unremarkable dawn.

Mossman was pointing out to his right, quietly commenting over the intercom that he'd seen something three or four miles away to the south of their position at about the same height. He thought he'd seen the brief silhouette of a large four-engine aircraft weaving stealthily downwards through layers of broken cloud. Kelly took control while his co-pilot and radio operator watched the southern skies intently where the aircraft had been spotted.

"Perhaps its one of the Hudsons," articulated Gaul over the intercom.

Mossman shook his head and grunted emphatically into the mike in his facemask.

"Uh-huh. Four engines, definitely."

Their first clue came from somewhere else. Unusual movement in the wave patterns below them began to show on the sea's face – a series of merging 'V's etched for a few minutes on its long, rolling surface. Broken cloud a thousand feet or so below them precluded their sighting of the cause, but from experience both pilots suspected a large ship or ships. Then it was exposed, ploughing a determined course just north of east: a convoy of ships, eight long lines of deeply laden vessels, each line set up for twelve plodding transports of one sort or another. Here and there, cutting a white swathe through the grey seas, the dark shape of a grey-blue camouflaged naval vessel turned and metaphorically prodded some of the slower or out-of-station merchantmen onwards. It was noticeable that most of the lines were incomplete – empty spaces – mute evidence of recent death and deep, crushing destruction, no doubt delivered after dark by a deceitful hidden enemy.

Not wanting to be fired on by the convoy's naval escort, Kelly, in control, climbed the Hudson, banking sharply away from the lines of ships towards the south. From their present course he guessed that the depleted convoy was headed for either Liverpool or Glasgow intending to round Malin Head, which jutted out from Northern Ireland's welcoming coast, promising safety and the delight of sleep in warm, dry beds for those who eventually made it.

The two Hudsons they had seen earlier during the night had now closed with Kelly's machine, once again in a loose 'V' formation, rocking their wings gesturing 'Hello' in the daylight – still no sight or sound from the two missing aircraft. Just fifty miles or so off Ireland's west coast the cloud was broken, the air becoming unstable as they caught up with the tail of another intense winter depression that was presently dumping its cargo of cold rain onto the partially neutral island ahead.

Its plan silhouette was visible for barely a split second as the large aircraft turned, steeply banking downwards across their path, right to left, about a mile or so ahead, sliding from one thin cloud layer into another below. In the instant available they could discern that its dark shape bore the faint white outlines of German markings on its exposed undersides, and it had four engines.

"Jeez!" Mossman breathed. Kelly had seen it too and pulled

the Hudson sharply around, hoping that the two following machines in their loose formation were sufficiently awake to his manoeuvring. He guessed that the German machine they had just spotted was descending through the cloud, hoping to report accurately on the convoy they had seen a few minutes earlier.

"Wireless! Man the turret – quick!" Kelly barked urgently through the intercom.

Pushing his charts away, Peter Gaul moved quickly down the fuselage towards the Perspex-shrouded mid-upper turret with its two .303 machine-guns. Then he remembered: they were not carrying ammunition, in the interests of weight-saving, allowing for more precious fuel to carry them across the Atlantic. Plugging in his intercom, Kelly swore silently as Gaul's comments crackled in his headphones.

They could not attack what they had now identified as a large Luftwaffe four-engine Focke-Wulf Condor; but they would certainly attempt to upset its reporting activities, shouted Kelly above the increasing engine roar. Kelly was familiar with the machine: the Germans had developed their four-engine Condor from a pre-war civil airliner. With a range of over two thousand miles it could easily patrol Britain's Western Approaches, leaving from their base at Merignac, near Bordeaux, in western France, curving north-westwards out into the Atlantic around Britain, before final landing at Kjeller in southern Norway, a few kilometres from occupied Oslo.

Mossman glanced quickly around at Peter Gaul, who was standing behind his seat, his eyes grimacing above his facemask. They had strict instructions from Atlantic Ferry Command not to attack or become involved with any enemy aircraft en route, giving away their presence in a place where the enemy would not normally expect to find them. It would not take the German intelligence people too long to make a reasonable guess at why such types of aircraft were somehow way out in the empty ocean. And there was always the chance that the enemy, aware of regular movements of aircraft, could arrange a well-timed ambush in future, a waste of experienced crews and a vitally needed aircraft. They all knew that the Condor was armed; intelligence passed to all military aviators was that the machine was fitted with a twenty-millimetre cannon plus four or five machine-guns, and also carried bombs. Mossman turned towards Kelly, his eyes now wide above his facemask.

"You do know the bloody thing's armed, don't you, Skipper?" Michael Kelly glanced pointedly across at his co-pilot,

"Yes. I do know."

Throttles open, the Hudson plunged noisily down through broken cloud. Kelly intended to make for sea level, hoping to see the silhouette of the reconnoitring Condor etched clearly against the cloud base above them. With no ammunition for their guns he really had little idea how he was going to take any disruptive action against the huge, well-equipped German machine. Emerging from the lowest layer of cloud at two thousand feet, still plummeting seawards, Mossman and Gaul glanced about urgently, looking up for the big machine, which the Germans regularly employed to stalk and spy on vital convoys as they approached Britain's shores. Out of range of the guarding naval escort's anti-aircraft guns, the Condors would circle the convoy safely for hours, radioing its position, course and speed back to their base. Grateful U-boat commanders would position themselves, lying in wait as a wolf pack across the convoy's reported path, receiving crucial information that would enable them to plan concerted attacks. Recent months had been nothing short of disastrous for the merchant marine in terms of vital tonnage and men lost in the deep.

"Seems like we've lost him, Skipper," grumbled Mossman through his mike, looking, eyebrows raised, across at his captain. Thin-lipped behind his facemask, Kelly nodded, still looking avidly about hoping to see something of the machine and its crew of armed spies. Circling a couple of times between the sea and cloud base brought no sighting.

"OK, we'll resume our course and climb back; I hope the other two haven't lost their way." He opened the two throttles and boost controls to climb power. The cloud became more broken as they climbed eastwards. Once settled on top of a scattered white layer, they caught sight of two moving dots towards the far south-east horizon, which seemed to be performing some odd antics.

Minutes later they could see their own two Hudson bombers performing an unusual aerial waltz with the apparent agility of fighters; now and again one would dive into the thin cloud layer then re-emerge seconds later, climbing hard. The second aircraft would then cut in on the gyrating performance, undertaking a similarly risky manoeuvre. Within a few minutes they were at the same location, a couple of thousand feet above their waltzing colleagues. Circling, they watched below, worried. Gaul shouted something almost unintelligible over the intercom.

"The bastard's there, Skipper, look, at three o'clock. See the shadow, just in the cloud?"

Looking off to his right and pushing both throttles almost fully open, Kelly banked the machine hard to starboard looking down through the cockpit's right-side screens. Both he and Mossman saw it together: the dark-grey outline of a large four-engine aircraft just below the surface of the cloud, like some predatory shark cruising shallow waters. Now and again they could see bursts of fire from the Condor, its machine guns sparking anger at the two cavorting Hudsons.

"The buggers are teasing it, look, stopping it from turning south!" shouted Mossman, gesticulating towards the whirling machines. It was true; Kelly could see that each time the Condor attempted to turn south, presumably to make its escape towards its home base near Bordeaux, the two Hudsons performed some highly dangerous and risky flying for such large aircraft – finishing with a steep pull-up through the translucent cloud just ahead of the Condor's nose.

"Stupid buggers; it's those two bloody Poles, isn't it?"

The Condor's attackers were like small birds mobbing a larger bird of prey that was intent on stealing their young, thought Kelly. The two young Polish captains had also received the same instructions about interaction with enemy aircraft as had Kelly. Since their participation in the Battle of Britain the vengeful bravery of Polish pilots was well known, as was their ignoring of orders and excitable, heroic indiscipline at certain times.

At their level, in the thin cloud, the two Condor pilots would not have been able to see the cavorting of the two Hudsons once they had dived and were submerged in thin surrounding cloud, but the Hudson crews could see the Condor's sinister shadow against the lighter sky as they pulled up almost under its nose.

"It must be most disconcerting for them," said Kelly with

deliberate understatement, smiling slightly; still turning the Hudson in a steep bank, watching.

"I wonder how long he's been out on patrol. He might be short of fuel, could be desperate to get home." He looked at his own fuel gauges. They did not have the luxury of loitering too long either, and he hoped the other two Hudson captains were conscious of their fuel situation.

Another five minutes saw all three aircraft back in loose formation droning eastwards; ahead a thin solid line sat on the ocean's horizon, visible through the thinning cloud. Its image slowly resolved into cliffs then emerald-green fields and brown earth, with groups of dwellings and barns clustered together here and there as the aircraft closed on the Six Counties coast. They took great care not to infringe the neutrality of its southern, Republican neighbour.

Within an hour of passing Ireland they had all made a good landing at Prestwick and were handing kit and their remaining rations to a pretty and petite young WAAF driver who was steadily loading them into the back of an ancient squadron-blue Morris van. Looking keenly about him, Kelly was partly relieved to see the missing fourth aircraft of his flight parked close to one of the camouflaged hangars, with its engine cowlings swung open and mechanics on ladders peering inside. The smiling WAAF driver said that it had landed alone forty minutes earlier; its crew had reported to the duty officer and were now having a cup of tea in the operations block. It would appear that the aircraft's young and extrovert French captain had made a favourable impression on the girl.

After completing delivery formalities and a debriefing by the unit intelligence officer over their meeting with the Luftwaffe Condor, all four crews were taken to the officers' mess, fed and then allowed to sleep – Kelly for fourteen straight hours after managing to wangle a priority call to Sarah. On waking, he contacted operations and spoke to the duty officer; there had been no news yet of the fifth Hudson. They'd tried ringing around other likely airfields for news but there had been nothing to report so far. The officer did mention, however, that they had just received a report concerning a wireless intercept, seemingly from a German aircraft. The story was that the aircraft had sent out a message en clair reporting they were almost out of fuel and were preparing to ditch. A rough-and-ready fix on the transmission suggested a position seventy miles south-west of Cape Clear, off the south-east coast of the Irish Republic. Coastal Command was going to investigate during a routine patrol. Sitting in the mess ante-room, a cup of lukewarm coffee in hand, Kelly knew that by now the missing Hudson would be long out of fuel wherever it was.

Awful, he thought, I hardly knew any of them, and now I never will. He recalled the crew's captain: an older man, English, with a large scar across his face and chin gained over Arras during the first conflict in 1916. He became conscious of a mess steward standing by his chair as he dwelt unwisely on their probable experiences as they tried to save the aircraft before finally ditching in the sea. The thoughts were too raw, too near his recent experiences with Cornucopia.

"Mr Kelly, Sir?" Kelly looked up, slightly surprised, and nodded. Smiling, the elderly, white-coated steward handed him a sealed envelope. It contained a request for him to visit the duty operations controller as soon as was convenient. Nodding, he thanked the steward, rose and left the mess, making his way through the bright winter sunshine among well-ordered roads and hangars to Flying Control.

A week later a Sunderland on patrol far into the Atlantic spotted a yellow dinghy with two men in it. The sea was uncharacteristically calm, just a long unbroken swell. Even as they taxied across its rolling surface they could guess at the worst. No movement from the two individuals sitting stiffly opposite each other in the half-filled boat. The two deceased airmen, one English RAF, one Norwegian, were lifted with difficulty from the bouncing craft and returned to their base near Stranraer. When identified, they turned out to be two members of the crew of Kelly's fifth Hudson and were buried with ceremony in a small churchyard looking to the hills and the sea beyond. The third crewman – the older, scar-faced pilot with the soft, west-coast Scots accent – was never found.

❖ ❖ ❖

Cecilia Grosvenor-Ffoulkes jumped down from the dull khaki-camouflaged Tiger Moth with its yellow-painted training bands and walked across the glistening dew-covered grass to the reporting office at the far end of the hangar. For about four months she'd been delivering new machines to pilot-training airfields from her base at Hamble, near Southampton. Having returned to England with her mother from Singapore in early 1939 – her Colonel father had remained there in his post under Australian Army command – she had been at a loss for something worthwhile to do. All talk was of a possible war with Germany; her fiancé, Harold Penrose, had joined the Royal Air Force, accepted for pilot training. Since learning to fly in 1936 she had accumulated a good few hours' flying her Gypsy Moth around England and the near continent followed by her flying adventures in Asia with Penrose while looking for the downed Empress Airways flying boat Cornucopia.

She had returned by car to the London Aero Club at White Waltham airfield one bright autumn afternoon some months earlier, hoping to run into some of her old friends, but she had been a little disappointed. Although it was a Saturday afternoon there appeared to be very few people about save for a couple of flying instructors she didn't recognise, and some very young mechanics. The wooden clubhouse was cool and smelt a little of damp and fresh creosote; in the fireplace a desultory fire flickered occasionally from within its tall red-brick surround. An elderly club steward hovered nearby. He was intrigued at the young woman's presence, not dressed for flying but in neat chequered skirt cut fashionably above the knee and a twin set – but no pearls. Her waterproof jacket and a bright matching chequered scarf were thrown across a nearby chair; her attractive round face was flushed pink from driving her open Riley sports car in the bracing air; which was now parked untidily outside. On one of her well-manicured fingers was a huge sapphire engagement ring; he noticed that she kept looking at it.

Relaxing in one of the tired-looking but comfortable chintz-covered armchairs facing the long windows she sipped at a warming brandy, alone, looking at the late sun and the dozens of flying machines drawn up outside. She remembered a lively time at the club during her training, four years earlier: it always seemed so full of young people laughing and enjoying the freedom of the air and the club's vibrant, sometimes risqué social life. But it had changed. The war was clouding everyone's view of the future. She saw an Avro Anson making a long, steady approach, its landing lamps glowing feebly yellow in the sunlight. After a faultless landing it taxied towards an empty space on the apron almost in front of the clubhouse. The silver-painted twin-engine machine with RAF markings lurched over the undulating turf until it came to a squeaking halt. Its two Cheetah engines ran on for about two minutes then clattered into silence, propellers jerking suddenly and awkwardly to a halt.

Ceci, as she was known to all her close friends, watched interestedly. There was movement in the cockpit, and then the cabin door at the rear of the machine popped open and the pilot jumped lightly down onto the grass, leather helmet still on, a small bag in one hand. One of the two mechanics she had seen earlier and a boyish-looking RAF officer strode out to the machine from offices further along the dispersal area. There was a brief discussion, then the pilot shook hands with the officer as he pointed to something further down the dispersal while the mechanic prepared to refuel the eight-seat communications aircraft. Although the Anson had proved inadequate as a coastal patrol aircraft, in its new communications role it had been a valuable and reliable workhorse.

She was dressed in dark-blue slacks and wearing an oversize fleece-lined leather jacket. The clubhouse door banged shut after her as she clumped in heavy flying boots towards the small bar area, throwing her leather helmet and bag onto a nearby chair.

"Hello, George, again! Seems only yesterday since you were making tea for me." A grin crossed the steward's creased and tired face.

"Hello again, Miss Helen. Didn't expect to see you back quite so soon. Another pick-up?"

"'Fraid so. Can't keep the girls waiting, you know what they're like, bloody impatient bunch." She took the freshly poured tea and walked across the threadbare patterned carpet towards the patch of late sun by the windows, gently shaking free the curls from her chestnut hair.

"May I join you?" The voice was cultured and friendly with just a trace of a foreign accent, the smile warm and infectious. She was quite short with an oval face and dark-brown eyes. Ceci smiled back.

"Of course," moving her empty glass to one side of the small table. The brandy had had the desired effect, warming and relaxing her. The girl sat down and, despite her thick boots and jacket, managed to make it an elegant exercise.

"By the way, my name's Helen Lorenzo," she held out a small, delicate hand. Ceci took it and looked into the girl's tanned, open face.

"Oh hello. Cecilia Grosvenor-Ffoulkes..."

The pilot interrupted, eyes wide.

"That's an awful mouthful, if I might say so."

It was not meant unkindly – the girl was smiling broadly, her dark-brown eyes twinkling.

"Yes, rather. All my friends call me Ceci, actually; it helps to speed things up." They both laughed.

"Are you a member here?"

"Not now," Ceci replied, "used to be, I learned to fly here and came back looking for lost friends, but as you can see, there aren't too many people about," she said with a sweep of her arm around the empty room

"Oh, so you fly, do you? Great fun – where do you fly from these days?"

"Well, nowhere now, actually. The Air Ministry commandeered my brand-new Tiger Moth almost as soon as I had collected it from de Havilland's. Anyway, I'm a bit rusty, haven't flown for about seven or eight months now. Wonder if I'm still up to it," sighed Ceci.

"That's interesting ... how many hours have you done?" Helen asked pointedly.

Ceci turned in her seat and waved to the steward.

"Can we have some more tea, please? And I'll have a cup too." Then, looking back to the pilot, "About six hundred hours now, mainly on Gypsy Moths. I learned to fly here with Paul Maddern – about four years ago – he taught my mother as well. Is he still about?"

"Paul Maddern! My dear girl, you lucky thing, he was quite a dish apparently, so I'm told by some of my girlfriends."

"Was? You mean he's no longer based here?" Ceci looked askance. There was a brief pause. Helen looked down into the steaming cup on her knee.

"Oh dear, you obviously don't know. I'm so sorry; Paul was killed about two months back. They think the young student he was with froze on the stick during instruction. Witnesses say the aircraft stalled on recovery from a spin, went straight in from three hundred feet, caught fire. Unusual. Sorry. No one survived."

Although now very happily engaged to Harold Penrose, whom she loved dearly, Ceci had very fond memories of Paul. He had been a lot older than her, an ex-RFC pilot and not only a brilliant flying instructor but also a gentleman – and a greyingly handsome one. Still in her teens and impressionable, Ceci had shared more than one late-night dinner engagement where she had fallen in love with him all over again. They had once spent an illicit weekend together in the early spring of 1936 and Ceci had had the devil of a job explaining to her mother where she had been. She'd never regretted the weekend and her gentle initiation. Annoyingly, she found out later that her mother had also had a fleeting affair with him some years earlier on his return from France.

"I'm so sorry you had to find out like this ...." Helen Lorenzo sensed that there was something meaningful in her bluntly delivered news.

Ceci's face was white. 'What a horrifying and unfair end,' she thought.

"It's alright, just a bit of a shock that's all. Poor ... dear Paul." She caught herself biting her lip, her eyes glistening slightly.

Helen changed the subject quickly.

"Listen; if you're really serious about flying again I might be able to help you. We need pilots with experience pretty urgently. I work for the new Air Transport Auxiliary, the ATA," she said, pointing at the shiny gold badge logo on her uniform jacket, "We have bases all around the country now – I'm down at Hamble, but the HQ is here at Waltham, just across the airfield. It's great fun, we're all girls at Hamble – we deliver new aircraft from factories to squadrons in the south or wherever else they're needed so that the RAF and navy don't have to use their own pilots. We've only been in existence for about a year. It was the idea of Gerard d'Erlanger, do you know him, by the way? He was a director at

British Airways; a great pilot, too. Anyway, when the Munich thing happened, he had the idea and the Air Ministry thought it was a good one. So the ATA was formed. Our CO's great too; Pauline Gower, she runs the whole show as far as female pilots are concerned, over two thousand hours, flown almost everything!"

Ceci looked up at her as the girl stood looking out of the window towards the west. Perhaps this was something she could do. Just then a gaggle of six camouflaged Tiger Moths landed, taxiing into a neat row on the other side of the airfield. Ceci and Helen watched together for a few minutes, then Helen turned briskly.

"Sorry, time to go. I'm taxi driver for that lot today, got to take them back to Hamble. Listen, if you're interested, I'm sure our unit CO, Harriet Brotherton, would love to meet you, why don't you come down one day and see what we get up to?" Helen left an expensively printed personal card on the table, plucked from her jacket as she left.

"I might just do that," called Ceci, smiling after her as she clumped out of the door.

She watched a bunch of laughing girls amble across the grass airfield towards the Anson. Using her hands as imaginary aircraft, one young pilot demonstrated some quite impossible manoeuvre to her colleagues to be greeted with howls of good-natured derision. They piled into the machine in their unflattering thick Sidcot suits, their faces bright and alive. Soon both engines were turning; Ceci moved outside to watch. She could see Helen at the controls; waving briefly for a moment, she gunned one engine causing the slowly moving machine to pivot about a wheel before lurching off, rolling like some ancient dowager towards the grass take-off area. When she went inside to collect her things, the steward was clearing cups.

"She's a live wire, that Miss Helen, always full of beans."

Ceci nodded at his comment.

"Very pretty, too."

"Oh that'll be the Italian in her – dark," he added. "I think she once told me her mother is English and her father's Italian, a professor or something at a university somewhere in the north of Italy. Must be difficult for her, being at war and all that, with mixed-nationality parents."

Ceci thanked the kindly man and with a faint smile on her lips put on her jacket and scarf. Roaring off down the narrow road that led from the busy airfield, she began to think seriously.

Three weeks after her encounter with Helen Lorenzo, Ceci visited the ATA airfield at Hamble. It was a lovely location, just outside an unspoilt hamlet, evocative of a past era with traditional shops: Serpells the grocer, Spakes the butcher and small Victorian houses scattered along its narrow main street leading down to the banks of the tidal Hamble River, which emerged clear into turgid Southampton water before diluting fully in the salty, tidal Solent. The hamlet provided billets for many of the ATA's pilots and staff, and importantly for them, offered a choice of four pubs: The Victory, The King and Queen, Ye Olde White Hart and the unit's favourite, The Bugle, plus a number of still partly active sailing clubs. Ceci had lunch with some of the all-female operations staff and pilots and immediately felt at home. Harriet, the unit CO, had a long talk with her after flying had finished for the day and Ceci decided on the spot that she would like to put her past flying experience to good use.

On a damp, cold and misty February morning she reported for

duty and training at the Central Flying School of the Royal Air Force at Upavon, remote on the downs in Wiltshire. Here she was to be assessed and given her ATA training before being sent to a unit for delivery duties. She would probably be flying light aircraft initially, like her Tiger Moth – collecting completed machines from the de Havilland works at Hatfield, or from Cowley, near Oxford, for example, then flying them to training airfields around the south of the country. As time went by, she was told, if she showed promise, she would undertake further training on heavier aircraft like the Spitfire and Hurricane, and be taught to fly twin-engine machines including Ansons, Hudsons or Oxfords.

❖ ❖ ❖

Prestwick's Flying Control office was flooded with light from the low afternoon sun. Smoke curled up from the duty operations officer's cigarette as he tried to make sense of a signal from the Air Ministry about conserving motor transport fuel.

"Good afternoon, I'm Michael Kelly – you sent a note?"

"Oh, Mr Kelly, of course. Please do sit down." Smiling, the elderly and bemedalled Flight Lieutenant waved him to a seat as he lifted a heap of official paper from one of the wooden chairs facing his desk, dumping it onto an adjacent desk where a bespectacled and matronly WAAF was trying to type, head barely visible above an encroaching wall of files.

"Thanks for coming in, I'll come straight to the point. We've got a problem and I wondered if you and your crews could help us out?" Kelly raised his eyebrows.

"The ATA are overwhelmed at the moment with aircraft deliveries from our own factories to the squadrons and I wondered if you could fly your four Hudsons down to White

Waltham. The ATA could manage to take them to the requesting squadrons from there; it's just that they don't have the manpower or time to come all the way up here to Prestwick to collect. Kelly thought for a moment. They would have to get down to England by some means anyway. They also had to find transport of some sort back to Montreal and then Gander in readiness for the next transatlantic delivery.

"I don't think that's going to present a problem. We have to get to Liverpool somehow for a sailing back to Canada. When do you want us to leave?"

The operations officer looked relieved.

"Any possibility you could leave first thing in the morning? I can advise your people of what's happening and arrange fuel, charts and any crystals needed for the radios."

Kelly called his remaining crews together before they all set out to tackle the local Scottish hostelries.

"Sorry, chaps, early start tomorrow, and an early night tonight, I'm afraid, but I can promise you a night in London's dens of iniquity tomorrow." Faces dropped momentarily. He hoped he would be able to make just a token gesture of hospitality to them before catching a train from London's Waterloo rail station for rural Hampshire, Sarah and the two children. He wanted desperately to see her and their children before returning to the bright lights of Montreal before as brief a stay as possible in wintry, inhospitable Gander.

Just after six in the morning the Hudson crews were delivered yawning and shivering to their aircraft for the two-hour flight to White Waltham, north-west of London, just off the main London–Oxford road. With just three-tenths cloud at four thousand feet the flight went without a glitch. Switching off, he and Mossman rose from their seats, grabbing their bags along the way. Out in a fresh breeze, they gazed about. The airfield seemed to be covered in aircraft of almost every description. A small crew van arrived, bumping across the grass; they piled in looking forward to a night out in London after a nap. Kelly decided not to join them in the van; he favoured a little fresh air and a walk to the flight offices.

Ahead of him a shortish, bulky figure in thick Sidcot suit and boots, leather flying-helmet in hand, walked towards the operations hut. He thought that the RAF must be letting things go a little despite it being wartime; the airman could do with a good haircut, his dark tousled hair blowing in the wind. Entering the corridor of the operations hut behind the pilot he noticed that his gait was not quite normal – couldn't quite put his finger on it. The pilot turned, holding a door open for him. It was a girl, he realised.

There was a brief glance of recognition and developing smiles.

"Michael! My goodness, what are you doing here?"

"I might well ask you the same question! By the way, the suit doesn't do you justice!"

She grinned broadly and attempted a curtsey in the heavy flying garment.

"Michael, how lovely to see you again. Are you flying?"

"Can't do anything else, girl. Just arrived from Canada via Prestwick, its great to be warm, or, rather, warmer. I'm with the Atlantic Ferry people. Just brought five – no, sorry, four – Hudsons across the pond. Regret to say we lost one on the way."

Her smile dropped for a moment then Ceci looked at him, pleased.

"Oh, it's really good to see you again, Michael, how are Sarah and little Beth?"

"Oh they're just wonderful; we've got a little boy now: Alistair, he's growing fast, nearly two and as you'd expect, into everything – and little Beth is no longer little. We're living down in Hampshire, moved out of London before it becomes too dangerous for the family. Sarah's still beautiful and busy with the children."

"That's wonderful! I'm based at Hamble with the ATA, only Class I at the moment though. Only trusted to deliver Tigers and Magisters. Harold's just got his wings, due to join a squadron in the next few days. We must get together soon." They touched briefly on their shared Cornucopia experiences; Ceci had been largely instrumental in finding and reporting the lost flying boat and its survivors including the injured Michael Kelly, Sarah, who was now his wife, and her daughter Beth. As they completed their delivery formalities they continued their light-hearted talk until Ceci had to dash outside to catch the taxi Anson back to Hamble but not before exchanging addresses and telephone numbers.

◆ ◆ ◆

Harold Penrose had done well at flying training, starting with Tiger Moths at No. 10 Elementary Flying School at Yatesbury, in Wiltshire, followed by a period of 'square-bashing' at Uxbridge, north of London, and more advanced training on North American Harvards. He was hoping to be posted on to fighters, either Spitfires or Hurricanes. He'd missed the Battle of Britain during his training, which had been interrupted by a period of illness: scarlet fever, but it was not a fighter squadron flying the iconic eight-gun Supermarine Spitfire that he was to join, but a photo-reconnaissance squadron based at RAF Benson in Oxfordshire. Despite having his flying log book annotated: 'Exceptional' by the CO of his training unit – a comment very rarely inscribed – he was bitterly disappointed at being given second-best in his view. It was, however, a view he was soon to change once the value of his new unit's work was revealed to him during some reconnaissance flying training from a bare, freezing and windswept coastal airfield: RAF Dyce in north-east Scotland.

Ceci was secretly pleased that he was not going to join a normal combat squadron. Although, she knew of the sometimes-greater dangers and risks that existed in flying an unarmed single-seater Spitfire fighter high over enemy territory with little except speed, height and pilot skill to ensure survival. And there was the constant and vital imperative to complete the sortie, bringing back crucial images that would aid intelligence-gathering for the fight against Hitler.

❧ ❧ ❧

Michael Kelly crept up the stairs of the red-brick Victorian farmhouse, managing to avoid the squeaky third and seventh treads; it was well past two in the morning. As he passed Beth's bedroom door he peered in. In the dim night-light the little girl lay asleep facing the part-open door; he gently pushed it further. She opened her eyes briefly, then closed them, fast asleep with a slight smile on her tiny face. Sarah had just got back into bed having been up with Alistair again. He'd been crying but was now settled and sleeping deeply and gently snoring. Michael came into their bedroom. Sarah's side-table light was on.

Turning, slightly startled, "Who ... ? Darling ... why didn't you say?"

"I didn't know myself until this afternoon, didn't want to raise your hopes in case I couldn't make it." He sat on her side of the bed holding her. She was crying gently as the tension slowly ebbed away.

Four days later he was packed and ready to go again. Sarah and the two children went to the local railway station at Whitchurch to see him off on the long and arduous wartime rail journey to Liverpool where he would board a ship for Canada. It would be at least a month before there was any chance that he would return home again.

The following day Sarah went up to London to have lunch with her mother, who insisted on staying there despite the increasingly obvious dangers of remaining. The children stayed at home with their newly acquired French nanny. Patricia, a bilingual young teacher had escaped from France in an overcrowded fishing boat with her soldier father just as the Nazis started to move westwards towards their home near St Nazaire.

The wartime Empire restaurant was very crowded, the din of knives and forks on plain white china and the hubbub of blurred conversations almost ear-splitting; it took a few moments for her to see her mother among a sea of uniforms sitting on the far side of the room at a small table. Opposite sat another, younger, woman in a light-blue uniform. A harassed and balding waiter led her over and pulled a chair out.

"Sarah! At last, I was beginning to think you weren't coming." She pecked her mother on the cheek; she was looking fit despite wartime rationing, bombing and the damp English weather.

"Darling, this is Daphne. You probably don't remember her, its years since you met, you were very young – she's your step-niece." Sarah held out her hand to a very slim, pale woman of about twenty-six with auburn hair pulled back in a rather severe style.

The handshake was warm despite first appearances.

"How nice to meet you again. I must admit I didn't remember you. You're in the RAF?" Then Sarah noticed the gold ring on Daphne's left hand.

"Yes, in the Women's Auxiliary Air Force, WAAFs in current jargon. I'm based up in Buckinghamshire at the moment; we haven't been there long, got bombed out of the last place, Heston aerodrome, in September." Sarah's mother intervened in a conspiratorial whisper.

"Daphne's engaged in some hush-hush work, top secret and all that."

Daphne smiled and her whole face lit up, totally altering her appearance. Stunning, thought Ceci.

"It's not quite as dramatic as that. I'm attached to a photographic unit. It's quite interesting at times trying to see what the enemy is up to."

"Oh, do you mean photographic interpretation?" nodded Sarah, "I should think it can be very interesting?"

"It is. Strictly between you and me – our problem is a shortage of people to do the interpreting at the moment; the whole operation has grown by leaps and bounds since Sid Cotton first set it up. Originally we only had two pilots before Dunkirk, 'Shorty' Longbottom and Robert Niven. You might have heard of their exploits. Now we are receiving film from a number of photo-reconnaissance ... er ... PR ... squadrons around the country. The growing insistence for more and more photo intelligence from the army and navy is creating a real problem for us." Daphne picked up her glass of water.

"How did you get involved in something like photography – were you in the business before the war, so to speak?" asked Sarah.

"Oh no, I joined the WAAF just after the outbreak of the war hoping to do something useful, duty and all that. I met this chap at the Air Ministry when I was being interviewed for a job involving translating – I speak French and German tolerably well; did modern languages at university – who said jokingly that I should stay out and become a model. I had a good figure then. Service food has seen the end of that," she grimaced. "Anyway, I laughed at such a preposterous idea and suggested that he learned to use a camera first!"

As it turned out, he could – at over three hundred miles an hour, it seems – he was a reconnaissance pilot back from France; he'd been serving in the Special Survey Flight helping the army's Expeditionary Force keep abreast of the German advances – just, by all accounts. Anyway, to cut a very long story short, he invited me to meet another chap after lunch who ran a specialist photographic unit at Heston aerodrome over in west London. He gave me some idea of what they did and how they did it, without giving any secrets away, I should add – and I was hooked. Mind you, he was very persuasive."

Sarah sat for a while picking at her food and listening to the din around her. The food was barely warm and the small portion of meat was tough, the dark-brown gravy congealing. She looked up.

"Do you think I could do photo interpretation?" Daphne stopped, fork midway between plate and mouth.

"Of course you could, I knew absolutely nothing to start with. We train people, you know. It's not the sort of job you can pick up in civvy street. Listen, why don't you come and talk with my boss, Peter Riddell? He could explain what's involved and I'm sure he could get you on board with minimum fuss." Sarah was excited by the idea; perhaps she should meet Daphne's boss, she pondered as her mother wittered on about the cost and rarity of fresh vegetables today.

"It sounds interesting, I'm sure I'd enjoy it once I understood what to do. I've got to do something useful, but I've two young children and my husband is often away, so it might prove to be a logistical nightmare. Still, I'd be keen to meet your man if it can be arranged."

"Let me have some dates when you could come to Danesfield, that's our new place near Medmenham in Buckinghamshire, or give me a ring later. Don't worry; meeting Squadron Leader Riddell isn't a commitment, just a way of finding out." Daphne touched her arm and smiled warmly as she spoke. Sarah was reassured.

Later, in a taxi taking her mother back to her flat in Bayswater, Sarah and her mother chatted about Daphne. Her mother warned her daughter about not putting her foot in it at some later stage; Daphne's husband was missing after an attack on some key bridges in France in an effort to hold up the German advance in May. He'd been flying with a squadron equipped with Fairey Battles; the aircraft had soon proved totally useless against the German flak and fighters and had been rapidly withdrawn from action. But not before a lot of courageous young pilots and crews had died, she went on. Daphne's husband had been declared killed in action only the previous month, after information from the Red Cross.

After helping her mother sort out some pieces of furniture and papers to be stored in the basement of the building where she lived, Sarah caught a bus to Waterloo station, boarding a very full train home packed with soldiers and sailors armed with large canvas kitbags and rifles. She was conscious of a number of the men looking at her admiringly. So she hadn't lost her looks and figure after the birth of Alistair, she thought, rather pleased. One very young naval officer, a schoolboy almost, offered her his seat, and gazing out at the cold countryside, she thought about Michael. Had he got away from Liverpool yet? The trains were so unreliable these days and there was always the danger of being bombed or strafed by an opportunistic German aircraft. Michael had told her of his chance meeting with Ceci at White Waltham aerodrome. It would be nice to see her and Harold again after all they had been through together; perhaps they could arrange a weekend soon. Sarah and Michael's farmhouse had plenty of room and it would give them an opportunity to catch up with all the gossip.

Five weeks later Sarah Kelly eventually made her way to Danesfield, a large sprawling country house set in acres of once-carefully tended grounds, which had been commandeered by the military for the period of hostilities. What had been originally set up by Sidney Cotton at the behest of the military, when they had finally recognised the gaping photo intelligence deficits in their organisations, had grown into a very large and expanding organisation. As Sarah was later to learn, just before the outbreak of war in September 1939, Ian Fleming, Assistant to the Director of Naval Intelligence, had asked Sidney Cotton, an Australian civilian at the time, to take on a secret intelligence reconnaissance job for them using his own private aircraft; a Lockheed 12A. The machine had been cleverly and secretly converted to take high-quality aerial photographs.

The story she heard was that the Admiralty was worried; the issue concerned the feasibility of German U-boats using ports or bays on the neutral Irish Republic's west coast for refuelling and support. Sid Cotton took off in his civilian Lockheed shortly after the meeting with Fleming; he and his co-pilot managed to photograph the entire Irish Republic's west coast from ten thousand feet and again later from two thousand – there were no U-boat refuelling bases evident, he was able to report to a relieved navy. A few days later Sidney Cotton had been brought into the military fold and made an acting Wing Commander with responsibility for a special RAF photographic reconnaissance unit: the Heston Flight, based at the former civil aerodrome in west London. Daphne mentioned how upset everyone had been in 'Sid Cotton's Air Force', as his growing photographic unit was called, when he had been forced to resign his commission a month or so ago.

"It appears from what has been said that there were a lot of regular officers who didn't like his go-do-it approach to problem-solving. He didn't dither about, just got on with things. He did some incredible things, you know. Once, before the war, he flew some senior German officers around Germany in his private Lockheed. What's so funny is that the aircraft's specially concealed cameras took photographs of sensitive areas of Germany while he was flying them about – they knew absolutely nothing about it. I think it's a dreadful way to have treated him. Without his ideas and energy the military would still be literally fighting blind." Sarah detected a note of outrage in Daphne's voice.

Her arrival at the newly named Photographic Reconnaissance Unit at Danesfield coincided with a new peak in photo interpretation activity and Sarah was both relieved and disappointed when met by Daphne and told that Peter Riddell was away at meetings with the Admiralty and Army Chiefs of Staff. The afternoon was spent amicably enough with various members of a relaxed but highly competent group of men and women, working very hard as part of the Special Intelligence Service, or SIS, as it was constantly referred to. As she left with Daphne that evening her mind was made up; she would do it even though it meant some weeks at Farnborough undergoing training. How would Michael take it, she wondered?

TWO

Over four months were to pass before the weekend get-together spoken of by Ceci actually took place. During those months Michael Kelly had completed six successful crossings of the North Atlantic, the last four in quick succession owing to the introduction of the new American Liberator bomber, which had been hastily modified to carry a limited number of government passengers or ferry aircrews wrapped in eiderdowns in its freezing bomb bay. It saved a dangerous, weather-dependent sea voyage fraught with the likelihood of U-boat attacks – anything from five days to two weeks in convoy to Canada; although flying was not without risks. Kelly had luckily just missed flying back to Canada a few months earlier in a Liberator that had ploughed into the two-thousand, eight-hundred-foot peak on the Isle of Arran in bad weather. Its crew and a number of Ferry pilots, a total of twenty-two, were killed as the aircraft disintegrated on the raw mountain-top. Kelly's last flight eastwards was in a PBY Catalina; a twin-engine amphibian machine destined for the RAF's Coastal Command and delivered safely to an RAF unit at Wigtown Bay, near Stranraer in Scotland. He'd enjoyed the challenge of the work but had no real regrets in leaving.

Kelly's wife, Sarah, underwent her very intensive training at the photo interpretation school at Farnborough, not too far from their home in Hampshire. It meant that she could be home each evening for the children, even though she nearly always arrived feeling utterly exhausted. Growing pressure at Danesfield meant that she was pressed into action before her training was completed. Occasionally it proved impossible for her to get home at all and she was forced to spend the night billeted in one of the growing number of wooden huts erected close to the main house. On evenings when she did finally return late, to Patricia's relief, both Alistair and Beth stayed close to her, demanding attention and insisting on sleeping in her bed. With Michael often away this presented no problem.

Ceci's flying skills advanced; her CO soon recognised her capabilities and had pushed her rapidly onto a Class II course at RAF Upavon and she qualified to fly powerful single-engine machines and had actually delivered a brand-new Spitfire from one of the Supermarine shadow works to a fighter squadron based at Tangmere, in Sussex, only a few days after returning from Upavon. The girls at the Hamble ATA Pool had to suffer Ceci's enthusiasm for that first Spitfire flight for a few days until she had to deliver two more. The thrill of flying such a machine did not pall but the experience had matured her outlook.

Just before fulfilling Sarah's weekend invitation, Ceci became a Class III pilot, able to handle simple twin-engine aircraft such as the de Havilland Rapide biplane, Avro Anson and Airspeed Oxford Trainer. She loved it. Her escalating qualifications gave her an opportunity to fly a wider range of aircraft to an extended number of destinations but she still harboured hopes of further training until, like Harriet, Hamble's CO, she would be allowed to fly heavy four-engine bombers.

It never failed to amuse her when she was greeted by ground crew and operations people at an RAF destination airfield or factory: they often had difficulty accepting that a woman had just flown the machine in and landed it all by herself. On one particular occasion, after delivering an Oxford to a navigation training school near Bristol, she was told she was not permitted to complete the delivery paperwork, only the delivery pilot was allowed to do that. It took a few minutes for her to convince an officious, elderly and dyed-in-the-wool RAF officer that she was the delivery pilot. He added insult to disbelief, going out the aircraft to check that no one else was on board.

But the harsh reality of flying in all weathers to meet the constant demands from squadrons made itself known tragically from time to time. Late one Tuesday afternoon, most of the girls were back in the rough comfort of the crew room knitting or playing cards, one was even cutting out a dress on the floor, and there were only a half dozen pilots still to report in. During the day the weather had changed gradually from benign sunshine with small white cumulus clouds bobbing along in a stiffish westerly breeze to a lowering front of dark-grey rain-bearing clouds.

The taxi Anson arrived just after five-thirty and made a reasonable landing in the developing crosswind; five laughing girls crashed giggling through the operations hut door dropping parachute packs and other flying paraphernalia around the operations desk. Ceci looked at the 'Delivery & Collections' board covering one entire wall of the cluttered, noisy room. There was one collection still incomplete. She saw it was the quiet and stylish Jane, flying a new de Havilland Mosquito from the Hatfield works north of London back to Hamble ready for onward delivery early on Wednesday morning to a squadron based near Exeter. Jane had been in the fashion business before joining the ATA, paying for flying lessons from her miserly salary at one of London's leading couturiers, "All fur coats and no knickers," she used to joke about many of their 'lady' clients.

She had phoned earlier in the day; she was still waiting for the machine to be made ready and would probably be late home for the planned party celebrating one of the girls' birthdays. As Ceci studied the board that listed the huge number of aircraft collections and deliveries they had completed that day the phone rang; it was Hatfield saying that Jane had just got airborne. The time was just after six-thirty. Most of the girls drifted off home to their billets in the village, the calls of 'Bye – see you in the Bugle' tapered off as the room finally emptied. With an irrational pang of concern Ceci stood and waited for Jane at the darkening windows; the two girls shared a small house right alongside the Hamble River with other girls from the pilot pool.

Steering around London's barrage balloons and flak batteries, Jane's flight should have taken her about forty-five minutes to an hour in the new, very fast twin-engine machine. After an hour and a half, Alison, the duty ops officer, rang Harriet, Hamble's CO, to report Jane's non-arrival. Harriet said she would come in; in the meantime they were to phone around other units on her known route to see if she had landed somewhere else, perhaps because of bad weather or mechanical problems.

Outside, the weather was taking a serious turn for the worse, becoming blustery with large raindrops beginning to fall, and ragged clouds tearing across the darkening sky. Across the other side of the airfield the windsock could just be seen, jerking horizontally at its mooring post. From the windows, to the north and west, the signs were increasingly ominous, lowering black cloud approaching menacingly. By 10 pm, in the dark, there was a full alert. Nobody had seen or heard anything of Jane since her leaving Hatfield. She would have been out of fuel two hours past; they never fully filled machines for delivery flights. The party at the Bugle that evening was a restrained affair.

Early next morning the army reported finding an aircraft crash site after a telephone call from a local villager, but there was no sign of any pilot in the wreckage, which was scattered for hundreds of yards along the top of a ridge lying between Andover and Hungerford on the Hampshire–Berkshire border; there had been no fire, the officer had said, just total and absolute disintegration. Owing to continued bad weather, the considerable number of assembled pilots stood, silent, hoping against hope that Jane had escaped safely but for some reason had not been able to contact them by telephone.

Later that morning the tragic facts were given to Harriet over the telephone by an army captain who'd spent some time at the site. Her face blanched as he told her the details. Jane had been found, eventually. She had been hurled bodily from the machine as it had broken up on impact and had rolled down the steep sides of the ridge's southern slope until she became caught in a mass of bare briar and brambles growing there. At first sight she appeared to be quite unmarked, her make-up perfect and intact, but for a small scratch on her left cheek. She'd always been a stickler for her appearance, on duty or not. Three months earlier Jane had coped bravely with the loss of her fiancé, who had been reported missing with his crew on an anti-submarine patrol in a Sunderland somewhere in the Western Approaches. She had been told of their last message to base, "Am attacking U-boat," followed by a position grid reference. Nothing further had been heard.

Just turned twenty-three, she was buried near her mother's plot in the graveyard of her local parish church in Norfolk. Her father stood, dignified and grey. Some of the ATA girls attended. Clutching Jane's tiny black kitten, Ceci sobbed alone in Jane's room in the shared house, shouting irrationally at God for his bloody unthinking cruelty. The small cat jumped down and sat looking out of the window, washing itself, unperturbed.

Three weeks later the inquest surmised that Jane's aircraft had been forced lower and lower as the weather front had advanced south-eastwards until eventually she had been obliged to complete her delivery enveloped in turbulent cloud, although the inquest took account of the fact that she was a newly qualified instrument pilot. The only real clue to the accident was the pressure setting on her altimeter, found miraculously undamaged in the remains of the destroyed cockpit. It appeared to be set ten millibars too high, indicating to her that she was much higher than she really was; additionally, flying towards the advancing low pressure area would have made the situation worse. Had she set the altimeter incorrectly, or had the briefing people at Hatfield given her incorrect pressure settings? They would probably never know now. Another twenty feet or so, the investigators had calculated, and she would have just cleared the cloud-obscured ridge with its stunted trees instead of piling into it at around two hundred miles per hour.

❖ ❖ ❖

Harold Penrose wore his new RAF pilot's wings and pilot officer's single thin stripe proudly. After further training with his new squadron he had undertaken two reconnaissance flights for one of Benson's two PR squadrons' special long-range Spitfires. The first had been a piece of cake, a high-altitude photographic run over the docks at Kiel in northern Germany then, turning south at thirty-seven thousand feet, over-flying and photographing further dock facilities near Hamburg at the request of the Admiralty.

His second sortie was low level; he had been ordered to take oblique photos of new construction taking place at La Pallice on the Gironde River in western France, thought to be developing U-boat facilities. As he readily admitted, this second sortie no was cake-walk. The Germans were well equipped with fixed and mobile flak batteries around the site. Some of their shooting proved accurate, as evidenced by one torn hole in the Spitfire's port aileron – fortunately without adverse handling consequences. Almost before he had come to a halt from his hair-raising sortie, the Spitfire's fuselage side panels were off and two oblique cameras had been removed; its rolls of vital film being quickly sent for developing. At Danesfield, using their special stereoscopic viewers, the identical twin sets of pictures were scanned and interpreted before a rapid report was compiled with accompanying photographic prints and was forwarded to those responsible for targeting at Bomber Command HQ and the Joint Chiefs of Staff Intelligence Group in London.

✦ ✦ ✦

The weekend proved to be a great success. Somehow they had all contrived to arrive early on the Friday evening at the small Hampshire hamlet where Michael and Sarah had made themselves a comfortable home. Amid much laughter and storytelling, the evening meal, courtesy of their farming neighbour, was admirably supported by four bottles of now-rare red burgundy; by eleven they were all spent. The last log glowing a pale orange-red as they sat within its warmth; a bottle of good brandy bought by Michael on his last trip from Montreal provided a fitting conclusion to some hectic and at times worrying months for all of them. Outside, a penetrating frost covered the remains of dead perennials; a brittle white carpet was spread across the lawn and hedges that surrounded the red-brick house with its large picture windows.

Sarah looked around the cosy, shadow-filled room; Ceci and Harold were close together on one sofa, her head in his lap, eyes closed, his staring blankly into the distance of the ebbing fire. Michael sat at her feet on a cushion, his metal right leg almost in the hearth, head resting back against her legs, totally relaxed. Beyond the tall windows with their blackout curtains the sound of German bombing could just be heard from the south, probably Southampton or Portsmouth, she thought. The dog, Snoots, a young black Labrador owned by Harold, lay like a draught excluder across the door, his ears twitching slightly at each distant concussion.

The rest of the weekend was spent relaxing and walking along country lanes, visiting the small township of Stockbridge, sat astride the Test's multitude of chalk tributaries as they meandered their way through the Hampshire countryside, crystal-clear and loaded with fish. However, the war was ever present; seemingly constant flights of aircraft spread a rumble of sound across the near-cloudless ice-blue skies from the airfields at Middle Wallop, Chilbolton and Thruxton. The three pilots among them glanced up as each machine passed overhead, conscious of their need to return to duty within a few hours. Late on Sunday evening Harold left for Benson on his AJS motorcycle. There had been a call from his squadron adjutant just after late breakfast ordering him back in time for an early-morning sortie on Monday.

Sarah and Michael went for one last walk with Snoots, whose energy seemed to have unplumbed reserves. Ceci and Harold were left alone in the house. They had four hours before an unclear future settled its mantle on them again. Bright sunlight filled the small bedroom. As it moved steadily across the heavens it warmed their gentle lovemaking. She lay stroking his back, her neck melting under his kissing until, aroused again, they gave mutual pleasure to their precious partner.

Mid-morning on Monday found Sarah and the children alone; their nanny, Patricia, had gone to see her father, who was based, with other French military survivors from Dunkirk, at a training base in Devon and would not be back until midweek. Michael had received a phone call from a rather officious civil servant ordering him to report to the Atlantic Ferry offices in London for some reason or other; they'd recommended that he take his overnight kit with him.

Young Alistair sat on Sarah's knee as she prepared vegetables from the garden, upset that his daddy had gone again. Beth, old enough now to accept the situation, sat looking quietly at a large picture-book in the corner of the kitchen. The family tabby cat sat on the large high-back chair beside the stove washing and purring gently. Sarah had not the heart to break the news to them that Mummy too would be absent on a regular basis from now on. She had reached a stage where she was now fully entrusted to scan and read the aerial photographs so riskily gathered by the PR pilots from Benson, and now from an RAF Coastal Command station at St Eval, down on Cornwall's north coast, and also from remote

Wick, way up in the north-east of Scotland.

❧ ❧ ❧

Helen Lorenzo had been trying to contact her father in Bologna, where, as far as she knew, he still held a professorial post at the University. Being half-Italian – with an English mother - she had to be careful; they were at war now. Red Cross officials were sympathetic but had told her that it may prove difficult under the circumstances; however, they would do all they could to help and would be in touch. Before joining the ATA she had been subjected to a great deal of questioning from the security services about her parentage and loyalties.

Professor Elio Lorenzo had spent most of his academic life studying the life and work of Leonardo da Vinci, the sixteenth-century philosopher, artist, engineer and pathologist. Helen had last seen her father in early June 1939 when she'd been for a brief visit to Italy before German hegemony had made travel to the continent too risky. Her visit was to try and persuade him to come back to England with her; he had been outspoken about Mussolini's Fascist politics for Italy and had been warned by local party officials about reported inappropriate comments. Even as she boarded the boat train for Dover she knew somehow that it was probably a lost cause. Since her mother had died, her father's once-strong attachment to England had almost evaporated; he was bitterly upset and disappointed that his wife had left him alone so soon in an increasingly turbulent Italy. To counter his grief and disappointment he had immersed himself deeper in his academic researches.

She vividly remembered those few glorious summer days; the warmth and pure cobalt skies as they had wandered together along narrow shady streets and across wide sunlit piazzas in Florence and Siena. One afternoon they had watched silently together the gloss of heavy summer rain on terracotta roofs drying slowly to matt in renewed sunshine as they sipped rare English tea under a large green umbrella. Siena was her paternal grandfather's home; she'd always loved it. To her it seemed to her to have more intimacy and discretion than Florence.

Her father was, as usual, engrossed in his work, even on holiday, talking incessantly as they walked, about Leonardo and his latest theories or a new discovery. He'd been very excited, she recalled, after being given some very ancient documents and notebooks that had been secreted in a wall cavity in a building near to where Leonardo had once lived. The building was being repaired by local artisans. One of them, a student, working part-time, knew of Professor Lorenzo's deep interest and expertise in ancient documents, and had brought them unannounced to his department at the university in Bologna.

Helen only half-listened as he spoke with passion about the unique human who had dominated his waking hours for nearly four decades. This time his enthusiasm was driven by the new material from the student. Listening more attentively, she gathered that the work appeared similar in approach and style to Leonardo's but so far there had been no way to accurately date it. Over the years, from childhood until finally leaving home after her mother's unexpected death in 1937, she had lived with Leonardo da Vinci, at mealtimes, during walks, while picking olives or almonds in the summer holidays, even as bedtime stories. At times Helen felt she knew almost as much as her father did about the man who had managed to seriously enrage the Pope with his work on the human frame and its organs.

His interest in the newly discovered drawings and text was for the moment presenting a challenge to widely accepted theories, both his own and those of other scholars with whom he had selectively shared the papers. It appeared that the work was undertaken by a hitherto unknown late-sixteenth or early-seventeenth-century engineer, Pietro Azzaro. Professor Elio Lorenzo's increasingly strongly held view was that the ideas and drawings were the work of a man who may well have studied under Leonardo for a period but who had, for whatever reason, moved on to develop his own ideas outside the great man's close circle, perhaps at the time that da Vinci went to work for a duke in Milan. From the documents it was evident that Azzaro lived in, or came from, the city of Lucca, an old Roman town of narrow streets with thick encircling walls that lay south-west of Bologna on the opposite side of Italy's Apennine backbone.

The papers and notebooks depicted some of Leonardo's engineering concepts with comments; there were copies of his helical helicopter design as well as the parachute. But what had caught the elderly professor's attention was a neatly wrapped bundle of different concept drawings and seemingly explanatory text for what could only be described as an aeroplane. The text was coded; he had tried the obvious trick of looking at it in a mirror. He knew that Leonardo had sometimes encrypted his writings in this fashion. But it was to no avail; the notes were not in some simple mirror form of writing. More intriguing, explained the professor to his patient daughter as they sat, he with coffee and she with iced water, in the shade outside a small taverna, were eleven fragile and loose pages of detailed and complex drawings alongside the indecipherable Latin text.

"They showed," he said, "an aeroplane in a configuration that would be easily recognised today. Except," he held his finger up for emphasis, "for the wings; they are like nothing we have ever seen before, anywhere! I went to see an old friend who used to work for Marchetti, the aircraft builder; he was a senior draughtsman in the Varese design office back in 1934. He's retired now."

She watched his face grow florid with excitement. He was challenged by the material that fate had handed him. Putting his empty cup down, he reached over and tore a page from her diary and began to rapidly sketch the aeroplane he had memorised from one of the Azzaro drawings. An accomplished pilot, Helen was familiar with most aircraft shapes and their controls, and her father's sketch appeared little different from them. Until he filled in the detail of two larger-than-normal wings positioned conventionally either side the narrow fuselage. The wings were very thick and straight with none of the beautiful plan form curves adopted by many modern aircraft designers. But, as he progressed, totally engrossed in his sketching, it became evident why they were so thick and straight. Incorporated almost full-length into each wing, along its leading edge, there appeared to be a long, hollow drum-shaped object. Her father went on:

"The drum appears to be hollow but around its circumference is a series of what look like aerodynamically shaped vanes, like an aircraft's wing section, creating lift. The vanes you can actually see on his drawings are only exposed to the air on the wing's leading edge and upper surface. We have to assume that the drum is mechanically rotated somehow inside the wing. There can be no other purpose for positioning it there, but we don't see how the drum with its part-exposed vanes are rotated, or what they actually achieve by rotating. My colleagues and I have presumed that it's what generates lift to support the machine. It's quite unlike anything we have today."

"It's true," she nodded, "after all they didn't have any form of self-powering mechanical engine then, did they? Not even steam; manpower would have been the only option." He held his hands out in acknowledgement. She went on:

"But no doubt the coded text describes some form of engine and how it interacts with the drum, how it turns it. From your sketch, it's the only thing likely to provide lift to get the machine off the ground. There is no propeller or any other form of propulsion shown in any of the drawings."

They sat for a few moments looking at the torn-out diary page with its firm black lines. Helen knew only too well the accuracy of her father's observational powers; he would not have made a mistake over his interpretation of the Azzaro drawings.

"But my child, even if they were able to turn the drum with its vanes mechanically, and assuming that the materials and fixings of that time were strong enough, how would it provide sufficient lift? Marcello from Marchetti has a great deal of experience in this area, but he is unable to explain it satisfactorily, and he doesn't have a clue about the formulae that appear also in code on the backs of the eleven drawings. But, what he does suggest is that the airflow and vortices created within such a rotating layout are likely to be very complex and ways would be needed to manage these to gain any efficiency from what might at first glance appear to be an innovative, alternative-powered flying solution. I ask you: how would Pietro Azzaro, a man from the late-fifteenth century, have known about such things that we hardly understand today – with nearly fifty years of flying and experimentation behind us?"

She paid and they left the shade of the table; as they did so Helen picked up the diary paper, folded it carefully and put it in her handbag for safe keeping.

❖ ❖ ❖

Ceci continued to enjoy the challenge and variety of her work with the ATA despite unsocial hours that often precluded her spending time with Harold. They were unsure about planning their wedding. The war was not going well, and uncertainty and tiredness plagued their discussions on the subject. They'd been tempted to just go ahead; almost everyone in their situation, it seemed, took the plunge without too much thought.

"After all," some of her girlfriends had said, "with the war on you just don't know how long you've got to be happy." Every so often they were able to snatch a weekend together at some discreet hotel or bed-and-breakfast in Sussex or near to her base at Hamble. Ceci usually wore a cheap brass ring on her left hand; she felt it somehow gave legitimacy to their sleeping together. It had never worried her before, out in Asia. And just sleeping together was often exactly what they did. They were often so tired that making love was incomplete as one or both just fell asleep, something neither would have done before the war; they'd always had an energetic approach to this aspect of their relationship.

The workload for aircraft collections and deliveries was growing and the girls were kept very busy despite problems with weather and occasional unserviceability with machines. Ceci was making regular collections from the Supermarine shadow works at Cowley in Oxford, taking Spitfires to desperate southern front-line squadrons in 10 and 11 Group of Fighter Command to replace lost machines and for use in training new young pilots. One afternoon she was given the task of collecting a new Spitfire especially developed and modified for long-range photo-reconnaissance, or PR operations, as the jargon had it. It was intended for a PR unit in the far south-west. Painted cerulean blue, a deep shade, the machine was fitted with additional fuel tanks in the wings and behind the pilot that gave it a radius of action of about eight hundred and fifty miles.

The special Spitfire, designated by the factory as a PR Mk ID, was quickly dubbed by pilots and ground crews alike as the 'flying bowser', carrying, as it did, over one hundred and fourteen gallons of highly flammable petrol. All the guns had been removed along with its radio, together with anything else that served no real purpose in a role that required superior speed and height to ensure its pilot's survival. The Cowley factory fitters and riggers had spent inordinate amounts of time polishing the beautiful machine, fairing off rough cowlings and panel joints, and even rivet heads. The result was a Spitfire that could fly at something over twenty-five miles per hour faster than a standard armed Spitfire fighter and could climb more rapidly and to much greater heights – forty-four thousand feet had been mentioned. On arriving at Hamble all the pilots inspected the new machine as Ceci quoted its phenomenal performance figures.

Overnight, instructions were changed. The new aircraft was now to be delivered to the recently established PR flight at Wick on the north-east tip of Scotland, intended for photographic intelligence-gathering in the North Sea and along the rugged Norwegian coastline. The Germans were known to be operating supply routes along it with coastal tramp steamers; also, the hundreds of coastal indentations in the form of fiords and bays were thought to be providing welcome shelter for larger units of the German navy. In view of the urgency and the aircraft's very extended range it had been decided that Ceci would make the complete delivery rather than take it to another ATA base for onward progress. The weather was benign as she took off from Hamble and turned north intending to fly direct to Dishforth, a bomber station in Yorkshire, where, if she was lucky, she might get lunch; then on to Wick over the Scottish highlands.

As cloud began to progress across her northerly path, she decided to take advantage of the machine's capability for reaching extreme altitudes. Tightening her oxygen mask and selecting near-full boost for the Merlin engine, she began a climb that left Newbury and its racecourse thirty-two thousand feet below. By Oxford she was pulling back the boost and cruising gently at just over two hundred and thirty miles per hour at thirty-six thousand feet. Looking out of the clear blister canopy in full sunshine she could see as far east as the Thames estuary and beyond, including London, between gaps in the cloud crossing slowly below her as a new weather front started to slither across the land. To the west, fragments of the Bristol Channel and River Severn reflected occasional golden shafts of sunlight. Passing just to the west of Nottingham by her dead-reckoning navigation, she saw that the surface was completely obscured by a solid layer of brilliant-white cloud cover. It seemed as though the world had been coated with an uneven layer of pure snow, riven here and there with gently folding valleys. After fifty minutes Ceci began looking for a hole in the solid white through which to descend, ready to make her approach to RAF Dishforth. Looking about carefully as she turned a full circle she realised that there were no holes; she would have to make a careful instrument descent and hope that the cloud base was at least a few hundred feet above the high ground in the local area.

A momentary thought of Jane's final predicament crossed her mind. Like her she had had no formal instrument flying training. Gently Ceci pulled the throttle lever back, setting the propeller to fine pitch. The Spitfire's long nose nudged gently down below the crisp distant horizon as their descent began. The thick white layer waiting to receive her enveloped the machine as she sank into its soft curling folds, the view from the canopy a blank grey-white with beads of moisture streaking back along its clear surface. Monitoring the artificial horizon, the airspeed and her rate of descent, Ceci watched as the machine's altimeter slowly unwound: eight thousand, six... five... three and still descending.

At two thousand feet the cloud was as thick as ever. Approaching one thousand feet she levelled the Spitfire off, applying gentle power. A quick look at her notes indicated that the airfield was at about two hundred feet above sea level. Once again she pulled back power and allowed the aircraft to continue a slow gentle descent. At eight hundred feet the cloud thinned temporarily. For a few seconds she thought she was in the clear. She had not reckoned on the frequent fogs that settled in the Vale of York, ready to catch unsuspecting aviators.

Descending to five hundred feet, she could see fragments of farmland now and again, occasional houses or a village. But the fog was alive, swirling, driven by a light breeze from the east. Ceci reviewed her situation, she had enough fuel to reach Wick, perhaps the prudent thing to do would be to climb back again above the murk and resume her course. Just as she decided to do exactly that, a tall, sturdy stone tower surrounded by slate roof tops appeared in a break, a hundred feet or so below her port wing. She smiled to herself. By pure chance she'd recognised Ripon Cathedral from a visit made while attending Girl Guide camp five or six years previously. Ceci actually hated camping with a bunch of girls; it was so uncomfortable and dirty, but her father had insisted. She had,though, enjoyed the visits and activities that had been arranged that summer – one had been to Ripon Cathedral – they'd spent a whole day there, picnicking in the grounds surrounding the historic monument.

From her briefing notes and chart she knew that Dishforth lay about five miles or so to the east of the great church. Banking the aircraft gently, paying careful attention to her compass, she progressed slowly across the barely visible vale. With no radio, common for ATA deliveries, she announced her relief and presence over the airfield with a slow pass along the runway at two hundred feet. Below, off to one side of the runway threshold, there was a great deal of activity, a large crane with accompanying trucks was removing the remains of a burnt-out aircraft from the churned and muddy airfield. With a flash of green from an Aldis lamp aimed at her from the control tower she made a perfect three-point landing, weaving as she taxied towards an airman waving a pair of gloved hands. Switching off, Ceci thankfully undid her straps, slid back the hood and lowered the cockpit's small side door. The Spitfire's unusual colouring attracted some interest but less so than the sight of a young, slim female pilot emerging from its small cockpit. Taken trophy-like to the mess for lunch, she ate self-consciously surrounded by a group of young Wellington bomber crews watching fascinated by this apparent wonder-woman in dark-blue uniform and flying boots. She had great difficulty convincing some of them that there were many other girls delivering all sorts of aircraft, including bombers, and that she really could not spare the time for a night out at the local pub – she must get on to Wick, if possible that afternoon.

❧ ❧ ❧

Michael Kelly's meeting at the London HQ of the Atlantic Ferry Organisation proved to be a bit of a shock. There had been some changes at the top and new arrangements for managing the despatch of aircraft from Canada to war-torn Britain had been set up. Don Bennett was leaving, and rumour had it that he was going to join Bomber Command in some special pathfinding role aimed at aiding the accuracy of bombing targets in Germany and elsewhere. Michael Kelly did not like the sound of the new Ferry arrangements, and his thoughts turned to what else he could do. He was too old for fighters or even bombers, at least according to current thinking, he'd tried that option before and been turned down. He unsure if it was his age or the fact that he wore a prosthesis below his right knee that had influenced the selection board – it certainly couldn't have been his wide flying experience.

Somewhat depressed, he stepped out into London's Kingsway. A light drizzle had begun, and he walked slowly until he came to a pub. Inside it was heaving with uniforms and noise of all types as he struggled to make his way to the bar. Ordering a beer and Scotch, his slight Aussie accent attracted the attention of his neighbour. Kelly noticed the New Zealand flashes sewn to the man's uniform shoulder and the wings displayed on his left breast. They began chatting. The young pilot had arrived to fight by a very roundabout route: initial selection and some flying training in New Zealand, interrupted by a long Pacific sea voyage to Canada's west coast disembarking at Vancouver, followed by a near-four-day rail ride across the Rockies and eastwards to an airfield in the middle of nowhere in Ontario province. Here he continued his training in specially adapted Tiger Moths, then Harvards, until finally he was awarded his coveted Wings and shipped off to England to join a squadron, glad to be free from Canada's frozen wastes but not the hospitality of its nubile young women.

He'd been assigned to a unit based in Bedfordshire operating Lysanders: army co-operation aircraft, or 'Lizzies', as they were affectionately called. Kelly rolled his eyes. He knew the type, it seemed a dead-end job and he said so. The young pilot shook his head in disagreement.

"Oh no, Sport, it's very special, I've only been there a few weeks, further training, you know. But the flying looks to be quite a challenge. Sorry, can't say much more except we spend two weeks of each month at a forward RAF airfield in Sussex, near the coast."

Michael Kelly looked knowingly at the young man. From his comments and the way he'd delivered them he suspected that there was something special about this pilot's squadron. He wondered if it was an opportunity for him – he'd never make it to fighter pilot now. He also knew that he could demonstrate above-average flying skills if he was given an opportunity.

"What's the name of your CO?" Kelly said pointedly.

"Sure, that's no secret, it's David Balfour but he's in hospital just at the moment, got shot up a bit a couple of nights ago landing in France; bugger, now I've told you." Kelly grinned, touching the man's arm in reassurance.

"The adjutant is perhaps your best bet; he's a pukka sort of bloke – name's David Rawlinson."

Kelly's eyes widened.

"You know him?" answered the young New Zealander.

"I might do, what does he look like?"

The description tallied with that of the navigator Kelly had had as part of his crew on board the Cornucopia the day they had ditched in the Bay of Bengal.

"Oh, I know him, I know him very well," smiled Kelly. "Can you get a message to him? When are you going back?"

It transpired that Brian Coombs, the young New Zealander, was returning to his unit in Sussex that night ready for ops the following night. They spent an enjoyable evening together drinking; Kelly borrowed some paper from a barmaid and wrote a note to David Rawlinson, asking him to make contact. Just before eleven, suitably merry, they vowed to stay in touch and went their respective ways just as the air-raid sirens began to wail for the second time that evening.

Above, the characteristic unsynchronised drone of German bombers covered the dark eastern part of the river and docks, the now-familiar crump of explosions gradually working their way westwards across the City and on towards the West End. In the parks and down on the Thames Embankment anti-aircraft batteries fired incessantly, rarely catching a raider in their salvoes. Searchlights wandered, probing the darkness occasionally lighting up a bomber or defensive barrage balloon swaying aimlessly in the night air. Kelly wondered about his mother-in-law, still living stubbornly in Bayswater. Reaching home in the early hours of the morning, he fell unwashed and reeking of beer into bed beside his snoozing wife. Sarah was not impressed.

The body of the young New Zealand pilot officer was unmarked. He had been found lying, seemingly asleep, just beyond the wrecked houses and shops in the remains of a park flower bed. The policeman who found him was all too familiar with the circumstances.

"Blast killed him, I think," he said solemnly to the ARP warden helping him to lift the lifeless young body onto a stretcher ready for the ambulance.

"Walking about during an air raid; not to be recommended!" Checking the uniform pockets for identification, the policemen placed all items into an envelope: money, ID card, a handwritten note, and so on, and sent them on to the New Zealander's squadron based at RAF Tempsford, not too far from Bedford.

Days later Flying Officer David Rawlinson took the envelope from his 'In' tray and emptied the few items onto his desk.

"Poor old Brian came all this bloody way; for it to end like this is a bloody waste," He muttered the words angrily under his breath. The squadron had had a rough time lately with casualties and two deaths in the past three days as a result of flying accidents. 'To be killed having an innocent and well-deserved night off in London was the last straw,' thought Rawlinson. He picked up the grubby, folded piece of paper. With surprise he saw that the note was actually addressed to him. He cast a glance at the bottom of the page, where it was signed, 'Best regards, Michael Kelly'.

✦ ✦ ✦

Ceci enjoyed the attention she was getting from the young aircrews in RAF Dishforth's mess. After a rather public lunch in the dining hall surrounded by young men, she made her way to the station's Flying Control, where the latest meteorological information was displayed. It wasn't too encouraging: strengthening south-westerly winds would develop over the coming hours bringing rain as an advancing weather front splashed across the UK. Outside, however, the sun had broken through occasionally and the mist that had made her arrival a little dicey had dispersed in the developing breeze; scattered around the airfield were Wellington bombers. One of the young 425 Squadron bomber pilots insisted on driving her out to the dispersal where her Spitfire sat, its long nose sniffing the wind ready for action in the atmosphere for which it had been conceived.

The bomber pilot was clearly impressed and chatty as he walked around the machine while Ceci did her pre-flight checks. Thanking him for his help, she climbed onto the aircraft's wing and slid back the large, clear Perspex hood, lowering the small side-access door of the cockpit.

"Good luck with your trip," he smiled shyly up at her from the tarmac. She smiled back at him as she pulled her helmet over her ears.

"Will you be back this way soon?" She had to lift her leather helmet from her ears to hear him as he repeated the question.

"Oh, I'm not sure; we don't normally deliver this far north from my pool, I'm based down at Hamble...perhaps." She smiled shyly back at him. He nodded, disappointed, waving as she closed the door and pulled the hood almost shut. Ceci could see that she had had some effect on the young man. He was quite short, but good-looking with wavy dark-brown hair, and a broad smile that showed perfect teeth. 'I'm promised to another,' she thought, 'but if I wasn't?' Taking off her left glove she held her hand up so that he could see her engagement ring glinting in the sun. He saw and gestured understanding, laughing awkwardly.

The ground crew had the battery trolley plugged into the machine as she did her pre-start checks. With the Merlin engine turning over and mag checks and run-up completed she waved away the chocks. The two airmen yanked on the ropes, the chocks slid easily from the wheels accompanied by a 'thumbs-up' gesture from one of the ground crew. The power of the machine never failed to surprise Ceci as she taxied carefully across the grass towards the runway threshold, weaving every so often so that she could see what was hidden beyond the Spitfire's lengthy engine cowl.

Short of the runway, she stopped to carry out her pre-take-off vital actions and await a 'green' from the control van. Ceci ran through the short list of actions: boost pump, on; blower, on max; radiator gills, open; elevator trim, neutral; rudder trim, full left. Satisfied, she allowed the aircraft to creep a little closer to the runway. The airman in the control van watched her from the glass dome in its roof, then gave her a green light to proceed.

Turning onto the runway she opened up the engine to 2,750 revolutions, keeping the boost at plus six. The propeller bit hard into the cool air, dragging the Spitfire forward with tremendous acceleration, her right foot holding on the rudder to counteract the Merlin's powerful torque, which, unchecked, would have pulled her rapidly off course down the runway. Within seconds the tail was up; the perfect roar of the engine filled the air as she streaked across the airfield, loving the moment. As the main wheels left the ground her hand fell to the undercarriage lever. As they began to retract, the machine accelerated to one hundred and sixty miles per hour in a moderate climb. Still climbing, she banked the Spitfire hard around to the right aiming to over-fly the airfield as she set course northwards for Wick. Glancing down, she noticed the crane and attendant loaded trucks pulling off the churned muddy area where burnt aircraft remains had lain when she had landed.

Each dispersal was occupied by a black-painted Wellington twin-engine bomber tended by diligent ground crews readying them for their grim night's work somewhere over the dark continent. Long snakes of trolleys followed crawling tractors around the dispersals, each trolley loaded with lethal iron bombs whose latent energy bursting among German homes and factories could only be imagined. The last two dispersals, one of which she had just vacated, were empty, and walking away towards the group of hangars were the figures of the two airmen; just behind was the attractive young bomber pilot looking up. She waggled the Spitfire's wings. The second dispersal should have contained a Wellington too, but it was now burnt beyond recognition its remains bumping along on the back of a truck across the airfield's uneven surface.

The flight north began well; she climbed up through broken cloud that stretched in layers from four thousand to eighteen thousand feet. Below her the sun occasionally dappled the rich Borders farmland with patches of light and warmth. The distance to Wick was just over three hundred nautical miles; with a partial tailwind she expected to be on the ground in just over an hour. Approaching the Firth of Forth at nearly twenty thousand feet she became aware that she was cold. Such heating as was available was clearly not functioning properly in the cockpit and she was not wearing anything special apart from an additional jumper under her fleece-lined leather jacket. Her feet and legs were frozen with nothing much to do. Looking down, she could see ahead, through breaks in the cloud, the city of Edinburgh spread along the river's southerly bank. The huge grey-painted Forth railway bridge crossing from South to North Queensferry stood out clear, an unfailing landmark. A trail of white steam made its way southwards as sluggishly a train edged gingerly across. Upriver she could see a number of large ships camouflaged in shades of grey at the Rosyth Naval base linked spasmodically by wakes from smaller vessels criss-crossing the water. The cold was getting to her. Closing the throttle slightly she commenced a descent towards the river's northern shore, hoping that it would prove to be warmer nearer the earth.

She'd heard the noise on a number of memorable occasions while on the ground at Hamble as, above her, fighters had fought with twisting contrails over the Solent and Southampton. The dull, reverberating noise of machine-guns and cannon had become implanted in her mind as she and colleagues had watched the lethal jousting four or five miles above them. The outcome was often immediately evident as one of the small blurred dots began a desperate final fall, trailing smoke and sometimes erupting in flame. Now and again a parachute would blossom from an even smaller descending object that had broken away from a burning aircraft. It was a noise she was hearing now, suddenly much louder and clearer as she continued her descent over Rosyth.

Momentarily fascinated, she watched a stream of sparkling tracer pour past her starboard wing, followed by a Spitfire banked hard to the left as it shot past her; for an instant she could see the top of the pilot's face peering at her above his facemask. The fighter then flicked over to its right diving sharply downwards. Then it occurred to her. She had been mistakenly attacked by a friendly aircraft. Watching as it dived, her attention was suddenly taken by huge creamy, almost perfect circular eruptions in the brown water surrounding the grey ships moored mid-stream. Still watching, she saw the cause: a flight of six or seven German Dornier bombers were unloading their lethal cargo hoping to catch the anchored naval vessels asleep. Their pencil-thin fuselages, adorned with heavy black crosses, suddenly scattered like petrified partridges as a flight of three Spitfires swept around up-sun above them. From the leading edge of their wings she saw occasional bright-orange flickering as the Spitfire pilots depressed the gun buttons on their control stick's hand-grip. Ceci turned rapidly away, to the south, trying to get far from the incredibly fast confusing action taking place a thousand feet or so below her. Seeing for the first time the white puffs of anti-aircraft bursts surrounding the German machines, she continued to bank hard around against the sun, holding her gloved hand up to shield her eyes from its glare. As she did so there was an incandescent flash.

❖ ❖ ❖

Michael Kelly met Cornucopia's erstwhile navigator in the Unicorn pub in Chichester after David Rawlinson had received the note found on Brian Coombs's body. After warm, genuine greetings and an exchange of general gossip, Kelly opened up.

David was keen to find a way of recruiting the former Empress Airways captain and friend into their special operations squadron. At this stage he was unsure of the situation, his CO had been injured quite badly while on the ground in France and had been lucky to find the will, let alone the strength, to fly the machine accurately off the black field, somehow making it across the Channel with two Special Operations Executive women couriers on board. Rawlinson described how he had realised that something was seriously wrong as he had watched the Lysander wallowing dangerously, flying very slowly on its approach to their airfield in the early dawn.

"I could hear that the engine was just idling as he came over the airstrip and in the occasional light from the goose-neck flares I could just see David's silhouette leaning over against the cockpit side, head down just as the machine hit the ground for the first time. It bounced high but he managed to open the throttle a bit to help hold it off. It bounced heavily again two or three times, then ground-looped, coming to a halt in a pile of hay; fortunately it was unbaled, left by the farmer the previous afternoon. I ran out, when I got there the two SOE women were out of the rear cockpit looking at David, trying to undo his straps and holding his head up. He was soaked in blood and coughing something awful. Incredibly, he was protesting loudly, trying to carry out his shut-down drills in that state."

Kelly sat slightly open-mouthed.

"Then the meat-wagon arrived with one of the flight commanders. We managed to lift him out – he'd been shot twice, once in the back of the head, the second through the shoulder, but he was conscious. He said something about being betrayed, that there had been German soldiers hiding in the hedges alongside the field."

"How is he? Have you been to see him?" Kelly felt a surge of sympathy for the injured and heroic pilot. Putting his glass down and swallowing, Rawlinson nodded.

"Went to the hospital this afternoon, not allowing visitors in to see him, but he's stable and mostly conscious."

"I suspect he'll be out of action for a while," suggested Kelly softly. David Rawlinson nodded as he got up to refill their glasses. The pub was crowded and it took a while.

❖ ❖ ❖

His transfer from the Atlantic Ferry Organisation to the RAF was swiftly arranged. Michael Kelly reported for duty a week later still wearing his dark-blue Atlantic Ferry uniform, which drew some enquiring looks in the mess for a couple of days. He'd been given the rank of Flight Lieutenant acting Squadron Leader in recognition of his extensive flying experience and navigation expertise, but the pay was less than he had become used to as an Atlantic Ferry pilot. Sarah was pleased with some aspects of his change in employment – now he was able to get home most nights in the Morgan three-wheeler car he had acquired from somewhere; its Matchless V-twin engine signalling its approach. She said she was more concerned about him in the Morgan than when he was flying; he did have a tendency to throw the powerful, light, two-seater around at unnatural speeds along the narrow, high-banked country lanes, with little thought for his own, or indeed other people's safety.

Despite his new rank, Kelly recognised that he was a virtual novice compared to some of the younger men of lower rank who flew dangerous and discreet missions into France during moonlit nights – collecting or delivering agents either by parachute or landing in remote, dark fields – always susceptible to betrayal and capture. The squadron was equipped with a mix of matt-black-painted machines including four Lysander army co-operation aircraft, four Hudsons, two Whitley bombers, lightened and converted for parachute-dropping, and a commandeered, five-seat Percival Proctor communications light aircraft. His briefing with Rawlinson, the temporary deputy CO and squadron adjutant, made him aware of the nature of their work and how risky it could be, as exemplified by the fate that befell their seriously wounded CO, David Balfour. Getting used to the mix of machines for their respective work occupied nearly a month of near-continuous day- and night-flying including some very hairy night-landing practice in fields in the remoter parts of central Wales. There had been angry complaints from locals seemingly unaware that there was a war on.

The night was truly black for his first mission to France, Operation Cygnet, unforecast high cloud blocking sight of stars and moon; not even basic reference points were evident. There was some doubt about the weather; however, his crew was experienced, although a little perturbed at having to fly with a new skipper in such conditions, and as yet unproven in their line of work.

There was a tension in the air as the four crew-members were driven out to the shadowy aircraft. Operation Cygnet was to drop two agents by parachute at a location just south of St Pol, about fifty miles inland from Boulogne, using one of the squadron's elderly, twin-engine Armstrong Whitworth Whitleys. They'd been briefed to continue south after dropping the two agents, hopefully giving the impression that the aircraft was on a normal bombing mission and not something more surreptitious. A black car with slitted headlamps arrived with the two agents, a man and a woman, accompanied by a dark-suited civilian man and a WAAF Squadron Officer. They stood for a few minutes under the starboard wing. A few quiet words were exchanged in French followed by a gentle laugh and an exchange of Gallic kisses.

Settled down and with checks completed, Kelly started the two Tiger radial engines and prepared the machine and his crew for take-off. Once they were airborne the few goose-neck flares positioned to mark the runaway were extinguished as they climbed away into the opaque blackness on a compass course given by the navigator. The crew watched the enveloping blackness, totally alert, while the two agents sat quietly at the rear of the aircraft cold, uncomfortable, breaking the rules by occasionally smoking. One agent, the young woman, looked tired under the single dim yellowish lamp, but surprisingly relaxed and showing a radiant smile every now and again despite what she knew she must be facing in the way of danger and possible betrayal. Her colleague, a much older, aristocratic-looking man, seemed confident, sometimes exchanging a few shouted words with the woman in French; once, laughing, she hit him playfully. At nine thousand feet just west of Boulogne it was cold. Kelly levelled the machine off. Now and again a series of intense bright flashes could be seen further along the near-invisible coast. The RAF was attacking ships and ports with effect that night. After fifteen minutes he pulled back the two throttle levers and trimmed the aircraft for an almost silent glide towards their target lying some seven miles distant in the inky darkness; nothing showed below. At three thousand feet he switched on the two red 'prepare' lights in the aircraft's rear fuselage, warning his passengers that they were nearing the drop zone. The hatch in the machine's belly was lifted, the air sucking noisily at the opening. In the dim red lights the woman kissed the male agent briefly before sitting, ready, legs dangling just in the air-stream. He prepared himself, checking the straps on his parachute, then watching her.

A short burst of white Morse dots and dashes shot silently skywards; the ground reception committee was ready. Turning very slightly left, he could see a tiny, steady white light; seconds later he switched the green jump light on. She was gone in an instant, out, down and behind the aircraft, parachute opening almost immediately. Her companion followed within seconds, keen not to be separated by too much ground when they landed. With the hatch closed, Kelly gently opened the throttles and climbed away south-east towards Germany as flak batteries opened up somewhere off to their left, firing at a genuine bomber raid on a key railway junction. After fifteen minutes he banked the aircraft around steeply onto a reciprocal heading making a bee-line for the French Channel coast.

After debriefing and a very early breakfast he stood watching a blood-red dawn emerge from low clouds. In his bath he thought about the casual courage displayed by the two agents dropped low into the black night sky. Who were they, what was their brief, what drove them to take such risks with their lives? In bed with curtains drawn against the rising sun he heard the opening roar of an aero engine as the squadron started its day's work. He awoke cold, hungry and still tired just after one o'clock that afternoon.

❖ ❖ ❖

Harold was disappointed. He'd been airborne for almost two and a half hours, the cold and his wish that he had availed himself of a visit to the toilet before leaving did nothing to improve his state of mind. His briefing had been to photograph the result of Bomber Command's work the previous night, attacking industrial works around Mannheim. The problem was the weather. The Met boys had got it all wrong; below was ten-tenths cloud cover, not the four-tenths promised for the time of his arrival. He could dive below and photograph from low level but he had the wrong type of cameras fitted; not the oblique ones used for low level, but the vertical cameras ideal for capturing expansive images from high level. The decision was his as he circled over the area of his intended shoot. Turning slightly and glancing back he noticed that he was now leaving a long white contrail in his wake; if enemy fighters saw this he would have to run for his life. The contrails provided a superb pointer to his moving location for any enemy aircraft within fifty miles. Diving, he sought a level where the moisture in his burnt fuel and the swirling vortices generated by his wingtips would not condense in such a pointedly public fashion.

Listening intently as he turned up the volume control on his radio he could hear the wavering whine as one then another German radar emission caught his machine in the ether, providing its controllers with his changing position.

There were two of them. Swiftly moving black graphics against the clouds, racing towards his position and climbing hard. A pale trail of grey smoke followed their persistent progress. Stopping his descent, he turned smartly away aiming to narrow the angle of their interception but the new heading was taking him further into German skies, not homewards. Now he was not cold. He opened up the Merlin, full boost selected, climbing powerfully, intent on outrunning the two lethal pursuers. It was the PR pilot's standard evasion tactic; at his height there were no clouds to run to. He had to turn eventually. That was self-evident. Back towards the north-west, the Channel and home. Harold could see that such a course would actually reduce the horizontal separation between his Spitfire and what were slowly resolving into a pair of lethal Focke-Wulf 190 fighters. It was essential he gained height to compensate. It was a gamble, he knew, relying on height and speed to pull him clear of their murderous cannons and machine-guns.

He made a sharp turn; it slowed him slightly. The Spitfire's tell-tale contrail rigidly followed the tightly executed change of course until upper winds blew the virgin white lines into untidily dissipating daubs across the arc of blue sky. If they were 190s, they had an absolute ceiling of thirty-seven thousand feet; he could match that, he knew, and probably raise them two or three thousand feet – possibly more. His pursuers were now immediately below him as a result of his slowing turn. Some five or six thousand feet still separated them.

Harold maintained the climb. But, the Spitfire was reaching its limits, the altimeter hands slowed markedly as each few hundred feet were gained. At nearly 41,500 his reliable Merlin engine was slowly running out of steam, even with two powerful superchargers sucking hungrily at the rarefied air, snatching at available vital oxygen. The aircraft's handling had also become less precise. In the rarefied atmosphere the machine was beginning to wallow, sitting on an aerodynamic cusp between stalling and flying in the thin air. He turned slightly, careful not to upset the delicate stability of the Spitfire, trying to look down and behind him. The two German fighters had levelled off about four thousand feet below him, now a mile astern, tracking him exactly.

How long they could keep this up he had no idea. It was generally thought by Fighter Command that the Fw 190 had an operational range of about five hundred miles. Depending on where they had taken off, they could chase him to the French coast and beyond. After all, he thought, they could always refuel at one of the many Luftwaffe bases in northern France before setting off for their home base, wherever that might happen to be.

At 42,150 feet the Spitfire stopped climbing. Additional height would only come from lowering its weight; a result of burning off fuel. Every few minutes he gingerly turned the Spitfire again, keeping tabs on the two heavily armed fighters. They had lost ground to him. Approaching the Channel coast near the Belgian–French border, the lower cloud began to fragment, and it was possible to see the grey, chilly waters of the English Channel. Distance, he judged, was about twenty miles. Turning his head, he looked north-east along the curving coastline towards Nieuwpoort and Ostend; beyond those brutally occupied towns the image was haze-blurred; only a vague distinction between land and sea could be determined.

Harold turned his head back scanning the skies off to his left: nothing. He slowly turned his head again to scan the skies to his right. He gasped involuntarily into his oxygen-rich facemask. There were now two more fighters, this time only very slightly below his altitude. They were converging from the coast on his far right. Both were unashamedly leaving pure-white contrails in the cold, clean air. It seemed to him that the Luftwaffe was having a special counter-reconnaissance day. He knew that his progress across the continent would have been carefully tracked. His two original pursuers would have kept their controllers fully informed of the lone Spitfire's course, height and speed. In his headphones the wailing noise of a number of enemy radars emphasised his perilous situation. In turn the German controllers would have known just when to scramble intercepting fighters from airfields in northern France, well ahead of him, as he attempted escape. It seemed they were determined to catch this one and make a very public example of it. The two new fighters off to his right were intent on cutting off his escape. Looking down again, he could see that at some point in the past minute or so, the two original 190s had left the chase allowing their fresh colleagues a chance at a kill.

He was short of fuel. He'd being using it prodigiously, keeping ahead and above the Luftwaffe. Now he would have to fool his pursuers in some way so that he could turn further north, cross the Channel and land at the nearest available airfield. The irony was, he smiled grimly, his cameras were empty of pictures. The two fighters, still off to his right were slowly closing. He had no idea how they were managing to stay with him at this extreme height with all their additional armament, but it was, unfortunately, a fact. Harold recognised the need to do something fairly innovative to get away with his life. A few more gallons of precious fuel burnt meant that he was able to gain another hundred feet, the Merlin engine was performing perfectly in the conditions; as were the powerful BMW motors pulling the pursuing 190s.

Watching them carefully for a few seconds and judging the moment, he pulled the stick back firmly. Within a second the Spitfire had stalled in the rarefied air, even with full power on. He allowed her to have her own way: the machine dropped her port wing and plunged almost vertically. Speed built rapidly.

He searched his windscreen and canopy anxiously for the two 190s. There!

They had continued on their original converging course, surprised it seemed that the English machine had suddenly made such a violent and unexpected manoeuvre. Believing attack the best option for defence, throttle wide open and emergency boost selected, Harold soon covered the distance to where the 190s were now beginning to react. He aimed himself directly at the lead machine.

Its pilot glimpsed him. In an instant the 190 pitched up violently before rolling hard to the right. If Penrose had been armed, a two-second burst would have pumped enough lead and high explosive into the Focke-Wulf's exposed belly to make it and its pilot beyond any economic repair. The German machine fell away fast, its pilot fighting to recover control, unaware that the cerulean blue PR Spitfire had no teeth. Harold had no time to watch as he pulled hard around, pressed firmly into his seat by the growing forces. Still with plenty of speed in hand from his dive, he aimed himself at the second 190. It had turned away, its pilot no doubt intending to stay with his leader. He would only be able to see the approaching Spitfire in his rear mirror.

Intending to shock, even frighten the Luftwaffe pilot with some dangerous close-quarters flying, Harold hoped that the German would flee the scene as his diving colleague now appeared to have done, allowing him to finally get away.

The Luftwaffe pilot was keen to see where the blue Spitfire was, acutely aware that his life depended on it, so he believed. As the 190 banked hard left, its wings near vertical, Penrose was barely two hundred feet away, travelling much quicker. He was aiming to pass fast and close down the port side of the German and follow up with a steep diving turn to the left to clear himself from the Luftwaffe pilot's cannons and machine-guns.

It was the German's continuing steep and rapid left turn that instantly sealed the inevitable outcome of the rapidly developing situation. There was too little time for the Spitfire to react fully to the 190's swiftly changing direction in the thin air. The Spitfire hit the Focke-Wulf from above, just aft of the cockpit, its propeller slicing the tail cleanly from the rest of the German machine – the blades flying off into space. Mass and momentum carried the Spitfire through the mortally wounded 190's wings and remaining fuselage. Its pilot died in seconds from the impact of the Spitfire's port wing ripping through the cockpit, severing his trunk in two in the process.

Suddenly, Harold was in clear air. His engine roared like a wounded lion with no propeller to drive. His life-preserving canopy was partially gone, and he was conscious of the thin, freezing air taking immediate toll on his metabolism. His oxygen mask had somehow remained on his face. He must get out – the thought was instinctive.

The next few seconds ran like a slow-motion film; he was unbelieving of how ponderously things were happening. He tried to roll the machine onto its back with the intention of dropping out of the cockpit but it proved impossible; the stick was useless. There was no resistance in its movement. The ailerons weren't working. In his peripheral vision he saw the jagged aluminium tear where his port wing had once been, QED.

The noise; he pulled the throttle back and the engine cut completely. The terribly broken Spitfire was falling and beginning to spin awkwardly; gripping the sharp edges of the broken cockpit sides, he noticed that his gloves were dark-stained.

Nothing; couldn't move. His mind bellowed, 'Undo the bloody harness!' The gyrations were becoming wilder. What next? He tried to think but disorientation and cold slowed concentration on vital actions.

'Bloody hell, bloody hell, BLOODY HELL!' He shouted silently in frustrated rage into his oxygen mask. Panic was very close, then blackness, the mask disconnected forcibly. He was falling free, reaching terminal velocity in fourteen seconds. Fertile French farmland sat waiting six miles below; he was travelling towards it at a modest one hundred and twenty miles per hour, quite oblivious.

❖ ❖ ❖

Ceci watched, horribly fascinated as the Dornier bomber erupted in a brilliant white flash, a few larger pieces of debris arcing like fireworks from the mass of instantly boiling and turbulent grey-black smoke. It was only much later that she had time to consider in some detail what she had witnessed so closely. One of the attacking Spitfires, or possibly flak from the ships below, had scored a direct hit on the bomber's sleek cargo, primed and ready for immediate delivery in its open bomb bay. Its small clutch of five-hundred-kilo bombs had incinerated the machine and its crew in a brief instant. Apart from a huge patch of ragged smoke there was absolutely nothing left of the large machine and its three crew, save for a few of the larger pieces arcing down into the Forth below, unseen by Ceci. Now back over Rosyth she looked quickly towards the east, through layers of torn cloud. Fleeing below her were two bombers, one streaming smoke, Spitfires harrying them as they sought the sanctuary of the wide, empty North Sea. White flak bursts quickly curtailed her observations as Ceci realised she had become a target of an understandably nervous navy moored below. She climbed away north, hardly believing what had happened; all the time keeping a good look-out around the wide horizon.

She had been reported by one of the Spitfire pilots during his debriefing at Turnhouse. The young sergeant pilot mentioned seeing what he thought to be a deep-blue Spitfire during the action over the Forth Bridge and wondered what had happened to it. He had seen it only briefly after firing on it in error but was sure that no hits had occurred; it was too much of a deflection shot. He'd then become engaged with the Dorniers and lost sight of the Spitfire. The station intelligence officer made copious notes and promised to inform the worried young sergeant of any further gen. about the machine he'd mistakenly fired on.

The weather at RAF Wick was clear despite the earlier poor forecast. Her flight from over Edinburgh to her remote coastal destination had given time for her pulse to calm and for the adrenaline to dissipate somewhat. Turning finals with full flap at seventy miles per hour, she concentrated on setting the machine up for a three-pointer.

As the main and tail wheels touched down almost together she pulled the throttle fully closed the machine riding the uneven grass surface easily as she slowed with gentle use of the brakes. A small van rushed out like a terrier, bouncing across the field as she stopped the Spitfire, wondering where to taxi. An airman emerged wrapped up in a mix of unofficial clothing and climbed up onto the wing. She slid the canopy back a few inches, and the throttle back to idle. No wonder he was so wrapped up – the air was damp, near freezing. After signalled instructions she taxied to a distant hangar and shut down. The van followed her, and from it emerged an RAF officer, elderly with classic handlebar moustache and twinkling blue eyes. He wore a set of wings on his uniform, below which sat a double row of assorted medal ribbons.

"Hello, my dear. Good trip?" He held out his hand to steady her as she jumped from the Spitfire's wing onto the short, damp grass.

"Yes thanks. Bit hairy over the Forth though, nearly got caught up in a dogfight with some Spitfires and the Luftwaffe." Ceci smiled at the kindly gentleman officer, thinking that he must be from the Great War; he was probably considered too old to be in action now.

"Ah, so it was you, I thought it might be when I saw you land. We had a telephone report, one of the pilots based at Turnhouse reported seeing a blue Spitfire as he was diving on the enemy, says he fired on you by mistake. Were you hit?"

They walked around the aircraft looking for any damage. There was none.

"Well that's good, then," he said. "Let me take you over to operations, they can deal with the paperwork and then, no doubt, you'd like something to eat?" He smiled kindly at her; Ceci realised that she was quite hungry now. After a phone call to Hamble she managed to eat in the station's officers' mess. It was too late to attempt a return to Hamble that evening; she would try to hitch a lift with any aircraft going south tomorrow. The duty ops officer had said that there was a possibility that an Anson may be going to Squires Gate at Blackpool sometime the following morning. From there she would have to either travel by rail – just the thought of it made her depressed – or find another aircraft going further south with a seat spare. She spent the night in the WAAF quarters; there were no facilities in the officers' mess for females. As she closed her eyes she was overcome with an unusual feeling of foreboding.

❖ ❖ ❖

It was like a dream; falling interminably then waking, stomach in mouth, startled in the comfort and security of a solid bed. He knew he was already awake, his hands and shoulders hurting terribly.

Still falling; there was no bed. It was real. It was dark too; he raised his hands to his face. He couldn't find his eyes, appeared to be blind. Thoughts raced pell-mell and unconstructed through his brain. Recall!

What is happening? He was rolling over and over, that much he knew. Suddenly, the rushing air tore at his leather helmet, which ballooned, then was tugged off his face to the back of his head, the strap parted and it was lost.

France was growing very rapidly as his sight was instantly restored. Below, woods and farmland turned regularly with brief patches of sky. He knew what he must do but it was taking so long to bring his brain to function, to send the necessary signals to activate his arms and hands.

It would be quick, one minute falling free in the air, the next second nothing. Just a man-sized depression in the soft turf.

He inched his fingers to where the metal ring was positioned low on his chest, the cold streaming air ripping and rushing making concentrated movement difficult. Two fingers took hold like claws. He summoned his arm to pull. The pain was terrible. He couldn't pull. He must. The turf was now very near. The noise of his scream was obliterated as the canopy, released from its carefully folded bag, cracked open above him. Grunting in pain as the canopy inflated, he felt his earthward trajectory suddenly arrested. Like a pendulum he swung, just once, wildly to his left, then it was over. Harold Penrose lay cold, in pain, and damp from the wet grass that grew in the shadow of a densely wooded copse.

As he lay there, only the noise of the countryside filled his senses: a cow gently lowing, birds, wind rustling through trees and the distant drone of a vehicle. Above, the sky was a mix of blue and white rushing cumulus. Raising his head, he slowly became aware of how lucky he had been; the trees in the copse were mature, tall and sturdy. If he had landed in them his situation would have been even more precarious – or finally over. Lying back, he began to take stock.

Baled out over France. Where? Not sure where – somewhere west? Something wrong with right shoulder and hands. Instinct, need to hide. Parachute – get rid. Oh God, he ached. He rolled slowly onto his front, managing to raise himself to a kneeling position in careful and painful stages. His parachute was spread out between him and the shadowy trees while a fitful breeze picked and pulled at its folds. Biting his lip, he managed to undo the harness lock. The pain in his hands was terrible and his gloves left heavy red stains on the white silk.

Standing with difficulty, he kicked it into a rough ball along with his Mae West lifejacket, awkwardly, using his feet and one hand to pull its lines around the mass of expensive silk cloth. Still kicking, he manoeuvred the awkward bundle into the trees, well beyond the thin wire fence line that surrounded them. He desperately needed a pee. His damaged hands could not undo the buttons on his fly. The ripped gloves were bloodily stuck to his hands; he tried undoing his belt to drop his trousers but it was too much. He let go, at least for the moment it was warm on his legs.

Sitting, his back against a tree that gave him a view of the surrounding fields, he thought, 'What about Ceci? She'll be distraught when I'm reported missing. How will they break it to her? Where has my aircraft crashed?' The questions kept coming but he didn't, or couldn't, answer them. He was very tired; the grinding pain in his hands and the ache in his right shoulder dulled his senses to anything else. Early evening was settling on the landscape, and he tried to pull the leather jacket around him to keep out the chill. The zip was broken, no doubt ripped open during the fall, he mused.

Later, along the adjacent side of the field, a man in dark-blue dungarees was walking, wearing a misshapen hat. He seemed to be carrying a reel of something, his arm through its centre. Every so often he stopped and appeared to investigate something in the hedgerow. Two dogs, or was it three, accompanied the man. Penrose wriggled his back up the tree he had been leaning against. Standing groggily, he turned and moved further into the copse, staggering slightly. The evening sun was low and shadows among the trees had lengthened. If the dogs picked up his scent he was done for, but what could he do? He was in no real state to run anywhere. His mind tried to focus but it was difficult: the fall of nearly four miles in freezing, tearing air and the various pains around his body stifled his faculties.

Deliberately the man made his way along the perimeter of the field until he was walking along the fence line that bordered the copse. Harold stood concealed, watching. He stopped now and again, making running repairs to the fence as he progressed. The two dogs ambled about, noses to the ground, sniffing, ears up, tails wagging every so often. One, a medium-sized black-and-white collie, became agitated as it sniffed at the trodden area where Penrose had landed. The other dog, younger but of similar breed, joined in the excitement. Their instincts were aroused as they trotted forward inquisitively towards the trees at the edge of the hiding-place, tails now wagging furiously. The man looked up, watching his animals but suspecting their interest was rabbits or similar prey. Suddenly one animal bounded through the gap between the fence wires, tail up, then still, growling. The second watched, curious for a moment, then followed. The man had found another failure in the wire and bent to attend to a repair. If the dogs had found something it was of no concern to him. Rabbits and foxes were becoming an increasing nuisance in the area.

Harold watched, worried, as the dogs entered the trees; quickly they found the bundled parachute and started whimpering and issuing small barks. The man looked up. What was bothering those dogs today?

Standing, he held his hands up to shield his eyes from the lowering sun. Something unusual was exciting them. He'd seen the trail of smoke a few miles away as an aircraft had plunged to the ground, onto his neighbour's land. He'd not seen any crew bale out, though. Bending carefully between the wire strands, he walked up the grassy bank and into the shelter of the trees. The dogs were growling, hackles raised, at something lying in a bush about fifty yards away, at the base of an ancient ash. He knew immediately what it was; he'd seen one before after a dogfight over the area in late May 1940. It was a parachute rolled into a rough ball, partly concealed under some holly. The man looked about carefully.

A parachute in this condition needed a pilot. Quickly losing interest in the jumbled silk, the two dogs trotted off further into the wood, occasionally dropping their noses to sniff at the earth. With some trepidation the man followed with his heavy hammer at the ready, watching the dogs carefully as he went. A few minutes later they set up a great barking and snarling, teeth bared, heads raised, bouncing up and down on their front paws. Penrose stood stock-still behind another clump of holly that grew irregularly around the base of an elderly ash. They'd found him. It was inevitable, he thought. Then he saw the man approaching carefully and obviously a little afraid, hammer poised. He'd have to risk it.

"Monsieur, ici."

It was whispered. The man caught it, looked up, an expression of mild surprise on his face, but it was obvious that he could not yet see Penrose.

"Où, Monsieur, où?"

With a great deal of noise Harold stepped out of his concealment onto a clear patch of dead leaves and earth between the trees. The dogs' chorus rose in response. The man uttered a few sharp words and the dogs suddenly lay silent, watching, their noses active. Harold half-raised his hands as a sign of surrender. They hurt like hell. Unsure, they faced each other a few yards apart.

"Je suis Pilot Officer Harold Penrose, mon avion est ... er ... tombé." French was not Harold's strength. The man looked and half-smiled, stepped closer with the hammer firmly gripped in his right hand. He looked at Harold's half-raised hands in their bloodied, ripped gloves.

"Vous êtes Anglais, Monsieur, un soldat de l'armée de l'air?"

"Oui, oui; mais où est moi?" Harold hoped that his enquiry about his location had got through. The man took hold of Harold's right hand, gently pulling it down, looking at it.

"Vous n'êtes pas loin de Morlaix." Motioning to him, the man sat Harold down against a tree. The injured pilot appeared no threat, he thought, putting the hammer down but within his reach. Taking hold of the stained glove, the man gently tried to pull it from Harold's right hand. The pain was sharp and unbearable and he jerked the gloved hand away from the man's grasp, holding it protected under his left arm.

Near Morlaix, He tried to remember his French geography, then it struck him; his pursuit by the Luftwaffe had taken him almost clear across northern France. He was only a few dozen miles from the coast and the Channel .

"Bugger."

The man looked up askance. He took Harold by the arm and led him to the edge of the tree line, the two dogs trailing behind them, uninterested. Motioning Harold to stay concealed, he left, walking quickly and directly across the wide field towards the open gate at the far side.

Just visible was a bicycle leaning against one of the gate-posts. The man returned with a torn and ancient jacket. Tucked into its pocket was a paper bag on one side, a beret on the other. In his hand was a bottle, extracted from the paper bag, which he held up for Penrose. It was coarse red wine. He glugged, two streams of pale rose coursed down his chin and neck. Reaching into his trouser pocket the man withdrew a large penknife and opened it expertly. The blade was heavily worn from constant sharpening. Concerned, Harold jumped back.

"Non, non Monsieur, z'inquiétez pas, z'inquiétez pas, c'est bon ! Juste des outils! Et vous, ça va?"

The pilot relaxed a little; a few more mouthfuls of wine helped. The man put the knife in Harold's damaged hands, a gesture of trust; he indicated that he should cut off his badges of rank and wings from his uniform jacket. With his hands useless he let the man remove the incriminating evidence of his background together with his ripped scarf and shirt collar. His leather jacket was rolled up and hidden along with his parachute deep in the copse, well covered with branches and undergrowth. He put on the rough, thin blue jacket while the man rubbed soil into his urine-soaked blue uniform trousers and pulled the trouser legs over his flying boots. A dark-blue beret completed a temporary yet effective disguise.

Putting a thin knotted rope around one of the dogs, the man

handed the makeshift loop in the lead to Harold as they stepped out onto a narrow road bordered for the most part by high hedges and grassy banks. Now fully dusk it was the right time for workers to be wearily plodding home after the exertions of the day, thought Harold, as he allowed the dog to tug ahead of him despite spasms of pain while the man kept step at his side, pushing his squeaking cycle. The other, older dog trailed behind, tail down, eyes watching. Where they were all headed Harold had no idea but he was sure now that he was not going to be handed over to the Germans.

After fifteen minutes walking with occasional conversation in fractured French they finally rounded a long bend allowing a cluster of small houses to reveal themselves, one or two washed white with dark, tiled roofs. Harold could see a more substantial derelict property behind them, together with a group of barns huddled at the bottom of a grassy rise that led atop to thick deciduous forest. Above, dozens of crows circled, cawing raucously, alighting in branches for a moment then, dissatisfied, launching themselves again, adding to the noise. Beyond and to one side of the trees there rose a thin pillar of smoke, almost vertical in the evening stillness. The man pointed with his chin,

"A mon avis, c'est un avion Boche. Peut-être que c'est celui que vous avez descendu?" Penrose said nothing for a moment while he mentally interpreted the comments. Then, looking at the smoke, he nodded; it could be either his Spitfire or the German aircraft. Those adrenaline-filled moments high above the earth in the near-airless cold returned to him. He was still shocked at the past hour's events.

Inside the second whitewashed house the tiny parlour had a

good log fire roaring. A young woman was piling more logs into a wicker basket alongside the hearth; she looked up as the door opened.

"Papa, mais ... " There followed staccato conversation, back and forth. It was loud, as though he was not there; he watched their faces trying to glean some sense of what was being said, what his immediate future might be. It was soon obvious that the young woman was not keen on his presence. She was thin, her face lined with worry, her shapeless clothes hung on her, signalling an unusual loss of weight. The man motioned Penrose to sit while he and the young woman left the room; the argument raged on outside. The younger of the dogs crept towards him, and he carefully held out his hand tickling the cowering animal's ears. It slowly relaxed and lay at his feet. From upstairs there were more loud words and the banging of doors and drawers. She returned, thrusting the parlour door open and almost throwing a collection of clothes at him.

"Voilà," then withdrawing, closing the door firmly after her. He picked over the clothes; they were clean, some ironed but a little threadbare in places. On trying to remove his own clothes the problem of his hands arose. He sat for a moment wondering what to do next. Clearly she did not want him in the house; he was a dangerous liability, of that he was sure. Perhaps if he could get changed and have his hands tended he could leave after dark – taking their worries with him. The man came in and rolled his eyes.

"Je suis désolé, Monsieur, mais ma fille est très tendue." He was embarrassed, apologising for his daughter's behaviour. So it was his daughter. It had struck Harold she was too young to be the man's wife. He led the pilot through the house to a small kitchen at the rear. En route Harold stopped for a moment, turning towards the man.

"Où est votre femme?" He wondered where the man's wife was – it was obviously a house that had had a woman's touch. The man paused for a moment, and then shook his head. From the kitchen windows the farm barns and derelict house could just be seen, backed by the tall, dark trees on the rise in the near-darkness. The girl returned with a pair of scissors, her face expressionless as she glanced at him.

Pulling down the window blinds, she ran some water into a large, chipped enamel bowl and set it down on the scrubbed wooden table motioning him to sit by it. In the light of the flaring paraffin lamp she took his hand, gently studying the blood-stained gloves, then pushed one firmly under the cold water. The bowl's contents turned a muddy red immediately; he felt the tension in the dried, tight leather slowly release. After a few minutes she lifted his left hand, dripping, from the bowl and laid it on a towel spread across the table. Its worn whiteness was soon obliterated with his blood. From the cuff she began snipping carefully at the leather, pulling at the glove, which soon disintegrated from her efforts, and from the cuts and tears caused as a result of his collision.

The man watched, his back against the warm stove, smoking. As the glove was completely removed he stepped forward to look. It was a mess. Penrose's index finger was without a nail, and a large deep cut ran from its tip through the palm almost to his wrist. He couldn't move the finger. Other fingers were also cut and torn, some quite deeply. The skin on the top of his knuckles was ripped, not cut, as though torn through a coarse cheese grater. The cold water made the hand sting. Alert to the damage, he winced, trying to contain his pain. There was no sign of frostbite from his exposure to the high-altitude cold, he was relieved to see. His long, swift fall before opening his parachute had reduced his time in the sub-zero air.

At one point the girl looked sideways at him, not without sympathy. Gently but firmly she repeated the treatment with his right hand, which appeared to have suffered less than his left, but was in a poor state. Later that evening his hands had been covered in some sort of cream and heavily bandaged; he was unable to move the fingers on either hand and they throbbed uncomfortably. The woman fed him some chicken broth, wiping his chin from time to time; helping him change, the man finally led him out to the farther of the two barns after Penrose had insisted on putting his stiff, smelly and damp RAF uniform onto the parlour fire. In the dark the large double door was pulled apart; it was cool inside.

On an upper level a simple bed had been put together out of straw bales and loose hay with a few blankets. Bidding "Bonne nuit," he fell asleep within minutes. In his final waking moments his thoughts drifted back to Ceci.

❖ ❖ ❖

Ceci awoke early and managed to bathe and dress before most of the other girls in the WAAF accommodation at Wick were up and about. Packing her few bits and pieces into her compact leather holdall she quietly left the building and made her way across the station's central tarmac parade square to the officers' mess. Inside, a few officers were smoking in the ante-room; others were staring into cups of tea in the dining room among empty plates smeared with greasily congealed remains of recent bacon and eggs eaten by air crews who had returned in the early hours from a sortie over the North Sea. Her entry caused a mild stir among the quiet men and she was conscious of eyes watching her. A steward led her to an area partially screened from the main hall. Two WAAF officers were sitting chatting and smiled as she sat at an adjacent table.

"Hello, where are you from?" said one with freckles and a bob of ginger hair, a cigarette in her fingers. Swallowing and wiping her mouth, Ceci looked up.

"ATA, Hamble," she said.

"Hope to God it's warmer down there than it is up here," laughed the other, older woman. Ceci nodded noticing that the older WAAF had lots of rank on her shoulders.

"Just a bit, I'm trying to get back there today. Brought a Spitfire up yesterday."

"Oh, so you're the young lady responsible for upsetting all our men!"

The first WAAF rolled her eyes.

"Yes, I think it best you find a way home today, dear. They did nothing but talk about you yesterday evening in the mess, all hoping for a date. Can't have you muscling in on the few decent chaps that are here, there's such a poor selection anyway." Ceci grinned.

"I can't possibly have created that much of a stir." The steward came with more tea, which Ceci declined. "Who should I see about transport movements south?" she asked the two.

The younger WAAF, a flight officer, looked up, stubbing out her cigarette.

"Well you can talk to me when you've finished. I'm second i/c movements. I'm sure we can fix you up with something, although it won't be as fast as your Spitfire. Anyway, I've got a vested interest in seeing you on your way, there aren't enough men for both of us!"

The three women laughed; Ceci got up from the table and left the mess with the two WAAF officers walking quickly across the square towards the flying control offices situated on the airfield in front of one of the large camouflaged hangars. A biting easterly wind cut through the gap between the hangars, whining now and again through their supporting metal latticework.

Sorting through various signals and paperwork, the flight officer eventually came across to her, "I've got a Blenheim going to Squires Gate, near Blackpool, later this morning. You can speak to the pilot when he comes in, shouldn't be a problem."

Ceci sat in the warm office looking through old editions of various newspapers scattered about, left over from the night shift. Forty minutes later a pilot entered, slamming the door, and began discussing something with the control people. He kept looking over at her. 'Why do I have this effect on people?' she worried.

✦ ✦ ✦

"Monsieur, Monsieur, vite réveillez-vous, dépêchez-vous!" Someone was shaking Penrose wildly.

"What the bloody hell ...?" It was barely dawn and he was not awake. He looked up at the demented, unshaven farmer; his expression said it all. Pushing the blankets back, he turned to stand. It was cold and the farmer continued to chivvy him. He helped him pull on some old boots then anxiously led him, still dressing, out of the back of the barn. Pointing in the faint light at the tall hedge that ran beside a ditch up towards the forest behind the clutch of houses and barns, he motioned Harold onwards. Such conversation as there was, was in clipped, whispered tones; Harold had difficulty in catching it all in the cold, damp air. But the urgency of tone made clear that he, and they, were in great danger. The farmer raised a finger.

"Ecoutez!" They both jerked to a stop, listening. In the distance the sound of heavy engines could be discerned, their volume increasing in the still, grey-lit countryside. Thrusting a bag into his bandaged hands, the agitated man finally wished him, "Bonne chance".

From the few words exchanged within his comprehension, Harold gathered that the Germans had now found both wrecked aircraft. In the German machine were the incinerated remains of its unfortunate and dismembered Luftwaffe pilot. In the wreck of the English machine there had been no sign of human remains at all – but there had been reports of a parachute descending. Now they were looking.

Crouching down as he ran up the steeply sloping ditch, he splashed in and out of freezing water until reaching the end of the hedge. He realised the boots had holes in them. From there to cover in the forest he estimated was about one hundred and fifty yards. No distance normally for him but on this occasion the critical hundred and fifty yards was over higher, open ground; his silhouette would be easily seen from the road and from the approaching field-grey Wehrmacht half-track, full of heavily dressed infantrymen. He sat and watched them over the rim of the ditch for a moment or two.

From his vantage point he could see that they would be in the small cluster of houses, searching, in four to five minutes. He hoped against hope that his RAF uniform, cast on the fire in the parlour, had been totally destroyed last night. Move he had to; if he was caught here the fate of the farmer, his daughter and probably the rest of the small community would be grim. His own future would lack any firm guarantees, save incarceration or worse.

Watching, he thought his best plan was to wait until the Germans were actually in the houses. Once there, they would not have a clear view of the forest or the section of exposed hillside above where he sat hidden in the ditch, wet, cold and now rather hungry. As the clattering approached he could see finally that the convoy comprised two trucks and just one noisy half-track. It stopped out of his sight on the narrow road, and he could hear crashing, banging and guttural bellowing as the heavily booted soldiers stormed into and through the small houses below.

Into the farmer's small house they rushed with characteristic disdain, gratuitously damaging and breaking what possessions lay about while the inhabitants were pushed outside and lined up with other unfortunates from the cluster of dwellings. The farmer's two collie dogs' hysterical barking turned to growling as grey-coated stormtroopers barged into the kitchen heading for the door leading across the muddy yard to the two barns. Worried and confused, the dogs crouched, bellies on the floor, snarling with teeth bared, ears flat against their heads.

They were obstructing the soldiers. Two shots rang out from within the house, followed by a few seconds of yelping then another shot followed by a braying laugh and breaking glass.

Harold ran across the exposed stretch of field, all his aches and pains instantly gone for the moment. Running deep into the trees, he felt his breath coming in rasping gasps as the icy air tore painfully at his throat. He could still hear activity coming from his night stop; three shots, muted to some extent by distance and the trees, but he kept running, clutching the bag under his arm, his hands throbbing painfully. After twenty minutes of alternating running with fast walking among the trees he stopped, leaning and panting against a solid, broad oak with branches spreading close to the ground.

A fine drizzle was making its way through gaps in the canopy of sparsely leafed branches. For the moment it was insufficient to wet him but he was conscious that before long he could be soaked; how he wished he still had his leather, fleece-lined flying jacket. Sitting in the shelter of the oak's thin canopy on a pile of drying and decaying leaves, he tore open the crushed paper bag with his teeth, holding it clumsily between his bandaged hands. Inside were some fresh bread, cut slices of sausage and a very large piece of hard yellow cheese. The aroma from all three penetrated his senses; in no time he had eaten it all. Leaning back replete but with ears and eyes alert, he realised that gorging the whole lot was rather foolish. He had no way of knowing when he might be fed again.

The rain began to fall more heavily, a cold breeze now darted through the trees penetrating his thin jacket. Huddling closer to the trunk of his tree he began giving some thought to what he should do next. Ideally he should try to go north, towards the coast, perhaps steal a boat and try to cross the Channel – possibly be home in a few days – back at the squadron having beers and congratulations. Sleeping with his Ceci.

Refocusing his mind, he returned to his immediate reality. He was on his own, the Germans were looking for him and he had no food now; if he was not careful he would catch cold or worse if he got any wetter. Build a shelter, that's what they had been told during escape-and-evasion lectures. The forest floor was littered with fallen timber in a variety of sizes; he'd tripped more than once on his run. Harold started looking around for suitable material, kicking over and then lifting branches and trunks awkwardly with his stiff, damaged hands. Leaning some of the longer lengths against a convenient low branch growing almost at right-angles from the oak's mature trunk, he assembled a rough lean-to, managing to cover one side with loose branches still with their dead leaves attached. Throwing a few branches onto the floor of the crude shelter, he sat watching the increasing rain drip heavily off the trees. He had no idea how big the forest was, or where he was in relation to roads and surrounding villages and towns. Harold determined that while it rained he would stay put and perhaps tomorrow go back, if he could find his way, to the small community he had left in panic that morning. Looking down from the safety of the forest edge he would be able to see the houses and barns. If it looked all clear he would risk venturing back to the house, the farmer and his unhappy daughter.

❖ ❖ ❖

"Hi, I understand you're trying to hitch a lift south?" Ceci looked up at the speaker. He was young, well built and spoke with an American accent. Smiling, he went on.

"I can offer you a lift as far as Blackpool, Squires Gate today. Any good?" Ceci nodded emphatically.

"Yes, thanks very much, ready to go when you are."

He picked up her small leather bag and walked her towards the door. Opening it, he pointed to a worn and oil-stained Blenheim standing forlornly further down the dispersal.

"That's her, I'm afraid. I'm doing a favour and delivering her for modifications; why don't you go and have a look around while I finish up here and get the latest from the Met bods. See you in ten minutes."

Ceci turned to say goodbye to the ginger-haired flight officer standing watching her and the pilot from behind the ops counter. Smiling broadly she spoke, mockingly.

"Some people get all the luck!" Laughing and waving, Ceci left flying control, walking across the damp black tarmac to the twin-engine machine. Strapping in, they managed to introduce themselves. He was Flying Officer Paul Mossman, and had a deep American lilt to his voice.

The flight to Blackpool's Squires Gate airfield was uneventful and Ceci thanked Paul for the trip as she left the cramped confines of the aircraft. During the flight, conversation had been limited owing to the noise generated by its two large Bristol Mercury engines within a few feet of where they sat; the intercom was working only intermittently. Walking towards the airfield's flying control office, they fell into a natural conversation. Inevitably Ceci enquired where in America the young pilot came from. His response was quick, slightly hurt.

"I'm a Canadian, Ma'am, not a Yank! Came from Prince Rupert in British Columbia a while ago, delivering Hudsons and PBYs to White Waltham and Scotland. Got fed up with doing that so, finally, I enlisted in your air force and got posted temporarily onto a squadron flying these noisy machines," he split the word

'Waltham' into two distinct syllables: Walth-Ham; laughing, his hand swept around pointing at the oil-streaked Blenheim. Ceci looked interested,

"I have a friend who used to be involved with the Atlantic Ferry Organisation, you may have known him; Michael Kelly?"

"An Australian Guy?"

"Yes, he's a bit of a mix, I think – Irish and Australian. He's got a tin leg, lost his right leg in an accident with a flying boat two or three years ago." Ceci looked at Mossman in anticipation.

"Yup, I know Michael very well; we did a few trips together from Gander to Prestwick and Walth-Ham; fantastic pilot and a great navigator; tried to attack a goddamn Focke-Wulf Condor on our very first trip. We were unarmed; a bit crazy, I think." He laughed, remembering the encounter. "Do you know where he is now? I'd like catch up with him again; we lost touch when he left Atlantic Ferry."

They had reached the door of the flying control office. Inside Paul Mossman reported their arrival and Ceci enquired about any movements going further south and passed Mossman a piece of paper with her contact telephone number at the ATA Hamble. He studied the paper carefully.

"I'll give you a call if I'm down your way; please give my best to Michael. Ask him if he's caught any Condors yet." Still smiling, Mossman turned and shook Ceci's hand.

"Have to remember to act like a gentleman now I'm an officer," he exaggerated an upper-class English accent. "Joining a new squadron soon, not far from Oxford, might catch up with you then." Ceci watched him go, walking with a certain swagger out of her sight. 'What a nice chap,' she thought; 'quite a catch for some girl'.

"Sorry, Miss, got nothing scheduled for the rest of the day. Might have something in the morning. I can arrange transport to run you to the railway station if you'd like to try catching a train to London." The Flight Sergeant looked genuinely sorry.

"Silly, really," he went on, "one of your girls left just before you landed, at around eleven o'clock, in an Airspeed Oxford. You might know her; she's that famous flyer, what's her name?" He looked down at the logbook, his finger pulling down the morning's list of movements. "That's it," he looked up. "Amy Johnson, you know, she did all those record-breaking flights all alone to Australia and South Africa?"

Ceci looked up, "Amy. Damn! She's based at Hamble. I'm trying to get to there." Ceci didn't actually know Amy Johnson very well, save to exchange morning or evening greetings; their paths had not had any real opportunity to cross. 'It would have been ideal,' she thought, 'I could have hitched a ride and been home this afternoon.'

"Oh, bugger," was her unladylike response. The Flight Sergeant looked up in mock horror. Unknown to them both at that moment, Ceci had been spared her life, arriving just minutes too late.

The story gradually emerged when she eventually returned to Hamble, still cross at having to wait for a whole day until she was able to take advantage of a lift back to her home base. The following day hard information began to come through. Harriet took the call.

Sitting quietly with a cup of tea in front of her at the end of the day's flying she spoke white-faced to the small group of ATA girls assembled in the ops hut. The story she told was much as it had been given to her.

"It seems," she started hesitantly, "that Amy was suddenly seen parachuting into the Thames estuary off Herne Bay about four hours after leaving Squires Gate airfield at Blackpool the day before yesterday, at about three-thirty in the afternoon. Her aircraft was also seen to plunge silently into the muddy waters at the same time; in view of the time she'd been in the air it was probably out of fuel. A naval trawler on duty in the estuary saw her descending from low cloud towards the water and made good speed towards poor Amy." As an aside she mentioned, "I think they said the ship was the Hazelmere or something like that."

Harriet stopped for a moment, turning her face away from her girls while she regained her composure. She swallowed hard.

"Unfortunately, in its haste to get to her it ran aground on a sandbank and they lost some time in freeing themselves." There was muted sobbing from one of the group as they watched Harriet struggling with words.

"Apparently when they were about twenty yards off, the crew could make out that it was a woman swimming in the violent swells. Lines were thrown and a ship's lifeboat was launched. Just as they did so she was swept out of reach by the heavy seas. The ship's captain, a Lieutenant Commander Fletcher, I was told, very bravely dived into the freezing sea and actually managed to reach her. He was supporting her, and the lifeboat followed as fast as the seas and currents would allow." There was a collective intake of breath. Harriet stopped, took a sip of tea, her lips quivering, the words forming in her mind. "The next time the captain was seen, Amy was not with him. They were unable to save the captain.

I understand that he was also lost in the seas; he died trying to rescue our Amy."

Managing to hold her emotions firmly in check, blank-faced, Harriet rose from the table and walked with slow dignified steps to her office, closing the door firmly behind her. Through the frosted glass Ceci glimpsed her shoulders shaking. Taking their example from Harriet, the girls dispersed quietly to their billets. Some of the girls went up to London on 14th January to a memorial service for Amy at St Martin-in-the-Fields. Her loss had cast a sombre pall over the tight-knit unit.

THREE

Following a subdued weekend that saw flying continuing as normal, Hamble slowly assumed a happier atmosphere. Ceci made five new deliveries from the Castle Bromwich Spitfire works in the Midlands to a squadron based at North Weald, near Epping, and to Tangmere, just beyond Chichester. She was looking forward to seeing Harold at the coming weekend.

Ceci was called into Harriet's private office late in the evening. She had made two collections and deliveries that day, taking an opportunity on one to over-fly Michael and Sarah's house. She'd been showing off, and was feeling quite satisfied. Harriet rarely used her office except for dealing with routine paperwork, or sometimes privately remonstrating, comforting or congratulating one of her girls. Unsure what this summons might be for she was not left in doubt for long as Harriet quietly closed the door and sat her down.

Without waiting she spoke: "Ceci ... you've got to be strong. It's very bad news, I'm afraid."

Sitting perched on the edge of her chair, the colour drained from Cecilia's face in an instant. In that instant she knew what was coming.

"Benson phoned earlier. Harold's been reported missing on a recce trip over Germany." Ceci stared back, eyes wide, willing it not to be.

"At the moment there are no firm reports about him, it's possible he's OK, baled out, a prisoner ... or perhaps on the run."

Harriet knelt in front of the seated, statue-like girl, holding onto to Ceci's cold hands, fully prepared for what was to come; she'd had to deliver this sort of news before. Ceci swallowed hard; she was unable to breathe.

"What ... what ... no ... it can't, not Harold ... it ... how?"

The words would not come out; would not assemble. Harold. Missing. She tried to deny the link between the words. The blow was unexpected; it struck powerfully at her gasping emptiness, her breath still would not come. Her heart was pounding. Standing suddenly, she lurched towards the window staring blankly out across the airfield, Harriet holding her shoulders; ready. Then it broke, the tears flooding, her body tense, shaking uncontrollably, holding onto the cill.

Using her official car, Harriet took Ceci back to the distraught young woman's house; Wendy had been warned and took Ceci up to her room. She stayed with her all night. No crying, just looking out into the night. Nobody slept much.

◆ ◆ ◆

Sarah rubbed her eyes; perhaps she needed glasses. Looking through the magnifying stereoscopes at the matched pairs of photographs for ten to twelve hours a day was taking its toll, not only on her eyes, but also on her role as a mother. She was increasingly relying on the French nanny Patricia to care for Beth and Alistair as her work and growing responsibilities kept her more frequently at Danesfield. The previous week she had managed to get home on only three nights. The two children were crying and clinging as she tried to leave each morning with desperate pleas for Mummy to be home that evening. Patricia did her best but they both knew that for toddlers there was no substitute for Mummy at certain times of the day: tea time, bath-time, and bedtime in particular.

Sarah tried to make up the deficits with her two youngsters by involving herself as much as possible with their playing when she was at home, but often felt quite exhausted. Michael's rare 48-hour pass at home had been something of an anti-climax, although the children were so excited at the prospect of Daddy being home for two whole days. But, like Sarah, he spent a lot of time snoozing in a chair, trying to relax and was short with the children over their noise and wanting to do things with him just when he'd nodded off. In bed, sex was not even contemplated, although Sarah had dressed to entice one evening, her superb legs peeping from a long slit in her silk nightdress. In a way, she was pleased that Michael's valiant efforts were overtaken by sleep; she would have had to feign it anyway.

On Tuesday she was back at Danesfield. Over a snatched lunch in the canteen she overheard two photo-interpreters from another specialist section discussing the loss of yet another reconnaissance pilot on a photo sortie over Germany; it was the third one this month and it was only the 10th. Butting in, she asked if they knew where the pilot had come from.

"It seems he was from Benson again, second or third this month. Know anyone there?" asked the young sergeant. Everyone had become sensitive to losses and how information about them was released.

Learning of the loss of a loved one or close friend had become a daily reality for many as the war bore on into its third depressing year. But, even if one was conscious of the real possibility of loss, its occurrence always caught a wife, husband, lover, or friend unawares and immediately vulnerable.

"I do actually, he's a young reconnaissance pilot with one of the PR squadrons there, joined quite recently," said Sarah, worried, saturated with a cold, sinking feeling. The young sergeant looked across the table and empty plates at his colleague, wishing he'd kept his mouth firmly shut. The colleague turned, looking over at Sarah.

"I don't think they would have sent a new boy on a long sortie to Germany. Look, I've got a contact phone number for one of the squadrons there. Would you like me to try and give them a ring? You might be worrying for nothing."

Sarah nodded although she wasn't sure what she wanted. It might be nothing to do with Harold and that she was just being uncharacteristically pessimistic. Looking at her watch, she realised that she should be getting back to her desk; there were literally heaps of photos requiring attention.

"Which section are you in? I'll see what I can find out during this afternoon and let you know, if that's OK." The sergeant looked up at her as she rose from the bench. Sarah stopped for a moment, looking at him.

"I'm in the Aircraft & Airfield section, Hut 7B – Flight Officer Sarah Kelly, by the way."

"Fine, I'm Jim Savage. I'll be in touch if I find anything out ... and don't worry," he said gently.

Back at her desk a large pile of photos sat waiting. Her mind wandered from time to time as she wondered about Harold. What would Ceci do if anything had happened to him? She tried to cast the thought from her mind but it was difficult as she inspected a set of pictures that had been logged as from one of the RAF Benson squadrons. The pictures had been brought to her by one of her section's sergeants. She had been concerned at some buildings that had appeared in a very short space of time in an area that was largely uninhabited apart from an odd farm or two, among woods. Previous aerial photos of the area showed nothing in the same place, but that was nearly six months ago, she'd added. As far as they knew there were no German garrisons in the immediate area; only the German naval bases at Douarnenez and Brest, seventeen miles or so to the west on the Atlantic coast of Biscay. To Sarah it just seemed a funny place in which to erect three long, plain agricultural-looking buildings among fields, off a very narrow road not far from the tiny village of Sizun.

Although the pictures had been taken when the sun had been well up, thus eliminating a good deal of shadow; when enlarged, it was possible to just make out a run of what appeared to be telegraph poles coming away from one of the buildings, following the narrow road to a crossroads about two miles away. Here they appeared to join with other telegraph poles alongside roads that led eventually to Brest.

She could see that the telegraph poles were a relatively recent addition to the local landscape; the disturbed soil around their bases was a slightly different colour and no grass grew. This supposition was backed up when Sarah studied the route of the telegraph poles in more detail. Where the wires would have to run from one pole to the next, some trees appeared to have been disturbed, cut or broken to make a clear way for the wires; there had been no new growth and on one or two trees the branch structure was unusually irregular. Looking again at the series of duplicated photos under the twin stereoscopic magnifying glasses, she thought it unusual that there were no tell-tale signs of vehicles regularly visiting the new buildings, always a sure sign of something going on. The question was: how long had they been there and what were they for?

The three photos that lay in front of her had been taken more in error than by design – a reconnaissance pilot had left his cameras running as he left Brest at a much lower level than normal. He'd been taking oblique shots of the port facilities and shipping – a regular sortie. From his normal operating altitude of around thirty-five thousand feet above them, the barns, if that's what they were, would have scarcely caused a second look. As it was, taken from this much lower altitude, they impacted largely on the wooded landscape; Sarah had an odd hunch about them.

One other thing jarred as she picked up the folder of pictures. Sarah had noticed that most of the fields surrounding the buildings were inhabited by livestock, sheep and cattle and were well grazed, yet, two fields immediately adjacent to the buildings, both larger than most, had no animals in them whatsoever. The photos showed, however, that the grass in the fields was long and had not been grazed or cut for some time. Discussion with her own section leader led to an agreement to keep an eye on the area over the next few months and to request further regular monthly reconnaissance over the site, not far from Brest and Morlaix, by either Benson or a new PR squadron down in Cornwall at St Eval.

Hoping to get away early that evening, Sarah was returning to her office from the washrooms to collect her handbag when she saw one of the two young sergeants she had spoken to at lunch. He was looking for her, and on spotting her walked quickly over.

"I've managed to speak to a friend of mine at Benson in the photographic development section; he said that they had one aircraft missing on Tuesday from a PR op. over Germany. Mannheim, I think he said. He couldn't tell me the name of the pilot as they hadn't yet informed the next of kin. But he was a bit upset, I could tell. He mentioned that the missing pilot and he had had some fun together from time to time racing around the airfield perimeter track on their motorcycles." Her expression froze.

"Thanks Jim ... thanks very much, I think I'll try to find out more myself." She spoke the words slowly, distracted by the image that flashed into her mind of Harold leaving her home that Sunday evening to return to Benson, roaring up the road on his noisy AJS motorcycle and swerving about foolishly, showing off, until he had disappeared around the long bend that eventually joined with the Salisbury road. Speaking to her section head, Sarah got permission to take the following morning off. The Squadron Officer unimpressed in view of the backlog of work building. Collecting her handbag, Sarah turned off the office lights, locked her door and walked, unseeing, out to her small maroon Morris car and set off for Hamble in the dark, her face firmly set.

After a few miles the car began to lose power and sputtered to a stop. She'd run out of petrol. Her Service ration did not run to long trips around southern England. Standing looking around in the dark, she hoped that someone would pass soon and give her a lift to somewhere where she could obtain a few gallons, or civilisation of some sort, somewhere. The countryside was black, it was very late and little traffic moved about on country roads in the enforced blackout; over the adjacent hedge she could hear movement. Standing stock-still and slightly fearful, she listened, trying to penetrate the darkness. Relief flooded over her as she realised it was just cattle having a late supper, tearing at the grass. After twenty minutes nothing had passed in either direction and it was cold. Hunting about, Sarah eventually found a small torch in the glove compartment of the car. It offered a feeble light but was probably better than nothing. Bugger the blackout, she thought. She realised, on thinking back, that she had not passed any signs of habitation during the previous few miles of her journey. Best to keep going, she thought.

Half an hour later the dark shape of an isolated house loomed, set back on the opposite side of the narrow road. She walked over, her heels clicking on the hard surface, looking at her watch. Its luminous hands showed that it was just before one-thirty in the morning – 'My God, it's late'. The gate clicked loudly as it closed behind her. Seconds later a dog started barking furiously from inside as she walked the short gravel path. Reaching the door, she fumbled, looking for a bell or knocker. Without warning, the door was suddenly pulled open and a tall individual faced her; her torch had died, so she couldn't see whether it was a man or woman. She could see well enough to note that the individual was holding something threateningly in its hand. The interior of the house was unlit and the constant noise from the agitated dog made any form of communication difficult.

❖ ❖ ❖

Nanny Patricia came into the lounge with Alistair giggling and wriggling in her arms; they'd being playing and he still wanted to play. Michael looked up smiling from his chair, where he had been contemplating putting another log on the fire. Despite the laughing boy in her arms Patricia looked serious.

"Michael, I need to talk wiz you about somesing, can we 'ave a chat when zis leettle devil 'as gone to 'is bed?" Alistair rushed at his father, leaping into his lap. With an outrush of breath he looked up at her.

"Of course. Does it have to wait until then?" She nodded, pulled the blackout curtains across, switched on the standard lamp and went back to the kitchen to prepare the evening meal; food rationing made variety a problem but at least none of them were in danger of putting on weight. Her recent trip to Devon to meet her soldier father and his colleagues who had narrowly escaped the clutches of the Nazis – had put an idea into her head.

Later that evening after a rather quiet dinner, Michael, Alistair, Beth and Patricia all gathered around the kitchen table; Sarah had not yet returned from Danesfield. Alistair and Beth were bathed, read a story and put to bed. Michael was enjoying the last glass of his 'Canadian' brandy when Patricia came awkwardly into the lounge, sitting opposite him on the other side of the glowing hearth, she spoke.

Reporting the conversation two days later to Sarah, Michael Kelly told her of Patricia's wish to become an agent and to go back into France. Sarah looked horrified.

"Is she mad? A spy? We sometimes get feedback on what happens to agents they catch. We can't let her do it, Michael, she's much too young." Michael remembered the young woman he had dropped near St Pol all those months ago on his very first mission with the squadron; he'd never seen her again in all the pick-ups and drops they'd made subsequently. He still wondered at their courage.

"She is very determined, Darling. That visit to her father has something to do with it, I'm certain. She was very quiet, introspective, when she came back. Anyway, she wants me to arrange some sort of meeting with SOE or the SIS to see if she can volunteer. I've said that I'll try to help her through any contacts we have with SOE at the squadron but I have explained with some force that it's a very dangerous course to pursue." Sarah looked at him open-mouthed.

"You can't let her get involved with something like that, Michael, God, she's only just nineteen! Think what some jackbooted thug would do to her if she was caught spying."

He stopped what he was going to say. He didn't want to think about it. He looked at her and said,

"I know, Darling. From our perspective you're right but you didn't hear her, she feels it's her sort of destiny. She's very intense about it. I'm sorry but I've managed to arrange a meeting for her. Once she hears what is expected of her and what the risks are she may change her mind. Somehow I doubt it"

Within the month Sarah drove Patricia to the front gates of a large house set well back in secluded gardens surrounded by a high brick and flint wall near Guildford. Depositing her with her small case at the gate, she embraced the young woman and left, tearful.

❖ ❖ ❖

Harold Penrose's teeth were chattering and his stomach rumbling. He was damp but his hands felt a little better after an uncomfortable night spent shivering on the forest floor covered by a few leafy branches in his crude lean-to. The comings and goings of nocturnal creatures every so often kept him alert, fearing someone was creeping up on him. In dawn's cold, forest-filtered light he determined to go carefully back towards the small group of houses. Standing stiffly, he looked carefully about, listening to the noises in the trees, trying to remember the rough direction in which he'd run through these trees. Yesterday there had been no sun so getting his bearings took a few moments.

As he'd run the previous day he'd inexplicably noticed clumps of bright-green moss clinging to the sides of some trees. Somewhere in the distant past, perhaps during his young Scouting days, he remembered being told that moss usually accumulated on the north side of trees, buildings and roofs; he hoped he was remembering correctly. Treading carefully between the trees, keeping a close check on which side, if any, moss was growing, and taking great care not to step on broken branches, he set off. Now and again the flight of a bird would bring his heart up into his mouth; twice he jumped fearfully into the nearest thicket.

Despite feeling that he was on the wrong track, the natural compass afforded by the clumps of moss led him eventually to a place where he could see down and over the small hamlet. It appeared devoid of life; no dogs, nothing. From his position tucked well back inside the tree line he studied the surrounding countryside and the road snaking greyly through arable farmland. The Germans, it appeared, were no longer in the immediate vicinity; the whole area was silent of human sound.

Moving back inside the forest, he kept to his left until he reached the place where he'd entered its welcome cover the day before. Looking carefully about him again, he made sure that there was nothing untoward in the hamlet as far as he could see. Launching himself across the open ground, he attempted to run through the wet, heavy mud until he reached the shelter of the ditch with its long protective hedge. Avoiding deep water lurking at its bottom, he made his way almost silently down the incline to the rear of the two barns. Edging slowly around the second, he reached the yard across which stood one of the whitewashed houses. Off to one side he noticed two low mounds of freshly dug earth under the shelter of an ancient and empty apple tree. Remembering the sound of shots he'd heard echoing through the trees the previous day he became concerned that the Germans had possibly murdered the farmer and his daughter.

Guilt filled his heart and mind – his stomach turned. Had he caused this? Had his fateful presence here led directly to innocent people being killed? He turned and stealthily edged his way back around the barns. Coming across the small door through which he had taken flight under the farmer's guidance, he pushed it very slowly ajar until it creaked. Through the narrow gap he peered into the half-light inside. There was no one there. Opening the door further, he stepped smartly inside, pulling the door almost shut. Harold stood still for a few minutes, his back against the wall, trying to penetrate the gloom. Off to his left was the ladder that led up to his makeshift bedroom. He climbed up; the bed was gone, along with the blankets. It all looked quite natural with strewn straw.

He returned to the outside of the barn, moving around gingerly until he was opposite the small white house again. The mud in the yard was dry and beginning to crack as the sun rose into a clearing sky; bits of dried straw blew about in a gentle breeze that was laden with the rich odour of cattle. Silently he crossed the yard ending up outside the back door to the house; its glass panels smashed, long shards of glass lying about dangerously on the floor. 'Need to mind the dogs don't walk over that', he thought. His mind's sudden fix on the two dogs brought him up short; where were they, why weren't they barking?

He heard a noise from inside the house and stepped back from the door. There was someone inside, in the kitchen where she had gently attended to his hands. Moving silently, he edged sideways towards the kitchen window, with every sense alert. Through the nets he could make her out; she was working at the white porcelain sink, pumping water into something. He stepped forward and tapped gently on the window. Too gently – she carried on pumping. He knocked louder and she looked up, at first surprised, then angry. Looking at him for a few seconds, her face twisted and she burst into a tirade, running from the sink to the broken back door. After seconds it became obvious that she wanted him gone, as a stream of violent words whose meaning needed no translation echoed around the yard. But one word was increasingly repeated that he did know.

"Allez! Fichez-le camp." She wanted him to go, far from here; that was clear. She was crying as she shouted, gesticulating, wringing her hands. Unchecked tears coursed down her angry, contorted face. Then she was pointing at the two mounds of soil.

"Regardez-moi ça, c'est tout de votre faute, mes pauvres chiens, espèce d'Anglais de malheur!" He caught the word 'chiens' and the penny dropped: it was the dogs; the Germans had shot her two collie dogs, and it was his fault. Distraught and shaking, she collapsed onto a rough bench positioned to face the evening sun.

Unsure of what to do, Harold walked slowly over and sat at the far end of the bench, four feet from her. He couldn't just walk away and leave her in this desperate state. The bench was shaking with her sobbing, her face cupped in her hands. The shouting had stopped. He slid along and sat beside her. She seemed about to move away from him but then remained.

"Mademoiselle, je suis très, très désolé." He put his arm tenderly around her shoulders, trying to find suitable words in French to express his sorrow and comfort her. She didn't shrug him off but gradually gathered herself and stood up, wiping her face on her apron, and turned without looking at him and walked back to the kitchen, the broken glass scrunching under the thin soles of her shoes.

Penrose was unsure what to do next. Deciding to wait a little, he returned to the interior of the barn. The sun beating on its dark-coloured exterior and closed doors made it warm inside and he sat comfortably in the hay to contemplate the situation. Nearly five hours later he awoke. The farmer in dark-blue dungarees was standing over him, and slightly behind him on one side was his daughter. The man carried his hammer as when Penrose had first met him.

❖ ❖ ❖

Helen Lorenzo rarely got letters, but she had one today. The faded red postmark was smudged but she could just make out the date: it was from thirteen weeks earlier and franked 'Bologna – Italia'. The envelope had other postmarks, some English and all dated fairly recently, from London and Paignton. Another was a Swiss Red Cross, Geneva postmark, dated exactly five weeks earlier. Inside the buff envelope was a stark note on a compliment slip to the effect that the contents had been inspected by the British security services. She pulled out a creased letter on thick, coarse paper written in delicate Italian handwriting that she did not recognise. It was from someone called Paola but gave no address. Sitting in a patch of sun outside the ops room, she read the letter.

Paola, whoever she was, had taken the trouble to tell Helen that her father had been arrested by the Fascists, summarily tried on some trumped-up charges and thrown into jail in Milan. It seemed that he had continued to make derogatory comments in public about Mussolini and his associates, despite Helen's and his fellow professors' warnings, and had stubbornly refused to recant when given the opportunity. His office at the university in Bologna had, it appeared, been searched and all material taken as incriminating evidence for a further trial on more serious charges at some time in the future.

The last paragraph, however, had a specific message for Helen from her father. Paola had drawn an emphasising line around it; it was a short statement in Latin: 'Azzaro's skies are taken. New energies will lead to right's disaster if it turns above.'

The relaxing but stimulating discussions with her father in Florence and Siena nearly two years ago flooded back. She recalled the sixteenth-century engineer Azzaro and his aeroplane concepts set out in a clear hand on delicate parchment, and the way that they had aroused her father's enquiring mind to academic fever pitch. She had no way of knowing how much further her father had gone with his research; he was never a good family correspondent. In any event, since Italy had entered the war on the Axis side in mid-1940, there had been no mail. How had the letter from this Paola found its way to her here in England? Helen could only surmise that the Red Cross had managed to perform some sort of miracle.

But what did the message mean? Her Latin, learned at a convent school in Bologna years ago, was buried deep in her memory and needed resuscitating. She studied her hurried translation, which she'd undertaken with the help of a friend's son's Latin school dictionary. It meant little to her and she tried to recall the discussions she and her father had had that summer, for clues.

Somewhere she still had the simple sketch that he had drawn that warm afternoon to outline Azzaro's ideas for a flying machine, but where was it now? Two days later she had a flash of memory, mentally thanking St Antoine. In her mind she went straight to a small wooden soap-box she'd last seen in her mother's desk in the front parlour of the terraced house that she had owned before her death. The next time she had a few days' leave, she promised herself, she would go down to Paignton and see if it was still there in the house, which she had inherited. It was nearly two months before Helen had an opportunity to make the visit.

❖ ❖ ❖

Michael Kelly had always thought the Lysander was not a pretty flying machine but his recent experiences of its capabilities in terms of handling and short take-offs and landings had finally convinced him that it was an ideal vehicle for collecting and delivering passengers in remote and dark areas of occupied Europe on behalf of Maurice Buckmaster's SOE.

The aeroplane had a high wing and sturdy undercarriage

allowing for good downward visibility, and an innate ability to absorb the shocks of rough landings on darkened French pastures. The squadron had removed all the heavy armament and stub wings from the ungainly-looking machine and had made available an additional fuel tank, giving it a range of seven hundred miles. This tank was fitted to the underside of the aircraft; Kelly considered this a rather exposed place to hang what he considered a simple barrel of petrol.

Recent sorties to France had required him to both deliver and collect agents of the SOE. Their highly dangerous work was being undertaken a week either side of each month's full moon. The squadron's official base was at RAF Tempsford, near Bedford, but during the critical two moon weeks of each month they usually operated off an advanced airfield in Sussex close to the coast.

Out of moon they would spend time planning new operations, carrying out continuation flying training, mostly by night in the squadron's various aircraft, which now included a couple of Hudsons. They also undertook training of agents, or 'Joes', as they were known, teaching them how to assess a field's suitability for different aircraft and how to lay out the minimal lighting for landing, procedures for changing over Joes and any cargo, and importantly, protection of the site while a delivery or collection was under way.

At home with Sarah, he explained that he rarely had time to be frightened during a collection or pick-up; the concentration required for a landing or take-off from an unknown field, usually in near-darkness, meant that there was little mental capacity left for being scared. But he did admit to the constant background worry of whether the landing site might be a trap with Germans waiting, as they had been for their squadron commander earlier in the year. Sarah asked how he would feel if he was assigned to carrying Patricia into France. He had no answer and shrugged his shoulders as he helped her bathe Alistair and Beth; there had been very little contact with the young French nanny since Sarah had delivered her to the large house near Guildford months ago.

The two children often asked where Nanny Tricia had gone. She had visited them once while still in training, when the children had been all over her, and Sarah had also managed to meet her when they were both coincidentally in Baker Street in London. The young woman said very little about what she was doing and of course Sarah was unable to speak openly about her work for the unspoken and barely admitted possibility that if Patricia were ever captured she would be tortured and let information go. Both women knew the rules.

Tonight's delivery was a long haul and would require the 'barrel of petrol' to be attached under the aircraft. A wireless operator and local Résistance circuit organiser were to be collected from a field not far from Brest, the centre of German naval activity, with the U-boat pens at nearby Douarnenez under constant Résistance surveillance. The collection was to be made at a location near the small town of Callac in the Côtes du Nord region, on the south-westerly wooded slopes of the pretty Montagnes d'Arrée. The briefing officer said that the site should be fairly easy to locate in the moonlight as the selected field was to the left of an area where a road, a river and a railway line ran almost parallel for a short distance.

Michael studied the local area maps very carefully. The direct route as the crow flies was a non-starter; he would have to dog-leg around the Cherbourg peninsula and the Channel Islands to avoid detection and flak. That meant, he calculated, a distance of two hundred and ten miles against a fairly strong headwind going out: about an hour and twenty minutes in all, assuming he experienced no problems in finding the site. Take-off was scheduled for twelve-thirty in the morning, taking advantage of the moon's current phase.

Once airborne, he left the coast over Selsey Bill. Looking out to the west, he could see moonlight glittering on the Solent below as he set a compass course to take him to a point well to the west of Guernsey in the Channel Islands before turning south for Callac. The flight was uneventful and he crossed the French coast a little before time near the Ile de Bréhat. The weather was not co-operating, cloud cover was slowly increasing and the moon's frail silver beams were having difficulty in penetrating its serried layers. Timing his run from the coast and allowing for slightly less wind than originally anticipated, he gradually reduced height, conscious of the approaching high ground of the Montagnes d'Arrée, just ahead of him, near invisible in the reducing visibility.

The seconds ticked on; glancing regularly at the stopwatch fitted to the instrument panel, he finally began a wide circle, hoping that the reception committee would hear him and flash the appropriate single-letter Morse signal from the ground with a torch. Nothing burst up from the dark. After ten minutes he knew he would begin to attract the attention of the Germans with his persistent aerial loitering, and gave himself another few minutes before he would declare the mission aborted. Still nothing; disappointed, he finished the turn and straightened out, heading due north initially. Looking back one last time, just in case, he saw a quick flash of a light from the ground. Was it the reception committee? They were late; it happened sometimes, he was aware; delayed by the Germans, the curfew, even a tyre puncture, but it was very worrying all the same. Reversing his course, he turned back to where he had seen the light flash. As he approached the general area he waited for a repeat of the Morse code letter. It came. He thought about it. It wasn't quite right; the letter they had flashed was incorrect.

Banking around again, he cruised slowly back; this time the burst of Morse was correct. The signal was followed by three white lights positioned in a standard inverted 'L' layout showing him the direction of the landing area. He just hoped that the agent in charge had picked somewhere that was not full of ruts or cart tracks, and was not boggy.

Turning the elevator trim wheel full back for landing, he lowered the aircraft's big flaps fully. Putting the propeller to fine pitch, he set the aircraft up for landing, carefully monitoring his speed at sixty-five miles per hour. Ahead, the blackness was almost tangible, the moon was still co-operating in a rather desultory fashion, and only the slightly wavering torches offered any hint that someone was down there and that there was actually somewhere to land. In his peripheral vision on each side he could vaguely make out sloping ground and black, shadowy trees. Ahead was still black apart from the encouraging three pinpoints of white light. Within seconds he could just make out some features on the ground ahead and began to gradually flare the machine for a landing. Suddenly all the lights went out; how far he was from the ground he did not know for sure.

The landing was heavy. The Lysander bounced, and Kelly hoped that the field was a good length. Working hard at the rudder bar with stick fully back, he expertly recovered the machine's stability, and moments later was taxiing back to the end of the field in readiness for a quick departure, resetting the elevator trim as he did so, watching carefully about him.

For a moment he thought that someone was trying to light a fire; the flickering light off to his right was unusual. He thought it rather stupid in the circumstances. Allowing the noisy Bristol Mercury engine to idle, he jumped down to the ground, and as he did so he slipped his helmet up off one ear and opened the sliding hatch to the rear compartment ready to receive his passengers. As he turned back ready to climb back into the cockpit looking at where the reception committee would be coming from, the side panel above his head exploded into small pieces of Perspex shrapnel, narrowly missing his face. He suddenly became aware that occasional bullets were hitting the machine with thuds and clangs; he could see clearly irregular bursts of orange flickering coming from within the opaque silhouette of a thin stand of trees bordering one side of the field.

"Christ!" he shouted. Reinvigorating the engine, he began taxiing the Lysander rapidly down the field away from the automatic fire. As he taxied he became aware of a figure running near the port wheel, waving and shouting.

The man was not in any sort of uniform that much he could see, and seemed to present no actual threat. Keen to be as far as possible from weapons firing from his right, he kept the aircraft moving. It would mean a downwind take-off when he left, but he thought it preferable to being shot to pieces while attempting a conventional into-wind take-off from the downwind end of the field. Finally, he was able to make out the spikes of a boundary fence ahead, and opening up a fistful of throttle, he urged the machine to turn rapidly about its own length. The move caught the man running alongside by surprise; Kelly saw him fall and as he did so the main wheel appeared to run over his legs.

Two grey figures suddenly jumped out of the surrounding darkness and pulled the man upright and over the short distance to where the aircraft's rear compartment lay open. The injured man was screaming; Kelly could hear it above the engine noise, punctuated by the intermittent chatter of weapon fire. Turning and glancing behind, he could see the two individuals trying desperately to push the helpless man up the short fixed ladder on the aircraft's side. Two women were struggling without success; Kelly braked the aircraft, unstrapped himself and jumped from the cockpit. He heaved hard on the screaming man's buttocks: the man rolled into the cabin. The aircraft rocked as the other two, armed, female figures almost fell in behind the still-screaming man, pulling the sliding hatch closed.

'Three?' There were only two to be collected as far as he was aware. Too late now. The source of the automatic fire was moving closer. He could sense new hits on the aeroplane. 'No time to sort it out; get airborne.' He was now very worried at the increasing level of fire being aimed at his machine and conscious that just behind, between him and his three passengers, lay the aircraft's internal petrol and oil tanks. Looking ahead, unstrapped, he pushed the throttle fully open. The engine roared and the Lysander rumbled down the grass, the tail finally coming up. 'Downwind and three up, that's going to be interesting,' crossed his mind. He concentrated on getting the aircraft into the air quickly and safely as he approached the area where the original firing had been coming from. Now shots seemed to be coming from almost everywhere. Ahead and on either side of his anticipated take-off path he could just make out the outlines of dark figures, the firing momentarily increasing in intensity. 'We'll be lucky to get away with this,' he thought, as he coerced the overweight machine into flying. He became vaguely aware of odd noises from behind him, then shouting, and shooting from the rear compartment as they roared down the field. On the ground at one side the shooting had suddenly stopped.

They were up, but only just, the aircraft behaving most oddly, mushing along just above the stall, the huge radial engine bellowing out across the quiet countryside. Against the slightly lighter night sky Kelly could make out gaps in the black trees across their path ahead. Cagily, he banked the aircraft to the left, hoping to pass through the tree line secure from pursuing shots. Had they got away with it? Despite all the lead suspended for an instant in the night air, had the Germans failed to cause any real damage to the aircraft? He was briefly jubilant, the adrenaline surging until, through habit, his eyes scanned the instruments and fuel gauges. Their simple message was that precious fuel must be pouring from the tank or tanks into the night air... hit by some of the lead.

Passing through a slim gap in the trees, the aircraft was beginning to feel more manoeuvrable as their speed slowly increased. The shooting was over; he encouraged the heavy Lysander to climb. Any attempts to conceal themselves in the dark were defeated by the bellowing engine. Hopefully no Luftwaffe night fighters were being vectored into area after complaints from slumbering German generals. At three thousand feet he finally managed to secure his seat harness. They were heading north. Kelly could just make out the French coastline ahead, beyond the rising hills. The once-reluctant moon, now momentarily fully exposed, cast a pale silver path on the distant sea's surface. He glanced again at the fuel gauges, thinking quickly about the implications. It struck him as most likely that the long-range fuel tank exposed under the climbing aircraft's belly had been well and truly peppered by the automatic fire from the ground.

The additional weight of passengers, including one not previously accounted for, meant that he had had to use more power to maintain their height and speed, although, as the weight of fuel drained away this problem would soon right itself.

As always, fuel gauges were not to be trusted and he took a few moments as they left the coast to study their faces. Perhaps he should make a landing here in France. A night-time ditching into the sea in such an aircraft, with its heavy fixed undercarriage, could prove fatal for them all. The undercarriage was ideally positioned to trip the machine onto its back as soon as it struck the water at 55 mph. It occurred to him almost immediately that his life and those of his three Résistance passengers would be quite worthless even if they survived a landing in German-occupied territory.

They needed the shortest possible sea crossing back to England; adjusting his course, he headed for Start Point on Devon's steep coast, praying that the fuel would last for the next ninety nautical miles. Normally he would expect to use thirty gallons of petrol an hour; with the tailwind he estimated that the flight across the choppy English Channel should take about twenty-five to thirty minutes. If the fuel ran out their only option would be to ditch in the cold Channel waters. He'd put his lifesaver Mae West on when he dressed before take-off in Sussex. But what about his passengers? There would have been two Mae Wests and parachutes with separate harnesses left available in the rear cabin; hopefully two of them would have taken the initiative and put them on – it was part of their agent's training. The third passenger, however, would be without any life support in the seas if they should come down.

Nursing the engine carefully, leaning off the fuel mixture in an effort to make the precious and volatile liquid go further, he allowed the aircraft to continue its gentle, slow climb. If the fuel ran out, the higher they were the more time they would have to prepare for a ditching in the uninviting water. At five thousand feet he reduced engine revolutions to nineteen hundred and cruised on through the blackness silently praying while watching the softly lit compass. He switched on the IFF beacon, hoping that any radar watch would pick them up, confirming their identification as a friend, not a foe.

He was tense. There had been no noise from the rear compartment since the take-off and now there was a strong smell of petrol in the cockpit. Momentarily the aircraft jiggled about violently for a few seconds before resuming its natural equilibrium on a steady course. There was a brief, barely audible shout from the rear, then silence. But, he suspected what had happened in an instant. They had flown through the boiling wake of an aircraft somewhere out there in the dark. The level of turbulence suggested that the other aircraft was actually very close, or had been, just seconds before. Looking out, staring into the grey darkness, he wondered. It could be one of ours, or one of theirs. For those in the Lysander, it did not matter which; neither party would take the trouble to ask after their business before opening fire with machine-gun or cannon.

Looking again at the fuel gauges, he noted that one had dropped completely off the scale, its needle leaning lazily on the stop. The needle on the other was sitting well below the last digit on its black-and-white circular face.

Again it hit them, more violently this time, and lasted some seconds longer. Again there was a muffled cry from behind him, audible above the engine. The other machine must be quite large; he'd experienced wake a number of times before and was sure that whatever was causing the Lysander to react so boisterously was almost certainly wake turbulence from a big aeroplane, lurking, hunting. If it was an enemy machine and it found them they would be a sitting duck; at their height it would be able to manoeuvre easily about them, shooting at will. He pulled the throttle closed, the Mercury engine died to a gentle tick-over; the Lysander began a descent towards the luminous white caps below. He'd decided that flying low with the risk of engine failure through fuel starvation, followed by a quick ditching, was preferable to being unexpectedly blasted out of the sky by some unseen night fighter. Operating just a few feet above the sea may help to conceal them and would preclude a night hunter from striking them unexpectedly from below.

After twenty-one minutes Kelly began a gentle pull back on the stick and the Lysander began to rise from the sea's surface.

Crossing the coast just to the east of Start Point was signalled by a line of plunging white surf below. Calling on the special Darkie distress frequency, he was immediately given a course and distance to steer for Warmwell, an airfield south of Exeter near the coast. Overhead the airfield, as they were preparing to join the circuit, the labouring Mercury engine suddenly coughed twice and stopped. They were finally out of petrol. Kelly executed a professional dead-stick landing in the near-darkness along a single line of burning goose-neck flares.

As the Lysander rolled to a halt he breathed out, massaging his face where the mask had been rubbing on the bridge of his nose and his chin. Climbing down from the cockpit, he swung around and stepping up onto the first rung of the boarding ladder looked into the rear cabin; he was aghast. With light from his torch he saw that the inside of the small compartment was spattered red with blood and black with oil. There was also an overwhelming smell of high-octane petrol. Two figures lay bunched, seemingly carelessly intertwined down on the floor, squashed awkwardly into the tiny space. Sitting, barely able to hold its head up with eyes closed and bubbling fluids from the mouth was another person sticky with dark blood mingled with oil from the split oil tank. In one dripping hand an automatic weapon was securely gripped. On the far side of the cabin two equi-spaced rows of holes migrated across the compartment wall. Most of the Perspex was missing from the rear-cabin side-window frames as well.

Medics extracted the three passengers carefully. One, a man, was dead already, hit in the head and chest, the legs hanging awkwardly, both broken by the Lysander's undercarriage; the second, an older woman with short black hair, her body horribly riddled with bullets, died in the meat wagon on her way to the station sick quarters; she had muttered a few words as she had been lifted into the back of the vehicle but nobody had been able to make sense of the sounds she'd choked out on the blood bubbling from her mouth.

The last passenger, a woman, was still just alive when he had seen her lying cold, eyes closed on a blood-soaked stretcher, a medic crouched over her, pumping the chest continually. Despite her bloody state Kelly finally recognised her in the light of the medic's torch; it was the young, tired-looking young woman he had taken to drop near St Pol on his first operation with the squadron all those months ago.

In Warmwell's flight offices he slumped at the debriefing officer's table, mentally and physically drained. Apart from the RAF Intelligence officer there was another man in dark civilian clothes standing by the table as he retold his story. He wondered later how he had known that they would end up here. The desperate sight of the three passengers had taken all the gloss off their remarkable escape. It seemed pretty clear to Kelly that the Germans had been aware of the planned rendezvous and had prepared an effective ambush for the departing agents and himself. He still could not understand how he had not been hit personally, even more so when he visited the aircraft in the hangar the following morning.

The Flight Sergeant in charge of the unit's servicing teams took Michael Kelly around the part-dismantled aircraft. The long-range petrol tank had been removed from under its belly; there were eleven bullet holes punched through its thin aluminium walls. Scrap, the Chiefy had said.

"Any one of those bullets could have caused the whole shebang to explode! The tank would have been half-full when you were on the ground in France. The vapours would have been just waiting for a source of ignition, Sir." They turned their attention to the rest of the aircraft; under the open engine cowlings they could see the paths of various lumps of high-velocity lead that had nicked pieces out of cabling, the exhaust manifold and the levers that controlled the throttle.

"But no hit was life-threatening to the aircraft; bloody lucky, Sir, if you ask me." They walked around the aircraft, now and again pushing their fingers into the many holes in the fuselage and wings. The wreck of the rear cabin caused Kelly to stop and imagine the chaos and pain that that small space had endured for those few seconds or minutes barely twelve hours ago. The split engine-oil tank positioned between the cockpit and cabin had also been removed and most of the blood and human detritus had been flushed from the interior, but the holes in its side spoke of dark, penetrating horror.

"Thanks, Chiefy. It seems I've been very fortunate ... unlike my poor passengers," he said sadly, pointing with his chin to the damaged cabin before walking out through the hangar doors into the brightness outside.

"You have, Sir. You certainly have," the Flight Sergeant called after him. "It'll be ready for you to take tomorrow morning." Michael nodded appreciatively without turning.

❖ ❖ ❖

Helen did not have to think too long about the first part of the Latin message from her father. If, as this Paola had said, his office had been ransacked, then it was likely that all his research papers including the rare and valuable Azzaro documents had been taken. Initially her concern was for her father. The fragility of the ancient papers, with their indecipherable text and aeroplane drawings, figured next. 'So,' she thought, 'the coded Latin comments in the first sentence probably meant that the special papers had been taken by the Italian authorities.' The more she mulled over the second part of the message, the more confused she was about its meaning. Her father was obviously trying to communicate something pretty important to her. She planned to go on her next couple of days off down to her mother's house in Devon to try to find the drawing he had made in Siena, in the sun, all those months ago.

Paignton was full of military personnel. As she left the railway station she was amazed at the numbers of soldiers and airmen marching about the place; the small seaside town set squarely in Torbay had become an armed camp where recruits of all sorts were accommodated in requisitioned hotels; sent to have the corners knocked off them before they were given further, more explicit, military training. Eventually a bus arrived at the head of the queue and she managed to board for the long, circuitous trip to the end of a road of Victorian semis where her mother's house sat. Walking from the bus stop up the road's slight incline, she looked back and could see the sea sparkling in the sun above the rooftops. She pushed open the wooden gate and heard the familiar click as the latch dropped back into place as it slowly swung closed behind her.

Inside it was cool. The next door neighbour came in occasionally to clean and see that everything was alright. On the mat were a few letters. The same neighbour normally forwarded the post every week or so to Hamble. She picked them up, putting them on the dark-stained hall stand, which still wobbled slightly, and made her way into the front parlour. She pulled back the heavy curtains, and light flooded in, specks of dust twirling and dancing in its low, straight beams. The dark furniture sat unmoved. Memories flooded back. Helen sat on the sofa for a few minutes thinking about the past, her mother and father; their friends and family had sat and laughed in this very room at Christmas, birthdays and feast days.

A noisy car labouring up the hill outside woke her. It was dusk and she was annoyed at herself for nodding off when time was all too valuable. In the small desk set in front of the parlour window she found the paper with her father's sketch lying folded within the old wooden gift soap-box. Opening out the creased diary page onto the ornate mahogany dining table, she sat and peered at the lines he had sketched, hoping for divine inspiration.

She recalled the discussion that they had had about the machine; how her father assumed that the rotating drum in the wings would create some lift through its vanes enabling the machine to rise. Certainly unconventional, she considered, from her expert pilot's perspective. The only thing stopping it, she recalled, was the lack of an engine and doubts about the suitability of materials available to a fifteenth-century engineer. She spent the remainder of the evening looking at the sketch and reading again and again the letter from the unknown Paola. The penny would not drop, but she was tired, perhaps in the morning matters would crystallise. Despite the recent warm weather the bed felt damp, not aired.

Feeling a little foolish, she hunted out a hot-water bottle to put in the high double bed that stood in the larger of the two bedrooms at the back of the house, which had been her parents' room.

Watching out of the upper windows she could see the last vestiges of daylight softly surrendering to night. From the small landing window, she stood looking out to sea; there were no lights, unlike her childhood days, when she would watch the lights of the fishing boats and the big steamers twinkling from end to end, making their way up-Channel towards Southampton, Portsmouth and London.

The BBC Home Service brought news of further bombing raids on Germany and on England. In North Africa Rommel's Afrika Korps were making strides against the Eighth Army. Depressed by the news and her inability to interpret the second part of her father's message, she climbed into bed and lay down with the light out, blackout curtains drawn back, hot-water bottle at her feet, staring at the blank ceiling. She realised she was hungry but couldn't be bothered to go down to the kitchen again.

❖ ❖ ❖

Sarah Kelly was frightened. She stepped back from the front door as the shadowy figure brandishing some sort of object moved out of the confines of the dark interior of the house. As she staggered backwards she slipped slightly on the porch step, dropping her small, unlit torch as she grasped for the wall for support. It clattered briefly as it hit the tiled floor and burst into light. Reaching down, Sarah picked up the comforting thin beam of light, and standing, focused it on a tall, thin man with a heavy five-o'-clock shadow. He raised a scrawny left hand to shield his eyes from its beam. His face was round and grey in complexion, the skin tight and drawn about a narrow, thin-lipped mouth.

"What you want?" The voice was an octave too high for a man, the teeth stained, and she noticed one was broken as he spoke. Sarah tried to settle her anxiety before speaking.

"I'm so sorry to trouble you at this time of night but my car has broken down and I wondered if I could use your telephone?" He turned slightly, looking back into the hallway of the house. The dog was still erupting somewhere to the rear.

"Hans! Shut up!" The dog slowed through a series of yelps and growls until it was finally silent. He moved towards her. It was a hammer in his right hand. "You cannot come in; we do not have telephone, now please to go way, I do not like stranger here this hour."

Sarah started to ask where the next nearest village or house was, but the man raised a finger to his mean lips.

"Please to go; now please!" He turned back into the hallway, slamming the front door in Sarah's face. The dog started to bark again and she heard the man bellowing at it from inside, but not in English.

How odd, she thought, as she walked back down the short pathway to the gate, recovering her composure. Funny too, she could see etched faintly against the night sky a telegraph pole growing out of the hedgerow against the road and two thin lines running to it from the house. 'No bloody phone, my foot!' she cursed, as she stumbled back into the road and walked back towards her car, intending to curl up inside and hopefully sleep until the milk wagons began in the early morning. As she tried to get comfortable on the narrow seats she wondered at the strange attitude of the man. There was something not quite kosher, she thought. Almost since the war began, nearly everyone's attitude had changed; people were putting themselves out to be helpful and co-operative, making the best of things. And another thing; she had detected a slight accent now and again in the few words spoken by the man. And who would ever call a dog 'Hans'?

She awoke shivering and stiff. There was a cool dampness inside the car and condensation trickled down the window as she rubbed it with her fingers, clearing a watery patch to look outside. "Damn," she exclaimed, alert, sitting up quickly. The reason, she quickly realised, for her awakening was just disappearing around the bend a hundred yards ahead of her stationary car. The tractor had a sole occupant sitting atop its seat set between two large muddy tyres as the machine rumbled noisily around the bend and out of her sight. Opening the car door, she struggled out. Her legs were stiff with the cold and from the cramped position they had been held in for nearly five hours. Brushing herself down, she searched for her handbag, extracting a small silver-backed hairbrush, a birthday gift from Michael two years ago, and commenced brushing her long, blonde hair, crouched and looking in the car's wing mirror. A quick swipe of lipstick completed the presentation exercise. Renewed, she looked up and down the road for some form of transport.

It was thirty minutes coming but she was grateful to climb up into the vibrating cab of the milk lorry as it completed its rounds of the local farms before heading into Petersfield.

The driver, a happy soul for the time of morning, dropped her at a roadside transport café where he said she would be certain to find help with getting fuel for her car and probably a good breakfast. For once in her life Sarah ordered a complete breakfast, the generously shaped proprietor managing to find two superb eggs to go with the home-cured bacon. The all-male clientele were fascinated to have a tall, slim blonde WAAF officer in their midst at such an hour, and seemingly well able to put away a man-sized breakfast.

Of course they were only too anxious to help in any way they could; within an hour she was back at the little red Morris with five gallons of agricultural petrol being glugged into its tank. The young driver would accept no payment for either his time or the illicit fuel now feeding her engine. But he did get to her to promise to come again to their 'breakfast club', soon. Smiling, she agreed as he roared off in his heavy truck, the rich smell of diesel trailing behind. An hour later she was at Hamble having a morning cup of coffee with Harriet, the unit CO.

Sarah thought it wise to familiarise herself with the situation before going into Hamble village and Ceci's billet. Harriet told her all that they knew of Harold's missing status, which was not much. They both knew that in time the Red Cross would send a signal announcing his capture or death, or the Résistance would send a message by some clandestine means announcing he was alive. Either way, they were aware that there could be no time limit for information and Ceci would have to be strong and keep busy. It was a tough regime, but the only one.

The day was bright, the sun sparkling on the Hamble River's rapid tidal flow. Knocking on the dark-blue door to Ceci's shared house, Sarah was apprehensive. She heard someone bouncing quickly down the stairs. The door opened and there stood a smiling Ceci.

"Sarah, what are you doing here? Come in, come in, I was just going to make some tea. Will you have some?"

Sarah was a little taken aback. She had expected a red-eyed girl sniffling into a handkerchief, inconsolable. In the tiny kitchen a blackened kettle was just beginning to whistle on the ancient gas stove. Pulling another cup and saucer from the wooden dresser, Ceci placed them clattering on the scrubbed kitchen table. From the window a narrow beam of sunlight divided the table neatly in two.

Ceci pulled out a rickety beech chair, its woven rush seat worn and tattered, motioning Sarah to sit while she poured the bubbling water over the leaves in a large pale-blue teapot.

"You seem in fine form, Ceci. I was expecting something different when I heard that Harold had been reported missing since Tuesday." Ceci looked her in the eyes as she momentarily stopped pouring tea into the two cups.

"Harold's OK." It was a definitive statement.

"Oh! Have you heard from him? Has he been in touch?" The young aviatrix looked away for the moment then sitting, faced Sarah, leaning towards her across the table.

"He's been in touch with my heart; I know he's OK at the moment – he's alive. It's a feeling. I know you don't understand but I just know he's OK."

Sarah looked askance. Was she in denial, she wondered? Over tea, as they talked, it became abundantly clear to Sarah that Ceci was totally convinced that Harold was alive somewhere; a prisoner, perhaps, or on the run; where, she did not know but there was no doubting the total conviction in her eyes and talk. Certainly she was worried about how he would come back to her but there was absolute belief in his survival. Ceci said she intended to go back to delivering aircraft tomorrow.

It was not the reception she had expected but Sarah too was convinced of Ceci's belief; the more they talked the further the patch of sun moved around the table. Later that afternoon, with a somewhat lighter heart and a full tank of petrol in the red Morris, Sarah left for home and the children, aware that she should have called her section chief at Danesfield about her delayed return.

◆ ◆ ◆

Harold Penrose eyed the farmer and his heavy hammer with concern. Perhaps it had not been such a bright idea to return to the house and village. "Bonjour Monsieur, vous allez bien?" Harold wondered; asking after his well-being was hardly the act of a man about to inflict violence. There followed a stilted conversation in a mix of French and a bastardised version of the classic language from Penrose. He heard of the brutality of the Wehrmacht troops as they had searched the area, and the delight they had taken in killing the two dogs and frightening the inhabitants. At least no one had been arrested and carted away to the Gestapo HQ in Brest.

For safety's sake they agreed he would stay up in the forest. The farmer would provide a waterproof sheet with which to make a shelter able to withstand the rain and to help insulate the few blankets available from the damp ground. The girl Véronique would bring hot food once a day to a concealed hole in a rotten trunk lying just inside the tree line. It would keep him alive until arrangements could be made to have him collected by the local Résistance circuit and put on a route back to safety and England. Waiting until just after dusk, Harold and the farmer carried the blankets, waterproof sheets, an oil lamp and supply of food up the hillside and into the forest, trudging carefully half a mile or so into its subdued interior, guided now and again by a pale torch beam. The farmer helped Penrose for a few minutes, and they erected a simple structure of branches bound together with strong twine and covered it with two of the oil-cloth sheets. The floor space was lined with the remaining sheet, and the blankets were thrown on top. Lighting the oil lamp, the farmer hung it from a convenient twig extending from one of the simple structure's branches. They shook hands, the man patting Penrose on the shoulder.

"Bonsoir et bonne chance; à demain." Penrose wished the farmer goodnight, patting him gratefully on the back.

Sitting with the unopened dish of stew on his lap, he listened as the man moved back though the forest, every now and again a dry twig snapping in the darkness. How long would it be before he could be on his way, he wondered. Before leaving the house the daughter had come downstairs and shyly given him some additional clothes to help ward off the penetrating damp and coolness of the forest floor. As he'd left she had raised herself on her toes and kissed both his cheeks.

He was glad of the additional clothing when he had finished the lukewarm stew and lay under the blankets trying his best to sleep. It would not come. The adrenaline was still circulating in his body; at least anyone approaching his well-concealed hide would signal their presence through the twig-snapping alarms set by the farmer around his crude bivouac. Above, somewhere over nearby fields a barn owl was screeching coded messages to its mate as it patrolled the dark landscape seeking prey. It was a disconcerting sound and he hoped it would fly to alternative grounds before long. Lying, knees drawn up, thinking of Ceci, he eventually fell into a troubled sleep.

❖ ❖ ❖

The Spitfire completed its photo run over Brest before turning to head north-east towards the grid reference given by the unit intelligence officer at his pre-sortie briefing. The pilot looked carefully at his chart; from twelve thousand feet there didn't seem to be much to interest the intelligence bods back at base, just a range of low hills, some fields and farms and lots of woodland; nothing of military significance as far as his human eye could see. Approaching the site, he switched on his vertical cameras and, unusually, flew two runs – each one at right angles to the other over the location marked on the chart, which seemed to be some fields with livestock and a few farm buildings. Normally he would have only undertaken one run; two usually meant that the enemy was alerted and ready with flak, but here there were no defences, no apparent interest in him. When he had finished, he opened up the Merlin, releasing the energy of over a thousand horses to the propeller; it pulled him firmly towards the coast, across the Channel, home.

The photos from the sortie were anxiously awaited by the navy; what was left in the harbour at Brest? Sarah was pleasantly surprised when Daphne arrived one afternoon at her section. She had been temporarily assigned to help clear the backlog of photos requiring interpretation. Over recent weeks, interpretation work for the Aircraft and Airfields Section in hut 7B at Danesfield had been near to overwhelming. With growing numbers of new reconnaissance squadrons and the increasing capabilities of new aircraft like the bowser Spitfires, every opportunity was being taken to photograph the enemy wherever he may be, on land or sea. The navy section received their pictures of Brest; Sarah received pictures of her remotely located barns.

Placing the two identical images under her magnifying stereoscopic viewer, she immediately saw that some things had changed. The field immediately adjacent to the last of the three barn-like buildings had been mowed. Checking the scale of the photos, she could ascertain that the mowed strip was about thirty feet wide and about two hundred feet long running roughly east to west. It was possible to see dark tracks in the mown grass. She assumed that the mowing, quite recent, was probably caused by a tractor. Looking carefully at the barns, she saw that what appeared to be large double doors were open at one end; it was just as well that the pilot had made two runs in opposite directions because one picture gave her a tantalising glance just into the barn's interior.

The height at which the photos had been shot gave little away. Further enlargement would probably fragment the image to a point where nothing could be positively identified, but she thought it worth trying. An hour later and with much complaining from the photo development section the enlarged images were in her hands. Just protruding from the open door were some blurry human figures standing facing a flat oblong object that from shadows underneath she could see was raised off the ground. The flat object appeared long and extended into the interior of the barn. What she could see did not make a lot of sense at present. Off-centre of the object there appeared to be a dark, wide line, almost a third of the object's width. Using additional magnification and intensive study, she thought that the line was probably something physical on the flat object; not a painted mark.

Sarah called Daphne to take a look. Sitting and peering for some minutes, Daphne studied the pictures. With her greater experience she pointed out to Sarah a very faint curved shadow showing around the end of the mark, suggesting that whatever it was, it was solid and casting a shadow onto the surface of the rectangular thing. They both looked intently at the images again. Whatever it was was still worthy of further reconnaissance when aircraft were visiting Brest or Douarnenez. Their section leader agreed, somewhat reluctantly, and an instruction was passed to Benson to revisit on the next sortie into the area – preferably at low level.

The weather proved unfavourable for most of the next two weeks with low scud blowing up the coast and inland from Biscay on a regular basis. There was, however, plenty to keep the two young women busy, often working late into the evenings with Sarah's children now in the nannying hands of the wife of a young fighter pilot from a nearby Hurricane squadron.

Over a rare dinner together at home late one Saturday evening, Michael Kelly talked to Sarah about his visit to the hospital in Exeter, where the young female agent had been taken after their harrowing flight back to RAF Warmwell.

"She didn't recognise me, neither from our first trip nor from my pick-up three weeks ago. I didn't think she would make it then; she was in such a mess, blood everywhere. It's amazing, she had been shot no less than four times. Fortunately no vital organs were hit but she'd lost a lot of blood. I'm staggered at the courage of these people, where do they get it from?" He told Sarah that he had invited the young woman, Geraldine, to tea when she was better. Sarah put her hand over his on the table.

"Thank God you weren't hit, Darling, none of you would have returned, perhaps." He leant over and kissed her, then said,

"Have you seen Patricia lately? You mentioned you'd seen her in Baker Street a while ago, nothing since?" Sarah shook her head. "No, there's been a complete lack of news from her since then. Perhaps she's in France now?" He thought for a moment.

"I don't think so; I've been around the squadron most ops nights, even if I've not been on a delivery or pick-up. I think I would have known if she had been sent over. Having seen the state of that brave young woman in hospital I am beginning to wish that I'd not helped Patricia to connect with SOE. If something happens to her, how will I face her father? He thought she was quite safe with us, it's ...." He was swallowing hard; eyes slightly moistening.

"Darling, don't. You told me that she was intent on doing something, her destiny, you said. I really wonder if we could have stopped her. If you hadn't helped she would probably have made suitable contacts some other way. I thought about talking to her on our way to Guildford but I could see that her mind was not for changing,"

Sarah interrupted and tried to look reassuringly into his eyes as she spoke softly. They both felt responsible for her. During the night they made love and Sarah spent the remainder of the darkness in his arms despite his gentle snoring. It was the first time for many months.

❖ ❖ ❖

On each of the following few days Harold Penrose went to the hiding place in the tree trunk, varying his time. It was proving to be the highlight of the day. There was nothing else to do except walk about in the forest. Once or twice he plucked up courage and went as far as the opposite side out of curiosity, but from its dark interior all he could see was more rolling hills, more woodland and an occasional distant farm. On one occasion he had been lost for some minutes but managed eventually to retrace his steps with some considerable relief. On the sixth day, instead of a hot meal wrapped in insulating cloths there was just a damp note in French on a scrap of paper pushed into a torn and used envelope. It was badly written in pencil, a pencil that could have done with sharpening, and he sat for ages trying to make out the words in the unusual handwriting and wondering what it meant. Finally he came to the conclusion that he was invited to visit the house after dark that evening and to carry all his possessions with him. Could this be the move, he wondered.

While it was still light he decided to dismantle the shelter. He didn't want it to be a hostage to fortune for the people in the village below. He kicked the branches about to make them look more natural. Using a stiff branch he tried to brush out the marks of his habitation on the forest floor, adding piles of dead leaves and debris to the site. In the twilight he felt satisfied and, using the remains of the twine, pulled together a bundle of oil-cloth and blankets ready for his departure.

At the tree line he stopped, watching the small community below. There were no lights. In the distance the barn owls had started early, swooping about the two barns behind the houses. Unsure, he decided to leave his bundle under a bush of holly just inside his forest entrance. Unencumbered he would have a better chance of escaping if the note should prove to be a trick.

Over the top of the damp field he walked in complete darkness, managing to retain his balance in the soft soil. At the ditch he decided to risk walking along its top edge, avoiding the boggy interior; it had taken ages to dry his shoes after his last venture through its wet depths.

Arriving silently behind the barn farthest from the whitewashed house, he crept around its wooden walls; they smelt strongly of preservative. Now and again there was a scuttling as some small animal made a hasty, unplanned escape from his advancing feet. Moving carefully he made it across the short distance to the second, smaller, barn. He stopped short. There was a noise, a footstep from inside. Approaching the small narrow door from where he had left its warm interior with the farmer days before, his every sense was aroused and alert. Was it a trick, had he been lured into being captured by the farmer or his daughter?

Time ticked by as he stood silent and still, waiting for the other party to make a move. Ten aching minutes went by then there was a sort of 'grumpf' from somewhere inside. 'No human, that,' he thought, and edged closer to the door.

With his ear to the crack in the door he listened ... to chewing. The barn was currently home to some calves, inside, out of the frost-prone weather. Looking across towards the house there was a thin sliver of light from around the side of what must be a poorly drawn blackout curtain. He could also smell wood smoke; etched faintly against the star-littered sky above him a narrow chimney poured a thin stream of pungent smoke with an occasional spark. 'So, there's someone home.' It was confirmed.

Penrose tried to look through the narrow slit of light but could see nothing but sun-bleached flowery patterned wallpaper. The sound of low conversation escaped from inside. With one ear to the window frame and listening carefully for a few minutes, he thought he could detect four different voices, three male and one female, all speaking French, now and again interspersed with the clink of a glass. He was ready to risk it and knocked carefully three times on the repaired kitchen door. Inside, conversation stopped abruptly, and then someone spoke sharply. The kitchen door was unlocked and opened a few inches; a quiet voice said, "Qu'est-ce que vous voulez?" Penrose thought for a few seconds, "C'est moi, Monsieur; pilot Harold."

Suddenly another voice in highly accented English said, "Ah, Monsieur Penrose. Please come in, we 'ave been waiting for you." Inside the kitchen were the farmer and his daughter. The former made clear that the other two men were from the local Résistance circuit; one wore dark, heavy work clothes soiled with mud. He was short and thick-set with a toothbrush moustache and black, bushy eyebrows below a thatch of untamed black hair. The other man was dressed in a well-worn blue suit; a raincoat lay over the back of one of the kitchen chairs. He was thin and wearing a pince-nez on a narrow nose in a long face; the teeth were yellowish. His thinning hair was also black and slicked back. It was this man who had invited him to enter the kitchen in passable English.

The girl motioned Penrose to sit close to the stove, smiling as she did so. Its warmth soon helped to relieve the tension caused by his coldness. The thick-set man, Frederick, shook his hand, nearly crushing his damaged fingers, and said something unintelligible while nodding with his head and eyes upstairs. He left the room, clumping up the narrow stairs to the bedrooms above. Claude, the thin man, explained that Frederick was upstairs to observe the surrounding area from the front and back bedrooms. Standing with his back against the stove, he went on to explain that within two hours a car would arrive to take him on his first steps towards home. Penrose gathered that there were two general options being considered. One was to take him to a safe house near Quimper, a small fishing town on the west coast in Biscay, to link up with another airman, who, it appeared, had somehow managed to escape alone out of Germany, across Belgium and into France, where he had been finally picked up exhausted by the Lille Résistance. Hopefully the pair of them could be smuggled aboard a fishing vessel and, again hopefully, make their way across the Channel to an English port. To Penrose it sounded all too simple. And so it proved to be.

Taking off his pince-nez, Claude laid them carefully on the table, rubbing his eyes for a full minute. He went on to explain some of the problems as the assortment of glasses on the table were refilled. It seemed that the Germans always inspected fishing vessels before they left harbour and often an armed soldier or sailor would be present on board for the whole of the trip. Also, Penrose was concerned to learn, the Germans always accompanied the small fishing fleet with an armed vessel able to fire on any fishing boat that decided unilaterally to leave the confines of the agreed area of fishing. Penrose leaned his elbows on the table looking at the grubby and torn map spread out; the cognac flowed like a warm, reviving stream down his throat, causing him to cough violently for a moment. The others smiled.

The second option sounded little better. It would require

Harold to be entered into the Comète escape route leading eventually to the Spanish border somewhere up in the wilds of the high Pyrénées, far to the south. The two airmen would be accompanied by two Résistance members all along the route using normal rail services to Bayonne, then a bus to a small village and a safe house nestling in the foothills of the Pyrénées. From there Claude described the route as a combination of cycling and a non-stop overnight climb over the mountains in complete darkness crossing the Franco-Spanish border in the process. If everything worked to plan they would be met at another safe house well inside Spain by a British Embassy car from Madrid.

Claude was at great pains to point out that over such a long route in occupied France the risks were high with the possibility of many identity checks along the way. But, he went on, they had had some successes in recent months and had finally delivered naval and army escapees to Gibraltar in the past two weeks. Harold chose not to ask how many escapes had been thwarted en route. Claude promised to send word to England that Penrose was safe during one of their routine radio transmissions. What he did not tell him was that they needed to verify his identity before proceeding much further; at least one Résistance circuit in the area had been infiltrated, betrayed and captured through bogus escapees.

❖ ❖ ❖

Once the weather showed signs of improving, the two photo-reconnaissance squadrons at RAF Benson were back in action; there was a backlog of reconnaissance sorties that needed to be completed urgently, including further coverage of the German navy's Brest facilities. One priority sortie would take the opportunity to over-fly the site near Sizun. The flight was planned to allow for coverage of the Brest naval base from above twenty-five thousand feet. The aircraft would then fly out into Biscay some way, descending to sea level before flying back to Brest at wave-top height. The tactic was intended to avoid enemy radar cover and hopefully catch the port defences unaware. The pilot would flash through rather than over the port, taking more low-level pictures with his oblique, sideways-looking cameras then continue at low level inland to the location of the three identified barns. Again with his oblique cameras the pilot would attempt to take pictures of the barns from very low altitude, routed in such a way that if any of the barn doors were open they may get a fleeting photographic glimpse inside.

With no apparent defences in the immediate area of the barns, after their photography the pilot intended to continue flying at low level, following the contours of the land until over the coast then, opening up the engine, would streak, still at low level, across the Channel avoiding the occupied, flak-ridden Channel Islands. Both the robust young pilot and his elderly briefing officer were well aware that the second part of the sortie was particularly hazardous. While no known flak defences surrounded the barns, they were thick on the ground around Brest harbour, reflecting the importance of the facilities to the German navy. In the immediate vicinity were Luftwaffe airfields including one at Rennes where Geschwader 53 were based, operating the highly effective Bf 109G fighter. If they were scrambled after his inevitable alerting of the defences at Brest they would be ideally placed to catch him as he flew the few miles from Brest to the small group of barns, and beyond. The young officer was confident, however, that with an element of initial surprise and the superior speed of his specially modified PR Spitfire – just over four hundred miles an hour flat-out – he could get away with it. Together the two men plotted carefully: routes, headings and timings for each leg of the sortie. Accurate flying was going to be crucial to its successful completion.

With the battery trolley connected and a thumbs-up from the ground crew's engine fitter, the four-bladed metal propeller turned slowly as the Rolls–Royce Merlin engine gathered life. A gust of blue smoke erupted from its two rows of exhaust stubs, set uniformly down either side of the aircraft's long cerulean blue cowling. Under the clear Perspex bubble canopy the pilot watched dials and gauges, monitoring the health of the roaring engine ahead of him as he pulled the strap of his helmet tight and adjusted his seat. Within minutes the machine was airborne; without delay the Spitfire started its heavenward climb on a south-westerly heading.

An hour or so later the aircraft was undetectable over Brest at just over twenty-seven thousand feet. With the vertical camera clicking away behind him capturing vital images for the Admiralty, he took unusual trouble in making his two passes over the site, each at ninety degrees, the second run heading out due west into the wide, open expanse of the Bay of Biscay. Below he could see the ragged headland of Ushant with its satellites of rocks and small islands divided by treacherous channels and tides. As he descended to sea level some thirty miles out, his location was briefly betrayed by condensation trails streaming back from the machine as it entered a level where benign moisture in the atmosphere condensed to white with the passage of his aircraft.

A close trio of U-boats out of Douarnenez, crossing the bay on the surface in company for better defence against air attack, saw the ethereal white scores across the blue between rows of cumulus as the PR Spitfire turned gently and tracked eastwards back towards Brest. A coded report was radioed.

A few feet above the surface of the ocean he switched on the oblique cameras in the machine's fuselage at just under half a mile from the port's main entrance. By now they would have been able to hear if not see him; flak was already pouring into the sky, black puffballs scattered randomly far above him. Fixing his eye on a point ahead, he lowered his seat irrationally for additional protection and, gripping the stick and throttle firmly, hoped that the two opposing cameras would justify the risky tactics he was about to employ. Crossing the port entrance from seaward he had a brief instant to observe grey-helmeted machine-gunners situated in small nests strung along the quays. They had him in sight and were loosing streams of lead in his direction.

He was very low and realised that within the next few seconds he would have to expose himself dangerously as he was forced to gain height to clear taller dockside buildings and cranes; there was rising ground ahead. Across the water, with a mix of ships moored or manoeuvring, he began to pull back slightly on the stick encouraging the Spitfire to hurdle over vessels and buildings, swerving violently at one point to avoid a momentarily unsighted string of black cranes, stark against the sky, inanimate along one empty quay. Now and again he was aware of hits on the aircraft but could not afford to look anywhere but ahead.

Breathing out, he was across and was beginning a shallow climb turning slightly left when the aircraft suddenly lurched violently sideways. Straightening the machine with some difficulty, he glanced quickly to his right; a gaping wound had appeared in the aircraft's starboard wing just ahead of the aileron. The aileron controls had become stiff and jerky to move and he was now experiencing some vibration and difficulty in turning the machine. He hoped the damage was limited to what he could see: torn aluminium skin protruding into the slipstream. Thinking about it, he pondered whether the obvious hit by flak had bent or somehow partially jammed the aileron controls as they passed through the wing. The inability to move the stick smoothly across the cockpit caused the Spitfire to lurch oddly at each attempt to alter direction. At low level this presented a problem; loss of control at only one hundred feet above the ground left little room for correction if something went wrong.

Now, beyond the inland outskirts of Brest, he was flying over countryside but his worries over the condition of the aircraft had meant that he had momentarily lost his way. Fortunately the engine was pulling strongly and all of the instruments showed that everything was healthy in that department. Looking up, he scanned the sky above for signs of enemy aircraft; he wanted to climb to gain a greater perspective of the surrounding farmland in the hope of picking up his proper track towards the barns from Brest. Half a mile away, off to his right, he glimpsed a ploughman stop his team of horses to watch, incredulous, as the Spitfire snarled low over the fields.

The time from Brest to the next reconnaissance location, according to his notes, would be just over four and a half minutes at two hundred and fifty miles per hour. He must be just about there, he thought, looking anxiously ahead as the Spitfire edged carefully higher.

"Damn!" he muttered as he flashed over a small road just clearing a run of telegraph poles; three long barns sat unobtrusively in an adjacent field. Moving the stick carefully, he banked away to his right, still climbing gently. After a few seconds he judged a reverse turn-back would bring him over the site again. Reducing speed, he edged the stick across the cockpit. The aircraft banked jerkily around, vibrating heavily from the turbulence caused by damage to the starboard wing.

Sat square in the centre of his windscreen was one of the barns, the other two masked momentarily by the line of trees following the road. He realised that he would have to push the aircraft hard down once past the trees to give his cameras a clear shot of the barns.

Opening the throttle a little, he tried to ignore the aircraft's growing vibrations as he studied the approaching trees and barns, noticing now that on two of them the end doors were actually wide open. He switched on the two oblique cameras. Men were running from somewhere within the surrounding trees, some turned to face his approach with weapons held up, firing flickering orange bursts, telling of lead loosed dangerously in his direction.

Over the trees, he pushed the stick forward very slightly. Soldiers ahead threw themselves onto the muddy grass or ran from his path into the trees expecting to be strafed. 'Strewth ... I'm bloody low,' he thought, looking for the briefest instant sideways across at the barns as he tore past their wide-open doors below the level of their roof peaks, the propeller whirling barely ten feet from the earth's surface. In seconds it was over; pulling back on the stick, he zoomed up to clear the trees at the far end of the field, then, turning in a series of unco-ordinated jerks to the north, he switched off the cameras. Still climbing slowly to clear the range of hills between him and the coast, he allowed the Spitfire to accelerate while he scanned the sky about him.

The problem was, the machine was vibrating madly as speed increased. Instruments in the panel in front of him were becoming an unreadable blur. Turning for a moment, he looked at the damage to the starboard wing, recognising that what should be an invisible smooth airflow around its polished surfaces was now being severely disrupted by the jagged tears in the upper, and presumably, lower, taut aluminium skins. Reaching over the top of the hills he could see waves in the Channel glinting in the distance. He slowed the machine to clear the worst of the vibration.

Glancing down inside the cockpit, he spent a moment watching the vibrating airspeed indicator as he progressively reopened the throttle. The Merlin was delivering healthily but now, at two hundred and seventy miles per hour, the Spitfire was shaking almost uncontrollably and there was a problem holding the machine straight and level, the right wing tending to drop as speed was increased. Scanning the skies quickly again, he sought enemy fighters; there were none. With luck, he thought, he might just get away with it, back to England, but he would have to restrict his speed to less than two hundred and twenty miles per hour. Anything the Luftwaffe had was much faster than that, he knew. As he allowed the machine to slow, the vibrations fell to within acceptable limits; while it was very uncomfortable for him, he recognised that prolonged violent vibration could adversely affect the aircraft, possibly causing failure of some key component. Now, thankfully, over the sea, he let the Spitfire settle gently towards its rolling surface; it was flying that required absolute concentration. Even at his reduced speed, one wrong move, a cough or a sneeze would lead within a second to an enormous splash and a final note on the squadron ops board: 'Missing.'

He estimated his flight time to be about eighteen minutes to the coast of Devon or Dorset; there was a brownish haze hanging in the sky ahead. From his height just above the waves all he could see was the blur of water pouring past him below. His concentration was absolute, and he was no longer even bothering to make a hasty scan of his instruments.

Just ahead, into the water off to his port side, the pattern was momentarily fascinating. Seconds later, there was another. An instant row of water spouts that dissolved into the waves. He looked up for an instant into his rear-facing mirror looking for the perpetrator. Breaking hard away to his right and above him a Bf 109 was swooping upwards as it turned away preparing for another run-in. A second machine was already firing down on him. He felt and heard thuds through the airframe. As in the first attack, some missed shots raised pinnacles of water just ahead. Moving the stick carefully and very slightly to the right with a touch of rudder, he glanced again up to the mirror fixed atop the windscreen frame. Nothing.

Momentarily turning, looking back to his left for an instant, he caught the briefest of glimpses of an aircraft diving down again on him. Watching ahead, now and again glancing into the mirror; a second later it re-entered, orange flashes erupting every few seconds. When he shut the throttle suddenly the Spitfire slowed as though brakes had been applied. The 109 overshot; confirmation came by way of a shoal of bullets striking the sea well ahead of the slowing Spitfire.

Judging the moment, and keen not to give the second attacker a chance of shooting his slow-moving machine, he opened the throttle fully, disregarding the vibrating consequences as speed built. Pulling back gently on the stick, he intended to give himself more manoeuvring room above the sea's surface while trying to avoid the attention of the two attacking 109s. The leading German, alerted to the temporary loss of its target, pushed its nose lower to pick up the clumsy, slow-manoeuvring blue Spitfire just as it rose up from the sea's surface.

The German was moving very quickly as it overtook. With incredible reactions the young Luftwaffe pilot banked sharply left to avoid a collision. He missed the Spitfire by mere feet. Still carrying the energy of its dive, the German machine continued briefly seaward, its plan-form momentarily silhouetted black against the setting sun. Its port wingtip struck the sea.

There was no time to watch. It must have been spectacular. The Spitfire pilot was now seeking his second pursuer. He glanced for a split second behind, closer now to the ocean's surface. Again nothing. Watching carefully he awaited the inevitable second, avenging attack. Nothing came. He wondered if the remaining German had seen enough, perhaps decided that low-level attacks were not worth the candle. He hoped so and pressed on northwards at reduced speed.

The coastline sat levitated above the surface of the horizon; it was a trick of atmospherics, he knew; a temperature inversion. The last few minutes had been free of action and he'd been able to concentrate on flying straight while allowing the Spitfire to gain a little extra height.

Over the coast in a flash, he did not recognise anywhere below him. He called on his radio. It seemed to have been a victim of the enemy's shooting. Not a squeak could he raise, as he twiddled the TR9 radio's knobs. He just hoped his IFF was working, identifying him as friend, not foe; having survived a Luftwaffe attack he did not want to be finally despatched by his own side. It had occurred to him on his journey that the damage done to the wing may present problems as he approached to land. He wondered how the Spitfire would handle at their normal approach speeds.

"Best thing ... try her out at altitude ... see if anything happens ... then ... I've got some height ... to sort it out," the words were soundless from his moving lips. Over the greening fields the young Canadian pilot continued to gently climb the damaged aircraft until, reaching three thousand feet, he carried out a slow-speed handling trial, standard practice with a damaged aircraft. It didn't.

It didn't handle at slow speeds. The flaps were inoperative and it seemed that there was also a problem with the undercarriage; it would not come down. Prudence suggested that he should take the machine back to the coast, point it out to sea and bale out, but the photos were almost priceless, he was certain. He had to land her somewhere – and bloody carefully too.

He conducted a further set of tests to determine just how slow the Spitfire would fly while giving him sufficient control for landing. At one hundred and ten miles per hour she was proving difficult to handle; the right wing kept dropping, the growing jerkiness in the aileron controls proving a hazard in helping him to catch the wing drop. For safety's sake he felt that an approach at one hundred and twenty miles per hour was probably giving him just enough margin for adequate control. He was conscious at the same time that this speed would be fifty to sixty miles per hour above the Spitfire's normal landing speed. He would ideally like a long runway if he was able to get the undercarriage down using the emergency high-pressure air system.

Cruising around, he began to recognise some of the area over which he was flying. He worked out that he had crossed the coast near Bridport in Dorset. Somewhere to the north, not too far, he knew, lay two airfields: Yeovil and Yeovilton. Turning the machine with jerking difficulty to the north he watched the slowly rising ground ahead, looking for an airfield – any airfield. After four long minutes he saw one, its black and camouflaged hangars casting deep shadows on their lee side in the evening sun. Looking about carefully for other aircraft, he slowed the engine and began a careful descent towards the long sward of grass with its attendant wind-sock and control tower.

With no radio working he flew along the line of the runway, fish-tailing the machine with the rudder. The normal sign of an emergency without radio – rocking an aircraft's wings – was unavailable to him, he being unable to move his stick freely. At the end of the runway and at three hundred feet he affected a stuttering turn. The stick was becoming increasingly difficult to move. From the tower came a steady green light signalling permission to land. Making a close circuit of the airfield, he caught hold of the emergency undercarriage lever and pulled. There was a series of crunching noises from somewhere in the aircraft's belly; the pitch of the aircraft changed slightly, to nose down, and out of the corner of his eye he saw one of the red indicator lights on the panel turn green. The second light, representing the starboard side, stared back unblinking red indicating that the leg and wheel had either not come down or had dropped partially but not locked safely into position.

In the aircraft's damaged state, and without a working radio to enquire how it looked from outside, he decided to continue with a landing, intending to hold weight off the starboard leg as long as possible during the landing run. The problem, he knew, was the speed at which the landing would have to be made. And the possibly catastrophic outcome should the leg collapse allowing the wingtip to dig into the ground with a possible cartwheel to follow, engulfing him in flame. He released the canopy catch and moved it back an inch.

Turning gingerly to line up with the runway, and feeling surprisingly calm, he slowly reduced speed, watching the picture unfold through his thick, bullet-proof windscreen – momentarily distracted by a green flare launched from somewhere near the control tower. He was approaching the threshold of the grass strip at a hell of a lick, he thought. Once over the boundary hedge he cut the magnetos, and the Merlin stopped dead. Watching the rapidly approaching grass, he just had time to turn the fuel cock off and pull off the master electric switch. He was in the hands of his maker – and the skill of the aircraft's builders.

Flaring the machine just above the ground, he waited for it to settle. His higher-than-usual speed precluded the normal sensations that would prompt him to take appropriate actions to keep the machine running straight and true. As their speed reduced, control over the aircraft's attitude followed suit. Even with the stick pulled fully over to his left, the starboard wing insisted on dropping. The port wheel touched the ground first, however; just as it did so the starboard wheel followed and for a second or two it seemed to him that both undercarriage legs were safely and firmly locked down, wheels in contact. The red light still glowed.

In an instant the starboard wingtip struck the ground; the leg had collapsed, torn from the aircraft. Then came a vicious swing to the right. The port undercarriage, tired of such misuse, parted company. The Spitfire was on its belly pirouetting down the green in a cloud of grass sods. Recent rain had made the surface little better than a skating rink. The aircraft continued turning with little apparent loss of speed as it hurtled towards the far boundary fence. The pilot sat powerless, hoping for the best; at least she had not flipped over – yet. The legless aircraft continued to whip around and around. His head was being thrown from side to side – only momentarily could he make out the direction they were heading in. Two hundred yards away, well to the right of the runway, on the airfield boundary stood a solid tree. It was immediately clear to him how things would end. He tried pulling back on the canopy but the turning forces made it impossible.

Two seconds passed, the port wing struck the base of the tree. Everything stopped in an instant. He was thrown harshly sideways, his face striking the side of the canopy and its rails; blood poured down his face, into his eyes and mouth. His sole concern was to get out: fear of fire.

Reaching up, wiping the flow of blood from his eyes with his right hand, he sought the canopy edge. A man possessed, he pulled at the canopy. It moved a foot or so then stopped. With both hands he caught hold again, heaving with all his strength. Above it all, he heard the clanging of a bell in the distance. A strong, hot smell assailed his nose behind his oxygen mask. The canopy moved another few inches and seized in distorted rails. It was enough. He tried to pull himself through the gap. He couldn't.

"Harness, you arse!" He shouted at himself, turning the quick-release buckle. The straps flew from his shoulders as he pushed up and out of the cockpit, the side door stuck shut. The lower two blades of the Spitfire's propeller were neatly bent back under the crushed engine cowlings from where wisps of smoke were leaking, curling upwards, black and pungent. Still he could not get out; his parachute was still attached and jamming against the narrow gap. Falling half back into the cockpit he used both hands to release himself from the silk-filled pack that now threatened his escape. Squeezing and turning, he fell onto the wing. The clanging fire engine rushed, bumping incredibly fast across the uncut grass towards him. In its wake were assorted other vehicles, including an ambulance, its distinctive high-pitched, toy-like bell also signalling urgency. He stood briefly alongside the broken aeroplane swaying slightly, looking back. His route was plain to see, carved deeply in places, scoring the soft brown soil. Some two hundred yards back one undercarriage leg lay without a wheel. Further back still he could see other bits and pieces in his wake.

"You alright, Sir?" the RAF fireman, out of breath, ruddy-faced and ready for action, asked as the young Pilot Officer slumped down on the wet grass some yards from his once-beautiful cerulean blue aircraft.

"I'm OK, thanks," he said quietly, looking up at the man's incredulous face.

"Thought for a moment we might 'ave to take you out of there in a bucket the bloody rate you was goin'." The fireman smiled slightly as he pointed to the partially open cockpit. "Bloody lucky she never flipped."

"Yes," he whispered, sudden tiredness filling his voice; he lay back on the grass looking up into the sky. "Bloody lucky," he mumbled. A medic from the ambulance gave him a quick check-over, stopping the bleeding from his head and face with cold, clean bandages. He sat up partially, leaning on one elbow looking at an approaching group.

"Don't get up, old man, I'll get some chaps with a stretcher," the squadron leader knelt beside him. The young pilot looked anxious.

"I'm back from a recce flight, can you get the cameras out? There's important film there." The senior officer followed his gaze to the broken Spitfire lying on its belly, part-covered in fire foam in the soft earth.

"Don't worry, old man; we'll get them out somehow. Where do you want them sent?" The pilot looked up at him and managed just three words.

"Benson, 's urgent," and collapsed unconscious.

The squadron leader telephoned RAF Benson, advising that they were sending an aircraft over with cameras recovered from a damaged PR Spitfire; he gave its registration number and also let them know that their Canadian pilot, Pilot Officer Paul Mossman, was suffering from mild concussion and other minor injuries and had been taken to a nearby civilian hospital. He promised to let them know when there was further news.

FOUR

Ceci and Helen had been given a rare 48-hour pass by Harriet; the weather forecast may have had something to do with the unexpected reward; the prediction was rain, low cloud and boisterous south-westerly winds for the next day or two as a deep depression passed across the land. They drove from Hamble in Ceci's Riley; thin drizzle sought out every hole and split in the car's worn fabric hood. Arriving at Sarah and Michael's house and taking the key from under the doormat, they luxuriated in hot baths well above the two inches decreed by government. The children were being looked after in the village by a retired schoolteacher who knew just what interested young children and kept them busy. The young wife of the fighter pilot who had stepped in when Patricia had left had also moved away to her parents after her husband had been shot down and listed as missing some weeks before.

Tomorrow, Sunday, Sarah had been promised a day off; she'd been working twelve to fourteen hours each day for nearly three months and it was beginning to tell on her and the two children. She arrived home just before nine to find Michael off operations for a couple of nights despite it being within the moon period; Ceci and Helen were gossiping while preparing a late dinner. The meal was simple and satisfying. None of them felt particularly hungry; tiredness was the predominant state. Michael and Ceci washed up while the other girls put Alistair and Beth to bed with a story each; neither child remained awake to the end of the tale.

Finally, they all sat around in the lounge chatting, wondering how best to make use of their rare and valuable time off.

After a late breakfast, Michael took the children splashing through muddy puddles to the neighbouring farm to see the lambs and a newborn calf. With time on her hands for a moment Helen took the opportunity to empty the contents of her somewhat battered and voluminous handbag onto the kitchen table. Giggling over cups of tea at the sheer diversity of things scattered over its surface, Sarah watched as Helen rationalised over odd items that were kept and not thrown. Ceci came in and joined Sarah in comments jokingly made about some of the items; one broken earring, a leaking fountain pen, a small bag of red elastic bands and seemingly endless numbers of boiled sweets in shiny wrapping paper, now almost unobtainable in rationed Britain. Ceci, smiling widely, remarked that she hoped Helen took account of the extra weight of her handbag when calculating her aircraft's centre of gravity before each new delivery. Helen took it in good part, and then she came across the diary page folded and tucked inside a now-distinctly off-white envelope.

Unfolding it, she spread it onto a clear area at one end of the kitchen table.

"What's that, Helen, a compact navigation chart?" Ceci laughed, as she moved around the kitchen to get a better look at the firmly drawn lines across its surface. Sarah peered over her shoulder, warming the teapot in her hand. Helen briefly explained the history of the drawing and that it was something her father had drawn some years ago from memory. Sarah put the teapot down and sat looking carefully at the surprisingly detailed freehand sketch.

"Its odd, isn't it?" remarked Ceci. "It looks like an aeroplane but there's something not quite right about it." Sarah nodded.

"How old did you say the original drawings were, Helen?"

"My father thinks the designer, a chap called Pietro Azzaro, was a student at some point working under Leonardo da Vinci. There were some of Leonardo's original ideas in among the ancient papers."

"So ... it must be from about the middle to end of the sixteenth century, Helen?"

"Well, my father is convinced it's about that period, perhaps a little later. What's so amazing is that the aeroplane drawings are almost as you would expect to see today, the layout and so on. Except, here, look at the detail of the wings, there is something very different here. It's like a ... well, my father said, a cylinder with some sort of aerodynamic vanes attached to its surface. He believes that the cylinder is hollow and that somehow it was intended to be rotated, the airflow presumably creating lift for the machine.

"Problem was, of course, they had no engines to drive it." Ceci piped up.

"It seems way ahead of its time. Has anybody else seen it?"

Helen explained further about the letter she had received some weeks ago from the unknown girl Paola in Bologna. Sarah reboiled the kettle and made tea, saying,

"Perhaps Michael would have some ideas. We must show him when he gets back with the children."

Helen carefully refolded the paper back into the tattered envelope and finished sorting the wheat from the chaff into her handbag; it was about as full as before. Minutes later, two rather wet children and a damp, worn-out father came into the kitchen. The children were full of what they had seen and demanding jam sandwiches for an early lunch. After a quick meal the children were left playing upstairs in their bedrooms. In the lounge there was some desultory chatter before Michael and Sarah fell asleep together on the worn sofa; the two other pilots read magazines and chatted quietly.

In the hall the phone rang. Michael jerked wide awake. Helen got up.

"I'll go, Michael, leave it to me." They could hear a few brief words from the one-sided conversation in the hall.

"Oh hello, Harriet. No, no, it's Helen ... What ... really! Hang on; I'll get her, just a minute." Putting the phone down onto the worn mahogany hall table, Helen came into the lounge with a smile on her face.

"Ceci, it's Harriet. She wants to speak to you."

Ceci rose from her comfortable position curled up in the largest armchair and disappeared into the hall. Helen stood just inside the door waiting.

"Hello, it's Ceci. Got a rush job on?" There were a few moments of silence then, "Oh, thank God, thank God, I knew he was alive. Thank you so much for calling, Harriet. Yes, yes, I understand, no, that's OK; see you Monday morning. Thanks again, Harriet, bye bye."

Ceci came back into the lounge, where by now everyone was fully awake.

She was laughing and crying together, huge clear tears of joy and tension release pouring down her smiling face.

"There's been a message from France. Harold's OK ! He's safe.

Oh my God, he's safe. He's with the Resistance somewhere." She collapsed back into her chair looking frantically for a handkerchief, still laughing and crying. Michael jumped up.

"Bloody marvellous! This calls for a celebration." On his return from the cellar with a bottle of 1936 Champagne the two girls and the children were gathered around Ceci laughing and talking; glasses clinking together, bubbles flashing red and orange from the log fire alive in the grate.

❖ ❖ ❖

The weather had not improved much by Monday morning as Sarah made her way across the puddle-strewn car park towards the main entrance to Danesfield House. Passing through the enormous house, she made her way across cinder paths to her hut. On a table next to her desk was a mountain of large sealed buff envelopes; she knew that their contents would keep her and her girls busy for some days ahead. Inside were both high- and low-level black-and-white photos of various Luftwaffe airfields and their aircraft; pictures riskily captured by PR squadrons from the south of England. Parcelling out the work of studying and interpreting the pictures to her section of three WAAFs, she took the major portion herself, keeping a particular envelope to one side.

While sorting the work into roughly even amounts she made a point of quickly looking at the content of each photo batch. One batch was marked as taken by a Benson PR squadron aircraft indicating the time and date with a location code. The code on this particular batch was the area around Morlaix, Sizun and Callac near to where they had seen the three barn-like buildings. For no particular reason Sarah had continued to think that there was something illogical, or at the least odd, in building three plain-looking barns in this particular location but the earlier photos had not produced anything tangible to support her suspicions.

When she opened the envelope a selection of pictures slid onto the table, where her stereoscopic lenses stood. One staggering fact soon became apparent; the pictures were of incredible quality, and more importantly, taken from extremely low level. In one, the detailed facial features of a grimacing German soldier with a Schmeisser machine-pistol rising in his hands could be clearly made out as the aircraft had passed. In another, individual blades of grass could just be made out in some parts of the picture as the aircraft had made its rush across the end of the three barns, one with its doors fully open, another with doors partially open.

The insides of the open barns were very brightly lit; just within the doors of one stood a group of white-coated figures, their faces turned towards what must have been an ear-shattering sound as the Spitfire shot for an instant across their narrow field of view. One or two of the faces wore expressions of horror or surprise, now fixed permanently by the camera.

It was the final three photographs of the batch that caused Sarah's pulse to quicken as she made a sharp intake of breath. Her previously unjustified interest was now apparently fully vindicated. One picture captured the entire interior of one long barn. Down the centre she could make out what looked like three rather small aircraft, their wingtips almost touching either side-wall. They were coloured a pale green, not camouflaged, probably some protective undercoat, she surmised, remembering facts from her infrequent visits to shadow aircraft factories, asking questions about technical aspects of aircraft to aid her interpretation duties.

She spent most of the morning studying each of the pictures quickly through different levels of magnification to gain an early understanding of their content and any immediate implications for the enemy's capabilities. Later, more detailed studies would be undertaken, probably with the help of other experts.

The aircraft nearest the barn door was facing the opening, slightly off centre, so that some aspect of the machine's side profile was visible. On cowlings that contained an engine of sorts she could make out a dark stain running along its length, but interestingly there was no propeller where one should have normally been. She mentally filed away a fact: the tell-tale stain could only be the result of exhaust gases from an engine. A possible conclusion from such a germ of evidence was that the engine had been running, and probably running for some time in view of the darkness of the stain which was well illuminated by the barn's overhead lights. The question was, had the machine actually flown or was it still undergoing ground testing? Looking at the undercarriage and the wheels, in particular, did not help her conclusions. They were in dark shadow under the fuselage and little of value could be made out; she was looking for mud and dirt on the tyres and undercarriage.

What really struck Sarah was how small the aircraft appeared to be in comparison to the men standing nearby. Were the Germans developing a new midget fighter, she pondered. If they were, she thought it would almost certainly have some distinct advantages over a conventional fighter. The Germans would never waste time and vital expert engineering resources on something that would not give them a serious advantage. Just being smaller would make it a difficult target. She decided to call the section head of her group and show the new evidence, but before that she would have a good look at the other pictures first.

The next picture showed an alternative view of the interior of the same barn a fraction of a second later. Such shots, she knew, always gave valuable alternative perspectives and lighting angles, often making further evidence available or helping to confirm something not clear in only one picture. Yet another shot was obviously captured as the aircraft was between barns. It showed a strip of grass lying between them and two figures standing, one facing the camera the other turned slightly away. The second individual was smoking; the picture clearly showed a curl of smoke from a cigar in his right hand, but it was too large to be a cigarette. This man was dressed in a pale uniform with shiny badges of rank attached to its epaulettes and wore a peaked hat. Sarah made a further mental note to study this later in greater detail to determine what rank he was; it could have implications for understanding how important the apparently new aircraft were. She looked at the other man, who was shortish, tubby and balding with a pair of glasses pushed up onto his forehead and wearing a white coat partly unbuttoned at the front. It was the stance of the short man that attracted her attention and made her look more carefully. The stance was that of a naughty schoolboy suffering blows – verbal blows – his whole attitude was subservient, cowering.

The next picture in the sequence showed the adjacent barn with one door fully open, the other only partially so. The interior was, like the other barn, brightly lit but there were no complete aircraft standing there. Instead there were what appeared to Sarah to be large pieces of aircraft; to one side there were two large objects being worked on by some men. Could they be the wings? She looked back, carefully studying the first two photos: they were wings. The objects had the same form as those attached to the completed aircraft. Very used to studying aircraft in photos, she was surprised by an odd-looking structure that from her quick initial studies appeared to be set into nearly the full length and width of the wing, looking at its plan view. Further into the second barn, with increased magnification, she found something not too clear about halfway down its length. It also appeared to be a wing form but seemed to have a huge rectangular hole cut right through it; she could see part of a man working through the aperture. To one side two other blurred figures were carrying or perhaps lifting a longish object that from the way the light caught it appeared round and cylindrical.

"Goodness," she said out loud, "It can't be." The other three girls looked up from their work. Picking up the telephone, she called her new section head requesting a visit to her office. The penny had dropped; the coincidence was uncanny. She needed to get in touch with Helen – despite the need for secrecy.

❖ ❖ ❖

Returning to the squadron, Michael Kelly made his way to David Rawlinson's office and told him of Ceci's news about Harold Penrose.

"I wonder if we can arrange a pick-up, David? Can SOE or SIS make contact with the Resistance group concerned? I'd volunteer to go in and fetch him in one of our Lizzies."

"I'll speak to them this morning, Michael. I've got a couple of bods from there due later; it might be possible, but I know what they'll say: 'It will have to be fitted in with all of the other rendezvous etc, etc.' You know what they're like at times, especially now."

"OK, but see what you can do, David. Oh, by the way, how's David Balfour? Any news of him leaving hospital? I visited him a few days ago, before the weekend, and he seemed to be pretty good to me." David Rawlinson stood.

"I'm afraid David won't be joining us again. The quacks say his injuries, particularly his head injuries, make it impossible for them to pass him 'A1' fit for flying. It's affected his nervous system in some way; his reaction times are too slow and he doesn't have full range of movement in his neck."

"Christ, what bad luck; is it a permanent?"

"'Fraid so. They intend to give him a desk job somewhere and we'll be getting a new CO."

Michael Kelly left the offices and walked slowly towards the squadron flight offices pondering the fate of his erstwhile CO and considering how lucky he personally had been when he had been ambushed during the recent pick-up. On the operations board he was listed as flying that night but he would have to wait until later that afternoon before he was briefed. In the meantime he redirected his steps to the Met office to forearm himself for a likely sortie into France in the dark.

❖ ❖ ❖

While waiting for a call from Helen, Sarah got in touch with Daphne, who worked in another section based in the main house. Daphne was acknowledged as one of the experts when it came to photo interpretation, regardless of the genre. Half an hour later the slim flight officer walked smiling into Hut 7B, propping her umbrella into the corner by the door and rubbing her hands together.

"So, what have you got, Sarah, something good?"

Sarah explained the detail behind her concerns and the link she had now made between the recent low-level photos and Helen's father's copy of bits of the Azzaro sketches that she had revealed to them over the weekend, together with the technical comments proffered by Michael Kelly when he'd been shown them in their kitchen. Daphne sat and spent a long time looking at the set of pictures. She asked a few questions about the location of the barns, how long they thought they had been there and whether there had been any sign of construction traffic before or after their appearance. Sarah filled in the gaps as best she could. The last question was an interesting one; surely signs of construction would have been plain to see, even some weeks after completion. These were substantial barns that would have required men and materials in sizeable quantities – and they would have left lots of evidence, she thought.

Daphne beckoned, "Sarah, look at the interior in this shot, look particularly at the walls of the building, just here, see?" Daphne pointed to a very short stretch of wall exposed between some what looked like tall cupboards.

"It doesn't appear to be brick construction. What are those diagonal crosses fixed to the wall?" Sarah looked up. Daphne grinned.

"These are prefabricated buildings, Sarah. No wonder they appeared so quickly, and with little discernible mess. Whoever wanted them wanted them quick. The buildings have been manufactured somewhere else, brought to the site and rapidly assembled like children's Meccano. These small aircraft are obviously of vital importance to the Germans. They've chosen somewhere completely out of the way to develop them, significantly, not in Germany, where all of their engineering expertise is based. They are far from any bombing raids and no one, not even we, would think of looking for something like this here. It seems that whichever PR pilot forgot to turn off his cameras after leaving Brest all those months ago has unknowingly done us a favour. Your insistence on pursuing matters is a credit to you. Well done! We need to get some of these pics over to intelligence at Bletchley Park or Baker Street. They may have ideas about the odd wing structures you've identified, and indeed the oddly small size of these machines. One other thing: there is little sign of these aircraft having flown. The grass around the barns appears to be quite long. No tyre tracks or landing skids in wet grass – that's interesting." Daphne got up from the table where the pictures lay.

"You need to get some duplicates of these made available for those who need to know; treat everything from now on as top secret. Please let me know when your friend Helen arrives from Hamble, I'd like to meet her." Sarah walked with Daphne to the door of the hut and watched as she walked smartly back to Danesfield House under her umbrella. 'Amazing woman,' she thought, 'you'd never think she'd lost her husband recently.'

❖ ❖ ❖

Sitting in the back of the Citroën as it cruised quietly through the blackout seemed almost surreal to Harold Penrose. The car had arrived at the white-washed house shortly before two in the morning, considerably later than they had anticipated. In the car was an unnamed driver, a woman; Claude sat beside her, a Sten gun concealed carefully down the side of his seat. Bertrand, a tall man with very wide and bushy eyebrows, and dressed all in black, sat with him in the back of the car. Nobody spoke; the woman concentrated on driving the unlit car through the narrow blacked-out country roads towards Quimper. Now and again she stopped, Claude got out, taking his weapon, and silently walked a few steps up the road, peering ahead. On his return, he would just nod and they would continue.

On the outskirts of Quimper the car finally stopped, and the engine was switched off. Harold noticed that they had pulled into a narrow driveway overshadowed by shrubs and naked trees. He was ushered silently out. Claude and Bertrand leaned on the car doors, silently closing them. The woman driver executed a carefully judged three-point turn and departed the way they had come, into the darkness, leaving the three men flattened against a tall privet hedge alongside a narrow footpath. In the black they listened carefully. The Germans did regular patrols and anyone outside during curfew was liable to be shot on sight if detected. There was nothing; Bertrand led the way, Sten gun thrust forward, sniffing ahead. Harold followed closely with Claude bringing up the rear, pistol in hand, constantly looking over his right shoulder.

Trying to contain the noise of his heartbeat, Harold pushed himself into the wall as the growing noise of marching boots approached their momentary hiding place in the shadows of a garden wall surrounding a dark, silent house set well back from the road. Only the jackboots crashing onto the damp road surface could be heard, none of the troop of eight Wehrmacht soldiers spoke, or sang as they conducted their mobile vigil. Eyes shut,

Harold heard the feet finally disappearing along the road; he felt a solid nudge as Claude urged him to make haste after Bertrand, who was now twenty yards ahead. They seemed to walk for ages, every so often darting for cover behind a wall or hedge as the sound of a patrol echoed somewhere down dank, unlit streets. Finally Bertrand turned into a narrow ginnel between two large houses fronting onto the road. At the rear of one darkened house he tapped distinctly three times on a curtained window. The three men stood, hearts pounding and out of breath, waiting for some response to a seemingly inadequate announcement.

From a small door to the left of the window came the sound of a sliding bolt. The door cracked open a few inches and a voice whispered:

"Er ... Oui ... Bertrand, c'est vous?" The heavy-set Frenchman looked towards the door uttering, "Oui." With the whispered confirmation, the door was opened just enough for the three men to enter a very narrow hallway lit by a glimmer of light from a partially open door. At the end Harold could make out a set of equally narrow stairs rising at the far end into darkness on the floor above. The man beckoned them forward, turning right into a room with a paraffin lamp alight. The three travellers reached up to cover their eyes from its relative brightness.

Harold took stock; it was a sizeable kitchen with dark wooden shelves covered with white and flowery crockery and pans of one sort or another on the wall opposite. An ornately carved, glass-fronted dresser stood against another wall. As they sat, the man opened one of the dresser doors, pulling some glasses from its packed interior, placing them on a large, solid wooden table. Harold noted that the man had a Sten gun on a sling around his neck, ready for any trouble. There were quiet greetings and they sat around the table in the warm room, glasses held firmly, sipping Calvados.

There was a brief discussion between Claude and the householder, Raymond. After a few minutes he stood, inviting Penrose to follow him. Shaking hands gratefully with his two escorts, he thanked them for their care in his best schoolboy French. They smiled at him and patted his back as he left the room following the man along the hallway and up two flights of steep stairs. On the landing there were two doors. Raymond ignored these and walked to a small window at the far end of the landing. Looking out, Harold see could see little except the vague outline of houses opposite and one or two trees that grew in what he assumed to be gardens in the space between. Raymond slid the lower sash of the window up; it seemed to move effortlessly and silently – it was obviously well used. Bending as he straddled the cill, Raymond stepped through and stood on a gently sloping roof outside. Harold looked then followed, his arm supported by Raymond as he did so. To the left of the window was what appeared to be a type of dovecote attached to the wall of the house. It was a grey-white in the darkness; Harold could see dark contrasting circular holes in its front face where the presently slumbering birds would make their entrances and exits during more reasonable hours.

The man was struggling with something and muttering barely audibly. There was a loud 'click'. Then the whole dovecote opened, hinging away from the wall leaving a sizeable opening. Raymond climbed through the hole with Harold scrambling through close behind. Inside was a modest-sized room. Raymond pulled the dovecote closed, and inside, a paraffin lamp was expertly lit and hung from the rafters above. It smelt musty, and it was cool and very damp. Alongside each of the two unplastered gable-end walls was a single wooden bed with a pile of blankets on each thin, stained mattress.

In the centre of the room, under the smoking oil lamp, a small, wobbly table stood with two equally unstable spindly chairs. Walking around his new accommodation, Harold picked out the bucket with a lid in one corner and a bowl and water jug standing alongside on a wooden box. The room had no plastered ceiling; above him only the undersides of the grey slate tiles protected him from any inclemency. Raymond grinned apologetically, bidding him goodnight, pointing him at one of the beds. He left the same way as they'd entered, locking the dovecote behind him. As he sat on the bed in the dim, flickering light Harold suddenly realised that access to and from the room could only be made during the hours of darkness if secrecy was to be maintained. Curling up under the blankets, having availed himself of the use of the bucket, he fell into a deep sleep. It was just before four-fifteen in the morning and his head was pounding.

❖ ❖ ❖

Helen was met by Sarah in the reception area of Danesfield House. The receptionist called Daphne while they chatted, then all three women went into the small conference room on the first floor. Pouring tea for the three of them, Sarah was interrupted by a knock on the door. Outside were two men in plain greyish civilian clothes, one with a Homburg held in his hand. Each carried a small, brown attaché case with the civil service coat of arms embossed on it. Introducing themselves formally, one was from the Ministry of Aircraft Production, the other from some scientific institute working within SIS. It later transpired that he was a senior scientist at the National Physical Laboratory at Teddington to the south-west of London. Outwardly they appeared fairly typical civil servants; steady but uninspiring.

Daphne initially took control of the meeting, opening the discussion by asking what further help Danesfield could give in determining more information about the 'midget' aircraft, as one of the men had termed them. The expressed view from one of the civil servants was that a further attempt to gather photographic evidence by reconnaissance aircraft may prove a waste of time. The Germans now knew that we would have some information about their activities and would no doubt take measures to safeguard the site, possibly by introducing a flak battery to keep prying aerial eyes away. The other man doubted that they would introduce anti-aircraft guns at this stage, as it would draw attention to the site, suggesting that it was important and that they had something to hide.

"Keeping the prefabricated factory doors closed would probably be as good a step as any, and increasing a discreet guard on the location," suggested the SIS man. He went on, "We need to get some people on the ground who know something about aircraft and could gather intelligence unobtrusively, perhaps in conjunction with the local Morbihan Resistance." Sarah looked around the table as she passed additional copies of the key photographs, much enlarged. It occurred to her that she had almost stumbled on a major intelligence issue and was now at the centre of a vital information-gathering exercise.

Looking at the photos, the SIS man pointed out some features on the tiny aircraft that gave them cause for concern. What Helen and Sarah had interpreted from the reconnaissance photos and from Professor Lorenzo's drawings as a rotating drum with vanes attached proved to be just that. Using the photographic blow-ups of the aircraft in the barns, the man pointed out some details which, when explained, made sense of the shapes that had been seen inside the second barn, in particular. The long cut-out slot in the wing had been designed to accommodate the rotating vanes.

He spent some time explaining the technical features of the aircraft as they had been assessed by their experts. As he pointed out at the outset, he had to make clear the detail of the machines to help Danesfield in their future interpretation work; it may be that the programme discovered by Sarah was also being conducted elsewhere.

Their discussions lasted well over four hours. Sandwiches were brought to them at lunchtime but were left largely untouched; all of the girls were impressed with the concise explanation given by the man from the Ministry of Aircraft Production, and became totally engrossed despite the technical nature of the explanations.

He started with some drawings on a small blackboard in the corner of the room. It became apparent as he progressed with his explanations that the rotating drum with a series of aerodynamically shaped vanes fixed to its hollow perimeter were turned by the main propulsion engine. The hollow drum-shaped objects, with their vanes, were fixed lengthwise into each wing very near the wing's leading edge. As the vanes rotated at high speed within the wing structure they created lift without the wing having to move fast forward through the air as with conventional aircraft. Importantly, the vanes also provided thrust, pushing the aircraft forward, so eliminating the need for a conventional propeller.

To Helen, an accomplished and experienced pilot, it quickly became obvious how such an arrangement could benefit an aircraft's slow-flying and load-carrying capabilities and she began to fire questions at the man, who smiled gently and continued to build the story of the unique aircraft and what its implications could be for the enemy – and the Allies. He went on:

"It's almost certain that what the pilot of Benson's reconnaissance aircraft has captured are pictures of small-scale test machines; they are endeavouring to prove the design concept and engineering with scaled-down aircraft, which are almost certainly being used for detailed evaluation." He turned to Helen, "Your father's open invitation for others to study the drawings when he received them, sharing them with other academics for comment and so on has unfortunately led to Pietro Azzaro's concepts being taken rather seriously by both the Italians and the Germans. There is no blame attached to your father – he was following normal academic research protocols. I think it probable that one of his 'trusted' colleagues has seen an opportunity to ingratiate himself and passed the research papers to the Fascist military authorities, who clearly have co-operated with the Nazis. Your poor father's arrest is almost certainly a sham to stop him talking further about Azzaro's concepts. I have to tell you, Miss Lorenzo, that we are taking discreet steps to see if we can help your father in his predicament, but I cannot hold out any immediate hope." Helen nodded sadly, wondering how her father was coping with incarceration. The SIS man took up the story.

"The key issue at the moment is how far has the enemy got with their testing and evaluation. From your photographs we can see no real signs of an aircraft being tested, any runways or repetitive marks on the ground. But; you should be aware that our aerodynamic experts suspect that an aircraft configured like this would not require normal long runways or lengthy grass strips. In fact, some calculations already undertaken based on current evidence and some hypothesis suggests that these small test machines could get airborne in only a few dozen feet, making them almost impossible to detect through ground-state interpretation."

He continued, after taking a long sip of lukewarm tea:

"We do know that the engines have been run extensively – the scale of discolouration on the engine cowlings indicates this – and we think that the aircraft has actually flown on some occasions. What I'm leading up to is this: you should search earlier reconnaissance pictures for signs of relatively short take-off strips, perhaps no more than thirty to fifty yards. It may prove difficult because the aircraft are estimated to be very light and are unlikely to leave any conventional take-off or landing tracks like a normal military machine." Sarah stood up instantly; her chair falling over backwards with a clatter.

"Oh, do excuse me but I've just remembered seeing some pictures from a previous sortie a little while ago. I thought it a bit odd at the time. I'll go and fetch them." She had left the room before any of the others could utter a word, the door banging closed behind her.

Turning to Daphne, the SIS man smiled, "Your colleague

seems very perceptive. Has she been here long?" Half-laughing, Daphne replied, "She only joined us about a year ago. Never actually completed her training at Farnborough, but she's proved incredibly useful and very quick on the uptake."

Standing, she went to see if there was any more tea in the small teapot; it was empty. Opening the door, she called for one of the young WAAF administration staff, requesting fresh supplies; the two men stood and stretched their legs looking out at the gardens beyond the tall windows and the rows of neat Nissen huts with their maze of interconnecting cinder paths.

Sarah was away some time and Helen and Daphne covered some ground with the two ministry men over ways of keeping in touch, particularly as any reconnaissance would possibly be ground-based, or from very high altitude from now on. After twenty minutes Daphne telephoned Sarah's office to enquire how much longer she was likely to be. One of the photo-interpreters answered, saying that she was now on her way back. The door flew open and she rushed in, breathless, with a buff-coloured file under her arm.

"So sorry I've been so long." The others looked up at her. She was agitated, they could see. "I had to take a phone call while I was over there; a girlfriend's air force fiancé was reported missing some days ago and was picked up by the Resistance; apparently she's just heard some more about him: they are trying to get him out of France by boat, somewhere in western France. She was so excited I just couldn't get her off the blower." Sitting opposite the two men, she was flushed, eyes bright.

Sarah had managed to locate in her files the single picture from a previous reconnaissance sortie that showed some of the large field next to the barns as being recently mown. She also found a note clipped to the shot that she had written at the time with the dimensions of the mown patch clearly recorded. It said: 'Mowing – 50 feet x 100 feet not completed – WHY?' The two men sat down quickly, poring over the black-and-white illustration. Nothing was said, then one, glancing at his colleague, turned and pulled a large and powerful rectangular magnifying glass from his attaché case. Taking turns, they studied the photograph from just about every angle. Daphne poured the new supply of tea into five cups. The two men suddenly stopped what they were doing; taking the full cups and saucers in their hands, they sat back and looked across at the three women.

"I think that there is little doubt that at least one of your aircraft has flown. Look." He held the photograph up in such a way that the daylight fell obliquely across its shiny surface.

"You can just see very, very faint parallel marks in the grass's surface. They're not visible for the whole length of the mown area but they all start from about here," he pointed to an area close to the last barn structure, "and tend to peter out about here." His bony, well-manicured finger marked a spot that Sarah reckoned was about sixty to eighty feet from the origination point. He went on.

"You mustn't blame yourselves for missing this clue. We didn't see the tracks until Miss Daphne moved away from the window over there, allowing the daylight to strike the print in a particular way. I think we might reasonably assume that at least one machine has flown on a number of occasions, and that, ladies, is a cause for some concern." His voice was measured, unemotional.

The two men stood, looking like a double act. The taller civil servant spoke.

"Ladies, if you will forgive us we must make tracks for London immediately. What you have found here is very interesting and, we suspect, vital to the future German war effort. We will be in touch. In the meantime, please treat this issue as top secret. All photographs and reports relating to this matter must be withdrawn from any local files that you have and placed in a secure safe with access by only yourselves." Daphne, as the senior RAF officer present, took responsibility for the information and promised to meet the conditions set – they were little different to the standard levels of security Danesfield already applied to sensitive material.

As the two men were leaving, the man with the Homburg suddenly stopped halfway down the stairs towards the hall. He turned, looking up at the three girls.

"Can we please go back to the meeting room again?" It wasn't said as a request, it was an instruction. The five of them turned and walked back up the stairs in silence and along the polished brown linoleum-covered corridors to the room they had just vacated. The door was shut firmly behind them. 'Homburg' spoke.

"Flight Officer Kelly, you said you took a phone call while you were away earlier; something about a girlfriend's air force fiancé attempting to escape from western France by boat; being helped by the Resistance, I believe." Sarah nodded affirmatively.

"He is a pilot?"

She nodded again – yes.

"It has occurred to me that this pilot could be very useful to us in finding out more about the aircraft and its unusual wings.

He is, as I understand it, in a location in western France. He is therefore likely to be quite close to the very site we have been discussing, is he not?" Sarah's face drained of colour.

"We don't actually know where he is, precisely."

"Not to worry, I can find out through my contacts within the SIS or MI9. May I have his name and squadron, please? If he is in the area and he's a flyer, we should try to make good use of his expertise while he's actually there." Sarah gave 'Homburg' Harold's name and squadron details. She and Helen both tried to speak at once; the thought of Ceci's fiancé being deliberately put into further danger having survived some sort of escape from his aircraft and the Germans filled them with worry.

Agitated, they tried to make their point but the man brushed off their concerns, politely telling them that the war unfortunately demanded more of some than of others. Despite the smile, his voice was clipped and had a hard edge to it. He turned to the door. His parting remarks made clear that they were under no circumstances to impart this conversation to anyone; least of all to the young lady concerned.

"Ladies, thank you for your kind assistance, it's been most useful. We will find our own way out. Please don't trouble yourselves. Goodbye." The door closed softly behind the two men; the three girls looked at one another, speechless for a moment or two.

"My God, why did I have to open my big mouth?" gasped Sarah slumping into one of the chairs surrounding the conference table.

"You weren't to know Sarah; it's no good blaming yourself. Anyway, I won't be able to look at Ceci without huge feelings of guilt from now on." Helen blew her nose and stared out of the windows, the sky pink with evening.

◆ ◆ ◆

The weather had not let up for two days; low clouds and steady rain with a blustery wind had made the grass airfield at Hamble a quagmire in places; at least one aircraft had become bogged down while trying to take advantage of a lull in the weather to depart. The girls sat around the crew room knitting, sewing, playing a noisy game of cards or just reading. Most were bored with the enforced inactivity, knowing full well that the list of urgent deliveries was building a backlog that would require many late-evening deliveries when this particularly slow-moving depression cleared the south.

Helen sat watching the rain while sorting through her bag again. The buff envelope with the letter from Paola was kept in a side pocket; she pulled it out to reread. Secured to it with a large brass paper-clip were the hand drawings her father had made of Azzaro's concept aircraft. How was her father, she worried. Like the SS, some of Mussolini's Fascists delighted in sadistic, bullying cruelty and she was too aware that her father was not a physically strong man. Staring blankly out of the window, she tried to see her father's face, remembering the time they had walked together in Siena that last summer before war broke out. Her library of memories spilled open, bringing volumes of happy images from years past: her mother laughing at her father falling into the lake at Como trying to retrieve Helen's toy sailing boat; a grand gathering at home around a table laden with food to celebrate a wedding anniversary or birthday. She let the pictures roll, watching her parents, uncles, aunts and family friends enjoying life before the lunacy had begun, and before her mother's unexpected death.

Tears fell copiously.

They dropped onto the coarse paper of the creased letter, soaking where they fell and causing the ink to blur. Ashamed and embarrassed, she turned further away from the room, not wishing her colleagues to see her sudden uncontrolled release of emotion. Ceci, sitting across the room lazily scanning an old copy of Punch, saw the gently heaving shoulders. Walking discreetly across the room, she stood near, shielding Helen from the room's activities. Turning slightly, Helen looked up, forcing a smile at Ceci and fumbling for her handkerchief. Nobody had noticed. Eyes dry, Helen resumed her confident, professional composure, reading again the words so carefully written by the unknown Paola.

It was now, at this moment, blatantly obvious what the second part of the Latin text meant. The English translation was fixed in her mind after her numerous attempts to unpick a meaning from her father's cryptic message, 'New energies will lead to right's disaster if it turns above'. The previous evening they had been listening to the BBC Home Service after dinner. The evening news broadcast had included an excerpt from Churchill's speech in the House of Commons that afternoon. In unmistakeable fashion, his stirring and dramatic delivery talked of the right of the Allies to fight to banish Nazism from the face of the world. It was his use of the word 'right' that had struck a chord with Helen. It dawned; 'right' in her father's context meant them, the Allies – they were in the right and, according to his Latin text, facing disaster 'if it turns above'.

The drawing lay on her lap. The curved arrows he'd drawn showed how the long vanes in the wings would turn to give lift to the wings. It was in front of her, starkly obvious, she now realised.

If the vanes turned and lifted the machine it would be above them – turning. The bit about new energies could either mean the advent of the internal combustion engine, something that could not have even have been imagined in the sixteenth century, or it could mean new energies in the sense that the Germans had decided to take the concepts and, with their typical efficiency, make them work.

Either way her father had undertaken sufficient research to realise that the Azzaro concepts, implemented with renowned German efficiency and ruthlessness, would give them a huge military advantage over the Allies. Sitting quietly, she wondered; was she contriving an answer to the puzzle – or was it the real solution?

◆ ◆ ◆

Michael Kelly sat nonplussed in the CO's office; the squadron adjutant was on the phone in the outer office having a coldly polite argument with the Ministry of Supply about some equipment that had not yet been delivered, despite a requisition made two months earlier. The one-sided conversation droned on and Kelly looked out at the activity on the airfield. Riggers and fitters were working on some of the aircraft assembled on the dispersals off to his right, no doubt readying machines for their night's work. To his left he could see a group of RAF Regiment personnel changing shifts at one of half a dozen anti-aircraft gun pits established around the airfield. He was not on ops; they were in a moonless phase, when flying in their line of work was not usually undertaken unless there was a real emergency. The moonlight was usually vital to their navigation and flying operations into small, unlit fields. He was looking forward to getting home and hoping to spend a few hours with Sarah and the children. He pondered the unnatural life he was leading: flying to France by night, landing in enemy-held territory, dropping or picking up agents with the constant risk of betrayal or discovery, then, if he was lucky, returning to a comfortable home where they all tried to ensure that the war remained outside the front door. It was a strain and one that so many aircrews had to deal with in his own squadron and in Bomber Command, whose flights of heavy bombers took to the night skies with such intent, fear and fortitude.

The phone call ended with some false pleasantries then the office door was thrust fully open. David Rawlinson's face was etched with worry lines; he was not the same carefree young man who had been Kelly's navigator on the ill-fated Cornucopia.

"Michael, sorry to keep you waiting. You must be wondering what the bloody hell's going on!" He shouted through the open door.

"Corporal Cannon, see if you can rustle up some tea for Squadron Leader Kelly and me." The response was muted but affirmative. Rawlinson sat down opposite Michael Kelly, smiling across the cluttered desk.

"Wish I could get back onto operations. This administration lark is definitely not for me." He pushed the untidy mix of papers into a clumsy pile to one side of the desktop, some falling off its edge and left where they fell.

"Good news and bad news, Michael. David Balfour has officially been taken off flying duties; had a confirming signal this morning. He's being sent away for a long convalescence somewhere up in Yorkshire. Off the record, I believe that his injuries from that bloody awful night will ensure that he will not fly in command again. Pity, he's a bloody good pilot and we're going to miss him. That's the bad news. The good news is that the AOC wants to see you at Group HQ, High Wycombe tomorrow morning at eleven. If my intuition is correct, you are in for an interesting meeting."

Corporal Cannon knocked and brought in two chipped cups of tea without saucers on a worn tin tray, placing it on the desk between the two silently watching airmen.

"Will they be alright, Sir?" she said, looking over the top of her thick glasses. "There's no milk left and you had the last of the sugar this morning." The overweight corporal closed the door as she left.

"What's your best guess, David?" Kelly picked up one of the scalding cups blowing across its dark, brown surface while watching his erstwhile navigator's face.

"I think, well I hope, actually, that you return after a good lunch tomorrow as the new CO of this squadron." Rawlinson grinned at the effect his words had.

"You're being a bit optimistic, aren't you?" laughed Kelly spilling hot tea onto the desk's scratched varnish surface. "I've not been in the Service long enough, let alone flown enough ops to justify it." David Rawlinson stood and walked over to the window, pulling closed its metal frame in an effort to reduce the throbbing noise coming from a Whitley running both engines for testing before a sortie that evening.

"But you're the man on the spot. You've easily flown enough sorties to know what we're about. You've experienced the risks and you've led men before. Anyway, we've got two good flight commanders in Geoff Standish and Ben Kendle; they will give you all the support you need. And ... if you can get me back on flying operations, I'll support you as well!" They both laughed.

Michael Kelly talked it over that evening; Sarah was quiet and a little withdrawn as they ate supper alone; the children had been fed and bedded earlier. She wanted to tell him about Harold but knew that she couldn't; not even her husband.

At twenty past eleven the next morning David Rawlinson's prophecy came true. Sitting quietly with his back to the large picture windows in the huge, sunlit office, the AOC had sought out Michael Kelly's views on him being appointed CO of his present squadron and asked if he wanted any particular people to join him. Kelly requested the Canadian Flying Officer Paul Mossman to be posted to his squadron and for Flight Lieutenant David Rawlinson to be relieved of his administrative duties as deputy CO and de facto adjutant, and returned to navigational duties with the squadron as commander of C Flight. The AOC approved the requests immediately, asking Kelly to take the matter up with Personnel in London, with his approval and to arrange matters without delay. Over a rushed lunch, the AOC talked over some of the issues that concerned him and the direction that the war was taking. In the space of forty minutes the newly appointed CO had learnt more about the war effort in the air, and how some matters were to continue for the foreseeable future, than he had learnt in the previous two years.

Returning to the AOC's office after their meal, Michael Kelly picked up his hat and small attaché case and made ready to leave. The AOC sat down and indicated that he should do likewise in the chair across the broad desk.

"Er ... one other matter, Kelly. I've recommended you for an award, the Distinguished Service Order. I heard about your ambush when you were rescuing those poor Joes a couple of months back. An appalling bloody business for you, I can imagine. I understand that you've undertaken a number of rather interesting nocturnal tours over France over the past few months, fortunately with better outcomes. Very commendable, well done. A DSO is the least we can do." Kelly rose, put on his hat and saluted.

"Thank you, Sir, thank you very much." He turned smartly and left the AOC's office; on the way out the attractive WAAF secretary gave him a wide smile; she'd known all along. Even before the appointment was gazetted most people in the command knew of the changes: that evening there was a huge and tumultuous party in the mess, every one seemed happy with the morning's outcome.

❖ ❖ ❖

Harold was bored. He could see across to the opposite row of houses by carefully pushing up one of the roof tiles in his attic room. Highlights of the day were meal times. Breakfast at an ungodly hour in the morning while it was still dark; dinner was had downstairs after dark when he could negotiate the awkward dovecote entrance and landing window without being seen. He had been waiting four days for the other airman to arrive so that they could move off towards the coast and the prospect of a night-time sea escape. He sat for hours wondering about Ceci and how she must be worrying. Had the Resistance been able to transmit news of his arrival and that he was alive and not in German hands? That evening, feeling warm and full down in the house, he sat watching Raymond decoding a message while the radio played some lively dance music from Paris.

"I must ask you somesing, 'Arold. I'm sorry but we must finally know 'oo you are. It is embarrassing but ... " Harold nodded, understanding.

"Go ahead."

"Er ... Well, can you tell me ze serial number ov ze plane zat that you was flying?" Harold sat up.

"I think so ...Yes ... it was CN 0092 or something like that." Raymond nodded.

"Zat's good, now, what is ze name of ze pub in Oxford where you pilots like to go in ze evening?"

"It's the Grapes of Wrath in London Street." He smiled as he remembered one or two entertaining nights there with his fellow pilots. The diminutive Frenchman wrote down his answer then,

"OK, now ze last, what is ze name of ze cat zat lives in ze officers' mess?" Harold burst into laughter.

"It's called Gobbles!" Raymond smiled broadly.

"Sank you 'Arold, but I sink you understand; we 'ave many problems with false pilots 'oo are German and zey are betraying our peoples."

There was a quiet but distinct three taps on the window. The lamp was partially doused as Raymond held his fingers to his lips. He moved quickly out of the darkened room into the narrow hall, towards the front door. Harold heard the bolts being withdrawn and a slight squeaking as the heavy door was pulled open a few inches.

" C'est vous, Claude?" There were steps outside.

"Oui, c'est moi." As Claude came into the kitchen the oil lamps were turned up and Harold rose, shaking hands. There was a staccato discussion between Claude and Raymond over

Raymond's notes, which were lying on the kitchen table. Claude smiled.

"So, everysing is OK?" Harold nodded. They all sat eating soup, tearing chunks of bread from a large loaf, watching the fire in the huge grate engulf the notes.

"We 'ave some new instructions from London about you 'Arold." Supper finished, they were sitting on hard chairs around the glowing embers in the fireplace. Harold looked up inquisitively.

"London want us to take you to a place in the country." He smiled. "No, I'm sorry, 'Arold it is not an 'oliday. Ze Germans are developing somesing, a new type of aircraft I sink and zey want us to 'elp you look at it and to take photos."

"That's OK, Claude, if you have a camera I can certainly take some pictures and make some notes of what I see. Is there some cover near the aircraft's airfield where we can get some good shots?" Claude shifted awkwardly on his chair.

"Of course, if it was going to be zat easy, 'Arold, I would be very pleased." He wasn't smiling. "London want rarzzer more zan zat, I am afraid to say. Zey want us to get you inside ze 'angars to take ze photos. If possible, zey want you to try to steal a machine and fly it 'ome."

Harold's eyes were wide with amazement.

"Bloody hell, that's a pretty tall order! Where is this bloody place? What sort of aircraft is it?"

"At ze moment I know very little but we 'ave sent two men to zee area to see what is involved. It will mean, I am afraid, zat you will have to stay here for anozer night, zen we will move you again to somewhere perhaps a bit more comfortable." He pulled out a packet of Gauloises and handed them around. Although a nonsmoker, Harold took one, choking fitfully during its life. 'Bugger, why can't I just go home like any other escapee?' he pondered between coughing fits.

❖ ❖ ❖

Kelly hadn't done any ops since his meeting two weeks ago with the AOC. Organising the squadron the way he wanted it done had taken a little time and there had been some new pilots to train in their unique ways. Fortunately they had both come from night fighter units so flying by dark was nothing new.

His was going to be the first op in one of the recently delivered twin-engine Hudsons; he was well fitted to undertake this particular first with his wide experience of delivering Hudsons across the North Atlantic to Prestwick and beyond, during the early stages of the war with the Atlantic Ferry Organisation. They were going to take six agents, or Joes, as they were collectively known, to a field to the east of Lyons near Loyettes, intending to collect five, including, unusually, a child. There had been two previous attempts at this operation, code named 'Claret', using two Lysanders, or 'Lizzies', as they were affectionately known, on a twin operation but poor weather on one occasion and a failure to show by the reception committee on the second gave some imperative to early completion of 'Claret'.

Kelly and his navigator, Rawlinson, were late out to the aircraft; the six Joes, both male and female, were already there in a small knot gathered around the Hudson's door in the deepening dusk. A couple of SOE minders were present, smoking and chatting with the six agents. It was almost as though they were going away for a picnic, not into the jaws of danger, and torture if betrayed or caught. Greeting his passengers confidently, Kelly made to climb the short ladder to board when he noticed two of the agents standing a little away from the group talking quietly with one of the SOE minders. He could see that they were both women and even in the poor light he could see unmistakeably that one was Patricia. Stepping back down onto the grass, he walked over to her; the SOE man stepped a little closer, partly blocking his way. Speaking over the man's shoulder, "Patricia ... hello, how are you?"

"Michael! What a coincidence. Are you taking us tonight?" He nodded, a little shocked.

"How are Sarah, Beth and that naughty little boy of yours?" She was smiling, somehow confident, the moonlight catching her eyes and teeth. It was unreal, he thought. He didn't want this. It was as though they were just passing the time of day at a bus stop. With a little luck he was coming back tonight; she was being left behind in an occupied country doing a very risky job.

But he sensed something. It wasn't the same Patricia, their nanny; this was a young woman who had not only gained confidence in her training, but who knew what to do and was certainly going to do it. The SOE man moved slightly aside. Michael stood facing her. There was a bit of a lump in his throat. She could be his daughter; he would not let his daughter do this. He could hardly trust himself to speak.

"I hope you'll be able to collect us in a few weeks, Michael. We're going to be alright, you know." She turned, "This is Marianne, we'll be working together for a while on a new circuit. She's been before, knows the strings, I think you say."

"Yes, I'll come and collect you Tricia; be careful ... and you too, Marianne." He kissed her, Gallic fashion, on the cheeks, holding her for a moment by the shoulders. Entering the cabin, he clumped forward, past Rawlinson preparing his charts and calculations, and sat down heavily in his seat. 'My God,' he muttered almost silently to himself. Completing the pre-start checks, he asked his navigator to ensure everyone was on board, strapped in, and that the door was closed securely. Responding to his signals, the ground crew pulled away the trolley battery starter as the two engines turned steadily. After final checks at the runaway threshold they swung around facing down the thin row of smoking goose-neck flares, the night sky waiting. The roar was followed by increasing acceleration as the Hudson's tail came up. Keeping her straight, they lifted off the damp, sweet-smelling Sussex grass, turning gently left to cross the coast. Landfall was at Cabourg, near Caen, their usual point of entry into France, away from coastal flak batteries and easy to recognise in the moonlight. Nothing stirred; rivers and larger streams two thousand feet below reflected occasional bursts of silvery light. Elsewhere the darker shapes of woods and copses showed, among them the blue-grey score of a road weaved through the landscape.

Well north of Macon they saw a potential problem. An ethereal white mist was forming on the land below them. Looking down, they could see that, as they progressed south, the milky patches were becoming more frequent and opaque. The still, cold night was ideal for mist patches. Kelly was too aware that the landing location was close to a river where mist was likely to form easily on such a night. They droned on, he and Rawlinson watching the increasing frequency of ground mist but also alert to the possibility of night fighters, both Allied and German. Behind, in the darkened cabin, each Joe sat silent with their thoughts, some smoking, one or two dozing or giving a good impression of doing so, the others just sitting, occasionally watching from the small cabin windows.

Just to their right it burst; a huge gout of white-and-orange flame erupting about a mile or so ahead, well above their altitude. The mass of flame started to fall earthwards and smaller pieces followed, their flames dying quickly. Horribly spellbound, they watched the remains of the unfortunate aircraft gather pace towards the quiet countryside. As it struck there was a further violent orange explosion.

"Don't think anyone got out, do you?" Rawlinson looked across at Kelly.

"Didn't see the sign of any parachutes, happened too fast, I think," the pilot replied. Kelly was watching carefully; the aircraft, Allied or Axis, had been surprised and attacked by a night fighter; there had been no sign of gunfire from the victim before the explosion. The moon and the superb visibility were ideal for such hunting activity by both the Luftwaffe and Royal Air Force.

Cruising watchfully onwards, they now estimated they were only fifteen minutes from their target field; navigation had been relatively easy over the moonlit terrain.

"It's just over there, Skipper. See, where the river turns slightly east ...." Here and there the moon's light was refracted by pools of water lying in some fields; it had been a week of heavy rain for central France and the last two clear daytime skies had been a welcome relief for its sodden and depressed inhabitants. Kelly turned the aircraft towards the field in question, throttling back and allowing the Hudson to sink gently and softly earthwards. Right on cue a single Morse letter appeared in white dashes and dots. Kelly responded by flashing the Hudson's downward identification light.

"If that's the field, David, it looks rather short. What's that at the end, the darker area, is it standing crop?" David Rawlinson looked carefully at the field; it was a narrowing rectangle tapering even further at one end where a sort of darker, greyish area lay. Suddenly three lights appeared on the ground, set out in the standard inverted 'L' layout indicating the start, finish and width of the landing area. Light A at the runway threshold was where Kelly would have to put the Hudson down, passing it on his left. Lights B and C were positioned at the upwind end of the landing strip, denoting its width.

At the risk of announcing their presence too widely, Kelly over-flew the landing area. He and Rawlinson took a good look at the shadowy field; beyond it mist was forming over the river and rolling slowly across the silent fields.

"Perhaps they thought we were bringing Lizzies again, not a Hudson," remarked Rawlinson. Banking the machine gently around, Kelly turned back in preparation for their approach; his navigator watched the surrounding area carefully.

"Get them all sat and strapped in and warn them it may be a bit hairy; this field is really on the limit." Returning quickly to his seat from the rear cabin, David Rawlinson secured his straps, watching the field with its three small lights move slowly across into the centre of the windscreens. Kelly was making a very flat approach, the engines roaring noisily as the aircraft hung on its propellers just above the stall; they would have to stop very quickly once down. He was familiar with the technique, once level with the first marker light the throttle would be cut and the machine would virtually collapse onto the grass, stopping quickly. They usually aimed to offload and load, and be off the ground again in something under nine minutes.

Descending, they could see mist rolling onto the east side of the field, fingers probing forward as they crossed a low fence; fifty feet beyond lay the first light. A split-second later Kelly had pulled both throttles fully back; the aircraft stalled almost instantly and heavily onto the surface of the field. The 'A' light flashed past Kelly's left side window as he applied gentle braking to arrest the machine as it blundered on across the uneven, and as they instantly realised, sodden, surface. He knew that braking was not going to stop them. Each time he tried, the wheels locked solid, skidding, ski-like, over the grassy surface.

"Bugger!" He exclaimed, as he worked hard at controlling the machine's direction as the field began to narrow. The change in surface colour at its far end that they had seen from the air was only fifty yards ahead and they were still moving very quickly.

"Hold tight!" Kelly applied brake pressure to the starboard wheel only, opening up power on the port engine. The Hudson slid sideways for a moment or two then suddenly whipped around, almost facing the way they had arrived.

"Not a very elegant arrival, David, ground-looping. Don't tell the chaps back home." He had managed to get the machine to slither around and stop just before arriving at an area of what turned out to be a banked-up potato crop. Raising the flaps, he opened up the engines to taxi back to lamp 'A', where the reception committee and its passengers would be waiting. Nothing happened; he tried again with more power. Nothing.

"David. we're stuck. The surface is soft mud under this top

layer of grass. Dammit; why don't they take more care over field selection?" Looking out of the cockpit windows he could see the thin layer of mist had now spread across the field, already passing, ghostlike, through the hedge on the field's western border and groping around the aircraft.

The six agents were rapidly offloaded without ceremony, by which time the reception organiser with his passengers had run and slithered to where they sat, stuck, engines quietly idling. The main wheels were sunk up to their axles in thick, brown goo. Every step was accompanied by loud squelching and soaked feet. This had happened before and all aircraft, including the smaller Lizzies, now carried a folding shovel to assist in just such a situation. All set to; hands and shovels working to cut a shallow trench through which the Hudson could taxi onto firmer ground. As they dug and scraped, the trench filled with water; they were all becoming caked in soil. Despite the water Kelly decided to try again. From within the cockpit he checked around outside, then opened up the two engines.

She rolled slowly forward displacing the water in the trench until she was back onto the grass surface. He kept her moving slowly up the field, trying to penetrate the mist lying as a semi-transparent layer just below the nose of the aircraft, intending to turn at lamp 'A' ready for take-off. Now the ground seemed firmer. She was responding more naturally to braking although she pitched and rolled terribly in some places along the uneven surface. At the end of the field, the following crowd of arriving and departing passengers watched as he commenced a final turn. The aircraft stopped, engines bellowing into the night as Kelly tried to maintain momentum. She'd sunk in again.

It was soon evident, even in darkness, that this time the problem was graver. The wet ground had just collapsed under the aircraft's weight; the top third of the tread of the port wheel was just visible above the bog. He cut the engines immediately there was a danger of the port propeller hitting the ground with the aircraft lying at such an odd angle. Jumping down from the cabin door, he surveyed the problem. Their first concern was the inordinate amount of noise they had made so far; surely every German for miles around would be alert by now?

Some discussion took place between the Resistance leader and the aircrew; it was decided that digging would not suffice on this occasion, the machine needed to be towed out of its undignified, lop-sided predicament. One of the reception committee volunteered to run across the fields to a farm about a mile away. He said they had some heavy horses there used for ploughing. Kelly, sceptical, sent him on his way while the head of the local Resistance circuit sent for more manpower from the local village. He knew that if they couldn't extract the Hudson and be airborne by three in the morning they would have to burn her and take their chances with the Resistance as escapees. They calculated that after three it would be too dangerous to be flying across the centre of France in the very early morning light. The enemy fighters would have little difficulty in dispatching the loaded Hudson. It was now almost one-thirty.

Twenty minutes later a crowd of people emerged silently from misty hedges in all states of undress; inhabitants of a small hamlet along the narrow road that ran past a field adjacent to theirs. One was the village gendarme complete with hat above his uniform trousers and dressing gown. With only a few words they began to dig around the trapped wheel, creating a solid route for when it finally rolled forward. David Rawlinson prepared all confidential papers for burning should events suddenly overtake them, although the reception committee head had indicated that there was a large force of Resistance fighters out, concealed around the field to fend off any possible German interference. It was normal, he had said, in very fractured English.

At two-fifteen in the morning the horses arrived. Four heavy-set animals looking none too pleased at having their well-earned rest interrupted at such an hour. Kelly supervised the attachment of ropes from the horses to strongpoint on the undercarriage. All the agents, including a young Jewish boy with his very worried mother and father, and villagers and the crew of the Hudson were placed around other parts of the aircraft and shown where to push without damaging the machine. The clock was ticking relentlessly. Time was tight. What if the Germans became aware of a disabled aircraft under their very noses? They'd been lucky so far, swirling mist providing some thin cover for their activities. With everyone ready the farmer climbed onto the bare back of one lead animal and jerked them into action. Initially she moved easily, rolling up the shallow incline that led eventually to firmer ground some twenty feet away.

But the horses had their own traction problems. Their huge hooves slid and struggled for grip on the soft surface. The Hudson rolled back. It was decided to spend a little time digging the trench rearwards from the wheels. One of the Frenchmen thought that if they could roll her back a little more they might be able to generate sufficient forward momentum when they all pulled forward together again. Kelly and Rawlinson kept looking at their watches; it was now twenty minutes to three. Increasingly worried, the navigator had undone an inspection panel over water drains in one of the fuel tanks and was draining off some of the volatile fluid into their empty coffee flasks in preparation for burning the aircraft.

All was ready; with everyone pushing, the reluctant Hudson slowly moved backwards until the machine was at the very end of the newly extended trench. Stopping for a couple of minutes to get their breath, they prepared.

"Un, deux, trois, poussez!" the gendarme shouted, his muddied dressing gown adding a touch of farce to the scene. As one they leaned into the job, pushing, the four horses causing the ropes to become suddenly bar-taut. The Hudson rolled forward easily this time, almost rushing towards the upward incline pushing a bow wave of water over the sides of the trench. Barely four feet from the end of the slope they finally came to rest, energy and grip expended. Two large logs were thrown quickly behind the wheels to stop them running back into the water-filled slot. There was a rapid confab by the aircraft door. Kelly thought that they may be able to taxi her out from this point as the ground was beginning to level off; he would then follow Rawlinson's instructions, via small torch, to the best route onto the makeshift runway, avoiding soft ground.

The engines were started. Wasting no time, he opened them up to full power. The ground vibrated beneath the watching crowd. She moved. They rushed forward, heaving against her structure, Rawlinson just in time pulling two volunteers clear of the slicing arcs of black swirling blades. They were out. He kept her moving. With torchlight reflecting eerily off the patches of white mist, he followed his navigator's careful steps towards the runway. A further burst of throttle helped her around. The mud-spattered Hudson sat waiting, looking down the field. Returning agents and the young boy with his parents clambered aboard. As he turned to check all was OK before closing the door, Rawlinson saw the girl Patricia running towards him. Like all of them, she was covered in mud.

"It is for Michael," she shouted, then kissed him full on the lips, "Bonne chance, David." The aircraft door was closed as they bumped with increasing violence, half-blind across the mist-strewn field. In the darkness of the rear cabin startled eyes were wide open wondering at the next few seconds.

The sky to the east was turning pale as they gained height. Lights could be seen rushing along on the road that ran close to their departure field.

"We need to improve the training of heads of Resistance reception committees. That field was quite unsuitable, wet or dry." His anger stemmed from his pent-up relief; it had been touch and go. David Rawlinson passed a new compass heading to Kelly nodding in agreement. He never mentioned the kiss.

FIVE

Harriet called Helen into her office early. It transpired that she had had a call from SIS late the previous evening requesting Helen attend a meeting at SOE in Baker Street in London's West End the following day. Harriet, already short of pilots for deliveries and collections, was interested to know what was going on.

"Sorry, Harriet, it's something to do with my father and I'm sworn to secrecy; Official Secrets Act and all that." Harriet smiled across the room at her and nodded knowingly. "OK, Helen, be as quick as you can and don't get yourself into any trouble. They're sending a car for you at lunchtime. It must be important!"

At one o'clock a huge, khaki camouflaged Humber staff car drew up outside the ATA offices and Helen got in to the inquisitive stares of some of her colleagues from the flight office windows. The journey north to London was relaxing, the young woman army driver managing a steady pace through the warm, sunny early afternoon without chatting too much and Helen nodded off once or twice. Just before three-thirty she stepped from the car and through the unprepossessing sandbagged entrance to SOE's HQ.

Inside, an elderly policeman guided her towards the reception's high oak desk. She gave her name and was asked to wait a minute. A man's voice addressed her, it was 'Homburg'; he walked across the narrow space, hand outstretched.

"Very good of you to come up to see us, Miss Lorenzo. Your

friends are upstairs." She shook hands and smiled briefly at the civil servant. His was damp and cold. 'I didn't have much of a choice,' she thought, as he led her towards a flight of stairs. On the second floor they entered a small room with two large desks and a few wooden chairs. The room was full of cigarette smoke plus a senior RAF officer, an army officer, two other men in civilian clothes, Sarah Kelly and Daphne. She took the last remaining chair and sat expectantly. Someone opened a window.

The RAF Group Captain stood and pulled some curtains away from a blackboard fixed to the wall behind him.

"Well, ladies and gentlemen, thank you all for coming. I've arranged to have some tea delivered shortly, so that'll be something to look forward to. Now, over the past two weeks or so we have been studying the pictures so cleverly identified and interpreted at Danesfield, and have been talking to some of our boffins about the unusual aircraft found in such an unlikely place in western France. One piece of information you all might be surprised to hear is that we have identified the two men standing outside the barns. One is no other than Reich Marshal Hermann Goering; the other is Dr Helmut Koenig. This tells us something about the importance of this project for the Germans. The fact that Goering was present at what at first appears to be a set of small aircraft workshops in an obscure, rather remote location suggests something of the project's value – and no doubt has something to do with Germany's future war strategy. This fact underlined by the inclusion of Koenig. He is known to have participated in a number of aircraft-related scientific programmes. He has, we believe, worked extensively since before the war with Willi Messerchmitt and with Ernst Heinkel, two of Germany's most prodigious designers and manufacturers. Koenig has a sound reputation for innovation." There was a knock on the door and tea was brought in. The three women were a little stunned at learning of Goering's presence coincidental with that particular PR sortie.

"One further thing before we get down to discussing matters and making some decisions. The young Canadian PR pilot from RAF Benson, Pilot Officer, ah, apologies, now Flying Officer Paul Mossman, the airman responsible for getting these remarkable pictures has recovered well in hospital and is now on a spot of leave. He'll be joining a new squadron at RAF Tempsford shortly. OK. Let's get on. Our research friends from Air Ministry have been giving some consideration to the type of aircraft you clever girls have discovered." He beamed at them.

"What I'm about to tell you is strictly top secret. You will not discuss this with anyone outside of this room. I'm sure I make myself clear; you are all sworn under the Official Secrets Act."

There was no mistaking the seriousness of his tone.

"We have managed to make a one-fifth-scale model of the aircraft you have discovered. I have to tell you that, despite the model's crudeness, it flies; in fact it flies very well and has proved remarkably manoeuvrable. We are building a larger model at the moment for further tests but from this first flying example we can make some guesses, fairly accurately I think, about how it will perform. The rotating vanes partially identifiable in the reconnaissance photos are just that."

He pulled a large blueprint sheet from a roll on the desk in front of him and pinned it to the blackboard. It had a three-view drawing of an aircraft not dissimilar to Sarah's machines.

"This drawing shows how our people have interpreted the photographs of the aircraft. The wings, as you can see, have this rotating set of vanes," he pointed, "positioned near the wing's leading edge and running almost the wing's full span on either side. We assume that the vanes are rotated by the main engine positioned conventionally here near the nose of the machine; probably through shafts and a gearbox." He looked around his audience for signs of comprehension. "The rotating vanes suck in air, here at the leading edge," he tapped the drawing with a thin wooden stick, pointing to the leading edge of the wing, "and push it back over the wing, in doing so creating lift. Importantly, Ladies and Gentlemen, the lift it creates is greatly in excess of that produced by a normal aerofoil wing section passing through the air. In fact, our boffins believe that the lift coefficient from such an unusual system could be as much as a two hundred per cent above that generated by conventional wing shapes. The rotating fan also creates thrust that actually drives the aircraft through the air. As you see, there is no conventional propeller!" He banged his pointer onto the nose of the machine where normally a propeller would be positioned.

Everyone sat back and looked at the drawings in some amazement, even those whose experience was outside practical aeronautics. Helen, as the only pilot in the room apart from the Group Captain, began to raise some questions.

"If the air is being forced over the wing by the horizontal vanes it must surely mean that the wing can fly at very low speeds without fear of stalling." The Group Captain looked up from sipping his lukewarm tea.

"You're absolutely right, Miss Lorenzo, well done! Yes, it does mean that the wing cannot stall because the airflow over its upper surface doesn't separate from the top surface, as happens at the point of stalling in a conventional aircraft wing moving too slowly through the air. One other important thing you should know is that the rotating vanes do not have to turn very fast to create the required lift and thrust. Our estimates at the moment suggest only one thousand revolutions per minute; it should be possible, therefore, to fit such an aircraft with a comparably smaller engine than a conventional machine ... and it will probably be much quieter and have greater duration for a given amount of fuel."

"So, a full size machine such as captured in Flight Officer Kelly's photos would probably be OK on very short take-offs, even when very heavily laden?" Helen looked around the room; she was the only one asking questions. The group captain looked across at her, smiling again.

"Trust a pilot to see the possible advantage in such a system. When you add up all of facts about this machine you begin to get some sort of idea as to what 'Gerry' is intending for this aircraft. Let me hand over to Colonel Blacksmith from military intelligence; he's put together some fairly plausible thoughts on the matter. Colonel ...." Helen's mind wandered as she remembered the Latin text her father had passed on via Paola's letter: 'New energies will lead to right's disaster if it turns above.'

The colonel stood and moved slowly and carefully around the side of the room until he stood squarely in front of the group. Sarah guessed he was about fifty. He was well built and had aged handsomely, with silver-grey hair, and a salt-and-pepper moustache; he wore two rows of medal ribbons across his left breast and leaned slightly on a highly polished stick with what appeared to be an ornate silver knob on top. It occurred to her that he had probably served in the last awful muddy conflict with the Germans. He cleared his throat.

"As you know the Germans' great success in the spring of 1940 was largely down to their Blitzkrieg strategy, rolling rapidly through France, Poland and Belgium. It certainly caught us and the French on the hop for a while – and the speed of their advance gave them a problem too, eventually, getting supplies through to their leading army formations. Transporting troops, ammunition, fuel and food along roads crowded with other military formations, not to mention the refugees, made life very difficult for them for a while. Well, I can tell you now that they have learnt from that lesson. The concepts handed to them by the Italians, and stolen originally, I believe, from your father, Miss Lorenzo, have obviously been taken seriously by German scientists and aeronautical engineers. We believe that they intend to develop this unique aircraft for a specific type of operation.

"As Group Captain Hawkins has pointed out, it can fly very slowly without stalling, it can also fly relatively quietly. It can carry a disproportionately heavy load for its size and it is capable of very, very short take-offs, and landings, probably from crude, unprepared, short grass runways. With all of these attributes, a full-size version would make an ideal military resupply machine, able to take very large quantities of men and materiel to where it is needed, much more quickly than by road transport. You will no doubt appreciate the vital value of this type of capability in any future Blitzkrieg operations, whether in Western Europe or indeed in Russia or the Balkans. There are, however, limitations associated with this form of propulsion, we believe: it cannot fly fast and it would have to be protected by fighters. We think it unlikely that it would be fitted with anything in the way of real armaments, which would detract from its primary load-carrying capabilities.

"Our people have assessed the lifting capacity of a machine of about the same size as our new Lancaster bomber to be thirty thousand pounds, that's fifteen tons. The Lancaster, for those who don't know, regularly carries around fourteen thousand pounds in bombs, around seven tons. It also requires a long, firm runway to get airborne with such a load. To be able to take off and, importantly, land with twice that much weight in troops and equipment, on very short, unprepared runways or grass strips such as you would find in an active battle area would offer a huge logistical advantage to the enemy. It does, of course, raise the question of what sort of military operations Germany has in mind where such a machine would offer that sort of key logistical advantage. We may believe that Hitler has given up any thoughts of invading us for now; his Operation Sealion, we know, has been put back into the cupboard and is gathering dust, but we should keep the possibilities and advantages to the enemy offered by this machine in mind for the future. And talking of future, all references to this matter will be covered by the codeword 'Azzaro'." Sarah and Daphne looked across at one another slightly stunned, then Daphne made a point.

"If they are able to do that then we need to target their factory, don't we? And ... theoretically we need to extend our photo-interpreting activities to include almost any field, anywhere, on the basis of your suspicions of its capabilities?" The colonel nodded.

"You're right, but we would like to see how far they get first and then, if possible, capture a test machine before they put it into a full-size production. We might in our turn be able to use such a machine within our own plans for when we return to mainland Europe. Now, any more questions? OK. Let me now hand you over to one of our civilian colleagues working with MI9."

The young man with unkempt gingerish hair and a pale, open face, who had looked out of place in such a gathering, remained seated, turning slightly to look at his audience.

"All of you now know that we have identified an RAF pilot now in the hands of the Resistance as being able to help us. We have already communicated our wishes through the usual channels. The intention is for the local Resistance to get this pilot to the barn's location east of Brest, not far from a small village called Sizun, and to work out a way in which they and he can obtain further information and if at all possible capture a machine and fly it to England."

There was a sharp intake of breath from Sarah Kelly. The young man paused momentarily, then continued.

"We are leaving the Resistance to set up the operation as they see fit; our colleagues at SOE will, of course, provide whatever help they can: weapons, specialist equipment, diversions and so on. Obviously there are a lot of risks attached to such a venture, not least the fact that the area is now likely to be well guarded after the latest low-level reconnaissance – and we do not know how much fuel the experimental machine carries and what its duration is ... clearly there's no point in stealing one if it cannot actually fly to England."

They all nodded in unison.

"However, we must take some action soon. If they complete their testing with these scale machines and put a much larger version into production, it could, for example, deliver one hundred and thirty heavily armed troops, typically in night-time operations, right into the heart of our major cities landing in any of the Royal Parks, Richmond Park, at Windsor, possibly even larger recreation grounds or school playing fields, perhaps, and so on ... not to mention a situation such as in North Africa, where, if Rommel's men were able to leapfrog the Eighth Army in sufficient numbers, they could attack it both from behind and in front. The Prime Minister has expressed an interest in this matter, and my boss at MI9 will be reporting matters to him as we proceed."

Group Captain Hawkins drew the meeting to a conclusion, insisting that everyone kept alert to the possibility of these new German aircraft being used at some near-future stage. However, he made clear that there would be no further reconnaissance flights over the three barns.

◆ ◆ ◆

As they left the French coast the new dawn was well and truly broken. They had flown low, and well to the west of the direct track home to avoid alerting the Luftwaffe airfields that lay in a tight pattern in the Pas-de-Calais region north of Paris. Kelly had given instructions that the agents in the rear cabin should watch through the aircraft's windows for enemy aircraft. Unlike other Hudsons employed by the Royal Air Force, machines in the special duties squadron had had all armaments removed to reduce weight and to assist with a little more speed and load-carrying. The landing was normal but their arrival caused some comment from the reception committee over the state of the machine and the fact that everyone was covered in mud. The agents, the Jewish family, including the young boy, complete with a small black-and-tan dog somehow smuggled on board, were all taken by car to some unspecified secret destinations. The ground crews walked around the aircraft, muttering at its filthy, mud-encrusted condition.

The debriefing with intelligence and SOE seemed to take ages. There were so many questions. Both Kelly and Rawlinson were tired from lack of sleep and the expenditure of so much nervous energy while on the ground near Loyettes. It was clear to all from this and some other previous deliveries and collections that some Resistance heads of reception committees had forgotten their SOE training in assessing the suitability of fields for night-time operations. Despite their tiredness the two men managed to stay awake for breakfast before a bath and a welcome bed. Michael Kelly sent up a silent prayer of thanks for their deliverance: they could just as well be stuck in some safe house in France trying to arrange their escape if things had gone the other way – or worse.

The Hudson sortie to Loyettes was the last for that moon period and the squadron were packing up to return north to Tempsford awaiting the moon's new phase in a couple of weeks. Kelly was not looking forward to overseeing the squadron's administrative work and had requested some help. Keeping his finger on the pulse while he was operating for half the month out of a forward airfield in Sussex and undertaking sorties himself, then trying to co-ordinate training of Joes and pilots when back at Tempsford for the remainder of the time was not working out.

His request arrived two days after they were back at Tempsford. There was a knock on the door and in marched a face he knew in RAF uniform with Pilot Officer rank.

"Good morning, Sir." He threw up a smart salute, his face wreathed in a huge smile.

"My God! George Hudson! How the devil are you?" Michael Kelly instantly recognised one of his passengers from their ill-fated flight in the Cornucopia. He motioned the new officer to sit.

"You requested some help and I'm afraid I'm the best the Air Ministry can supply at short notice," he said, removing his cap and relaxing into the only other serviceable chair in the untidy office. Kelly stood, opened the door and requested tea for two from the surly corporal in the outer office. It arrived quickly, complete with milk and sugar on this occasion.

"I hope you've not been dealing in black-market rations, Corporal. We've never been able to have milk and sugar together." It was meant as a joke but the overweight young woman failed to see the twinkle in Kelly's eyes and started to protest her innocence.

"So, what have you been up to since we met last?" George Hudson took a sip of tea.

"Well, nothing very much actually. After I'd lost Lilly when Cornucopia ditched, I didn't go back to Penang straight away. We'd a good local manager at the plantation and I thought I could leave it to him for a while, get myself sorted out. Anyway, by the time I wanted to go back it was too late. We were at war; getting out to Penang was proving to be an impossibility, so I made arrangements for the local man to continue running things until matters changed for the better. Later, once the Japanese had poured through Burma and Malaya, and taken Singapore, I was rather glad that I didn't go. Someone with whom I had been trading in raw latex in London heard that I was back, at a loose end, and kindly introduced me to some friends. I was a bit out of touch with people in Blighty, lunches, dinners that sort of thing. Anyway, most of them were in the process of joining up and I followed, lemming-like, and here I am, an admin walla."

"Its great to have you with us, George. Give me a day or so to show you the ropes and I intend to hand the whole squadron admin over to you but I do need to be kept informed of important matters, operational, personnel, and spares, and so on." George Hudson nodded enthusiastically.

"Let me take you over to the mess and find you a room; after lunch I'll introduce you to our flight commanders and the people down at the hangar, then we can decide how to tackle this mess," Kelly said, looking, eyes raised, around the paper-strewn room.

Two evenings later Sarah and Michael Kelly invited George Hudson to a quiet dinner at home, where George instantly made friends with their children. Over coffee Michael asked after Helen and the odd-looking aeroplane they had seen sketched on the diary page by her father when she had last been at the house. Sarah got up to clear away the last of the coffee cups, remarking that she hadn't heard any more about it; leaving the room quickly with her hands full, to avoid any further questions.

❖ ❖ ❖

They heard that the other airman had been captured by the SS when they'd managed to infiltrate a Resistance cell around Caen. It was thought that the circuit had been betrayed by a woman whose husband was being held in the notorious Amiens prison by the Germans. No doubt she believed them when they promised him better treatment and possible release at some later date. The move had obviously shocked the group Penrose was with; they became even more tight-lipped and justifiably paranoid. This was beginning to present problems, as it was going to be necessary for them to co-operate with at least one other Resistance circuit based in the Morbihan region if they were going to stand any chance of capturing the experimental aircraft. Privately Harold thought the scheme outlined by Claude and Raymond was a mad one. If the Germans had taken the trouble to establish the whole thing out of the way in so secret a manner, they were going to have the area under careful observation and well guarded.

It was now Sunday and the Morbihan group were going use the fine weather for an innocent excursion and picnic. They intended to see how close they could get to the barn site under the guise of a couple of young lovers out for some time alone. After her muddy arrival near Lyons, Patricia was sent a week later to work as a courier and radio operator for the local Morbihan Resistance circuit, who were trying to expand their operations and were short of key people. Being the youngest female in the group, Patricia was chosen as the 'girlfriend': the male role was taken by a rather thin boy aged about nineteen with straw-coloured hair and near-black eyes. His father had been taken eight months earlier and sent to a labour camp somewhere in Germany; he'd been a skilled engineer.

On two bicycles they rode along almost empty roads. The only other traffic being mainly German military supply trucks, they kept a mental note of what they had seen. Concealed in the saddlebag of his bike was a small Leica camera. If they managed to get close enough to the barn site they hoped to take some pictures of the surrounding area to help with future planning to capture one of the German aircraft. Naturally, every picture taken would include one or other of them as the main subject just in case the Boche should take the camera and study the content. It would hopefully appear to be quite innocent; two lovers taking souvenir pictures of a sunny day out together.

Information on the whereabouts of the three barns was not very precise. They knew it was on a narrow country road not too far from Sizun. The SOE had not been able to deliver the aerial pictures that would have helped them to identify the location with greater ease. Displayed in their tattered tourist guide for 1936, a number of small roads and tracks were possible routes in the vicinity; they had no way of knowing which was the right one, however. Finally they stopped in the small, isolated village of Kergudan. There was little activity in the late afternoon. It was warm in the sun, only the quiet buzzing of insects imposing on the area's serenity. They drank some water and looked about; over the wall of one house they spied a man peering at the two strangers.

"Bonjour!" Patricia called. The man acknowledged, then slowly made his way through a small gated opening in the garden wall and walked over to them.

"Vous êtes perdu?" They explained that they were not lost, just out for the day, enjoying the rare fine weather and having a picnic. Chatting for a bit, he then made to go, saying that they should not go too far up the opposite road towards St Rivgal; the Germans, he whispered, had a large military storage depot there and the area was closed even to locals.

The two 'lovers' waited until he had gone back into his small house, then casually walked, pushing their bikes along the road towards St Rivgal. Once clear of the village, they mounted and pedalled with renewed interest. As the road narrowed, evidence of some disturbance became apparent. Along some of the grassy banks that bordered the small road, huge gouges showing rich brown earth appeared. Taking a couple of sticks, the boy tried to estimate the height of the marks from the road's hard-baked surface. They both agreed, after a lot of measuring and discussion that the marks were possibly made by the huge steel bumpers seen on some of the larger German trucks. Where the road surface was very narrow the overhanging bumpers would probably have torn through the soft banks, scarring them. Their suppositions were partly supported by the imprint of large tyre treads found later in one area of the road where it seemed an erratic stream passed over or under the surface, making it soft.

It was at this point they decided to hide the cycles over the top of the banking where they could not be seen from the road, intending to walk through the fields that met the road on either side. It was getting late, the afternoon sun had lost some of its heat and they both realised simultaneously that they would probably not make it back to their friends and colleagues tonight before curfew. Holding hands in a show of true love, for the benefit of anyone watching, they continued. It was now less than half an hour from curfew, and time to conceal their progress.

They could hear its noise long before it came into view. Peering from within the bushes that grew piecemeal along the top of the bank, they could see, looking down, the dark-grey shape of a Wehrmacht truck swaying heavily like a heifer in milk along the narrow route. It ground noisily up through the gears as the road's incline increased approaching their concealment place. As it passed, the dimly lit outline of a red German face with cigarette poking out remained the parting image, together with the stink of raw diesel. The boy, Christian, said they should stay a while until the early hours before going further. Patricia, initially uncertain, reluctantly agreed and made a small hollow in the shrubbery in which to lie, alone. It was going to be cold later but that did not mean that standards were to be lowered, she thought. He sat a few yards away inside a bush, a thin jacket pulled about him. The night sky was clear and the earth lost its warmth.

"Patricia, Patricia." She had eventually fallen asleep despite the discomfort of her makeshift bed. His loud whisper indicated that it was time for them to move carefully along the direction of the road towards what they hoped would be the barn's location. Now and again a fox would bark somewhere in the woods high above them. Regular calls by screech-owls sent shivers through Patricia. They made their way stealthily across fields roughly following the route of the road off to their left. To be caught out after curfew in such a sensitive area would not prove a healthy experience, they were both aware. After forty minutes Christian stopped suddenly and lay quietly in the long grass. Watching him just visible in the darkness ahead of her, she did the same. Foxes and owls were still communicating through the darkness, but there was a new sound: humans.

❖ ❖ ❖

The pace of work at Hamble did not slacken. The demand for new aircraft for newly forming and established squadrons was relentless, particularly from Bomber Command. Allied airmen were taking the war to Germany at considerable cost in crews and aircraft; the new four-engine heavy bombers were crucial to the task. Ceci's flying proved above average regardless of the type she was scheduled to deliver or collect. She'd always made a point of preparing properly for each flight, reading and understanding the specially prepared ATA Ferry Pilot's Notes for each type in service, and ensuring that weather and other operations were OK. It had paid off on more than one occasion when an unexpected problem had arisen in the air.

Since Jane's death, Ceci had been allowed to take increasing responsibility for deliveries of the fast twin-engine Mosquito bomber, distributing the beautiful de Havilland machine to hungry units across southern England as far as St Eval in Cornwall and into East Anglia, which was now increasingly littered with new airfields for the RAF and the newly arriving Americans in the shape of the United States Army Air Force. Harriet accompanied Ceci on a couple of these Mosquito deliveries. They got on well together, almost as a mother and daughter, although the age gap was only twelve years. Satisfied, Harriet decided to send Ceci on the special four-engine ATA course at RAF Marston Moor, not far from York. Here she could qualify as a Class Five pilot able to make deliveries of the new huge and powerful four-engine machines at a time when their losses over Germany were worrying.

Ceci would follow in the steps of Lettice Curtis, the first female pilot in the ATA to be classified Class Five, followed soon after by Harriet herself. It was a qualification that they would share with only a few of their aviatrix colleagues. The training was to be undertaken on ex-operational Halifax Mk 1 bombers fitted with four Merlin engines; and it was arranged that all ATA pilot training was to be undertaken coincidental with training their female flight engineers. The four-engine heavies, which included the Stirling, Halifax and Lancaster bombers, required two on board for deliveries and on occasions had carried a rear gunner for safety's sake when training or deliveries were being conducted in southern England. More than one ATA delivery had been attacked by German fighters over England.

Their time at Marston Moor rushed past. Within five days Ceci had done four hours of dual instruction as well as aircraft familiarisation and classroom work; her male instructor was both pleased and surprised at her progress. On Sunday came the day when she would fly the large machine with only her trainee flight engineer sitting behind her. Walking around the aircraft with her flight engineer, she could feel a knot of nerves tightening painfully in her stomach. All seemed fine with the aircraft and they boarded, pulling up the metal ladder, then firmly closing the door. Her instructor watched, aware of how she was feeling. Running through the checklist together, their responses were taut. With all four engines running and the ground electrical power removed, she took a deep breath and affected a brief smile as she waved chocks away. Her instructor grinned back with a simple nod of encouragement.

Taxiing slowly around the seemingly endless perimeter track, she went through in her mind the vital and automatic actions required if something were to go wrong on take-off, such as an engine failure or a burst tyre. Either way, she now had the responsibility of another life on board, the charming and witty

Catherine, all the way from Argentina. She had met and married a wealthy rancher and moved from her birthplace near Worcester to start a new life breeding beef on the wide South American Pampas. Ceci swung the Halifax around with a burst of throttle and taxied forward onto the runway threshold, ensuring that the tail wheel was straight before applying the brakes. They spent a few minutes studying the engine gauges together. Everything seemed in order and within limits. Take-off checks were started: Ceci called them out; Catherine responding in her turn.

"Hydraulics?"

"Undercarriage uplocks in."

"Blowers?"

"Medium," said Catherine, calmly adjusting the levers.

"Boost plus twelve?"

"Set."

"RPM three thousand?"

Ceci slowly advanced the throttle levers, Catherine watching the four rpm gauges.

"Mixture rich?"

"Set."

"Gills – set half?"

"Set half, OK."

"Flaps twenty?"

"Flaps set twenty." The whine of their movement could just be heard above the roar of the four Merlins.

They were ready, the four engines straining to pull them down the damp, black tarmac stretching far away before them.

Final checks: Ceci adjusted the elevator trim wheel 'two notches nose up'. Rudder and aileron set to 'neutral'. Off to her left there was a green light from the ops caravan.

She glanced across at Catherine, thumbs up and raised eyebrows above her oxygen mask. Brakes off. Held straight with rudder and a brief touch of brakes, the Halifax gathered pace quickly in her unladen state. In no time, so it seemed to Ceci, she was pushing the control column forward slightly, encouraging the tail up. The power, the raw noisy power, still surprised her; she suddenly felt totally confident, the huge machine was hers and they were thundering down the tarmac. At ninety miles per hour the bellowing machine became light; at one hundred and ten miles per hour they were airborne climbing hard over the dark green landscape, the four Merlins joyously proclaiming their freedom. Her target speed in the climb was one hundred and forty. Catherine monitored the engines and, once settled into the climb, reduced their boost to plus six, selecting flaps and undercarriage 'up' on Ceci's request.

Up at five thousand feet she levelled off, allowing the speed to build to recommended cruise: one hundred and eighty miles per hour. Catherine performed her duties, reducing boost further and weakening the mixture to each engine. Below lay sunlit Marston Moor, the battlefield where Oliver Cromwell had first met Prince Rupert's Royalists and decimated them at the beginning of the English Civil War three hundred years before. Banking the huge machine smoothly left, Ceci commenced a series of simple manoeuvres as set out by her instructor. Each one successfully completed gave her further confidence for the most difficult exercise of all – getting the Halifax back onto the ground, ideally in one piece. They were ready to return.

Conscious that everyone on the ground would be watching,

she decided to join downwind into the Marston landing circuit. Turning away from the airfield, engine power reduced, they lost some height in preparation for joining. There were other aircraft operating much as she was in the circuit; they would have to keep a good lookout. Down to eight hundred feet and into the circuit Catherine called the speeds; at one hundred and forty miles per hour flaps then undercarriage were selected down, the aircraft responding with a slight nose-down pitch, providing a better view of the ground ahead. The two vital green lights glowed reassuringly on the instrument panel indicating main wheels down and locked. Turning right base from the downwind leg of the circuit, she began to feel slight tension rising.

"Be prepared for an overshoot if I don't get it right first time." Catherine responded calmly, "You're doing fine."

Across to her right through the windscreens she could see the thin black tarmac strip slowly moving around to her front as she held the machine in a gentle right bank. On finals, and lined up neatly with three quarters of a mile to run, she concentrated on holding the runway in one fixed place in her windscreen. Catherine adjusted engine boost and called the speeds.

"One hundred and fifteen." Near the ground the air was gusty. Ceci made allowances for the wind slightly from her right. The Halifax behaved impeccably as Ceci gently caught each wavering move as the huge, dark aircraft sank majestically down the invisible glide path, both girls watching the runway rise to meet them. Over the runway's painted numbers throttles were closed. There was the characteristic squeak as rubber hit tarmac at one hundred miles an hour. A blue puff of smoke whipped away by the breeze. It was a near three-pointer, no bounce. Using the rudder Ceci maintained a straight line down the centre of the runway, braking gently, and finally turning off at a convenient intersection onto the perimeter track.

"What was that you were saying about an overshoot?" laughed Catherine through the intercom.

"Couldn't have done it without you, girl!" responded Ceci.

Catherine was now standing alongside her in the cockpit, "You'd better believe it!" she shouted at the happy and confident Ceci.

They almost fell down the ladder together, laughing, proud of what they had done. Their instructors were waiting, standing back quietly, a little away from the ground crew, who were bustling around putting chocks in place, preparing to refuel the thirsty machine. They were smiling knowingly. They'd seen it all before and it was immensely satisfying. In the van going back to ops Ceci could say nothing. Gazing satisfied out of its open rear, she looked back at the dwindling image of the huge camouflaged bomber that she and Catherine had learnt to control together.

Over the next four days Ceci and Catherine completed another four hours together, both with and without an instructor on board, undertaking a mix of exercises that they had previously practised under instruction, including three-engine take-offs and landings, crosswind operations, short landings and emergency procedures. In barely four weeks, the weather had not played its part fully. It was all over; the flying, the classroom studies, and a last-night stand of beers all round. They could hardly believe that they had learnt to work together as a crew, entrusted to fly a four-engine bomber alone after barely eight hours of practical flying around the inspiring and beautiful Yorkshire countryside.

As they boarded the Anson that was to take them both back

to Hamble they experienced a mix of wild emotions. They had quickly formed strong bonds with their patient instructors, who took no account of the fact that they were 'mere girls' but treated them as absolute equals. They were young men, mature beyond their years; they had seen the Ruhr and Berlin and experienced the horror of those dark nights. A few quiet tears were shed as the Anson cruised noisily south. There was a huge party at the Bugle in Hamble that evening. Harriet was absolutely delighted; emotional, even.

❖ ❖ ❖

Christian stopped suddenly, very carefully raising his head above long, dew-wrapped grass. Ahead there were noises but no sign of human habitation, no lights, nothing. He turned and whispered into Patricia's ear. He proposed crawling ahead to try and find out how far away the Germans actually were. She nodded at his idea, unable to see the expression on his face in the dark. She would wait there for half an hour; if he had not returned or if she heard a lot of noise she was to make her way back to the cycles and wait. If he still had not arrived at the cycles by six o'clock when the curfew finished, she was to ride home alone.

He crawled away from her; for a brief while she could hear him rustling through the grass, then nothing. It seemed the foxes and owls had decided to make it an early night. There were no sounds now and the eerie quietness did not suit her. He'd left her at two-eighteen. She decided to wait in the cool and increasingly damp grass until three, then move off. Carefully she settled down, watching the luminous hands on the tiny gold watch given to her by her father for her eighteenth birthday. It had been four years ago in Benodet, in the sun on the sand by a blue sea. If they could have seen the future then, the gaiety that had filled that happy day might perhaps have been moderated.

Just ahead, about thirty metres, Christian could see the red point of a cigarette glowing brightly as each draw brought fresh oxygen to its tip. There was a cough, then heavy boots stamping about on a gravel surface. He watched the red pinpoint circulate, held in the mouth of the phantom. A few minutes later a new sound caught his ears. It was other boots approaching from some distance towards his location. Edging back, he continued to watch, concealed, like the makers of the noises in the dark. The boots stopped and there was a guttural greeting followed by a coarse laugh. The conversation continued for about four minutes during which a match was struck and he could briefly see two grey-helmeted soldiers in its arc of flare. He looked at his watch: gone twenty to three. He'd better make tracks back to Patricia.

As he turned carefully around he placed his foot on a broken dry hazel twig. It cracked noisily as his foot applied pressure. He lay still immediately, hidden in the grass. A voice shouted something in German; he heard the snap action of a rifle bolt. The shout came again and in the background there were new noises, more heavy feet stamping, approaching. Suddenly a bright light cast a powerful beam directly over his refuge. He remained flattened, concealed. Should he run, stay? He remained still, not even breathing. The beam flickered to and fro across the countryside, brightening the trees, disturbing the birds. Boots came towards him. Lights flashed about. More rifle bolts clattering. He could sense their nearness, just feet from him, shouting to one another.

He thought there were three or possibly four of them. Then

the light suddenly flicked off. The boots moved away off the grass, back onto a hard gravelly surface, where they scraped and clattered away into the distance. A mocking laugh, a few more guttural words uttered and the soldier was left alone again. Christian couldn't move; the German was now alert and any sound would probably set off the whole circus again. And they might find him this time.

He lay, still, coldness entering his limbs. It struck him that if he had to run now his legs would be too stiff to give him a chance. He stayed, dark eyes closed, listening intently. By four, dawn would be appearing and he would be unable to move for fear of being seen. He decided that he would have to risk a move. His watch said three twenty-eight.

Inching his way around, he was pointing back the way he'd come. Moving each leg and arm with infinite care, he began to crawl. In ten minutes he had covered barely thirty yards. He could see better now, he realised. Glancing up, he could see the eastern sky was perceptibly lighter. Risking everything, he slowly raised his head, looking back to where the guard was located. A faintly glowing cigarette was again just visible there, together with a shadowy human figure, unmistakably a Wehrmacht soldier with weapon slung over its shoulder. Over to his left the road was quite close at this point, and had a slight curve in it. From his slightly higher vantage point on the banking it was clear that from here anyone on the road could not be seen from the guard point. Crawling back to the cycles through the fields as the light strengthened would not only prove slow but also risk his exposure.

Crawling to the top of the bank, he rolled over its top and

silently down onto the road. Looking back confirmed that he could not be observed by the smoking soldier. Half-crouching and with feet clad only in socks, he began to run down the road to where he'd left Patricia. He knew, according to their agreement that she would have left some time ago and would probably be waiting at their hidden cycles.

They almost ran into each other in the semi-darkness. The man in the dark uniform with its Death's Head insignia recoiled sharply for an instant as Christian swerved around him and ran straight on and up the banking, his rushing silhouette briefly outlined against the lightening skyline.

"Halt!" Christian ran, the long grass and cold muscles slowing his stride. The first shot whistled somewhere off to his left, not close. If he could reach the fold in the ground ahead he would be able to run unsighted. Another shot zinged, nowhere near, off into the shrubbery. The third hit him as he reached the top of the rise, where the ground fell away. It may have been lucky or the work of a marksman. It was irrelevant. The outcome could not be altered. The few ounces of lead smashed into his twelfth vertebrae. It carried fragments of bone and cord up into his chest as it thrust through lung tissue before emerging well up on the left side of his breast to the accompaniment of a sudden spray of blood that resolved into a steady pulsing flow.

His brain acknowledged the situation. He knew he'd been hit but strangely there was no pain, just the thrusting impact and a thick, salty taste in his mouth. In accordance with nature, his nervous system automatically began shutting down areas that were not essential, preserving oxygen flow to his brain and heart as his lifeblood ebbed steadily from smashed tissue. In the fold he had fallen awkwardly; it was darker there. Sounds were coming into his brain, men shouting, a dog barking excitedly. He lay; it was difficult to breathe, his legs splayed unnaturally under him. He managed to move his right arm slowly up to the wound, his fingertips feeling sticky. Swallowing was increasingly salty and thick. He coughed; then it hurt. His brain registered he was dying, and quickly.

When the officer finally reached him, difficult to find in the dark undulating ground and bushes, he'd been clinically dead for forty-six seconds, his heart muscles fully relaxed. The officer stopped, and bending down in the darkness, called for a light. Another man, thick-set, breathing heavily, arrived over the rim of the ridge and shone a powerful lamp down at the body.

"It's not the sort of rabbit you were expecting to find, Gustav!" The second soldier stumbled down the incline as the SS officer searched interestedly through Christian's pockets in the torchlight. They were completely empty.

"No, Heine, but an interesting prize, all the same. Get this back to camp and we'll see what it can tell us, even dead." He pushed at the warm body with his boot, trying to roll it over, taking care not to get blood on the toe cap of his boots.

Patricia, anxiously waiting, heard the single shout and subsequent briefly dispersed shots as she hid in undergrowth near to where their two bicycles lay. Instinct told her not to move. She stayed. By six forty-five Christian had not returned. He wasn't going to come now. Believing the worst, she gingerly pulled one of the cycles from its concealment and carefully set off in the bright morning for Kergudan, where she had noticed a small café the previous day; there was bound to be a telephone there. Cycling into the rising sun proved difficult with tear-filled eyes.

❧ ❧ ❧

They didn't need an excuse for a party but recent events, promotions, joinings and awards dictated that while the moon was out of phase for special operations, it was an opportunity that would be criminal to miss. This was not to be an impromptu letting-off of steam, an all-male event where just about anything went – and often did; but a 'civilised event', as George Hudson described his idea, where wives, girlfriends together with any other young ladies would be invited for food, music and booze.

By eight on Saturday evening the mess was heaving. A local band was playing the latest swing sounds from across the Atlantic. George Hudson had shown hidden talent and had somehow found a supply of food and alcohol the variety and quality of which had not been seen since early in 1939. Undertaking the host's duties with some aplomb, Michael Kelly circulated the crowded room as best he could with Sarah on his arm. As squadron CO he was pleased with how things were shaping since his appointment. He made a point of speaking to all his crews, sharing a joke and talking with their lady guests, some of whom, he noticed, were very attractive. Undressing, later that night, Sarah remarked on it. He leered at her. She pouted and jumped into bed, naked, laughing.

They were a mixed bunch in terms of nationalities, including two Norwegians, a Pole, a Czech, two Canadians, including Paul Mossman, fresh from hospital after his hazardous reconnaissance flight, and a Dutch pilot recently escaped from Holland. Guy van der Beek had arrived literally out of the blue two days before, sent by the Air Ministry because he had much experience of night flying and spoke French fluently. He claimed to be the son of a Dutch diplomat, having spent part of his youth in Paris. On his second day he brought his dog, Hans, into the flight offices. It was a large, young Alsatian, which caused some amusement when it managed to get its head caught in a waste bin while looking for scraps, and ran about crashing into all and sundry. Guy was tall and thin, and they'd had to make some adjustments to the pilot's seat in one of the Lizzies so that he could fit in comfortably. Sarah liked his broad smile, confidence and natural ease with people, but something during their introduction set her mind searching.

The buffet meal was soon devoured, suitably accompanied by gallons of beer and an eclectic mix of superb wines for those with palates able to recognise them. Where all the wonderful delicacies had come from was a question Kelly was not going to address that evening. They spent some time catching up and chatting with Paul Mossman, who was under doctor's orders not to take alcohol; it did not seem to cramp his style or charm. Ceci arrived late with Helen from Hamble; they were mortified when they realised most of the food had been devoured by the hundred or so guests who had included, for a brief visit, the AOC. Later Sarah saw Daphne sitting with Paul Mossman, sharing a table in a corner. Oblivious to the couples dancing around them, they seemed to be having what appeared to be a lively conversation, she smiling constantly, he staring intently at her. Out of uniform, and made-up, Daphne looked stunning in a low-cut evening dress in a deep red, her hair beautifully cut and set; Sarah made a mental note to find out who had done it for her. By 2 am only a few hangers-on remained. It had indeed been a civilised event, but one that everyone had seemed to enjoy.

❖ ❖ ❖

News reached Quimper later in the evening. Penrose learned from Claude and Raymond of the disastrous outcome for the two Resistance people from the new Morbihan circuit after their attempt at gathering information about the experimental aircraft location. It seemed that the young man had been either killed or caught, probably the former. He had, it appeared, disregarded his instructions and risked not only his own life but also that of a female accomplice; more importantly his actions had put the whole project on hold. Now the Germans would probably increase the guard and make access to the general area much more difficult. The situation was communicated to London and they awaited instructions.

Harold was becoming increasingly frustrated with matters; he'd been effectively a prisoner in hiding for months and felt increasingly inclined to leave the stealing of an aircraft from under the noses of the Germans to someone else. On present performance, it was unclear when or if the Resistance would manage to assemble a proper plan. It was the sheer boredom that was most damaging; sitting for hours, reading, sleeping or watching the street below through grey-netted windows. The only positive aspect was that his French had improved, largely accounted for by his reading a number of old French novels and the Boche-censored daily papers – all painfully undertaken with the help of a battered English–French dictionary. Expressing his frustrations one evening, Claude pointedly answered that the alternative was one he was unlikely to enjoy either.

Harold agreed; being a guest of the Gestapo was something he would prefer to avoid. Claude also gently made the point that a number of individuals had put their own lives at considerable risk in giving him shelter. He, Penrose, was at least alive and living not too badly under the circumstances. Harold sat for a moment taking in the admonition.

"You're right, Claude, sorry. It's just that I feel so bloody useless, nothing to do all day, knowing people are risking themselves for me and I'm just stuck here not even paying my way."

Claude watched the young pilot over the top of his pince-nez, understanding; the sticking-plaster repair across their bridge sagging slightly

"I'm sure that what you were doing in your aeroplane was paying your way, Harold. Before too long I believe that you will have another opportunity to settle, as you seem to see it, your debt. I have some friends with a farm just north of Morlaix; if you want to stretch your body, if not your mind, they may have work for you to do in the fields. Your hands are healed?" Penrose nodded and it was agreed that a change of scenery may help.

Three days later the same black Citroën that had brought him to Quimper with the same incommunicative girl driver arrived at the house very early on a wet morning. Dressed as a local, Penrose walked out to the car with a small bag containing a change of fairly serviceable clothes and in his pocket a forged identity card, work permit and a little money. Claude and Raymond had spent patient hours implanting key French phrases in his mind, using the local Breton dialect. If Penrose were stopped at any point, his ability to answer promptly without falling over any linguistic hurdles was crucial to his and their survival. He was warned not to try to volunteer more than was asked for, and to keep responses to the required monosyllables only.

The wipers worked intermittently, squeaking annoyingly. He sat watching a distorted picture of soaking rural France pass in front of him. Once they were waved down and stopped by a gendarme in a dripping dark-blue cape; as they sat waiting at the narrow roadside a long, slow-moving convoy of German military vehicles passed them by. His driver watched each carefully; he could see her mind registering the type and possible content of each camouflaged vehicle. The girl spoke not a single word during their journey.

Remarking on it later, he learned that she was mute. Aude had not always been that way; only since she had witnessed the appalling and wasteful killing of her older sister by a German tank that had careered through the small village where they were living quietly in the early summer of 1940, managing to avoid most of the Blitzkrieg and the pointless destruction inflicted on large tracts of north-eastern France.

The journey to Morlaix took over two hours despite only being one hundred kilometres long. Penrose spent the final hour in some discomfort needing to relieve himself. The dismal weather, their being halted while waiting for convoys to pass, and their need to take to small backroads from time to time to avoid possible checkpoints added delay and frustration to their silent progress. Avoiding the centre of Morlaix, they finally found themselves on the last stretch; the few miles north to Terenez, situated on the edge of the Baie de Morlaix. Suddenly the girl turned right, driving inland along a muddy track part-protected by drystone walls, the Citroën finally stopping in a morass of a farmyard. Here, on rising ground, the rain was being driven near-horizontally, straight off the sea, and it was cold. Crowded over to one side and sheltering against a crumbling brick wall, a small herd of Friesians stood, almost oblivious to the rain, steam rising from their packed bodies, pendulous udders awaiting relief. Their gentle, mournful eyes watched the car and its occupants with passing interest.

The girl wiped inside the misted windscreen and pointed out to Penrose what appeared to be the farmhouse, its steeply pitched roof rising above the dilapidated buildings that surrounded the other three sides of the mud-filled yard. On opening the car door he was immediately challenged by the depth of mud and bovine deposits. His shoes would be engulfed before he had gone a yard. She opened her door, looking down from her side. Grimacing, she closed it. Starting the car, she edged it carefully forwards towards the house; she had no wish to get stuck. It briefly left two parallel furrows in the mushy surface until rain merged the lines back into the common mire.

Inside, feet wet and smelly, he stood in a darkened hallway of mainly dark brown; his shoes, left outside to wash in the rain, were propped up on a brick, no doubt left for that purpose. There appeared to be no one at home. Putting his bag on a chair, he walked up to a large, brown-painted door at the far end of the hall. It was the kitchen; inside a well-fed tabby cat lay curled on a coarse rug in front of a huge fire that had been banked high and from which plumes of grey smoke twirled up the wide chimney.

At the far end a full-length window gave a dispiriting view of wet farmland and low cloud. In front of the window a broad, battered table stood, stacked at one end with old newspapers, journals and bits of opened correspondence. The adjacent wall supported a massive brown cupboard, one door just ajar, white enamelware reflecting the little available light.

The cat stirred and stretched, rolling onto its back, toes curled and purring loudly. He watched it watching him through a pale slit in one half-open eye. On the wall above the stone mantle an old, round clock emitted a slow tick-tock. On the ancient black stove two large, heavy-looking pans sat, lukewarm. There was a strong smell of some sort of stew or soup, probably with onions. He turned and went back into the hall to see if he could see anyone in the yard.

Now, on the far side, the soaked cows were moving in a quiet line through a narrow doorway into what he assumed to be the farm's milking parlour. Someone must be there, he thought, looking for something to wear for safe, dry, passage across the yard. Borrowing a large pair of leather boots stiff with lack of use he made his slithering way through the surface puree, squinting against the driving rain towards the door where the last three animals were playing a sort of "No, after you, Claude" game. As he approached, he slapped the last on its rump; catalysed, its hooves clattered on the shed's brick floor as it scuttled nervously inside, followed by the last two animals, the whites of their eyes showing nervously.

The ceiling was low, and huge oak roof trusses gave a cathedral-like quality to the building; at the far end in the half-light a greyish head was moving, bobbing up and down. Pushing gently past the animals, Penrose made his way towards a round robust woman, red-faced and panting, watching each cow as it moved into its allotted stall. There were seventeen standing patiently waiting to be milked, water running off their coats, their tails and ears flicking now and again. The smell was evocative of those ever-golden summer holidays he remembered from childhood when his mother, widowed then, would take him down to the Quantocks in north Somerset to stay with her older sister and her tanned and dour farmer husband on their rented farm.

She turned and looked at him, not surprised. It transpired she'd seen him arrive but had been too busy to stop her work to see to him. He held out his hand.

"Oui, bonjour, Monsieur. Je vous attendais."

She took his hand in deference to English custom and shook it. Hers was firm and calloused. Just at that moment the far-end door burst open with a crash, and two boys of about twelve years rushed noisily into the shed, laughing. Clad suitably for the weather in black oilskins, they were quietened firmly by the woman and introduced to "M'sieur 'Arold, un ami d'Oncle Claude." He stayed and watched the three of them milk the cows by hand and later helped them to fill the stalls with dry hay for the night. The heavy milk containers were closed and rolled with deft skill out into the yard and left to cool. She walked down the rows of chewing creatures, looking at each one in turn; the two boys cleared up rotten straw or hay, washing buckets in a stone sink just outside the parlour door in the rain. It had taken nearly three hours and dusk was established. A single oil lamp was left burning brightly, securely fastened to a hook well above any inquisitive cow.

They all made their way back across the yard. The rain had begun to ease and way out to the west a thin sliver of deep-crimson sky sat low on the horizon.

❖ ❖ ❖

In no time at all the new moon phase was approaching. Kelly and his flight commanders prepared for a busy schedule over the coming fourteen days or so. Flying had not stopped while they had been back at their Tempsford base, but a reduction in its tempo had allowed all machines to be fettled to meet the squadron's enviable reputation in meeting maximum serviceability under pressure. George Hudson had taken over squadron administration with remarkable effect. He allowed nothing to stand in the way of their meeting operational requirements and had on two occasions been the subject of signal memos from the AOC responding to some complaint from a stores depot in Staffordshire about Pilot Officer Hudson's incessant and immediate demands on the system, which were 'quite unrealistic in current wartime circumstances'. Kelly showed George the correspondence with the AOC's postscript of support for their continuing to demand equipment and spares on a twenty-four-hour basis ... 'or he would want to know why'.

The first sortie on their return to Sussex was undertaken by one of the flight commanders, Ben Kendle. A pilot with wide experience, he'd joined special operations from a Beaufighter night fighter squadron, where he and his navigator had despatched six Germans in the dark during their last operational tour. Ben was quiet and reserved; known to be an excellent, careful pilot and pretty fearless if his record was to be believed. At Tempsford he was courting probably the most desirable WAAF on the unit, shy, bright and blessed with a superb figure, according to his envious colleagues. It was a pick-up only, a single male agent to be lifted by Lysander from a field that they had used before near St Victore l'Abbaye, north of Rouen, barely over the French coast.

Take-off was at one-thirty am. He was marked as 'Missing' on the ops board next morning.

Three nights later a young Norwegian pilot, Per Lindquist, failed to return from a sortie taking two Joes to a field south-west of Rouen, near Thevray, and aiming to uplift three Joes, two men and a girl. He too failed to return. The loss of two experienced pilots, especially Flight Lieutenant Ben Kendle, would have a serious impact on operations this moon phase and Kelly was very worried at the loss of the two in roughly the same area around Rouen. SOE were unable to provide any information as to the circumstances of the losses from their contacts in the local Resistance circuits but were still trying. Meanwhile, the work went on; Lysander, Hudson and Whitley aircraft sorties were mounted, delivering, dropping and collecting Joes and cargo from unmarked landing grounds scattered across blacked-out France, from Cherbourg down to Pau in the Pyrenees, on one particular occasion. Sometimes some of those sitting in the back of their aircraft were senior Resistance members; one or two had served as pre-war cabinet members in the final calamitous 1940 government.

Guy van der Beek flew his second Lizzie sortie to an easily identified field set neatly in a forest not far from Argentan. His outgoing passenger was a replacement radio operator for a Resistance group trying to overcome another disaster resulting from German infiltration. It had taken a serious toll on their number until the culprit had been identified and quickly liquidated. The changeover went perfectly and the Lizzie was airborne in less than eight minutes. During the returning passenger's debriefing at SOE's private house near Guildford he touched on why had his pilot taken such a long route home; initially heading east towards Paris before eventually turning north somewhere between Rouen and Le Havre, finally crossing the French coast near Fecamp. The passenger, a senior Resistance organiser in northern France, had been rather worried at their closeness to Le Havre – noted for its aggressive flak defences around the city's docks and port. The debriefing officer scribbled a note in the margin of his papers with a question-mark, intending to take the matter up with the special ops squadron concerned. It was overlooked.

On the Tuesday of the second week, with the moon beginning to wane, a Hudson with a full load of no less than eight Joes on its outward trip failed to return as scheduled in the early hours of the following morning. There had been a good deal of discussion about this particular sortie, some, including Michael Kelly, feeling that it should be the subject of a double- or even a triple-Lysander mission, in company if necessary. The loss of two Lysander pilots the previous week, not to mention their valuable aircraft, left Kelly and the SOE planners with few choices but to use one of their trusty Hudsons with a full passenger complement. In this case, however, there was some evidence as to what had happened.

The Hudson had taken off at 12.43 am. Another aircraft on a different mission towards the south of Lyon had followed about seven minutes later on an almost identical track across the Channel and over the Pas-de-Calais region. Fighter Command had tracked the two machines by radar as best they could across the Channel after leaving Selsey. That both were flying low-level across the water made identification difficult at times. As they climbed, some miles inland from the French coast, a single aircraft blip appeared weakly on their radar plot, seemingly taking off from one of many German airfields in the Calais area. The operators were increasingly worried as they watched the growing signal strength as the aircraft gained height, spear across the night sky directly towards the first Hudson.

The following Hudson saw the outcome graphically: a sudden violent fireball searing in intensity; burning wreckage scattering onto dark, featureless farmland below. The crew and its heroic passengers had stood no chance. The German night fighter, having completed its kill, returned immediately to its home airfield; it made no attempt to interfere with the second Hudson and yet it too must have featured on the German fighter controller's radar, being only a few miles in the rear of the first target. The navigator on the returning Hudson confirmed Fighter Command's estimate of the attack location: fifteen miles north of Beauvais, forty miles east of Rouen.

Later, checks were made on German night-fighter activity on the two nights when Ben Kendle and the Norwegian Per Lindquist went missing. Air Ministry records showed some activity but none indicated a specific attack on any special operations aircraft. The loss of valuable and trained crews meant that completing SOE's tasks placed all the remaining aircrews under increased pressure regardless of weather and moon conditions. The loss of eight trained agents, men and women, in one terrible attack left SOE's 'F' section facing a difficult period, unable to fulfil its obligations to its Resistance customers scattered across occupied France.

As a direct consequence, Michael Kelly undertook two sorties in one night, unheard of in the squadron's history, and only made possible because of the nearness of landing sites to the north

French coast. Fortunately both deliveries and pick-ups went like clockwork, with the moon playing its full part. The fortnight of the moon's full phase had ended with no further losses of crews or machines but it had been a salutary lesson. Before that dreadful fortnight, no pilots had been lost on special operations with the squadron.

◆ ◆ ◆

She was happy – very happy. A bland buff envelope had arrived that morning with a curt note from someone in MI9. There was no address but the department name on the letterhead, and no telephone number. On the sheet pasted to the letter was a typed note. 'Please advise my fiancée I am well and look forward to getting home. Harold.' Perhaps the Resistance had sent a message for him and MI9 or SOE had shown unusual compassion and sent it on; it was rather unusual, she knew. Since returning from Marston Moor to Hamble, Ceci had continued to deliver single- and twin-engine aircraft from shadow factories and airfields scattered across southern England. Then, one day, she and two other girls, together with their newly trained flight engineers, were given a new job. It was to ferry Lancaster Bombers from the A V Roe factory at Hawarden airfield, near Chester, to Bomber Command units across East Anglia, from Yorkshire to Essex. They were short of ferry pilots, and south-based ATA units were roped in to help.

Taken by Hamble's taxi Anson, they arrived late one evening just as the light faded from the sky. Arrangements had been made for them to stay in local digs with the families of workers at the Avro factory. The night was disrupted around one-thirty by German bombing of the Liverpool docks and, everyone said, they had made an attempt bomb the Manchester Ship Canal, but without success. A faint smell of burning was evident in the morning on the gentle north-easterly breeze as they were taken by official car to the airfield.

Neither of the girls had flown a Lancaster before and it was intended to give them some familiarisation with 'Bomber' Harris's latest weapon. They walked through the factory complex towards the airfield where, in isolated splendour in the early morning sunlight, sat a recently completed four-engine Lancaster finished with a matt-black belly and camouflaged topsides. The weak sun glinted on the cockpit and gunner's Perspex. Clambering up the short metal ladder into the aircraft they were assailed by the odour of the machine: hydraulic oil, petrol, dope and something that they couldn't quite put their finger on. Crawling over the two main wing spars that ran across the aircraft, they made their way forward to the cockpit and flight engineer's position. Looking around them in admiration, the girls all realised that this was something very different. It was exciting and, Ceci felt, quite magnificent. For four hours the pilots and engineers were shown all the cocks and taps: how to start it, run it, operate the various controls and systems, and in turn how to fly it. In the late afternoon the three pilots and their engineers had each made three take-offs and landings; it had been exhausting. Tomorrow they would begin deliveries to units on their own.

Ceci and Catherine was the second crew to make a delivery, taking their machine to RAF Scampton. During the following three weeks they and others, men and women, collected and delivered dozens of Lancasters to squadrons desperate to replace lost machines. Although much larger than anything else she had flown, with the exception of their Halifax training at Marston Moor, the aircraft proved very easy to handle, even for a woman, although care had to be taken in any sort of crosswind. Catherine laughed at the prospect of further deliveries and the disbelief they would cause when two women stepped down from the bomber – alone.

The sixth aircraft they were to deliver had developed obvious withdrawal symptoms after being taken from the place of its birth to a fighting unit. The early-morning pre-flight walk-round discovered a serious hydraulic leak from one of the main undercarriage jacks. It was a jack that, along with its sister, enabled the main undercarriage to be retracted into the bottom of the inboard engine nacelles. Ceci had suggested that they fly at slow speed to the unit in Norfolk with the undercarriage down and have the snag fixed there, but the Avro people were not happy with that.

"Should be delivered to them brave boys in tip-top working order, I reckon," said the foreman, scratching the top of his head with the end of a pencil, his clipboard papers rattling in the stiff breeze. The poor Lancaster was ignominiously towed back into the hangar and the offending jack changed. Just before lunch she was outside again, ready to go. Ceci and Catherine climbed confidently aboard. After their checklists, they soon had all the four Merlin engines turning sweetly; chocks were waved away and Ceci carefully manoeuvred the Lancaster along the narrow perimeter track towards the runway in use. Carrying out pre-take-off checks, they discovered a substantial magneto drop on the number three engine; it would not deliver full power, setting up a series of noisy backfires with engine revolutions falling off dramatically. They tried all the usual tricks, including leaning off the petrol mixture, but the snag remained.

Ceci had responsibility and decided to return the aircraft to the hangar for further investigation. They were met by long faces as they opened the door and disembarked down the ladder. The ground crew began stripping the side cowlings off the misbehaving No 3. Each spark plug was withdrawn and inspected. None of them appeared to be sooted up, or to have the wrong spark gap. Attention then turned to the magnetos; there appeared nothing wrong there, either and Ceci was beginning to feel a little uncomfortable at all the work she had engendered. Perhaps she had been wrong. Finally all the cowlings were closed and the engine was test-run with one of the works engineers checking the health of the Merlin. All seemed fine and the work was signed off on the usual Form 700, declaring the machine fit for flight.

The weather in the last hour had become increasingly miserable as rain driven by the earlier breeze spread slowly in from the north-east, gradually soaking the overalls of engineers working to find the problem. By the time they were ready to go it was raining steadily with a cloud base of about twelve hundred feet. Airborne, they hugged the cloud base for a few minutes before climbing on instruments into the soggy mass, gaining height to clear the southern arm of Pennines, which stretched across their route into Yorkshire. Monitoring her instrument panel, which duplicated many of the dials in front of Ceci, Catherine noticed that the oil pressure on the number three engine was unstable, surging up and down; the other three engines' oil-pressure gauges remained rock-steady as they climbed upwards. In cloud Ceci was flying solely on instruments, which required great concentration, particularly as the air was turbulent in places. Catherine did not want to distract her pilot unnecessarily. Finally, with the needle of the offending gauge flicking up and down alarmingly, she advised Ceci.

"We have an oil-pressure problem with number three, we should shut it down." Ceci, concentrating on her flying instruments, nodded, half-glancing across at the engine instruments on her panel.

"OK, do it from there, Cathy, while I wind on some rudder trim to compensate." Catherine acknowledged and pulled back the number-three throttle, boost levers and the engine's idle cut-off. As she did so there was a muffled bang from the aircraft's starboard wing, and heavy vibrations shook the machine. Continuing, Catherine pulled off all the fuel cocks serving the problem engine, finally reaching up and switching off the engine's twin magneto switches.

Where the number three engine sat, forward of the wing, its propeller still rotating, a dull orange glow shone through the rushing, moist air.

"Fire number three, pull the bottles!" called Ceci, her voice slightly higher than normal through the intercom. Catherine leaned over and pulled the toggle that would set off fire extinguishers inside the number three engine cowling to suppress any flames.

At nine thousand feet they burst into clear air, flying between two levels of heavy, ominous-looking cloud. Catherine moved forward into the cockpit, sitting on the folding engineer's seat that also doubled as the co-pilot's seat. Now there was no sign of fire but black soot showed, leaking out from around the cowling edges and spreading back across the top of the wing. The Merlin was dead but the propeller continued to turn, windmilling dangerously in the airflow. Ceci had been unable to select fine pitch for the propeller's blades; normally on a shut-down she would feather them flat into the airflow, stopping them from rotating. As it was, they were still in their cruise position; coarse pitch and the wind over their surfaces was causing the heavy metal propeller to rotate with increasing speed. Uncontrolled, it would create a new problem, a large increase in drag on their starboard side, pulling the aircraft hard to the right. As the Lancaster tried to turn, Ceci could feel the increasing pressure needed to keep the wounded machine flying straight. She found it necessary to apply all of her weight to the left rudder pedal to counteract the dragging, useless No 3 propeller.

They both knew they were in trouble. The clear space that was their limited world, flying between clouds at nine thousand feet, had a radius of about two miles. Both girls knew that they had to keep turning left. Turning right, in the same direction as the now-dead number three engine was a recipe for loss of control. Ceci's leg was in spasm.

The heavy air loads on the twin rudders, trying to counter the machine's urge to turn right, were beginning to overcome Ceci. Opening up power on number-four engine gave some relief, helping to pull the right side of the aircraft around. Catherine, back at her engineer's position, looked for some way to feather the blades on the runaway propeller. Slowing the aircraft down, Ceci spent time adjusting throttle settings on the three remaining engines in an effort to find a combination that would help her to keep the machine straight and level. Her left leg, straight, locked painfully into position, was aching like hell.

The runaway propeller's engine revolution gauge showed nearly three thousand, well above the normal maximum. With increasing vibrations, pilot and engineer knew that there was a real risk of the over-speeding propeller eventually tearing the engine out of the aircraft. The result would be catastrophic, and final.

"Cathy, you may have to jump."

Her voice was strained but calm as she fought the rudders, barely able to hold the Lancaster in a standard turn. Catherine looked up from struggling with various switches and electrical fuses in her efforts to find a solution to their dire situation. Reaching across, she picked up her parachute and clipped it onto the harness rings on her chest. Vibration was causing all the instruments to blur on her engineer's panel. Holding onto anything solid, she pulled herself forward into the cockpit. Plugging in her intercom lead, she shouted,

"I'm not jumping without you!" She ducked below the instrument panel, down and forward into the bomb-aimer's compartment in the nose. Through its clear Perspex she could see grey clouds below and above as they jerked around in the small amphitheatre of clear air. Bending, she lifted the yellow-striped lever and pulled. The circular floor hatch came away, leaving a neat hole to atmosphere through which she and Ceci could leave the stricken Lancaster. Then she had an idea. They had nothing to lose.

Climbing back up and into the cockpit, she sat again at her engineer's panel. Once she was plugged in she rapidly explained her idea over the intercom.

"Ceci, let's try restarting number three for a moment, it may enable us to feather the prop." Ceci, struggling and concentrating, said nothing for a few moments as she thought through the likely consequences. If they managed to restart the engine and it caught fire again they had no extinguishers to put it out a second time. If the engine proved controllable and its various systems worked, it might just be possible to feather the propeller blades, stopping them from rotating uncontrolled.

"OK ... give it a go, but be prepared to leave quickly." Her voice was strained. "I don't know how the engine is going to react to being started while turning at this speed." Catherine prepared the vibrating Merlin for action. Fuel cocks selected, boost pump and booster coil on. Pushing both magneto switches to 'on', she began to open the throttle fully. Before she had time to react, the turning engine started running, screaming wildly. The aircraft rolled quickly to the left. Ceci instantly grabbed the throttle lever, pulling it fully closed. Without waiting, Catherine pressed the feathering button. Slowly the blades turned, feathered into the airstreams. The vibration almost ceased completely as Catherine shut down fuel and electrical supply to the number three Merlin, finally flicking off its two magneto switches.

When they were on a level keel, there was a moment to take stock. Ceci, able to adjust the rudder trim, relieved her leg. The roar and draught from the open hatch in the aircraft's nose was discomforting but now they had a chance. Where were they? That was the next question. They needed to land. Below, ragged stratus lay over the Pennines, hiding the potential for granite clouds, as their instructors had described them.

Pointing west, they flew towards the Irish Sea. Descending

through the clouds with no real idea where they actually were could be disastrous. Heading west, towards the sea, keeping well north of the Welsh mountains, would allow a safe descent that should keep them clear of any lethal granite clouds lurking among the Pennine hills and valleys, which were covered by a mass of rising condensing moisture swirling in from the Atlantic.

Switching again to instruments, Ceci began the descent, concentrating hard. Catherine had worked backwards from their present situation to try to determine how they had flown and in which direction, taking account of the stronger winds at nine thousand feet. Help from below would not be forthcoming; the Lancaster's radio was inoperative, awaiting suitable tuning crystals at its new squadron.

The late-afternoon light dimmed further as they sank deeper into the grey gloom, rain streaming back across the windscreens. Two thousand feet was indicated on the pilot's altimeter; no sign of the overcast thinning. Swallowing hard, Ceci allowed the rumbling machine to continue very gently downwards. Both girls peered ahead trying to penetrate the impenetrable. The altimeter hands continued backwards, reeling off the numbers; numbers that could be decisive within the next few seconds. For an instant Ceci's mind flew back to Ripon, lost in cloud in the new cerulean blue Spitfire.

Below them, a single ship punched her head through steep seas, hurling green water back across her decks. Seven hundred feet was where the altimeter needles had finally stopped. The ship was the second thing Ceci had seen as they sank relieved, into clear but turbulent air. The first was the welcome sight of the white-strewn ocean. Carefully banking the Lancaster left, they turned back east, flying towards a barely visible coastline through fine rain. Over Liverpool Bay, Ceci adjusted their course, avoiding the docks and city with their attendant flak batteries and barrage balloons. Overhead Chester they prepared for landing back at nearby Hawarden. In the airfield's circuit everything worked. Despite the fire in the engine nacelle above it, the starboard undercarriage extended and locked down in concert with its port twin, as did the flaps. The control tower recognised an aircraft in difficulty by its one engine feathered, and squirted a bright-green beam of light upwards.

Left, off the downwind leg of Hawarden's landing circuit, Ceci peered across at the runway. It began to rain heavily again as she again banked the aircraft very gently, lining up with the runway at one hundred and ten miles per hour. She was glad of her practical experience at Marston Moor, practice-landing a Halifax on only three engines – now she was doing it for real. Adjusting the remaining three throttles to cope with the asymmetric thrust from only three propellers kept her on her toes as she expertly handled the bomber sinking calmly down the glide path.

Once over the threshold she called for throttles closed; Catherine obliged. Three Merlins lapsed into tick-over as she held the machine off, its speed rapidly declining against the wind. She pulled gently back on the column, with a little rudder to straighten her; there was a gentle, single bounce as the huge tyres turned, steaming into rotation on the wet tarmac. Taxiing back towards the dispersal they had left so confidently earlier, they were both quiet. It had been real; a challenging experience. Inside each of them had been unspoken fear but both girls were proud that they had coped without panic in a situation that most male pilots would have found testing. When they had stopped, they looked down at the assembled reception committee; there were worried looks. With the throttles closed, idle cut-off pulled, the magnetos off, the three engines clattered to a halt. The Lancaster sat silent, seemingly as relieved as they were to be safely back. The debriefing was short. Almost before they had clambered into the little van to be taken away to operations, the aircraft was connected to a tractor and towed tail-first into an adjacent hangar. Black, sooty streaks across her starboard wing told of a near-disaster somewhere over harsh Pennine moorlands. Four days later they delivered the Lancaster to a bomber station near Rutland with no problems. It was lost a week later over the Frankfurt.

❖ ❖ ❖

The Danesfield 'family' was still growing. Contractors were constantly erecting new Nissen huts for reconnaissance interpreters. Increasing numbers of PR squadrons and a growing realisation of the value of aerial photography by the army and the Royal Navy meant an ever-increasing stream of intelligence by way of photos landing on an increasing number of desks. The latest batch included the harbours at La Pallice, Brest, Douarnenez and Cherbourg, together with a series of low-level pictures of airfields on the Cotentin peninsula and around the Pas-de-Calais. The latter reconnaissance sorties were extremely dangerous: flying low, hopefully unannounced, across an enemy airfield was, most people thought, the height of folly. But the Air Ministry were keen to know how Goering and his Luftwaffe leaders were disposing their forces, and in particular, where the enemy's night-fighter units were established.

266

The sheaf of pictures that landed on Sarah's desk one morning was larger than usual. Looking quickly through each batch that related to enemy airfields, ports and aircraft, she began to allocate them to the girls and boys in her section. Since Hitler's attack on the Soviet Union they had noticed a reduction in the number of aircraft on most of the Luftwaffe's forward airfields. New free-ranging sorties undertaken by the RAF, usually comprising two Spitfires, and oddly code-named 'Rhubarbs', were aimed at disrupting enemy transport systems and attacking airfields, strafing aircraft and airfield installations. It was very dangerous work. The Germans had proved less than willing to rise and engage the RAF of late, possibly a reflection of their reduced numbers and the shock, in some respects, of their failure to destroy the Royal Air Force in the summer of 1940. Attacking German aircraft on the ground seemed a natural alternative, although Rhubarbs were beginning to prove costly in RAF pilots and machines. Late in the morning Daphne appeared, holding a small file of pictures.

"Sarah, thought you might be interested to see these; the navy section let me have them yesterday. Sorry, haven't had time to get down to you." The black-and-white pictures were high-altitude shots taken by a St Eval PR Spitfire during completion of a reconnaissance sortie over the north Biscay ports. The last three pictures on the film were taken directly over Sarah's three barns. There was a standing order for PR squadrons operating in the area to try to capture high-level photo intelligence of the area around Sizun.

Placing the duplicates under her stereoscope, she looked at the now-familiar site. Grabbing some earlier shots from the safe file, she began to compare current with recent past. There were noticeable changes evident to her expert eye. The two empty fields that never seemed to have any livestock had now been mown; that much was quite clear. The larger one had been cut, it appeared, quite recently. The one that she had observed earlier, some weeks ago, had been cut but its grass appeared to be longer than in the larger field. There were clear track-marks in the second field from the area of the barns to what was probably a general aircraft dispersal area; a discoloured patch some fifty yards away. At the end of the field, where the grass remained untouched, there was a disturbed patch as though something had moved off the mown section for some considerable distance. Daphne stood watching over her shoulder.

"What do you think?" Spending a few more seconds making up her mind, Sarah pushed her chair back noisily and stood.

"It seems probable that they are now using the second field, the more northerly one, for their aircraft take-offs and landings and that one aircraft has probably run off their mown runway area into the longer grass at the end." Daphne nodded, agreeing.

"My interpretation exactly, but have you seen this?" With the tip of her pencil she pointed to some blurry shapes almost hidden on the edge of the surrounding trees. Sitting again, Sarah looked carefully at the shapes. Although far from clear, their profile suggested anti-aircraft guns partially concealed. She'd seen similar objects in other airfield reconnaissance pictures. These, she felt, were definitely anti-aircraft or FlaK installations, probably 88s.

Together the two women studied the three pictures, noting an apparent increase in activity, not just as far as aircraft were concerned, but also in the number of trucks, part-concealed under trees, their positions in one or two instances betrayed by reflections off their windscreens. Interestingly, part of one of the barns had now been painted; the monochrome pictures suggested a crude attempt at camouflage but certainly it stood out less like a sore thumb in the countryside.

Casting her eyes wider, she could see that the narrow road that led directly past the barns had been widened in four places. Daphne said she suspected that they were deliberately constructed lay-bys in the road to allow traffic to pass.

"Probably traffic along this little road is increasing, or is going to increase." Sarah commented, sucking in her breath. As they walked back towards the main house Sarah commented on Daphne's auburn hair and how special it had looked at the squadron party. She was angling, none too subtly, she knew, for some comment from Daphne about her association with the young Canadian pilot with whom she had spent a good deal of that evening. Daphne looked a bit shy and smiled, blushing slightly.

"Oh, he's very nice, bit of a rough diamond. He's been in touch since and we might be going out to dinner next Saturday if he's not on ops." Sarah took her arm for a moment.

"Good, Daphne, good. Don't let him get away, he's a handsome chap." Daphne laughed, embarrassed.

"Yes ... yes ... he is, isn't he?"

Returning to her desk, Sarah booked a phone call to 'Mr Homburg', as he was now irreverently referred to by all who knew him at Danesfield. When the call came she outlined what they had discovered and arranged to send a set of prints to his office by despatch rider, the photos suitably annotated.

SIX

A rickety wooden cart was brought into the yard by the older of Madame Charon's two boys before he left for school; the horse was unhitched and led into an adjacent pasture. Harold Penrose looked around the yard; he guessed seventy feet by one hundred feet. The depth of the muck on its surface, he thought, about a foot. Whatever his estimates, it was an awfully large volume to shift. With no real strategy in mind he started shovelling the brown viscous gloop into the cart, the odour seeming to permeate his being.

Appreciative of his change of scenery and keen to help out, he'd commented on the state of the yard over supper the previous evening. Before he had realised it, he'd managed to volunteer to undertake the odious task. Madame Charon was more than pleased and ladled an extra portion of thick soup into his bowl with a beaming smile. The two boys watched his puppy-like attempts to please, smirking at one another. By lunchtime the cart was about full; from the many splits in its ancient planking small torrents of brown, odorous fluid ran onto the ground. The horse was hitched and the whole stinking mess trundled down the lane to a slurry pit in a nearby field. Risking being engulfed by the turgid mass, he pulled the large rusty pins from the cart's rear tailgate and stood back quickly as it fell, allowing the mass to slide into the pit, splashing and gurgling disgustingly. After lunch – bread, beetroot, some sort of cheese with a very rough red wine – he was back at work. Fortunately it was still bright;

the rain forecast by Madame Charon had not arrived. He worked steadily all afternoon.

He was about to finish and take the last of the day's excavations to the slurry pit when he heard it. It was an odd noise and he looked across the fields for its source, suspecting a farm machine of some sort, although shortages in fuel made this unlikely. He could see nothing working in any of the fields nearby. Then, briefly against a cloud, he caught sight of a small aircraft. At least he thought it was small; it might just be that it was far away. Now it was flying almost directly towards the farm and where he stood. His professional interest was aroused and he spent a moment leaning on his shovel watching the aircraft manoeuvring around the sky about half a mile away. Now he could see; it was a small aircraft. There appeared to be only one person piloting it, in an open cockpit. Harold then sat astride the top rung of the fence that bordered the open side of the yard, watching it. Something was different about it, he could tell. Gradually the machine, driven in his direction by the prevailing wind, drew closer.

The aircraft was flying very slowly and turning with very steep angles of bank quite contrary to all his flying training if one wanted to avoid a stall – particularly as the machine appeared very low. As it banked around for the third time he could see that the wings were different in some respects. The late sun now and again caught the glint of something flashing, fast turning near the leading edges of the wings. At the same moment he realised that, amazingly, there appeared to be no propeller at the nose of the aircraft. What the bloody hell was driving it forward then? 'Is this it?' he wondered. 'Is this the aircraft that the Resistance wanted me to find out more about, capture, even?' Still flying very slowly, the small aircraft suddenly veered away, disappearing behind trees and rising ground. Suddenly he knew this was what he was being asked to steal. Picking up his shovel, he set to work again, worried, intrigued and deep in thought.

❖ ❖ ❖

It was two days before the new moon phase but Michael Kelly left Tempsford early for their forward airfield in Sussex. The loss of three experienced pilots and their aircraft during the last moon-phase operations had left a large hole in their capability; the priority was to find new, night-experienced pilots able to fill their specialist roles. George Hudson had been up to the Air Ministry in London to talk to the air personnel branch with the backing of their AOC, to poach any suitable pilots from other units. Though there were some obvious candidates, their own squadron COs were fighting tooth and nail to keep them. Pilot Officer Hudson's efforts were being thwarted at almost every turn.

There had also been a lengthy meeting with SOE involving Michael Kelly and the squadron's intelligence officers about the loss of pilots, agents and aircraft. For SOE, the loss of a large number of expensively trained and some very experienced and important agents was very compromising. The discussion took note of the fact that before the last moon phase, there had not been any losses of personnel – pilots or agents – although two aircraft had been abandoned and burnt, one getting bogged down in mud, another apparently unable to be restarted after the pilot had shut the engine down while awaiting the late arrival of his returning agents.

A significant fact soon emerged: all the recent losses had occurred within the geographic area operated largely by the

Rouen Resistance circuit. Inevitably, as the facts were pored over, the question of intelligence leaks and betrayal were discussed and beginning to assume importance. It was always accepted as a danger but if it were the case they needed to find a way of locating the leak quickly. One approach was to keep all SOE requests for sorties absolutely top secret on both sides of the Channel with no release of information, even to pilots, until two hours before the sortie was scheduled to leave. Pilots assigned to specific sorties would not be allowed access to telephones or to leave the ops building until it was time to fly. It was a system that had been imposed on bomber crews and seemed to work.

Kelly admitted that normally pilots would probably be informed earlier in the day about a particular night operation so that they could prepare, and of course all the information for that night's sorties would be available to a number of people in operations for some hours before take-offs. SOE also had concerns over the way information was being passed to the various special-duties squadrons; was information being leaked at this point, possibly from someone within their own organisation? The discussion ranged far and wide and a number of new procedures were agreed and set up to try and keep information confidential until the last possible moment.

"After all," Kelly said, "it's hardly going to be the pilots leaking information. Their lives also depend on absolute secrecy."

Everyone present recognised that the other area where schedules of activity could be leaked was from someone within the Resistance circuit who had access to information radioed in code from London. The meeting lasted most of the day and Kelly returned to Sussex tired and frustrated by the more onerous operating conditions that had now been placed on the squadron by the loss of aircraft and almost irreplaceable pilots, and new worries over security.

Just before lunch the following day most of the squadron's pilots had arrived from Tempsford at their Sussex base and were assembled in the small, stuffy crew room. Michael Kelly set out the new standing orders concerning flight briefings and the need for increased security and vigilance. No comments were made but Kelly sensed real concern among his crews.

The first of the new moon's operations was scheduled for that evening; it was to be a dual Lysander operation into a new field that was close to a railway line and the River Risle, south of Beaumont le Roger. The squadron's briefing officer said that the location thirty miles south-west of Rouen should be easy to find owing to the rail lines and river showing up well in any reasonable moonlight. They were going to jointly deliver six agents and to pick up just two. It was planned that the first Lizzie into the field would drop its passengers and take off immediately. The second Lizzie would land once the first aircraft was airborne again. It would drop off its cargo of three Joes and collect two new ones bound for Blighty. The first machine would be piloted by Guy van der Beek, the second by Geoff Standish. Take-off was scheduled for eleven-thirty that evening after a comprehensive secret briefing.

All went well and according to plan. The agents were delivered and both aircraft returned home safely, the second Lysander with its two passengers, contriving to arrive home twenty minutes before van der Beek's returning empty machine. It had left the field seventeen minutes before them. 'A' Flight Commander

Geoff Standish was jokingly accused of pushing the throttle to the firewall in his haste to return, and risking damage to his engine; this he stoutly denied later in the mess over a plate of bacon and eggs. He countered by suggesting that Guy had been trying to fit in a quick trip to Holland to see his girlfriend instead of coming home as ordered.

Flight Lieutenant Standish visited the hangar late the following morning. He wanted the riggers to make some adjustments to the Lysander he had flown the previous evening. Both his and the other Lysander were receiving care and attention from their dedicated ground crews in preparation for the following evening's work. Walking about chatting with the airmen responsible for the aircraft's health, he was struck by something slightly odd. Guy's machine had light-coloured mud splashed over its main landing gear and on the machine's black-painted belly, adjacent to the tail wheel. It was the lightness of the dried soil that attracted his attention, standing out in stark contrast to the aircraft's overall matt-black finish.

It looked as though Guy had landed in a patch of wet ground on the field they had visited together. His own aircraft had odd bits of darker deposits here and there but they were nothing like the light dried mud stuck to Guy's aircraft.

"You need to be more careful, Sir, bringing back 'alf the bleedin' landscape wiv yer." Standish smiled as one of the riggers brought bits of broken branches from the side of the hangar to show him.

"Where did these come from?" he said, taking the broken stems from the diminutive airman.

"Oh, them's from Mr van der Beek's machine, we 'ad ter pull

them out of the tail wheel and undercarriage." 'Odd, how did they manage to get there? I'm sure there were no trees on their approach to the French field,' Standish thought.

Later, in the flight offices, Standish mentioned the branches and muddy condition of his aircraft to Guy van der Beek.

"Well, Geoff, if you will insist on us landing by dark on unknown fields you must expect aeroplanes to get a little dirty from time to time," he laughed as he spoke. But his eyes were not smiling.

"What about hitting trees, Guy? We can't afford to lose any more aircraft or pilots from hitting objects on the ground. As far as I recall there were no trees on the approaches to that particular field last night?" Van der Beek stopped for a moment.

"Well, I don't know, perhaps I was a bit low on landing here and hit the top of the trees at the far end of our runway. I'll be more careful next time, I promise."

After lunch Geoff Standish went for a walk. Trudging through muddy lanes, he then made his way across the farmland that stretched across their landing approach path. There were some young trees, but normally pilots would have been well above them when lined up to land, almost half a mile from the runway's threshold. He studied the trees carefully. There was no sign of any damage to their upper limbs, and anyway, he noted, they were of a different species to the twigs collected from the aircraft. To satisfy himself he walked back through wet grass towards the airfield. The hedge, just before the threshold of the airfield, was low and very recently trimmed. Whatever had been collected by Guy's aircraft had not originated from here either.

❖ ❖ ❖

Harold Penrose was almost enjoying his enforced stay on the farm.

He missed Ceci terribly but at least he was out in the open, not hidden and continually worried. His French was now sufficiently developed so that he was able to accompany Madame Charon into Morlaix on market day to carry her purchases, and for a change of scenery. There was, he admitted to himself, a certain frisson of excitement in sitting at an adjacent table to two German officers in a café. It was true he took a certain delight in studying examples of the 'master race' at close quarters, sipping coffee and brandy, their guttural conversation jarring on his ears. He and Madame Charon conducted a simple French conversation that failed to raise any interest with the Germans. She mentioned that Claude would probably be visiting them in the course of the next few days.

Work on the farm increased as better weather prevailed. Harold became an expert in fencing repairs and was able to milk the cows with the two boys, with whom he was developing a useful relationship; they were great pranksters. As time went on he became aware that the small aircraft he had spotted late that afternoon was appearing in the skies more frequently, often during the late afternoon or early evening. In the past week he had seen it on four separate occasions; each time it seemed to conduct a series of careful manoeuvres that included flying very low and extremely slowly over the countryside. Importantly, he noted that there now appeared to be two different machines. One was painted with a blue-grey camouflage effect, the other looked to be in natural metal.

On Sunday the ubiquitous black Citroën drew up in the finally clean yard. Out stepped Claude and a young woman, Claude grinning, making a show of how it was no longer necessary to wade through farmyard mess. As Madame Charon welcomed them into the parlour Harold realised that he had met the girl before, but where? Patricia smiled as she was introduced to Harold.

"I don't suppose you expected to meet me here 'Arold?" The penny dropped in an instant. "Patricia! Is it you? What on earth are you doing here?"

Sitting at the table, she told of what had happened since they had last met at Sarah's house that long weekend so many months ago. She'd lost weight, he thought. She was very pretty and he felt an odd male urge to protect her but it soon became evident that despite her obvious charms and demeanour, Patricia was a determined young lady intent on freeing her country from its oppressive occupation. Over dinner, which included a freshly killed chicken, Claude explained what had being going on, their communications with London and the plan to gain more information about the German experimental aircraft. Harold spoke of his observations of the strange aircraft that seemed to fly late into the dusk almost every day now.

Acknowledging this, Claude suggested that the Germans were being very circumspect in testing the machines; flying late in the day was probably a good time for them as Allied aircraft on day operations would probably be heading back home and there was less likelihood of the test machines being attacked in the air.

The local Resistance circuit had been considering the situation since Christian's death. Patricia told of the events and how she wished that she had tried to persuade him not to investigate the site further; they had, after all, got most of what they needed to know for the present: that the site was well guarded by day and night. Claude outlined an idea for Harold to think about. His suggestion was that they should somehow, the details were not fully thought through at present, he admitted, get Harold to a point near where the test aircraft were run up before take-off, or, alternatively, and depending on which way they were landing, capture the machine at the far end of the short airstrip after landing, remove the German test pilot from the open cockpit at the point of a gun and hold him hostage while Harold jumped into the machine and flew away. Harold was about to interrupt but Claude continued. If Harold was able to fly off the airstrip he should continue at low level to a location, still in France, where some inspection of the machine could be made, including photography and to check how much fuel was carried and whether it would be possible to fly it over water by night to an airfield in southern England. Finally Harold got to speak.

"Sounds an exciting plan, Claude, but just how feasible is it to capture the machine either before take-off or after landing? You can be sure that the Germans have lots of guards on the site, all armed to the teeth. And ... assuming I am able to take off without being blasted to Kingdom Come, where is this field I fly it to?"

"Yes, 'Arold, I know ze problems and we are still trying to work zem out, but you should remember zis: zey will not be expecting anysing; we will be holding zair test pilot and will zey really try to shoot down one of zair own experimental aircraft? I sink zat ze real issues are wezair we should use a small army of Resistance people to actually attack ze whole site, or we should infiltrate ze area at ze end of ze runway with just two or three people to help get you into ze aircraft after we 'ave removed zair pilot. We now 'ave some aerial photos sent from London of ze site and also a place where you can land which is not more zan twenty kilometres away. One uzair sing, we need to be sure of ze wezair. If ze wezair is bad zey will not be flying and we will be wasting our time."

Harold took a long swig from his glass; the red wine was rough as it coursed down his dry throat. Madame clattered about the kitchen preparing the fish for the evening meal.

"Well, Claude, it's an interesting idea, for sure, but it sounds bloody dangerous ... especially for me," he muttered. Claude smiled.

"Listen, 'Arold, we can arrange for a diversion of some sort to take ze Germans' minds off what we are doing." Patricia turned from looking at the encroaching dusk out of the window.

"One other thing, Claude, if we manage to steal one of their aeroplanes, and if in the process we kill one or two of their soldiers, what will they do to us by way of revenge? You know there are many stories of Germans killing whole villages, innocent men, women, children when the Resistance has managed something spectacular. It's already happened in this region." He looked up at her from his chair, gently stroking the side of his long, thin nose.

"You are right, Patricia, zair is ze possibility of reprisals if we are succeeding. London tells us zat zis operation is vital to ze war effort. Already many innocents have died for ze sake of France and freedom, I don't have any uzer ideas; if you do, please to let me have zem ... and soon."

They finished their meal in virtual silence.

Patricia stayed at Madame Charon's house overnight. Claude left after dinner, and the handshakes were muted. Harold went to bed but could not sleep, his mind churning over Claude's ideas to capture the aircraft. Before he left, Claude agreed to show Harold where they proposed he should land the experimental aircraft after its capture.

They met again the following Saturday but this time Claude had arranged for two horses to be made available for Harold and Patricia to ride across country to a location he had shown them on a pre-war tourist map. The horses were not chestnut thoroughbreds but a pair of working animals more used to pulling a plough or cart than taking an equine stroll through the spring countryside. Both creatures seemed to pick up a sense of adventure and began to act in uncharacteristically frisky fashion.

Patricia had learnt to ride as a very young girl and, despite not having ridden for some years, soon mounted and had the larger of the two horses under her control. Harold's only riding experience occurred when he was six and involved a small, fat donkey on the sands near Teignmouth; he viewed the whole idea with some trepidation. Together they left the farm and headed off south-east, avoiding the town of Morlaix, towards a tiny village: Botsorhel, which lay close to the Douron River. Patricia held onto Harold's reins as they walked side by side. A cool breeze was blowing in off the sea and they were both glad that they had taken Madame Charon's advice to wrap up well; she had lent Harold a thick waterproof jacket that her husband had worn about the farm during previous winter months.

Approaching the main road that ran east to west from Brest to St Brieuc, they watched from a rise in the land. The road was full of military traffic travelling both ways; beyond, they could see the railway track that followed the road for much of its route.

There were no trains running but Harold spotted a stationary train steaming quietly, standing part-concealed behind a line of poplar trees. Its wagons were closed but they could just make out about halfway along its length a flatbed truck with anti-aircraft guns mounted. They waited for almost half an hour, looking for a natural break in the convoys so that they could cross the road unobserved by Germans. Patricia made a mental note to report the traffic and the rail activity to the head of her group. A coded message to London would hopefully bring about disruption of German movements for a while; there was little doubt in her mind that the traffic was vital to the support of U-boat activities out of Brest and Douarnenez – and no doubt providing materials and weapons for 'Hitler's Atlantic Wall'.

Finally, crossing the road, the two riders continued their equine journey until Patricia and Harold decided that a brief stop for lunch was justified; it was nearly five hours since breakfast and the fresh air had enlivened their appetites. They sat together, just off the main road on the side of a farm track. A scrap of canvas that was normally placed under the rough saddle on Harold's horse provided an impromptu picnic rug.

With no warning there came the screeching of tyres on the rough road causing both horses to snort and writhe against their tethers. A German motorcycle–sidecar combination had lurched noisily off the road and roared up the track towards the two picnickers. Its crew of two dismounted and strode menacingly towards the pair sitting in the sunshine eating.

"Papiers!"

Patricia remained seated, feeling through her coat pocket before giving one of the soldiers her forged papers. Penrose stood up and likewise gave the identity papers Claude had given him to the other young soldier. Standing, facing them, he smiled, watching. They reminded Harold of Laurel and Hardy: one fat with all the appearance of being slightly stupid, a little clumsy; the other lean with a pinched face, helmet two sizes too large, his thin lips a callous curl.

They stood together by their vehicle comparing the identity papers, muttering conspiratorially in German. Their eyes flicked from one set of papers to the other. Nervously Patricia tried a smile, flirting slightly with the thin one, who had now shouldered his rifle. The fat one looked at their small bag of bread and fruit. Bending, he grabbed it off the canvas spread and laughed, making some ribald comment that caused his thin colleague to laugh uproariously. The fat soldier took the bag back to their combination and, half-sitting on the nose of the sidecar, began to push their lunch into his face; there was no finesse. Walking over to where Patricia still sat, the thin soldier reached down, pulling her to her feet. She stood, no longer smiling or flirting but white-faced and slightly defiant. He put his hand around her waist and pulled her towards him. Harold made to move towards him. There was a click of a rifle bolt action from the fat soldier. It had turned nasty.

"Hande hoch!"

From his basic RAF escape-and-evasion training Harold knew the German phrase to raise his hands.

Patricia was trying to ease herself from the attentions of the thin soldier, his oversize helmet now sitting on the petrol tank of the machine. He grabbed her by the arm and pulled her chin towards his face; Harold turned slightly, trying to see what the other soldier was doing. The rifle was firmly pointed at him from less than five yards away. Jerking her face away, she brushed his hand from her arm and pulled away from him. He swore something, slapping her hard across the face, grabbing her hair and pulling her viciously towards the cover of some small trees. Now she was screaming. He hit her again. She aimed a kick at his shin with her heavy riding boots. Blood ran from her eye and the corner of her mouth. Harold stood helpless, hands raised, under the barrel of a rifle aimed squarely at his back.

In the trees he threw her to the ground. She recalled smelling the damp earth and leaf mould beneath her, knowing too well his intention. His long coat was open and he was rapidly unbuckling his belt with one hand, pointing the rifle at her with the other, his right hand around the trigger. It was too clear what he wanted her to do.

She stared at him and slowly undid her jacket and the zip at the side of her slacks. Lunging at her, he covered her body with his. She could feel him crudely probing as, with her knees forced up, she reached unobtrusively down to her boots. He was excited and intent on other matters.

The knife was about seven inches long with a sharp, thin point. For some reason she had always known that she risked being assaulted and felt that the weapon could possibly protect her in extremis. He had arched his back ready to enter her. She stared up at him, oddly noticing the fresh green of the emerging leaves just above them; the knife firmly in her right hand out of his sight. As he lowered, ready to enjoy her, she thrust hard.

The knife plunged into his left side, sliding easily through the rib cage, severing the aorta and ripping the lung beside. His cry, mistakenly heard as one of ecstasy by the two other men, was his last. He collapsed onto her, his face resting on her shoulder, wearing a look of disbelief in his final moment.

Rolling sideways, she struggled to push him off to her side, covered in his warm blood. 'Stay calm,' she kept telling herself. He lay on his back, eyes staring to the heavens; very dead, mouth wide open from his final shocked utterance. To allay his comrade's interest she then performed a series of low screams and sighs suggesting delight at being pleasured by a member of the Wehrmacht . Raising her head, she could hear the other German calling what were probably obscenities and encouragement, no doubt thinking that he would be next to enjoy her.

Reaching out, she silently pulled her deceased assailant's rifle towards her from where he had dropped it, cocked. Continuing her passionate noises, she slowly sat and raised the weapon to her shoulder; through the trees she could just see the shoulder and bare head of the other man leaning lazily on the sidecar, still eating. Holding her breath, she squeezed the trigger softly as she had been taught during her agent's training. He died instantly, the unprotected skull exploding in a fine spray of bone and brain tissue.

Penrose turned, expecting to be executed. He, like the fat soldier, had no clue what had really been happening among the trees. She emerged, sobbing, covered in wet blood, her clothes pulled roughly around her. Holding her, he could feel her shaking, muttering something between the sobs. Gently she broke away from him, now businesslike.

"'Arold we must get away from here; first we hide the bodies and the machine." She nodded towards the scene of carnage she had created.

Together and with difficulty they lifted the two dead Germans onto the motorcycle combination. One was unceremoniously thrust head-first down into the sidecar with the two rifles; the other lay firmly jammed down between the bike and sidecar. It was heavy and they were both quite exhausted from pushing the temporary hearse deep into the trees, covering it with branches and brushwood.

"I will speak with Claude; we need to dispose of them properly before the damn Boche find them."

Slowly during the afternoon they made their way back to the farm; Patricia said nothing during their ride. Claude was waiting, having a Pastis with Madame Charon as they slowly clip-clopped into the yard. Penrose dismounted and helped Patricia from her horse. Inside the house the greeting smiles were immediately doused by the two rider's expressions. Claude stoked the fire with logs, the grate soon filled with bright red and orange flames licking up the soot-fringed chimney. Behind its firebricks the hot water boiler sat, absorbing the heat.

Grunting loudly, Madame Charon half-carried Patricia up the steep, narrow stairs clinging onto the banister. In the bathroom she helped the bloodstained, traumatised young woman to strip, pulling her own dressing gown around her. She ran water in the basin for a moment; it was still only lukewarm. Opening a cupboard, she took some soft, clean cloths and dampened them under the warm water. Sitting on the bath edge, looking at the pale Patricia leaning back expressionless in the creaking wicker chair, she tenderly cleaned the blood from her face and chest.

There was a question on her mind. She needed to ask it. She

had to ask it. How could she ask it? How do you phrase it to someone in this state? This was new.

"Un instant, Patricia." Madame Charon left the bathroom and hurried downstairs. Pulling Claude to one side, she started to whisper loudly, her face wild. After a few moments he stood back, upright, patting her on the arm. She hurried out of the kitchen and back up the stairs. Claude turned towards Harold. It was for a moment as though Claude believed that he had raped Patricia. Harold grew angry, calming as Claude turned to using his fractured English. The question arose again.

"'Arold, I need to ask zis question, it is difficult but I am sorry, I must ask it. " Harold looked, ready to answer, whatever the accusation was.

"'Arold ... did ze soldier rape her ... I mean did he ...? " Harold sat rigid, opposite him, across the heavy table.

"Claude, I couldn't see what was happening, one of the bastards had his rifle aimed at me. He took her into the trees, I do not know if he ... er ... entered her. Only Patricia ... knows."

Finally it was running, steaming and splashing into the cast-iron bath with a few perfumed bath salts found from a pre-war birthday present from Madame Charon's missing husband. Madame helped Patricia into the welcoming foam and left, closing the door carefully, carrying Patricia's bloodstained clothes. Her underclothes and blouse were thrown onto the fire; the rest were plunged into a bucket of warm water. They sat mortified over events, still unsure of her 'condition', as Madame Charon delicately put it.

Busying herself, she began to prepare the evening meal. It seemed to Harold to be a comfort reaction, rather as a cat would resort to washing after being frightened; a way of reaching back to prior normality. Forty-five minutes later Patricia came down the stairs, pushing open the kitchen door slowly, wearing a man's dark-red dressing gown, a white towel wound firmly around her head. They looked up, Madame Charon rushing from around the table towards her.

"Ma pauvre petite..." Patricia smiled slightly and sat on a chair pulled up to the fire by Harold. Madame Charon knelt at her side looking up into the girl's ashen face.

"Patricia; je ... " The girl smiled again, briefly touching the woman's worried face. She made clear that her condition had not changed; he was dead before the opportunity could be fulfilled. Claude stood, helping Madame Charon off her knees. Putting on his coat, he left, shaking Harold's hand and kissing Patricia on the top of her head as she sat staring vacantly into the flames. He was going to arrange for the disposal of the Germans and would probably be back in a day or two.

Returning to the farm late the next day in the now-heavily muddied Citroën, Claude had some news for both Harold and Patricia. First, he and some friends had found the two dead Germans and arranged to dispose of them by faking a road accident where the combination had plunged off the main road into a deep ditch and caught fire.

"I hope zey had planned to be cremated," smiled Claude with an uncharacteristic touch of black humour. Over dinner he passed on the instructions sent by SOE in London. Both Harold and Patricia were to return to England leaving in three nights from a field south of Callac near to the banks of Hyeres River. It would be just them in the Lysander returning to England;

the aircraft would be bringing in two new radio operators for other Resistance circuits in the north-west of France. Harold was surprised, wondering why he had waited for so long, then been told to steal an aircraft, and now this, he was to leave without any warning. Patricia sat, not saying anything.

❖ ❖ ❖

Life was proving a tad difficult for Sarah. Jenny, the young fighter pilot's wife who had been taking care of Alistair and Beth in her absences, was leaving. Her husband had been reported missing after a tangle with enemy fighters over France the afternoon before. No one in his squadron had seen what had happened to him once the fighters had been engaged. He was no novice; he'd fought all through the Battle of Britain with four confirmed kills. It seemed there had been no sign of a parachute or even a smoking aircraft diving down. Sarah had gone round to their small cottage about a mile from the airfield as soon as she'd heard the news. Jenny, red-eyed, let her in and offered tea. It was clear to Sarah that the fact had not sunk in; the poor girl was still in shock, denial, even. As she made the tea she talked matter-of-factly about the Red Cross; they had promised to find out what had happened.

"Bob may be alright, a prisoner or wounded, they said." White-faced, Jenny looked across at Sarah for confirmation. She was barely twenty, Sarah guessed.

"Let's wait and see what news comes from the other side, shall we, Jenny?" Stirring her tea, she put the spoon carefully into the saucer. Jenny did the same, looking out of the window at the Sunday-morning sunshine.

"I'm so sorry, Sarah, I can't stay here now. I'm going back to stay with my parents in Tewkesbury. It's going to leave you in the lurch with the children. I did so love looking after them. We were going to start a family after the war... It's just that ... just that this house ... we were so happy here ... I can't ... " The tears streamed down her cheeks from dark hazel eyes. She was so very young, unequipped, looking for comfort, miles from friends and family, alone and now, as far as she was concerned, totally lost, her man, her rock, missing. Sarah stood and walked around behind the girl, who was sobbing now, uncontrollably.

Putting both hands gently on her heaving shoulders, she said, "Jenny, come home with me now. I can't leave you here like this tonight. We can sort out your going home to your parents tomorrow but you're in no fit state to travel anywhere like this." Sarah lifted her from the chair.

"Come on, Jenny, get some things together and let's go home." Twenty minutes later they were on the road. After locking the tiny house before leaving, Jenny carefully, reverently almost, placed the small brass front-door key, with its good luck charm attached, under the doormat.

"He might not have his keys with him," she whispered, standing. Sarah smiled encouragingly. Jenny stayed three days; it gave Sarah a chance to find someone else to care for her two little ones while she and her husband were away so often.

Pauline came to stay. She was round, ruddy, of good humour and, in less than a day, totally adored by both children. Living in, she took control of the house and its running. Coming from a local family, her father and stepmother ran the pub in the next village. She seemed to solve all of Sarah's problems in one fell swoop. Pauline had been married for a short while, just before the outbreak of war, but her husband, an infantryman, had been killed on the beaches at Dunkirk during the final few desperate hours of the evacuation. He'd been machine-gunned by an aircraft while standing chest-deep in water awaiting a boat. His body had not been found before the last of the army had left. A rare weekend off allowed Sarah and Michael up to London for a show, followed by dinner on the way back, at a quiet restaurant in Farnham.

The signal from SOE proved a bit of a surprise for Michael. Sitting alone in his office with its window overlooking the airfield wide open, he wondered if he should tell Ceci of its contents. The instruction was for a delivery of two Joes to a known field near Callac, and the collection of a downed airman and a female Joe; unusually, a name was given: Flying Officer Harold Penrose; no name was given for the Joe. Delivery and collection were scheduled for Wednesday night, two days hence. Filing the signal in the safe, he thought hard about the matter, conscious of his own security rules, then stood for a moment, staring out at the expanse of grass with various aircraft scattered about, some with mechanics working on them poised on ladders and gantries.

During their last week at Tempsford before moving south again for the new moon phase, they'd had two new Lysanders delivered to replace those recently lost. The pilot situation had not improved, however; they had had only one new pilot join them – to replace three lost, and he was untrained in their special work. Michael decided not to contact Ceci about the imminent return of her fiancé but to keep it to himself for the while. He was less concerned about her leaking information and possibly compromising the sortie than worried that something might happen to delay Harold's return. Recent disasters with the Lysanders were colouring his rationale, he knew, but there was no point in getting her excited, and then having something go wrong.

The new moon phase was three nights old and Kelly had flown each night along with his two remaining flight commanders and some of the other pilots and navigators. Despite the operational workload, the aircraft were standing up well to the demands placed on them. A combination of Pilot Officer George Hudson's insistence on prompt response for parts and spares made the engineering officer's job of ensuring maximum serviceability much easier. The ground crews, unsung heroes, were doing a wonderful job; he made a mental note to reward their unstinting efforts with some sort of party when they all returned to Tempsford in a couple of weeks.

On Wednesday, early in the afternoon, the schedule was altered to take account of new instructions from SOE and MI9 for the now-named Operation Giselle. The number of agents to be delivered into Callac had been increased that night, so now they would have to use two Lizzies instead of one; the field in question was too short to accommodate a loaded Hudson, which would have carried all six Joes with ease. Geoff Standish and Guy van der Beek were on standby; two hours before take-off they were informed of the detail of the sortie. Both pilots had been to the area around Callac before and they were familiar with its geography and the particular field in question. The weather, according to the Met, was forecast to be good until early dawn, when there may be some mist forming, but they should have little trouble from that quarter. Geoff Standish would take and collect three passengers and arrive first at the field. When he was loaded and ready to leave the field he would call in the second aircraft by radio to deliver; it would then fly back to base empty.

Passing overhead the small town of Callac, Standish flew south following occasional silver reflections from the small river. As he calculated his timing to the site a precise burst of a single Morse letter met his downward gaze. Below, the field's shadowy shape became familiar as he turned gently back towards Callac intending to land towards the south to benefit from a slight breeze from that direction. As he turned the aircraft he could make out the classic positioning of the three white torch lights, and prepared the aircraft for landing. The moon was quite bright and he decided not to use his powerful landing lights on the first attempt. If he had to go around for another attempt he would probably use them but felt no point in illuminating now, potentially alerting every German within ten miles to his presence.

Over the edge of the field he cut the power as he passed the single white light on his left marking the beginning of the landing run. The ground seemed solid and he braked firmly bringing the ungainly machine almost to a halt before pushing left rudder and brake pedal over and applying a fist of throttle, causing the Lysander to swing around, heading back to the landing threshold ready for quick take-off. As they taxied he heard the hatch on the rear cockpit slide back as his three Joes prepared to exit the machine. The accommodation was very cramped and they would no doubt be pleased to get out and stretch their limbs. As the aircraft rocked gently to a halt, the three agents poured down the fixed boarding ladder and ran with the reception committee's grey shadows into the surrounding darkness.

Within seconds Harold Penrose and Patricia were being encouraged up the ladder and the hatch was slid shut. There were a few muffled words from inside.

"Au revoir. Bonne chance!" responded the head of the reception committee. Quickly completing his pre-take-off vital actions, Standish pushed the throttle lever firmly forward while simultaneously making a quick radio transmission calling in van der Beek. Roaring healthily, the big monoplane rumbled down the narrow grass strip and was soon into the air clawing its way skywards. The message flew instantly through the ether and the second Lysander landed within three minutes of Standish and his two excited passengers becoming airborne. Van der Beek glanced around as his three passengers almost fell down the ladder and, like earlier arrivals, were whisked away with only a backward glance and wave. Leaning out and down, he shook the hand of the Resistance leader and, closing the cockpit window, followed Standish into the air.

Geoff Standish climbed to only seven hundred feet before levelling off, not keen to gain too much height for fear of roaming night fighters, Axis or Allied. Intending to fly back in company with van der Beek, he continued south a short distance then made a wide circle over the sleeping countryside, aiming to fly south of Callac, where he hoped to pick out the other machine as it became airborne. The field was right on the nose below him and he congratulated himself for such an accurate piece of flying in the near-darkness. Passing to the east of the landing site he could just make out the dark shape and occasional exhaust flare of the second Lysander as it rushed down the grass. In the fragmentary moonlight it was difficult to track but now and again he could see it climbing and turning slowly on an easterly course, not for England. Circling, Standish watched, originally intending to follow van der Beek across the Channel and back to their forward airfield in Sussex.

But the Dutchman did not immediately head north, continuing instead along a track just a few degrees north of east. With van der Beek's Lizzie about half a mile ahead and now slightly above him Standish could see its opaque outline quite clearly against the softer dark night sky. Following, dog-like, for nearly thirty minutes, Standish was becoming increasingly concerned at the leading Lysander's failure to turn north for the sea and home. Increasing speed, he intended to fly carefully past the other machine and flash his torch at its pilot, perhaps to get some reaction.

He thought that possibly van der Beek's compass was acting up, or there was some other problem that was making him pursue his current unusual and potentially dangerous heading. Just as he began to slowly gain on the lead machine in the dark, it slowed and began descending, passing just ahead of him. Looking down as he passed, off to his left Standish could see it dropping towards moon-dappled farmland turning slowly left; now and again a fragmentary moonbeam would reflect from its polished canopy. From the ground he thought he caught a brief flurry of red flashing lights; possibly from a car. Standish followed, banking his machine around in a large circle, watching carefully, his engine gently ticking over. It looked as though van der Beek had a problem and was making a forced landing in a very large field. Glancing quickly at his chart using the torch, he estimated that they were somewhere near Lisieux, south of Le Havre and south-west of Rouen.

The moon slid stealthily behind an encroaching bank of solid cloud and Standish lost sight of his colleague within a few seconds. Circling the area, he kept looking, his two passengers wondering why the Lysander was behaving so peculiarly over enemy territory. Finally, unable to discern just what was happening in the blackness below, Standish made a quick note of his approximate position then turned to head north, intending to fly low over the marshlands and ox-bows of the River Seine as it wound its way westwards from Rouen until finally emptying into the Channel. There was no activity over the port of Le Havre; its flak guns were silent but he had no wish to alert them and covered the route between the two cities, hugging the ground until crossing the French coast somewhere near the village of Veules les Roses.

He arrived at the squadron's forward airfield just after two-thirty on a cold and dank morning. Patricia was met by two people from SOE, a man and a rather stern-looking woman in a dark-grey full-length coat, her hair pulled back into a tight bun; she was, no doubt, not keen to be standing about on an exposed airfield at such a time in the morning. Taking a brief moment to say goodbye to Harold and Standish, Patricia was driven swiftly away, yawning heartily through the window. Harold Penrose was warmly greeted by Michael Kelly, who had remained in the ops room until his crews had safely returned. He took Harold to the mess for a very early breakfast, which was followed by a welcome bath and an opportunity to sleep safe, under guard. Kelly made clear that he was to speak to no one about where he had been and what he had been doing, and that he was strictly bound by the Official Secrets Act. An appointment with MI9 and the SIS was scheduled later that afternoon; Harold was technically the responsibility of Squadron Leader Kelly until then.

About an hour after Standish had returned, the second Lysander landed and taxied to the dispersal area. Van der Beek climbed down from the cockpit looking pale and tired. The unit intelligence officer had been briefed by the flight commander about his observations of van der Beek's machine over France and was a little surprised to be talking to the tired Dutchman. The pilot begged a cigarette and they began the debriefing. The delivery had gone well and he'd been airborne from the field south of Callac in less than ten minutes. On leaving the area he reported that he thought he had seen the shadow of another aircraft and, fearing a night fighter on patrol in the area, had climbed to only about two thousand feet and proceeded towards the coast aiming to leave France over the Ile de Bréhat as usual. However, he said, still believing himself shadowed by a night fighter, he decided to turn east for a while before heading north again for the French coast, the Channel and England. He also reported that his compass appeared to be malfunctioning. The intelligence officer made notes about the sortie and left the pilot to return to the mess and his breakfast.

❖ ❖ ❖

Unusually, the meeting with MI9 and the SIS took place at the Citadel, the centre of wartime operations close to St James's in London. A secure room was arranged and Harold arrived feeling a little tired and numb from recent events, also slightly bemused at the attention he was getting. Smartly dressed now in a new RAF Flying Officer's uniform obtained that very morning, he sat in a comfortable sofa opposite three men in armchairs: two civilians and an RAF Group Captain. He was offered coffee and it was explained that they were still waiting for another member of their team to arrive. Within a few minutes the door opened and a young WREN ushered an out-of-breath Flight Officer Sarah Kelly into the room. Harold did a double-take.

"Sarah!" She was less surprised; the intelligence people had indicated earlier that Harold Penrose had returned from France and would be attending their meeting. The three men looked on as Harold and Sarah laughed and smiled at one another. Standing, Group Captain Hawkins took control.

"Well, Penrose, you may be wondering why you have been suddenly plucked from your comfortable rural life in France and returned to England?" There was a sparkle in the group captain's eyes and a slight smile about his lips. "We thought it prudent that we fill you in on some of the details about the aeroplane you have been observing from Madame Charon's farm, so that you are better equipped to fly it when we send you back over the weekend."

"Back, Sir?" Harold looked around at the others; the MI9 man was nodding.

"Yes, I'm afraid so, old chap; we'd still like you to steal the aeroplane with the help of the Resistance and bring it home so that our boffins can take a look at what the Germans have been up to. I'm so sorry; was that not explained to you before you left?" The group captain knew full well that it hadn't been.

The following two days were spent initially at a government research establishment at Teddington, just outside London in Middlesex, then later at Boscombe Down in Wiltshire. The scientists there had spent some time making working models of the machine whose pictures had been collected by the young

Canadian PR pilot, Mossman. Harold saw the model machine fly but clearly they had some way to go in development; after two short flights it had crashed to the ground, causing significant damage. But the model was a useful proof of concept, they all agreed. It was then back to the classroom and Harold was able to provide information about his observations of how the piloted machine flew, as seen from his vantage point at the Charon farm.

That it would fly very slowly was not in doubt: he had seen it and the calculations completed by the boffins suggested that an aircraft configured as depicted in the photographs would be difficult if not impossible to stall. They spent time talking about the likely flying characteristics of the machine, remembering that on some German aircraft the throttle operated in the opposite way to British machines; it could be a real safety issue if in the heat of a moment he pushed or pulled it the wrong way. There was a worry over how much fuel the aircraft could carry. Inevitably they all agreed that successfully stealing a machine would be pointless if it could not be ferried back to England, ideally under its own power. They had no idea what sort of engine was employed to drive the wing-mounted rotating wing fans and could only make educated guesses at fuel capacity, consumption and duration based on the size of the machine and where fuel tanks might be positioned based on similar-sized small aircraft.

At Teddington, poring over sheets of dense calculations, the head of the aeronautics research department suggested that he should aim to fly it at about seventy miles per hour, or about one hundred and twenty kilometres on German instruments. It then struck Penrose that the machine's airspeed indicator would be calibrated in metric units and that he would have to learn the German for all of the likely cockpit instruments and the information they would provide. There were no photographs of the cockpit and its contents available, so, it was jointly decided that all possible options were to be covered; it was a long list. The aircraft's rate of climb was thought to be quite good from Harold's own observations but it was suggested that he fly only two or three hundred feet above the sea if he did manage to get away.

If escape was achieved with sufficient daylight, escort fighters would provide cover against attack; it was almost certain that if the machine was successfully stolen, the Germans, on realising, would alert every fighter airfield in the north of France to stop him reaching England. And when he did reach England the RAF would arrange for him to be met by an aircraft of one sort or another capable of matching his slow airspeed to escort him to a suitable airfield. Fighters like the Spitfire or Hurricane would have a problem matching his low speeds; an alternative aircraft, possibly a Lysander, would be able to guide him to the chosen airfield, being vectored onto him by the RAF's experienced fighter interception service. Harold was informed that landing speeds had been estimated at around fifty to sixty kilometres per hour, possibly a little less.

The detail of how they proposed to steal the aircraft on the ground was going to be left to the local Resistance circuit but would be a combined operation, co-ordinated with the SOE, who would arrange with the RAF some diversionary activity to occupy the Germans, and to provide the escort cover if Harold managed to get away. He knew that any attempt to snatch a machine would have to be at the end of the day; dusk would hopefully provide some cover for his escape and the chances of any fighter escort in near-darkness was slim.

Their proposed plan included Claude's originally suggested option to fly the aircraft to a selected field only a few kilometres from the three barns airfield near Sizun and to hide there for a day or two in the woods that almost surrounded three sides of the landing ground. With luck, the Germans would assume that the machine had escaped directly across the Channel. It would be the field that he and Patricia had been making for before their disturbed picnic meeting with the two German soldiers. In that situation they would take the opportunity to photograph every detail of the German aircraft before Harold attempted a take-off and flew it to England. In this way, if for any reason he did not manage to make it across the Channel, they would at least have a clutch of relevant pictures and some dimensions on which to further calculate information, and to build their own version of the unique aircraft.

Before leaving Teddington, Harold was given a file of papers that would provide him with most of the information thought relevant to the aircraft and its operation. The papers had been cleverly laid out as a brochure from a well-known English heating-boiler manufacturer, with information about pump speeds, heating levels and graphs appearing to relate to a boiler but actually referring to key operating information for the unique aircraft. Only Harold and the Teddington and Boscombe boffins were aware of how the brochure layout could be interpreted.

He was to be flown back to the field near Callac on Sunday evening; the group captain agreed, against his better judgement, he said, that Harold should be given a few hours with his fiancée.

Late on Saturday afternoon, his mind full of key information, an official car took him into Hampshire and the home of Sarah and Michael Kelly; Ceci arrived just after eight in the evening. She had no idea that Harold had returned home, albeit briefly. Her face lit up as she was shown into the kitchen, where he stood waiting; there had been no intimation to her of his return. Within seconds she was sobbing tears of happiness as he held her close. Discretion dictated that the others leave them for few minutes as they kissed and held each other.

Later, Sarah busied herself around the kitchen with Pauline's help, the two children running to and fro with the general excitement of the situation. Harold mentioned as casually as he could that he would be returning to France soon.

"Harold! You've only just got back, how can they send you out again?" Her happiness clouded, Ceci sat in the lounge next to him on the sofa, the log fire roaring in front of them.

"When are you going? Why?" He looked at her worried and tense face. "I'm going soon and will be back as quickly as possible. It won't be like last time. Everything is arranged. They're expecting me. I have a little job to do, then I will be back. Please don't worry, Ceci, it'll be OK, I promise." He smiled and kissed her gently but she was not convinced and spent the whole evening holding onto him, watching him. They spent the night in each other's arms; Harold entered her gently and she responded with passion as they made love during the dark hours. Later, the following afternoon, he suggested that they should get married.

Harold was scheduled to leave for an airfield in the early evening, where he was to receive a final briefing with SOE and SIS, and to be introduced to the Resistance member who would accompany him in the Lysander back to Callac. SOE and the intelligence services, between them, hoped that they had formulated a viable plan for stealing the aircraft.

❖ ❖ ❖

The orderly corporal was instructed that there were to be no interruptions during the meeting. Michael Kelly sat in his large, wooden swivel chair behind his desk, moving it slightly from side to side as he spoke. His flight commander, Geoff Standish, sat on the edge of the sturdy well-used oak desk smoking a pipe and facing the other participant, David Rawlinson, perched comfortably on the arm of a dark-brown leather chair that had clearly seen better days. They were there with fresh tea to discuss the odd behaviour of their Dutch squadron member, Guy van der Beek.

To date, no one had tackled the Dutch pilot about his landing near Rouen. Intelligence had advised against it for the moment and he had been given the impression that they accepted his story of a possible night fighter lurking and a problem with his steering compass. Geoff Standish mentioned the light-coloured mud and bits of trees he'd seen on van der Beek's aircraft in the hangar after their dual delivery and collection some weeks earlier. And they discussed the fact that van der Beek had arrived back at base well after Standish, despite having left the drop-off field well before him. One other fact that had come to light was that the Chiefy in charge of Lysander maintenance could find no fault with the compass after a compass swing, or any other instrument in van der Beek's aircraft.

They agreed that van der Beek needed to be watched; everyone felt that SOE as well as the SIS should be brought into the picture.

Kelly spoke with his contact at SOE requesting a meeting as soon as possible. In the meantime van der Beek was to be given three days' leave – he was due it shortly anyway – and not to be allowed to participate in any further operations until something had been sorted out. Kelly was aware that the loss of yet another pilot meant that further pressure would be placed on the squadron's remaining crews in meeting their special commitments. The odd behaviour of van der Beek had raised serious suspicions; too much rested on their clandestine sorties being carried out in total secrecy to allow a security leak.

The operation that was to take Harold Penrose and the SOE radio operator to France was code named 'Cri-Cri'. English connotations for such a name were not of the best, it being interpreted as Cry–Cry, suggesting tearfulness and failure by Harold and Michael. However, once it was explained patiently by the head of SOE's French operations that the French for grasshopper was Cri-Cri there seemed to be a certain logic to the name for such an expedition – hopefully hopping in and hopping out again. The sortie was scheduled to depart their forward Sussex airfield at eleven-thirty on the Sunday evening; the delivery Lysander pilot was to be Flying Officer Paul Mossman.

With the kitchen clock showing half past six, Ceci clung to Harold, begging him to be careful. Outside, the driver of the official car waited patiently as final goodbyes were said. She watched as he closed the door, and the car, with its slit headlamps, moved away from the house up the curving driveway to the lane and main road beyond. By seven-fifteen they were entering the RAF airfield and driving slowly towards the operations room and aircraft dispersals where the Lysander sat, black and near ready.

They were a little early; only the fitters were about the aeroplane, checking and filling fuel and oil tanks. Michael Kelly appeared out of the surrounding dusk; he and Penrose walked across the damp grass to the ops room, where a boiling urn provided hot water for tea. Harold received his final briefing.

Sitting and looking out of the dark windows, Harold thought of Ceci as he watched the moon begin its long ascent. She'd been very brave and he was lucky to have such a plucky young woman as his future wife, he knew. Ceci had told them all over dinner the previous evening about her incident with the Lancaster; he'd sat open-mouthed listening. He considered for a moment that she was actually better qualified than he was in flying terms; he was, after all, only qualified to fly single-engine aircraft.

A car pulled up outside and two people got out, one carrying a small bag. It was Patricia. She closed the ops room door and turned towards him.

"My God, Patricia. You're not going back?" She half-smiled.

"And you too, I see, 'Arold. We need to be more careful, I think. People will begin to talk!" Despite her recent experiences she still kept a certain sense of humour. Paul Mossman shook hands with his two passengers and the SOE representative, helping Patricia and Harold climb aboard the Lysander and closing the hatch once they were seated and strapped in. Climbing up into his cockpit, he prepared to start the engine, one of the aircraft fitters turning the handle that provided energy to the inertia starter. Everyone else moved away and watched silently. With a final wave from pilot and passengers, the Lizzie moved off towards the runway, which was lit for his take-off by a few paraffin-fuelled goose-neck flares, their pungent, thick smoke catching the watchers' noses now and again.

Invisible in the dark at the far end of the grass runway, the watchers heard the engine note rise as Mossman commenced his take-off roll. Against the well-spaced flickering flares the aircraft could occasionally be seen as it progressed down the field, its black form finally climbing into the night. Completing his post take-off checks, he allowed the laden aircraft to climb slowly, heading towards Selsey Bill on the coast, their normal point of departure for France. The RAF radar plotters were just able to catch the radar returns from the Lysander as it gradually ascended, levelling off at two thousand feet. The Met men had warned Mossman of the possibility of thunderstorms moving north-east into Finistere from Biscay as the night progressed, but he hoped to be well clear of the area before they put in their dramatic appearance. Behind, Harold and Patricia sat looking down at the sea, its luminescence easily visible from above as small waves ran unimpeded up-Channel. As a pilot, Penrose was less relaxed than the trusting Patricia; with no access to the aircraft's controls he was distinctly uncomfortable.

Manoeuvring around the Cherbourg peninsula and Nazi-occupied Channel Islands, the aircraft descended to only a few hundred feet as it approached the French coast. Far out to their right they could see occasional brilliant flashes of lightning as prevailing south-westerly winds drove the dark, menacing and saturated cumulonimbus clouds towards the mainland out of the Atlantic.

Keeping a good lookout about them, Mossman began to time their run from the coast to the landing field. Glancing up to check on the scattered clouds and the moon's position, he was stunned to see a dark-grey shape barely one hundred feet above them on a similar track. How could he not have seen it earlier, he wondered, and was angry with himself. Not wishing to draw attention to them by manoeuvring out of the aircraft's blind spot, he sat for a moment watching the machine droning along unaware above them.

It was British; looking hard, he could just make out the roundels on the underside of the wings. It appeared to be a large four-engine bomber; Halifax or Stirling, he wasn't quite sure. Friendly or not, Mossman knew that in the dark all cats are grey and it would probably open fire if they were observed. As they were now both well over French occupied territory, he could be sure that the tail gunner should be fully alert to possible enemy night-fighter attack. It struck him that the machine above was travelling quite slowly, certainly not at its normal cruising speed, where it would easily overhaul the Lysander. Even in the darkness he could see that the aircraft had its flaps partly extended, aiding its handling at such a low speed. However, it was continuing to move slowly ahead above them. Soon they would be exposed to the vigilant downward stare of its rear gunner if they continued as they were.

Still peering through the Perspex canopy above him, he saw something that increased his worries tenfold. As it slowly moved ahead of them, Mossman could see the bomber's huge bomb-bay doors opening in its belly.

At that moment the huge aircraft banked slightly right and their paths slowly diverged; Mossman held his breath. He surmised that it was going to bomb a target around Brest from very low level; a night precision attack, probably one of Don Bennett's

Pathfinder crews. Their own target, a field, should be four minutes away and Mossman began preparations for a landing, keeping an eye on the ground ahead for some sign of recognition. Already high-level cloud was obscuring the moon, and the land below was becoming increasingly difficult to interpret in the growing shadowy darkness.

Then he saw it: the road, railway and a small river running parallel for a short distance. The field, he knew, lay slightly to the south and left of this landmark. Studying the ground, he waited for the single prearranged Morse letter to be discreetly broadcast into the night sky. Nothing. Flying back over the area, he studied the ground again; still nothing signalled to his searching eyes. Perhaps the reception committee had been delayed or had called off the delivery due to circumstances beyond their control; the German-imposed curfew was often a problem. Flying around the area at low level for too long was going to attract attention, but he decided to make one final pass over the field. Approaching, he noticed the black shape of a rapidly moving vehicle on the road, its shaded headlamps flashing on and off in quick succession for few seconds. Odd, he thought, was it the reception committee late to receive, or was it a trap?

Opening the throttle while rapidly raising the Lysander's flaps, he climbed away back into the almost safe blackness and headed north, back towards the Channel coast. Out beyond the coastline, over the Channel and deep in the dark, he circled for few minutes, then made a decision. Heading south again, he recrossed the coast and again began to time his approach to the field south of Callac. A well-timed break in the growing overcast allowed him to pick out the field again. On this occasion a single Morse letter curved up towards him through the dark in a series of white dots and dashes. Acknowledging briefly with the aircraft's downward identity light, he again went through his preparations for landing. The first lamp in the field was in its usual place, as were the other two, marking the end of the landing run. Shutting the throttle fully on passing the first lamp on his left, he allowed the aircraft to settle onto uneven pasture. With a stiff breeze almost directly on the nose, the aircraft slowed rapidly; turning, he taxied bumpily back up the field, hearing activity in the cabin behind him.

Once they had stopped, Harold was out first, helping Patricia down the ladder with her small bag. The head of the reception committee, his hair and coat blowing in the idling prop-wash, reached up to Mossman and shook his hand, apologising for their delay, indicating that he was placing a package in the rear cabin. Before hurrying away with the reception committee, Harold and Patricia managed to wave up at Paul Mossman, sitting high up in his cockpit. Pulling his facemask away, he smiled broadly down at them, shouting something they couldn't hear above the clattering of the slowly turning engine. All secure, the Lysander was soon racing down the field towards the two lamps forming the foot of the standard inverted 'L'. Being much lighter than on arrival, it was soon airborne and turning left, heading north again.

Back in Sussex, Mossman made his usual classic three-point landing. With the engine shut down, he climbed stiffly down from the cockpit and made his way up the ladder to the rear cabin. A sizeable box lay jammed awkwardly on the floor. It was heavy and difficult to catch hold of but he managed to lift it and placed it with a thump on the ground. One of the aircraft riggers cut the cords securing the lid; Mossman lifted the flaps. Inside, in the torchlight, were cheeses, paté, red wine, some Chanel No 5, and other goodies quite unobtainable in England since before the war started. It was a token from grateful Frenchmen and women in appreciation of the dangerous work undertaken by the squadron. Sharing out the contents of the box, Paul Mossman made sure he got a bottle of Chanel No 5. It was for Daphne.

❖ ❖ ❖

Worried, Claude hurried them stumbling in the dark across a ploughed field towards the road. Partially concealed against a low hedge, the ubiquitous black Citroën waited. In the driver's seat sat the mute girl. Seeing Harold, she smiled and nodded a greeting as they piled into the car. Driving unlit and swiftly along the narrow road, they briefly saw the black silhouette of the Lysander against racing moonlit clouds as it turned over them, heading north. Keeping to narrow, muddy sideroads, they progressed towards the farm near Terenez that they had both left so thankfully only a few hectic days ago.

He tried to relax; beside him Patricia had actually fallen asleep, she seemed to have no fear, he thought. They came suddenly to a halt and Penrose was immediately wide awake. Claude got out, leaving the front passenger door slightly open. He carried a Sten gun as he walked silently and cautiously ahead around a long curve in the road, finally disappearing from sight. Harold looked carefully about in the intermittent moonlight. It must be the darkness playing tricks, he thought. Sitting more upright and alert, he stared around the shadowy scene and down a narrow cart track that went off through some trees and bushes to his left. It seemed vaguely familiar. Eyes suddenly widening, he realised that it was familiar, even in near-darkness; it was the very place where he and Patricia had stopped with their horses to eat a picnic barely two weeks back. Somewhere, just a few yards down the track, they had left the two German bodies in their motorcycle combination. What had Claude done with them, he wondered. Through the open passenger door he imagined there came a faint odour of burnt rubber.

Claude, shadow-like, returned, silently and slowly beckoning the car forward. Gently pushing the front passenger door closed, he walked alongside the slowly moving Citroën, his weapon at the ready. As they rounded the curve, ahead lay the main Brest road. From time to time shaded lamps of a vehicle would pass across their limited field of view. Everyone knew that they could only be German vehicles at this time of the early morning.

Suddenly Claude raised his hand and the car stopped, the mute girl studying his every gesture through the windscreen. Staying within the shadows afforded by trees, Claude moved almost up to the main road. They could see him watching, his head turning this way, then that. Suddenly he raised his hand, its whiteness easily visible; the girl tensed and engaged a gear. As his hand flashed down she pushed the accelerator to the floor. Roaring, the car shot forward into the darkness ahead, crossing the main road in a series of resounding thumps and lurches. Harold was thrown back into his seat, Patricia awoke and reached out for his hand, mumbling. They had stopped in a very narrow tree-lined lane opposite. The driver turned off the engine and they waited, windows wound down. Three minutes later Claude appeared, opening the front passenger door, slightly out of breath, the Sten gun now slung over his shoulder. The remainder of their journey back to the Charon farm was uneventful despite the tension within the black Citroën.

She drove the Citroën straight into a storage barn, its doors left conveniently open. They all got out, struggling around in the darkness bumping into the sharp corners of farm implements and empty cattle stalls. Penrose helped Claude close the big, heavy wooden doors, dropping a large piece of rough timber into its metal hasps securing them. Inside the farmhouse they were greeted by a sleepy Madame Charon. They were shown quickly to their rooms and soon all were asleep except Claude. He sat keeping a watch on the surrounding countryside from two large windows at either end of the landing at the top of the stairs, smoke curling almost permanently from Gauloises hanging from his lips. When Harold and Patricia arrived down in the kitchen for breakfast later that morning, Claude, his attractive mute driver and the Citroën had been gone for three hours.

❖ ❖ ❖

Sunday at last, thought Sarah as she awoke with Michael still fast asleep beside her; the first time in some weeks. It was still early. Exceptionally, neither of the children had woken and the early chorus of birds came from the slightly open window. Down the hall Daphne occupied the guest bedroom that looked out over the orchard. Lunch was going to be interesting; she had persuaded Michael to invite Paul Mossman and David Rawlinson if they could manage to get away.

There was the vague drone of an aircraft somewhere overhead as she slowly and carefully got up and made for the bathroom. On her way downstairs she could see light squeezing from under the kitchen door; inside, Pauline was already dressed and had started to prepare a large piece of prime and illicit beef acquired from one of her father's farmer friends. Sipping a cup of tea, with her dressing gown drawn tightly around her, Sarah stepped outside into the garden. It was cool, the smell heavenly, fresh and full of the many scents of the countryside; as she sat on a damp garden bench she pondered man's need to kill and destroy in such a world.

By late morning Michael Kelly was playing in the sun-filled garden with two boisterous children, each intent on climbing all over him despite his tickling them until they fell off. Something that sounded like a disabled tractor approached the house up the curving drive until, finally, six inquisitive eyes, watching from over the garden hedge saw an ancient car finally lurch to a halt, steam pouring from under its bonnet and a pall of black smoke trailing its rear exhaust. Out clambered David Rawlinson and Paul Mossman, relieved, laughing and apologising for their noisy arrival. Ushered by Michael into the house, led enthusiastically by Beth and Alistair, all congregated in the kitchen, where Pauline was trying to organise the final elements of lunch. Daphne came in from the dining room, where she had been preparing the table.

Seeing the two uniformed figures, she did a classic double-take. Her face broke into a huge smile on seeing Paul Mossman standing by the stove, in his hand a small box with a huge red bow attached.

"Sarah, you never told me!" Daphne shrieked in mock anger, hands up to her radiant face. The children bounced around the company, their bright eyes on two packages held by David Rawlinson.

"Is there anyone here called Alistair?" David held up the

package, looking around the kitchen deliberately ignoring the small boy leaping up and down excitedly around his feet.

Eventually the teasing ceased and both boy and girl were tearing at the paper surrounding the impromptu gifts. For the next hour Alistair could be heard demonstrating the noise of an aeroplane as he flew his tin model Spitfire around the house and garden. Beth carried the rag doll carefully in her arms, talking to it as she went upstairs to her bedroom. Daphne and Paul went into the garden together. Unfazed, Pauline continued with her preparations, sipping now and again from a large glass of red wine, until, by one-thirty, all was ready. The lunch was long and relaxed, the meat supreme, with fresh home-grown vegetables, the first time they had enjoyed such a luxury for almost a year. Pauline had excelled herself; despite wartime rationing she had managed by fair means and foul to produce a meal that would have put even the Ritz in the shade, including some bottles of near-unobtainable Bordeaux.

The men volunteered to wash up. Pauline insisted on supervising. As late-afternoon shadows lengthened into early evening some of the company prepared to leave. David Rawlinson and Paul Mossman were returning to Tempsford, and Daphne, despite attempts to persuade her otherwise, intended to drive back to Danesfield to be ready for new batches of photos that would be delivered from RAF Benson and elsewhere early on Monday, after reconnaissance operations over the weekend. Before they left, Paul asked if everyone would please gather in the kitchen. Holding Daphne's hand self-consciously, she blushing slightly, he announced that they were engaged and were intending to marry as soon as they could both get leave. Sarah ran around the table and hugged them both; the others clapped and offered congratulations. Pauline found a bottle of whisky and they drank to the health and happiness of the couple. Daphne and Paul kissed each other goodbye; they had met just twice before.

❖ ❖ ❖

Claude had left a message with Madame Charon for Harold and Patricia. They were to have a meeting with members of the local Resistance committee in two days. They were to begin planning the detail of SOE's proposed capture of the German experimental aircraft and to communicate their needs for special equipment and possibly any diversionary activity by the RAF to London before the end of the week. Patricia had spent most of her waking hours in England discussing ideas and possible options with SOE and SIS personnel.

With some time on their hands the two decided to search for a new field in which to land the stolen aircraft, should that option become a necessity. Between them they had decided that the field selected by Claude and his Resistance colleagues was too far away, despite them not having seen it, and that a new option was wise even if only to ensure that no one else knew of its location. Betrayals and leaks within Resistance groups were a continuing concern and the fewer people who knew of a change of plan, the better. Sensing the possibility of exercise and of seeing and feeding off fresh pastures once again, the two horses enlivened as Patricia fitted the saddles and bridles, with Harold's assistance. The weather was much warmer than of late and they set off along narrow paths alive with May blossom across country. Madame Charon somehow guessed what they were setting out to do and suggested that they look eastward about twenty kilometres towards the River Kervegan. She had relatives with a smallholding near there and from visits knew something of the countryside.

Some hours later, having been stopped more than once by a German patrol asking for their papers, they arrived on the banks of a small river. As soon as they had dismounted, the two horses took the opportunity to quench their thirsts while their riders ate fresh bread, cheese and some fruit, all washed down with Calvados. En route Harold had noticed a number of potential locations where he thought a small aircraft could be landed and possibly be concealed within nearby trees. The river would provide a useful navigation mark, particularly as the operation was likely to take place near nightfall. With both animals and humans satisfied they remounted and rode slowly along the bank of the river. After a few minutes they came to an area where young trees had been allowed to grow, self-seeded, almost down to the trickling water's edge.

Through the thin stand of young trees they could see a sunlit open area with what appeared to be denser and mature trees beyond. Back on foot, they explored through the saplings, emerging eventually into an empty pasture with a myriad of wild spring flowers and fresh bright-green grass. It was sheltered from the winds by the trees and seemed an oasis of real calm. Towards the south the land dropped away slightly, with trees and bushes growing in profusion. On the other three sides, the field was hemmed in by taller trees; on the west side mature species were just bursting into leaf.

Securing the horses in shade under the young trees, they walked around the perimeter of the meadow. Looking carefully from its southern end they could see that the field would prove ideal, provided that there were no strong winds that could cause turbulence as air rolled up the rising ground from the south, swirling around the trees. It was a real concern for Harold; all the information about the experimental aircraft so far was largely theoretical and he had no idea how the machine would actually handle in gusty conditions.

Returning to the horses, they sat together in the sheltered sunshine, Harold finishing off the remaining bread and cheese. Patricia lay, eyes closed, facing up towards the spring sun; it was surprisingly warm in the shelter of the surrounded meadow. Lying back next to her, Harold fell asleep. It was not contrived, but he awoke to find his arm lying across her. She was watching him intently, not attempting to remove the wayward arm. Opening his eyes, he looked across at her. Behind, the horses were gently nibbling the grass, occasionally stamping their hooves. They were lying facing each other, his arm still across her. Raising himself slightly, he leaned over the young woman and spontaneously kissed her on the lips. Patricia smiled slightly and lay watching him. She reached out slowly, touching his face, stroking around his lips. Aroused, he knew he wanted her. Her eyes expressed similar feelings. Sitting up, he undid her jacket and blouse, gently caressing her breasts, kissing her neck. She responded, reaching down, undoing his belt. Near naked in the sunlight on the soft grass, they made love.

As they were riding back to the farm, they were both silent. She sensed he was troubled by what had happened. She knew also that he was engaged to Ceci. On the final stretch, with the farm in view, she turned towards him as they rode.

"'Arold, please don't feel guilty. You are not to blame. I did enjoy it, you know. Women have desires too." He looked askance at her.

"But, Ceci ... I shouldn't have, I've been disloyal ... it ..." She turned, reining in her horse, looking directly at him.

"'Arold, we are both adults, under strain – living in dangerous times. Some love and affection is not wrong in the circumstances. Don't worry, I will never mention this to Ceci. We have just enjoyed a little mutual comfort, no strings, just a way of releasing some tension, I think."

She was smiling encouragingly at him. He nodded reluctantly, riding on, still disturbed. Despite a past with many amorous affairs he felt desperately disappointed with himself. He had let himself down, taken advantage of a situation with Patricia and, worst of all, he had been unfaithful to Ceci. Although she may never learn of what had happened, it would always be on his conscience. But his principal feeling of guilt centred on the fact that he had enjoyed Patricia and wanted her again.

❖ ❖ ❖

Sarah leaned back in her chair, her back and neck aching from sitting over the stereoscope on her desk studying the seemingly endless twin sets of photographs, most of which had little or very little to tell. As usual they were the result of a normal recce trip over Brest for the navy. Despite being photographed from relatively high altitude, the barns were clearly visible; one now part-camouflaged, the other two still unpainted, standing out clearly in the rural landscape. But some things had changed. What had previously been two large fields had now become one very large expanse of grass. Quite clear were signs of disturbed earthworks where the original hedges between the two had been dug out, the ridge levelled. She could see dots of tiny figures working around the area and a vehicle of some sort. Comparing earlier pictures with this new batch she could see that the grass in both fields had been cut short. More interesting, however, were signs of traffic around the three barns. The grass was now well-worn by tracks, probably made by heavy vehicles. At the end of the tracks was a worn area with yellowed grass where lay rows of large regular-shaped objects in two separate groups some yards apart. Checking the scale of the pictures, she estimated the length of the objects in one group at around sixty to seventy feet; some of them were quite wide, others much narrower. Instinctively she knew what she was seeing – they were components for another prefabricated building of some sort.

She spoke later to a building expert from the economic warfare group, who made clear that the mass of material lying near the barns was likely to be for a very large structure, possibly three times larger than the existing barns or hangars. From what they understood already of the site, it seemed that the Germans intended to build a much larger barn or, more likely, a hangar. Its size, even unbuilt, suggested a need prompted by a much larger aircraft, or perhaps the intention was to accommodate a number of aircraft in its potentially cavernous interior. The second group of objects lay near to two enormous vehicles and were less easy to discern in detail; there were tarpaulins or some similar cover over the objects, which were much smaller than the first group studied.

Danesfield had recently installed a Swiss-manufactured Wild machine capable of improving the definition of high-altitude photographs to a point where significantly more detail could be seen than was normally available. The equipment had been taken over by the Air Ministry at the time the Australian Sid Cotton and his Aircraft Operating Company were absorbed into the RAF. Sarah phoned the machine's operator and requested some help with the pictures on her desk.

"It is a matter of some urgency. I understand that the Prime Minister has asked to be kept informed of matters relating to this location," she said, name-dropping. The operator was sending someone down to collect the photographs immediately and promised that any results would be ready after lunch. 'Must try dropping names more often,' she thought.

Returning from a late and rather frugal lunch, Sarah found a young airman waiting outside her locked office door. In his hand was a large, sealed buff envelope clearly marked 'Top Secret'. Smiling weakly with some relief, he handed the package to Sarah as she signed a receipt for the enlarged and more detailed pictures of the barns' site. Sitting, she carefully removed the small batch of greatly enhanced pictures from the envelope; at the second picture she stopped dead. Without taking her eyes of the image she reached for the telephone and called Daphne.

Together they studied the pictures. The larger group of objects was, as predicted by the chap from the economic warfare group, seemingly wooden components for either one or possibly two very large prefabricated buildings, roof trusses and beams. The two huge trucks on the site were now easy to identify: they were very similar to ones used by the RAF to transport large bits of aircraft such as complete fuselages or wings, known in the service as 'Queen Marys', no doubt because of their size. The vehicles were empty. Their loads had obviously been lifted and placed on the ground next to them. There were some figures gathered around one load, one a blurred-looking guard with possibly a rifle.

Using a large rectangular magnifying glass, Daphne studied the second load very carefully; at one end near the trees the covering tarpaulin had been pulled or blown back a little, exposing something she was unable to identify. Instinctively both women knew that they had to interpret their finds, and quickly. One of the Wild machine technicians was again asked to come to the office to see if it was possible to enlarge or gain better definition of the part-exposed load. After some minutes looking at the area of the photo he said it was worth a try but did not hold out much hope.

"It is likely," he said, "that the image will break up and be worthless for interpretation purposes." He left, taking the picture with the crucial area marked, promising to return as soon as they had got some results. Just before six he returned, a glow of success on his lined face. Containing their excitement, the three of them looked at the results. The enlarged area of the original pictures had begun to break up as the technician had warned, but after a number of attempts and experimentation they had managed a compromise that allowed some definition to be brought to the picture. Daphne and Sarah looked, gasping in unison.

The small area of the load exposed showed the end of what could only be a large aircraft wing with a rotating vanes system clearly visible despite the blurred quality of the image. They thanked the technician profusely and he left, unsure just what he had helped to uncover. Daphne and Sarah sat on opposite sides of the desk looking amazed at the pictures spread out in front of them.

"Obviously they have all but finished testing with the small aircraft and have built a very much larger version. It may explain why the two fields have been merged into one, giving them a greater take-off area for bigger machines," said Sarah.

"We'd better let Homburg know straight away." Daphne picked up the phone and within a few minutes was describing their find to him over a scrambled line. He was sending a motorcycle despatch rider to collect a set of photos and they were requested to attend a meeting at SOE in Baker Street in two days at eleven o'clock.

❖ ❖ ❖

Airborne, Ceci stared at the far southern horizon. Somewhere in the haze lay France and her fiancé, who had returned to undertake some dangerous activity to which she was not privy. The Spitfire cruised steadily over Salisbury Plain. Below, the bright green of new wheat and grasslands seemed to give her hope. Here and there the neat fields were scarred with dark gashes where the military had been practising for the future actions. The machine she was flying was the latest Mk IX and she was ferrying it to a naval station in Devon for assessment by the Fleet Air Arm. The navy had been using the Seafire, a variant of the Spitfire, for fleet and convoy protection and were keen to try the newer version on their aircraft carrier mock-up deck, laid out on the airfield. By the time she reached her destination airfield the sun was beginning its long fall towards an indefinite western horizon. Its deep-orange rays struck her full in the face, making visibility ahead difficult. Somewhere in her jacket, she knew, she had a pair of sunglasses but was too engaged in flying the machine in the thermally induced turbulence as the last vestiges of warm afternoon air rose from the land.

Over-flying the airfield, she noted from the ground signals by the control tower the direction of runway in use. As usual the Spitfire had no operational radio, a frequent practice for ATA deliveries. Turning above the airfield, she prepared to join the circuit on the downwind leg, descending to eight hundred feet. As she did so, Ceci selected flaps and undercarriage down, peering at the runway as it slid around and across into her field of view. Finally the black tarmac lay ahead, some two hundred feet below. The Merlin engine rumbled gently with an occasional 'popping' outburst as she sank gently down towards the threshold. Suddenly a red flare arced up from the control tower, a clear signal to abandon her intention to land. Pushing the throttle forward, she pulled gently back on the stick; as the Spitfire climbed away the undercarriage nestled quickly back into the wings, its flaps retracting.

Still climbing, she began a turn that would take her on a long circuit around the field at a thousand feet, enabling her to keep an eye on the control tower for further visual signals. The cause of her denied landing was even then lined up with the runway below. A twin-engine machine; she recognised it as a Beaufighter, with smoke streaming back from its stationary port engine. Ceci could just make out other damage to the machine staggering towards the airfield; in its wings were signs of battle, the fin and rudder were also missing huge chunks. What caught her eye particularly, as its pilot tried to maintain control, was the smashed Perspex of the gun turret located halfway along the machine's upper fuselage. Its two guns were pointing vacantly and uselessly upwards, the thin aluminium skin around the turret torn, large pieces flapping in the slipstream.

As it approached, it became increasingly evident that visible damage was not the only problem being coped with by its pilot. Fifty feet up and just over the runway threshold, Ceci could see the rotating disk of the remaining propeller decline as its engine was slowed to idle in preparation for a landing. Flying instinctively, Ceci continued her broad sweep around the airfield circuit, glancing continually across at the landing aircraft. As its only functioning engine slowed, it became increasingly evident that there was difficulty in maintaining directional control of the machine. From her position, turning at the upwind end of the airfield, she could see that the Beaufighter's undercarriage was not lowered and that whatever happened, it was going to end up tearing along the grass beside the runway on its belly. It lurched suddenly, perhaps caught by a gust of wind, and its port wing sank quickly towards the rushing ground. As the tip struck, it pulled the rest of the machine down, swinging energetically off to the left leaving a furrow of chocolate-brown in the emerald. With insufficient airspeed and no undercarriage the pilot was a passenger; he had no control over its direction with the tattered rudder as it ploughed, bouncing and swerving across the field heading towards aircraft dispersals occupied by machines being prepared for operations.

Ceci watched, horror-struck, as the skidding machine rushed relentlessly towards parked aircraft, flames now erupting from the damaged port engine and wing. No doubt alerted by the noise, ground crews immersed in working on their silent charges became aware of the flaming danger rapidly approaching. They ran, scattering as they went.

The explosion had an incandescent white centre for a brief instant, then a deep-red ball of boiling flame and black, oily smoke soared skywards. Only very small fragments of the machine reached the abandoned dispersals. She learned later from one of the local squadron crews that the Beaufighter's pilot had reported that his torpedo had hung up as they had left the target, a group of German ships, and remained precariously hanging under the belly of the aircraft. It appeared that they were bounced on the way home from a ship-busting sortie by a group of Bf 110s, suffering serious damage and crew deaths. From a very brief radio transmission received, it appeared that only the Beaufighter's pilot had survived the attacks but owing to his own wounds was unable to leave his seat. He died instantly in the explosion.

After landing, Ceci taxied towards a naval rating who was signalling to her with his arms. Shutting down the Merlin, she sat for a moment looking across at the far side of the airfield. A plume of pale-grey smoke still rose from the remains of the pyre. She wondered if any of its crew were married or had children? They all probably got up this morning, as on any other morning, ready to do their duty but not actually anticipating an end to life. Now they were gone in an instant, like so many others, horrifyingly cut down.

Leaving her aircraft she walked slowly across the long grass towards the ops block. Inside there was an atmosphere of near-normality; shock and loss were submerged beneath the endless comings and goings at the busy naval air station. The duty officer, a young sub-lieutenant, took the paperwork and signed for the Spitfire's delivery. He managed a brief smile of thanks as he looked up, advising her that an aircraft was due in in ten minutes to pick her up. She stepped back outside into the weakening afternoon sun to wait. The smoke had now gone; a group of figures were looking around the blackened grass at the site of the explosion. The taxi Anson arrived and she climbed aboard while its engines were kept running. One other ATA female pilot sat near the front of the aircraft, having been collected earlier from an airfield at Chilbolton on the way west to fetch Ceci. She began pointing at the scene as they taxied past but Ceci didn't expand beyond the fact that there had been an awful accident.

◆ ◆ ◆

It was decided that the meeting should take place at a location other than the Charon farm or indeed any other building that might attract the attention of the Boche. Claude instinctively felt that it would be much safer and more secure if the circuit's various Resistance members met secretly somewhere away from any local towns and villages. He had decided on a spot set in a clearing in woods just six kilometres from the farm. The weather forecast was good and spring was now in full bloom as the six men, two women, Penrose and Claude assembled in the shelter of the trees away from prying eyes and ears.

Sitting about in a circle, some on a fallen tree trunk, others on waterproof coats spread on the ground, they began discussing Operation Azzaro, their proposed raid to capture one of the small German experimental aircraft. After nearly two hours of sometimes animated and occasionally voluble discussion they had not agreed on a course of action although several had been proposed.

Having listened patiently for most of the time, finally Patricia spoke. She quietly explained the plan she had helped to formulate with SOE and some officers from a Commando unit while she had been in London recently. The plan required the RAF to undertake diversionary daylight bombing raids on local railway junctions and the docks complexes at Brest and Dinant with fighters attacking targets of opportunity during the course of a series of Rhubarb raids. This, Patricia said, had to be co-ordinated in such a way that the bombing raids and fighter attacks did not upset the flying activities of the Germans at the three barns airfield. As a trained radio operator she would keep SOE advised of events so that any aerial attacks could be planned at just the right moment. One of the things she noted was that they would require from SOE walkie-talkie radios that would enable her to talk directly to the leaders of the bombing and Rhubarbs. With this capability, she could call in or reject the attacks at just the right moment without frightening off any experimental aircraft testing by the Germans.

As regards the practicalities of stealing the aeroplane, she continued, they would observe the German flying program of the machines for a few days to further confirm at just what hour they undertook testing and how late in the afternoon or early evening flying activity usually ceased. These observations would be made as before, innocently, from the Charon farm; it seemed to be as good a place as any and would not require any new, risky activity elsewhere. With that information to hand it would enable the group to set a firm time for attacking the airfield, ideally catching one of the experimental aircraft on its last landing for the day. Claude made a good point.

"If ze wind is in ze sous-west, as is usual zis time of ze year, a landing machine would finish its landing run some distance down ze runaway, farthest from ze barns and ze Germans' centre of activities; it will take zem some seconds to realise what is going on."

After some questions, which Patricia was able to answer, matters moved on to how many Resistance members would be required to capture the aircraft. Again arguments developed between various group members, tempers fraying briefly: some advocated a major attack, a hundred or more fully armed Resistance fighters able to hold a sizeable German force at bay while the aircraft was stolen and flown off.

Again, with quiet determination Patricia brought order to the threatening chaos. Standing in the centre of the group, she presented an image of someone who was not prepared to be diverted by petty jealousies among them. She and Claude had anticipated a rift and discussed this aspect of the operation together for some hours the previous afternoon. In line with the advice given by SOE and the Commandos, they had decided to keep any force to an absolute minimum, thus keeping better control of events and reducing the possibility of security leaks. They also agreed that the alternative landing ground found by her and Harold would remain a secret for the time being; even Claude was not to be made aware of its location. Patricia gave the advice to Claude, who had pondered the matter over a couple of Gauloises, his rheumy eyes staring into the milky dregs of a Pastis glass as he had swilled it to and fro in the warm kitchen the previous evening. Finally, stubbing out his cigarette, he concurred, and they agreed that they would try to gain the co-operation of the others in accepting a compact force, maximum six, plus Harold Penrose, the pilot.

Once this aspect of the plan was calmly and slowly explained most of the group members fell into line supporting it, but two expressed displeasure and demurred. Patricia gave them both a feisty stare. Claude understood their motives; they were keen to take any opportunity to kill large numbers of Germans but failed to understand that that was not the point of the exercise. Capturing the aircraft was all-important; risking many lives, including any German retribution on the local population, was not. Much further detail was discussed and the meeting finally dispersed through the woods. Nearly everyone felt it had been a useful discussion. Now hungry, they made their way home ready to undertake any activity required of them. The one area where control and planning were weak was the weather.

A first step for Claude was to arrange to gain more detailed information about the airfield and its guards. Remembering what had happened when Christian and Patricia made an earlier ill-fated attempt, the man selected this time was mature and well-versed in field craft, a stockman and poacher. He was to make his way to the airfield the following evening and night and spend time watching activity there over the following twenty-four hours, reporting back to Claude and Patricia as soon as he had managed to extricate himself from the area. On the basis of his observations and those of Patricia and Penrose, watching the experimental aircraft activity from the Charon farm, final details would be agreed with the six Resistance members selected. These six were to include Claude, Patricia and four experienced Resistance members from one local group, including one other girl, and Harold Penrose, who made it clear he intended to take an active part in the raid and not be carried as a passenger.

Maxime, the man charged with infiltrating around the three barns airfield to gather the raid's vital intelligence, was small, stocky and said to be a crack shot. He was already wanted by the Boche for his part in a raid on a German supply convoy earlier in their occupation. Seven of them had managed to kill eighteen Germans before coming under fire from a following convoy. They all escaped with their lives, leaving four trucks burning furiously. Somehow their names and descriptions were quickly plastered on walls and other prominent buildings in the area as wanted fugitives with all manner of penalties threatened to anyone caught offering succour or shelter to any one of them. Despite this, he and two others had continued to disrupt German rail and road communications and survived nearly three years on the run. Maxime was taken by a local farmer on an ancient tractor as near to the airfield as the farmer was prepared to go – about four kilometres.

By the time he was left, in tall vegetation growing either side of a rutted, rarely used path hidden in the countryside, it was almost eight in the evening. A thin but increasingly persistent drizzle accompanied the coming darkness. By early morning the grey dawn was delivering heavy and unremitting rain. In a carefully constructed natural hide made during the night from branches and other handy shrubbery, he sat almost dry, watching the airfield through a pair of powerful German binoculars, making coded notes of everything he observed, including guards and any regular comings and goings of vehicles or people. He also watched the weather gradually change through the day, knowing that the front that had liberally drenched their area would soon leave, heading north-east into Belgium and northern Germany, offering in its wake a few days of near-settled weather.

By three in the afternoon the rain had stopped and increasing fragments of blue were being exposed overhead through broken and rushing cumulus. Fully alert, despite his cramped position and lack of real sleep, he saw German technicians wheel out one of the small aircraft from the oddly part-camouflaged barn, making it ready for flight. All day long since six that morning work had been going on at the far side of the field; ragged, soaked men delivered by truck at six o'clock were working on the large piles of timber and other pieces of structure that were assembled into neat piles. Through the binoculars he was able to make out what seemed to him to be large timber roof trusses and possibly wooden wall panels, some with windows already fitted.

The men looked wretched; no doubt they were prisoners, possibly Russian. The German guards stood about, rifles ready, occasionally shouting or hitting some of the ragged workers with the butts of their weapons. Two other men, civilians, Maxime thought, walked about the site. From their body language and activity he assumed the men were probably architects or engineers overseeing erection of the new structures.

At the time of the first flight late that afternoon, one end of what appeared to Maxime to be a large building had been erected, supported temporarily by substantial timber struts driven into the earth. It was positioned some way from the original three barns in a natural gap in the surrounding trees. The wind brought the low buzzing of the aircraft's engine to Maxime's ears. Through binoculars he studied it carefully taxiing towards the downwind end of the expanded airfield; he was amazed to have confirmation that the machine had no propeller to drive it. Its pilot could be seen quite clearly sitting in the small, exposed open cockpit wearing a white cloth helmet behind a small windscreen. Every so often he would glance down, perhaps looking at his instruments, thought Maxime. The machine spent some considerable time near the end of the runway with its engine running, the setting sun occasionally glinting off the long rotating vanes in its wings; then with a sudden increase in noise level it lurched forward down the short grass strip and was airborne very quickly; just over thirty metres, Maxime estimated. As the machine climbed away he watched it turn right towards an area where he knew the Charon farm lay.

Harold Penrose and Patricia had been waiting the whole afternoon doubtful of any sightings owing to earlier inclement weather. As the small herd of cows were brought into the yard just after four by the two Charon boys, one started shouting excitedly to his brother, pointing. The machine could be seen but not heard against the wind. They all watched its delicate manoeuvring until Madame Charon called the two complaining lads into the milking parlour. Penrose continued to observe professionally as the tiny aircraft flew a series of different headings, the last of which brought it closer to the farm. Now he could hear the engine noise occasionally against the wind. He continued watching with Patricia at his side, the aircraft heading at one point directly towards the farm, the noise of its motor increasing. Suddenly the noise decreased rapidly, the aircraft's nose pitched up momentarily, its speed dropping noticeably. Now, in a nose-high attitude, the aircraft began to slowly sink towards open farmland beyond. Just as suddenly the engine noise increased and the nose of the machine was now pointing even higher in the air. Harold gasped involuntarily. The aircraft's unusual and steep upward incline Penrose knew to be well beyond most aircraft's normal stalling angle. It would have brought any conventional aircraft spinning and crashing to the ground, unless caught early on in such a dangerous manoeuvre.

He watched, amazed, with the nose pointing about thirty-five degrees or more upwards. The engine could be clearly heard running hard, and the aircraft remained for the most part almost stationary in the air, neither rising or falling. His jaw dropped as he witnessed the next surprise, grabbing at Patricia's arm. The machine remained almost stationary, virtually hovering; unheard of in his experience. Then the small aircraft began to turn slowly through ninety, then one hundred and eighty, until unbelievably to Harold, it completed a full three-hundred-and-sixty-degree turn virtually on the spot while maintaining its height.

He knew beyond doubt that with such incredible capabilities and manoeuvrability it represented a real advantage to any military arm, offering flexible capability to deliver equipment and troops into small clearings or any other confined space. Eventually, after two more impromptu demonstrations some distance from the farm, the aircraft returned to a normal flying attitude, heading away from them, back towards where Penrose and Patricia knew the German airstrip lay. Stunned from his observations and realising the military implications, he pulled Patricia towards the farmhouse, insisting that she send a coded wireless message to London immediately describing what they had seen.

She refused, smiling patiently at his excitement. To send a signal immediately would alert one of the German radio detector vans known to have been long active in their area; besides, she explained, sending a message right away may well identify the farm as a place worthy of further inspection. In any event she would have to wait until her scheduled transmission time, due later in the evening. This would have its own risks attached as a transmission describing all that they had observed would be a long one. They set about writing a concise coded message in Morse that would include all of the facts ready for transmission. Patricia intended to ride her bicycle away from the farm for a few kilometres to somewhere quiet with her battery-powered radio set, in its small attaché case, tied onto the bike's rear carrier. It was vital that she transmitted on schedule; by eleven-thirty she was safely back at the farm, despite the curfew.

In London, at SOE's HQ, it was after two-thirty in the morning and the small room was full, cigarette smoke swirling around the hastily gathered group of men studying and discussing the content of Patricia's long transmission that evening. It was very worrying; the group captain had just finished a lengthy and somewhat trying conversation with the Prime Minister, who had been called out of bed.

❖ ❖ ❖

Michael Kelly wondered what to do next. Guy van der Beek was a problem but to confront him directly about his odd activities had been overruled by SOE. They wanted something planned that would force him to show his hand; give himself away, or perhaps direct them to other suspects or intelligence leads. The Dutchman, due back from leave later that day, would probably be surprised, possibly suspicious if he was not involved in the squadron's normal operations when they recommenced in three days, coinciding with the moon's new waxing phase.

One sortie that had been flagged up as a priority, among at least half a dozen by SOE, was the need to deliver some packages and a Joe to the area around Callac again. The frequency with which the squadron had been to this fairly remote field over recent months was beginning to concern Kelly. How long could they continue to operate there without arriving one night to find the Germans waiting for them as a reception committee, he pondered. Nevertheless, the job had to be done and the risks minimised. He knew that the packages were to contain some special walkie-talkie radios, American, he believed, together with some weapons. Group HQ had let him know that their delivery was absolutely crucial to a special operation that was to be undertaken imminently; it was emphasised that the Prime Minister himself was taking a special interest in the operation, he'd been pointedly informed.

Was there a way of using van der Beek on this operation that would not compromise it, but at the same time give them some clues as to his apparent alternative agenda? On Kelly's desk lay a piece of paper from the Air Ministry confirming the award of a Bar to a DFC. The notice applied to Flight Lieutenant Ben Kendle, his deceased flight commander, who had been killed on special operations over France a couple of months past. The award had been made posthumously. Not much good to Ben now, Kelly thought.

It was mention of Ben's name on the signal that launched an idea. Before joining the squadron, Ben Kendle had been a successful pilot and a flight commander in a night-fighter squadron, Kelly recalled. With the special radar equipment fitted into Beaufighters it was possible for the navigator/radar operator to guide the pilot onto a target aircraft in the dark; the outcome, ideally, was to identify it visually from close range and if it proved to be enemy, shoot it down without it ever knowing what had struck at it. Michael had met the CO of the Beaufighter squadron briefly when he'd popped over to see Ben while they'd been up at Tempsford. He'd been a very young squadron leader with over eleven night-time kills to his name, but shy and almost embarrassed at the mention of his success over a few short months.

Kelly lifted the phone and asked the switchboard to connect him with the young squadron leader's unit, which was based on an airfield somewhere in Somerset. Over a short telephone conversation the basis of a plot was hatched. Later, Michael Kelly informed van der Beek that he would be on operations in two nights but did not specify where or when he would be operating, in line with his recent new rules on security.

Rubbing his stubbly chin and sitting on the corner of the table, Geoff Standish tried to identify from memory, helped by the folded chart in front of him, exactly where it was that he had seen van der Beek's aircraft disappear onto the ground on the night of their dual sortie. After much trawling of his memory and rereading the notes he'd made at the time and the verbatim account he'd given to the unit intelligence officer on his return, he finally decided on the most likely point. He marked the spot with a pencilled ring.

Talking to Sarah at Danesfield, Kelly asked her whether they had any aerial pictures of the area in question; it was several kilometres square and did not appear to contain any towns or villages of note. Two hours later he picked up the phone. The Danesfield operator asked him to identify himself; satisfied, she put Flight Officer Kelly on the line. They both knew that their conversation would probably be monitored.

Unfortunately, Sarah told her husband, after a rapid search of their photo files they had only one high-level picture of the area in question, which was mainly rural with no main roads passing through it; also the picture was over a year old. As an aside she expressed a thought as to why such a picture should have been taken in view of its lack of strategic targets. She was sending a print to him by despatch rider that afternoon. The conversation ended with none of the usual endearments between man and wife but rather matter of factly, the courtesies of rank being fully observed. She could hardly conceal a smile as she put the phone down.

Later that afternoon Michael Kelly met with an elderly army officer working with SOE and they walked slowly around the airfield discussing possible options. Finally he put his plan to the army man, who agreed to do what he could but said time was very short for it to be co-ordinated fully with the Resistance. He pointed out that if successful, a second pilot would be needed on hand to fly van der Beek's Lysander home. One would have to be parachuted into the area that very night.

Paul Mossman left Michael's office somewhat taken aback; had never made a parachute drop before but was going to do so that evening from one of the squadron's Whitleys, and at night. His only training was a half-hour chat with a pilot from another squadron who had made a successful parachute jump resulting from enemy action during a dogfight. It was all they had time for.

Bemused and not a little concerned, Mossman climbed awkwardly into the Whitley with his parachute, wondering how he had suddenly got into this situation; he'd had no time to contact Daphne or anyone else. Sitting while the aircraft was prepared for take-off, he thought over the key points made by the SOE officer. His role was merely to fly an aircraft back from a field in France if ordered to by the head of the local Resistance unit. It had been underlined to him firmly a number of times that he was not to participate in any other activity which may occur involving the Resistance. Also, he was to remain in RAF uniform and if it proved unnecessary for him to fly the aircraft back, he would be uplifted at the first available opportunity by one of their own aircraft from the special operations squadron. The civilian had given him some code words with which to identify himself to the local Resistance circuit head. Given a standard escape-and-evasion kit and a new pistol just in case it all went wrong, he had also been made to memorise a telephone number where he might get help, but only in an extreme emergency.

Over the dim, shadowy French countryside the Whitley droned, lurching every so often in bubbles of turbulent air, heading for a point to the south-west of Rouen. A few miles from the drop zone the floor hatch was opened and Flying Officer Mossman sat poised to leave, the sole crewman in the rear of the aircraft waiting for the red light to turn green at the pilot's flick of a switch.

There it was. A white Morse signal from the ground confirmed the location and that there was someone there to greet him. Banging his elbow sharply, his expletive was lost as he exited the hole into the freezing night air, the static line yanking his parachute open a few feet below the departing aircraft. As the machine disappeared into the darkness the sounds of slumbering rural France rose in the quiet. A dog barked and a cockerel began its early matins as he swung gently and silently lower. Now and again a banging gate suggested a fair breeze blowing him sideways across the dark landscape. Looking down, he could just make out thick hedges, a small, nearly circular copse, around which the narrow, paler shade of a grey road curved. Suddenly he was mere feet from the surface of a pasture with what looked like ghostly dark-grey blobs scattered across its face: cows. He wasn't quite ready; it took all the breath out of him as he fell heavily, the parachute still full of energetic air dragging him towards a shadowy, dark mass of buildings. It caught, then collapsed, its folds snagged on heavy guttering surrounding one high black roof. As he pulled firmly on the parachute's lines in an effort to quell its independence, there was a resounding crash. Fragments of broken cast-iron guttering fell, just missing him. Suddenly, he was conscious of not being alone; two figures, breathing heavily, rushed towards him grabbing at the flailing parachute lines. They exchanged passwords, which tallied, and he accompanied them from the field. He'd never even seen their faces in the dark.

Van der Beek's sortie was to deliver one agent and some sealed packages. The location of the field to be used was kept from him until two hours before scheduled take-off. It was one that van der Beek had not used before, about twelve kilometres south of what had become their usual field near Callac. Kelly felt that an alternative venue served three purposes: first, it would make a change from one that had in most pilot's views been used to excess

340

over recent months, second, as Kelly put it to David Rawlinson, it was easier to identify from higher altitudes by the Beaufighter that was intended to track van der Beek, and third, if van der Beek had been somehow passing information to a local contact at the field very near Callac, the change of venue may help thwart it.

Just before van der Beek was due to leave, Squadron Leader Kelly phoned a discrete London number. When the phone was answered he uttered a simple statement.

"Did you hear the cuckoo this morning?"

The voice at the other end replied, in a dead monotone.

"Yes, it was spectacular." Michael put the phone down. This apparently ridiculous conversation confirmed what Kelly most wanted to hear before allowing van der Beek's sortie to continue. It meant that SOE had heard from a Resistance group near Rouen that Paul Mossman had arrived safely the previous night, and that there would be a hidden reception committee located strategically in the general area where it was thought the Dutch pilot had landed on an earlier sortie, partially observed by Geoff Standish that night.

By twelve-thirty in the morning the moon was up and bright. The Lysander, with van der Beek piloting and a male agent stuffed uncomfortably into the rear cabin with various parcels and packages, left the ground and turned almost immediately towards Selsey Bill. Skirting the Cherbourg peninsula and the occupied Channel Islands, the Lizzie soon crossed the French coast aiming directly for the new field. Looking out to his right, van der Beek could easily identify the old field near Callac, its characteristic shape outlined by darker woods in the moonlight. Tonight, at his altitude, and thanks to the moon's co-operation, it was possible to pick out the shape of individual cows lying or grazing in the field. He clicked the stopwatch, knowing how long it would take to reach the new field in the near-calm conditions. Glancing every so often at the watch's sweep hand crossing its green, luminous face, he scanned the countryside ahead. As the deadline drew near, flying slowly to reduce engine noise, van der Beek studied the ground watching for a signalled Morse letter that would prompt an acknowledging reply from him.

Circling and frowning a little, he watched the ground. No Morse letter signal had been forthcoming and he was becoming resigned to returning across the Channel with the drop not completed. A couple of miles away he could see the occasional flicker of traffic on a road highlighted against the countryside in the moon's silver. Perhaps the reception committee had been delayed by what could only be German traffic at this hour of the morning. He decided to fly from the immediate area in a very wide circular sweep that would take him and his passenger a long way out to the east, aiming to return to the spot within about twelve minutes. He gently opened the throttle and the Lizzie gained speed as he banked left across the shimmering silver-grey countryside. Looking quickly at his notes and watch, he reckoned he had about fifty minutes left of useful moonlight.

Flying around, he saw nothing to suggest life other than livestock occasionally moving slowly about in the fields below them. After eleven and a half minutes the aircraft was again approaching the designated area. Before van der Beek had time to scan the ground ahead a white light flashed up – – – , the Morse letter 'S'. It was correct and he flashed his own downward identity light to confirm his recognition. Within seconds the three cardinal points of the letter 'L' were picked out on the ground and he prepared to land.

He landed the machine with a jolt but it remained stable. Judicious use of the brakes quickly brought it down to a speed suitable for making a rapid U-turn, taxiing back up the narrow field towards the black stand of trees at the end. Behind him van der Beek heard the noise of the rear hatch sliding back, then the agent began lifting packages out and down to a waiting reception committee. Within minutes it was over. The head of the reception committee reached up to shake his hand and hand him an envelope. With a thumbs-up signal he prepared for take-off, pleased that his time on the ground had been barely eight minutes. He opened up the engine as he turned to face the two white lights at the far end of the field, the aircraft gained speed and was soon airborne, climbing away into a darkening night sky as the moon began to bow out behind a series of clouds.

Guy van der Beek continued to climb the Lysander slowly as he flew directly east, not north. He took care to keep below one thousand feet, not wanting to be tracked by RAF radar controllers sitting across the Channel. Tuning his radio to a discrete frequency, he uttered a brief greeting in German.

"Guten Nacht, Franck." The response was just two words.

"'Tag, Gert," came loud and clear through his headphones.

Above him, the Beaufighter's frustrated radar operator tried to locate the Lysander's blip on his small, pulsating green screen. It was proving difficult among the white ground clutter – signals that adversely affected the performance of the radar equipment when trying to track a target so near to the ground. The operator requested his pilot to descend, hoping that, being at or near the same height as their target, they would have more success in tracking the slow-moving Lysander. Lower down, the radar was proving even less effective as the reflected ground signals from the equipment's electrical impulses swamped the tiny green screen with a white mish-mash, making observation of the Lysander's blip impossible. Climbing again, the smiling pilot of the Beaufighter caught a chance sight of the black Lizzie moving across the dark-grey countryside below; he followed discreetly. As he did so he passed a coded message to the RAF controllers sat huddled in a warm, nondescript Nissen hut set off to one side of a silent southern airfield. He gave them the height, heading and estimated speed of the errant Lysander.

Van der Beek stayed on an easterly course, again watching his stopwatch. When the time was up he would scan the shadowy landscape looking for a tell-tale signal. In a litter of trees facing onto a long, thin field two German officers stood smoking in the darkness barely exchanging a word. One, a tall senior Luftwaffe officer, stood a few feet from the squat SS Major, barely visible in his black uniform; only the reflection of his cigarette in his thin frameless spectacles hinting at his location. Glancing at his watch, the Luftwaffe officer muttered a few words about lateness. Minutes later they both heard it; the gentle revving of an aircraft engine somewhere off to the west. It appeared to be quite low. The sound was intermittent in the breeze and overlaid by other occasional aircraft noises flying well above.

The Luftwaffe captain stood out from the shelter of the trees looking up towards the approaching sound; now it was quite close, he was sure it was their man. Reaching into the deep pockets of his leather coat, he pulled out a torch and, watched by the SS officer, walked out into the field for a few yards pointing the torch skyward. Fingering the button, he sent two long and two short red flashes into the night sky. The sky remained black with no physical sign of the aircraft, although both men and their small troop of four SS stormtroopers could hear the machine plainly; it was now almost directly overhead. Pointing again, he sent the red flashes upwards. The response was almost immediate. Van der Beek thumbed a long, white burst with the Lysander's downward identity light. On seeing it, the two pairs of soldiers illuminated their four red lights marking the extremities of a makeshift grass runway. The engine note quietened as van der Beek banked away to the left above them, preparing for a landing. Above him, turning carefully like a watching nighthawk in a wide circle, engines just purring, the pilot and navigator of the Beaufighter visually observed events, then sent a signal confirming the Lysander's landing location. Their signal acknowledged and their night's prowling completed, they turned north-west for England and another early breakfast.

Barely two kilometres away, eleven armed men of the Rouen Resistance group, together with Paul Mossman, followed the engine noise overhead and the occasionally discernible black silhouette of a Lysander preparing to land. Running silently along the side of an adjacent field, they split into two uneven groups intending to approach the landing field from either side. Watching the first set of two red lights, van der Beek allowed the aircraft to descend slowly into the gloom; he didn't want to use his landing lights unless absolutely essential. Beneath him, unseen, the eleven Frenchmen and one recently arrived Canadian jogged slowly onwards, unsure of just how many Germans would form the reception committee.

It was a good landing; on the field van der Beek was able to see easily as the moon momentarily broke cover through upper cloud layer. Taxiing back towards the downwind end of the field with its two red lights still illuminated, he saw figures emerge stealthily from the trees to his left. He immediately recognised the stature of the two men; one thin and willowy, the other heavily built. He could just see two German soldiers loitering by the red lights further up the field.

With hand signals and a single whisper, two of the Resistance men peeled off from one group to deal with the two German soldiers, silently, drawing knives from sheaths on their belts as they did so. The first victim merely grunted as the knife plunged up and under his left shoulder blade, into his heart and lungs. The second soldier, possibly alerted by his colleague's odd noise and gurgling exhalation, turned just as his assailant lunged. Frantically trying to pull his rifle, slung over his shoulder to bear, he fired once, wildly, into the night before the knife pierced his throat. As he writhed and flailed at his attacker, making horrible gurgling noises as he fell, the Resistance man fell on top of the mortally wounded soldier trying desperately to contain further dying sounds.

The leader of the Resistance group laughed out loud then uttered a series of expletives in German. The two officers, annoyed with the apparent indiscipline in their troops, looked up the field towards the laughter and shouting, assuming it to be from their men in the dark. They then turned their attention to the Lysander taxiing towards them. The machine bobbed to a halt. After a few seconds the pilot switched off the magnetos and the engine clattered to a halt, ticking as it cooled in the night air. He climbed down, glad to stretch his legs.

Guy van der Beek walked stiffly in the cold towards the two Germans; they exchanged guttural, muted greetings, full of false bonhomie. Reaching inside his flying suit and fumbling for a few seconds, he finally withdrew a bulging manila envelope, passing it to one of the German officers.

The second group of Resistance moved carefully within the shadows afforded by the thin trees bordering the airstrip. With a raised white hand their leader motioned everyone to stop. They were about one hundred and fifty yards from the aircraft; it was just possible to see some individuals moving about near it. At the end of the line Paul Mossman tried to contain his panting; he was obviously not as fit as he had thought himself, the air rasping in his throat. The silhouette of the Lysander stood blackly stark against the countryside; he could even smell its heat.

It was over in seconds. Trailing his small group, Mossman followed as they moved almost silently towards the aircraft. As they approached, someone began shouting something forcefully in German, then two or three closely spaced shots shattered the night. From behind, other shots rent the stillness. At the aircraft, men from his and the other half of the Resistance group surrounded the three officers, one Dutch, two German. Mossman, catching up, pushed through the gathered men and women, his pistol drawn; it made him feel better. A torch was focused on van der Beek's face.

"Good morning, Guy. Forgive us for arriving uninvited but we didn't want to miss your party. I must say, it's an odd location but perhaps midnight parties like this are traditional in Holland?

Kindly introduce us to your two hosts."

The two German officers were disarmed fully as the last remaining Resistance member joined the group, staring amazed at their bag of officers. She confirmed that the last two SS soldiers were dead; she held their two red torches in one hand, the other clutching a German machine pistol.

The two German officers had their arms pinioned behind them, their ankles securely tied; their faces were a mix of surprise and anger.

"Guy, can you explain why you are here in one of His Majesty's aircraft," asked Mossman, his face a few inches from the Dutchman's.

"I can, Paul; but not to you." Van der Beek looked away, his face pale in the torchlight. He was visibly shaking. One of the fighters searching the two Germans found the manila envelope and passed it to Mossman. Leaving it sealed, he placed it securely inside his inner flying-suit pocket.

Leaving three on guard, the rest of the Resistance group moved away to clear up the carnage of their night's work. One of them moved silently away to look for the car or truck that would have brought the Germans to the field; the others dragged four bodies from either end of the field, laying them out under the trees. It proved to be a small truck lying hidden in a sunken road a quarter of a mile from the field; it was not guarded. The four bodies were carried with difficulty over the uneven field and hedge. Two were placed in the front of the truck, the other two propped up in its rear. A large lump of plastic explosive was stuck securely to the vehicle's fuel tank and a detonator pushed into the soft, innocuous grey substance. A man was left behind to trigger it once he had heard the Lysander depart.

The two bound German officers were enraged as they were unceremoniously lifted and pushed forcefully into the cramped rear compartment of the Lysander. Van der Beek's hands and ankles were by then tied securely together and he followed the Luftwaffe and SS officers into a now very confined space. The burly SS officer started to shout in rage on realising that he was about to be transported to England. The head of the Resistance hit the man hard across the face with the butt of his Sten. Bleeding slightly, the German became more enraged and agitated, kicking out at the sides of the aircraft threatening serious damage to the machine.

Grabbing him by the throat, the senior Resistance man warned him in fluent German, in no uncertain terms, about the likely consequences of his continued actions. The Nazi spat and continued to thrash about in the confined cabin space, lashing out with his bound legs and banging his body about. With a final resigned nod the Frenchman grabbed the enraged German by his leather lapels and started to drag the man over the cill of the tiny rear cabin. Releasing his grip on the agitated German, the heavy man fell six feet onto the soft grass. Bound, and a little shocked from his fall, the man found difficulty in standing again; in any event his efforts to do so proved irrelevant.

Taking a large-calibre pistol from his coat-pocket and bending down, the Resistance leader placed the muzzle against the man's forehead, instantly pulling the trigger. There was no warning. The head was instantly thrust back, mouth unnaturally wide open as he fell twisted, blood soaking the soil from the remains of his head. For a moment no one moved; none of the Resistance fighters were openly shocked at the speed and nature of events. Mossman looked at the dead man; it had been a brutal and swift execution but wholly necessary under the circumstances, he thought. The Luftwaffe and Royal Air Force officers sat totally subdued in the rear cabin of the Lysander as Paul Mossman taxied it away towards a hint of morning growing at the easterly end of the grass strip. Once airborne, he turned onto a northerly heading, thinking about how he was going to weave among German coastal defences on his way back to Sussex. The dead SS officer was added to the passengers in the truck just before it erupted.

Their arrival at their forward airfield attracted quite a crowd of official greeters. Three large and armed RAF military policemen assisted both van der Beek and the clearly worried Luftwaffe officer down from the aircraft. The latter was taken to a waiting car; the bindings around his legs were removed for comfort but he remained handcuffed as he was driven away to a special reception centre near Richmond in south-west London for interrogation. Van der Beek looked embarrassed as he was led away to Michael Kelly's office in the charge of the remaining armed military policeman, accompanied by two SOE men, also discreetly armed, along with Michael Kelly and the RAF station commander. Despite the situation, the niceties were observed; tea was brought for all those crowded into Michael Kelly's small office looking out over the airfield, now painted with early morning sunlight. Nervously drinking tea and looking around from his position sunk into the sagging comfort of the tired leather armchair, van der Beek finally spoke.

"Gentlemen, a very clever operation. I congratulate you but you are all labouring under a misapprehension and have probably done irreparable harm to a very delicate situation." Nobody spoke as they sipped their tea for a few minutes. Then the policeman spoke.

"If you've finished, Flying Officer van der Beek, we'll be on our way." The military policeman assisted him from the chair and, accompanied by the two SOE civilians, the Dutchman was led outside to a black van with narrow bars at its small windows. Ushered inside, the rear doors were slammed shut and secured with a heavy brass padlock, the stockily built policeman pocketing the key before joining the army driver in the front. Before departing with their prisoner, the two SOE men stopped to exchange a few words with Kelly and the station commander before getting into their large Humber staff car, thanking them for their help. They would advise them in due course whether their interrogation of Guy van der Beek elicited information about any breaches in the security of their special operations. In the meantime they advised no further use of fields that had been in common use over the period that van der Beek had been with the squadron.

Paul Mossman sauntered across the grass from ops, having been debriefed by the station intelligence officer and one unsmiling civilian intelligence man who spent most of the time reading the contents of the large manila envelope, all the while sucking on his teeth. The intelligence agent indicated that he would no doubt wish to speak with him again, warning him in no uncertain terms not to speak to anyone about recent matters; nor was he to be permitted to take part in any special operations over France until they advised his squadron CO, Michael Kelly. He was pleased to take his leave of them and to be safely back home after his unusual and dramatic experiences. He was deep in thought as he crossed the road towards the squadron administration offices. The black van passed by, followed by the Humber. Looking out, expressionless, from one of the van's small barred windows was van der Beek; their eyes made brief contact but no recognition showed on either man's face.

SEVEN

It was set for four days' time. The weather forecast suggested a brief spell of fine weather over the following weekend before the next Atlantic low-pressure system shuffled damply and depressingly up-Channel between Brittany and southern England. Claude and Patricia had spent some useful hours assessing the information obtained by Maxime, who had been safely recovered from his hide close to the airfield, together with Harold's observations of the small experimental aircraft from the Charon farm. The airfield perimeter was now heavily and constantly guarded and Maxime confirmed that there were some additional flak defences carefully hidden in the trees alongside one edge of the field. The additional guards were no doubt due in part to the recently deceased Christian's attempt to probe the area some months earlier, and the growing number of prisoners now engaged in work on the site, plus the obviously increasing importance of the location as a temporary experimental aircraft establishment.

While preparing to leave his observation hide early in the evening and awaiting the dark, Maxime watched as a light aircraft quietly sank onto the airfield. It couldn't be anyone else, he thought, as he watched fascinated while a rather plump Goering lifted himself from one of the seats in the small machine and clambered out, stepping heavily onto the turf, greeted by a row of German officers, all saluting ferociously. Maxime watched through his powerful ex-German binoculars as the group walked rapidly across to the group of small hangars, disappearing inside, led by the ornately uniformed head of the Luftwaffe dressed in pale blue.

At one point in the visit, Goering and a white-coated figure appeared from the farthest hangar. Together they stood exposed on the field for a while, obviously talking; then Goering was stabbing a finger into the chest of the other man, waving his arm furiously, acting in a very agitated manner. They both finally went back into the hangar; the white-coated man walking bowed, in near-supplication, behind the rotund head of Germany's Luftwaffe. Twenty minutes later the Reichsmarschall made his way back and into the light aircraft and settled his huge bulk in. The door was shut, the machine started and it took off. Again a row of sycophantic Germans stood saluting as though their lives depended on it. They may well have done, Maxime suggested. Goering's second visit would no doubt prove of great interest to the intelligence services in England, thought Patricia, adding further weight to their theory regarding the importance of the new aircraft's development.

Maxime had also noted that work on the new, larger hangar structure had gone on throughout the night. Now and again a flicker of torchlight showed in the blackness as the malnourished prisoners laboured laying concrete and levering up large sections of wall to the vertical. Just after six in the morning they shambled listlessly away towards a row of open trucks, where a new group of dishevelled thin men stood shivering in the early light ready for another twelve hours' punishing labour. Before the last truck moved off, two lifeless bodies, grabbed by arms and legs, were thrown unceremoniously up onto the vehicle's tailgate; the two guards turned away laughing as the tailgate was slammed up and locked.

Later in the day a very large camouflaged truck arrived at the airfield, lumbering across the grass on enormous fat tyres towards the small hangars. Minutes later a smaller, open truck with what appeared to be darkly uniformed SS soldiers followed it. The twenty or so men dismounted, stretching their legs after what could possibly have been a long journey. Maxime noticed many of them were yawning. An officious, high-booted officer emerged from the second truck's cab and started to give orders to the assembled troops. Still watching, he then noticed a crocodile of prisoners making their shuffling way towards the three barn hangars accompanied by normal Wehrmacht guards. The line of men was led into the farthest hangar, the SS soldiers closing around the entrance to the building. He was still watching after half an hour; nothing had happened, although the troops standing about outside were obviously getting restless. Trying to relieve himself within the confines of his hide, Maxime suddenly heard shouts and, looking up, saw some prisoners emerging, bowed under the weight of what looked to be a substantial and heavy part of an aeroplane. As they turned he could see pale sunlight reflecting off shiny aluminium and a small windscreen set on the fuselage. It appeared to be a substantial part of one of the two test aircraft, the unpainted one. Struggling and staggering, the prisoners, induced by shouts and occasional blows from rifles, carried the small but obviously heavy load towards the larger truck. Behind the truck's huge camouflaged cab was a long, low flatbed on which were lashed some wooden trestles.

Finally, when they reached the truck, an attempt was made by the prisoners to lift the large section of aircraft onto the trestles mounted on the truck's flatbed. From his vantage point it was clear to Maxime that the emaciated prisoners were totally exhausted with their efforts so far; having to lift the machine up onto the rear of the truck proved to be beyond them, despite kicks, shouts and in some instances more beatings with rifle butts. Wehrmacht troops were ordered to help while the SS troops stood watching, some laughing and jeering. Eventually the fuselage was lifted up and onto the trestles and secured. Relieved, Russian prisoners staggered back from the load, some falling, completely drained. On the far side of the truck there appeared to be some sort of commotion. From where he sat Maxime was unable to see what was going on but suddenly a group of three SS men ran around to the blind side of the vehicle. Seconds later a burst of machine-pistol fire reached his ears. Maxime swore silently to himself, raging inside.

Throughout the morning more components of the small machine were extricated from the hangars and loaded carefully onto the back of the truck: the wings, followed by the tail and various other wooden boxes. All was securely fastened and covered by large grey-green tarpaulins. A guard was left around the vehicle and its load while the accompanying SS troops were fed and watered, standing around some sort of mobile field kitchen just below where Maxime hid. By two o'clock the huge truck with its dismantled aeroplane moved off, followed by the SS troops.

Harold's careful observations over a period of five days finally confirmed to him that only one of the small test aircraft was now being flown, in the morning, and sometimes, but not always, during the late afternoon and early evening. He knew that much depended on the weather conditions for their continued testing. The Germans would no doubt have accurate reports of approaching weather from their Condor patrols flying way out into the Western Approaches beyond Biscay and the Channel. If their own information radioed from England concerning good weather was to be relied upon, they would assume that the experimental machines would be operating in three days' time.

It was intended that Maxime, together with two of the Resistance team including Claude, plus Harold, would infiltrate the nearby woods and adjacent healthy pea crop that lay at the upwind end of the airfield during the night before the afternoon of the intended aircraft snatch. Hopefully, unobserved, they would lie up all night and during the next day, prepared for action late in the afternoon. Patricia would try to co-ordinate their careful infiltration past the guards with an arranged air raid on the harbour facilities at Brest, intending that the raiding aircraft should pass directly over the three barns airfield both on their way in and on the way out at relatively low level. She and the SOE knew it was a risky tactic for the bombers. The RAF were not at all keen; the bombers would have a fighter escort, at least on the outward leg, but set against the fearful threat posed by full development of the experimental aircraft, it was one deemed acceptable by all concerned. Their hope was that the deliberately low-flying, heavy aircraft would provide a major and worrying distraction for the Germans on the airfield who, it was thought, would be unlikely to fire on the passing bombers for fear of attracting attention to themselves. Both Patricia and her SOE colleagues at Baker Street had reasoned that it would at least keep the Germans worried and probably paying less attention to wider airfield security than they should for the few minutes that the bombers were in the vicinity.

The remainder of the Resistance team under Patricia were to fire some captured German mortars – they had managed to obtain exactly four rounds – at the airfield, aiming specifically at what Maxime had identified as a small fuel dump lying about two hundred yards from the main hangar site. If they managed to hit the fuel dump with the first two mortars they were to turn their attention to the hangars, then escape as best they could. It was agreed that the signal for the first mortar firings was to be given as the experimental aircraft was judged to have completed its final landing run and was taxiing at slow speed. The mortar team were to be dropped off late in the afternoon near to where the farmer had left Maxime to make his way to observe the airfield some nights previously. From the overgrown lane it would be necessary to move only a few hundred metres towards the airfield boundary carrying the home-made mortar and its stolen ammunition; the distance from their intended position to the fuel dump identified by Maxime would be well within range from that point.

However, the firers would be blind, hidden within the tangle of young and mature trees and thick vegetation growing profusely around the north-eastern side of the barns airfield. Using a local map, Maxime had done his best to pinpoint the location of the fuel dump he had seen, marking it carefully with a red cross. Harold, with his navigation skills, had sat for some time at the Charon kitchen table with a compass calculating the actual magnetic heading and estimating the range. One of the team, the young girl, would have to report where the first mortar round had fallen and relay the information by running the two or three hundred metres or so from where she would be hidden at the edge of the trees back to where their crude mortar weapon was sited, hidden in a small clearing. Hopefully they would then be able to adjust the weapon to make a hit with their subsequent firings. It would quite literally be a hit-and-miss arrangement, but as long as it kept the Germans distracted it would serve its main purpose.

It was intended that Patricia stay with the small mortar team and use the walkie-talkie radio sets delivered by air recently to call in a flight of waiting Typhoon fighters once Harold had got airborne and was seen to be well clear of the field. Again, working with SOE and the RAF, they had planned that the fighters would then strafe the airfield hangar's taking as much care as possible not to hit any of the prisoners working on the site, but all knew that some innocent casualties would be inevitable. From Maxime's coded observation notes it was clear that the prisoners' shifts were changed regularly at six in the morning and six each evening. Exhausted, the prisoners were herded brutally together ready to board trucks off to one side of the field. The newly arrived prisoners were disembarked at the same point and lined up for counting before being marched off to start their twelve-hour work shift.

During her previous evening's radio transmission to London, Patricia had requested that the RAF be warned about the prisoners and also instructed to watch out for the small experimental aircraft hopefully being flown by Harold. One of the Resistance group had a contact at the basic holding camp for the Russian prisoners and was hoping to be able to get a message to them warning of some sort of action that would require them to be alert and ready to take cover. It was a risk passing such information but they felt it a responsibility. To date they had not been able to pass the message securely. The RAF were instructed not to open fire if they were in any doubt about a target. Claude and Patricia intended that RAF Typhoons buzzing around the airfield would present an opportunity for the two teams of Resistance fighters to escape without too much trouble in the gathering dusk.

During the late afternoon and evening Harold Penrose and his team were scheduled to creep cautiously through the only crop field towards the airfield perimeter, ready to make their move, hoping against hope that the Boche would be testing the aircraft the following afternoon. They knew too that if by chance both machines were flying they were to wait for the last of the pair to land before moving out of their cover among the pea crop. Once it was at taxiing speed Harold and Maxime would break out, running towards it from the rear and on its blind side as observed from the German hangars across the field. They knew that there was always the danger that the German pilot would open up the engine and try to take off if he saw armed Resistance approaching from the front; they wanted to delay as long as possible any intervention from troops on the far side of the airfield, who, it was hoped, would be more engaged with the mortar attack on their fuel dump and hangars. The other two members of Harold's group had been briefed to fire on any Wehrmacht guards who may attempt to stop their planned events taking place.

Harold and Maxime agreed after some discussion that the best plan was to jump up onto the small machine's wings, one either side, aiming their guns at the pilot. It was hoped that, facing two weapons ready to fire, the pilot would acquiesce and get out of the machine without too much trouble, allowing Harold to jump in, turn the aircraft around, open up the engine and take off. Claude made clear to Maxime that if the pilot did not co-operate he was to be immediately shot where he sat; any delays to their plan were not to be tolerated. Harold wondered if he would be able to do it in cold blood; Claude looked at him, reading his thoughts and responding with a wry smile, telling him not be such a gentleman.

During previous days Harold had taken some time to re-familiarise himself with the fake heating-boiler brochure prepared by the boffins back in England, which actually gave useful information about the aircraft's anticipated performance as they had judged it. He'd also taken half a day to return alone on a bicycle to the field he'd identified earlier with Patricia. It confirmed its suitability as a possible landing site after the experimental aircraft had been taken. Once airborne, Harold's two Resistance helpers would abandon the pilot, dead or alive, and under cover of the mortar and RAF strafing attack, escape back into the pea crop and away from the area on foot by separate routes.

Claude agreed that Patricia should make her way alone to the secondary field after the raid to co-ordinate further steps, and to act as radio operator in case things did not quite work as planned. Claude pulled from his coat-pocket a tiny Zeiss camera with fast film so that she could at least photograph the machine in detail, even if Harold were unable to fly it back to England. Patricia was aware that SOE had arranged with Michael Kelly for a Lysander from his special operations squadron to be available on that evening to attempt a landing at the escape field. Using her walkie-talkie set to a discrete radio frequency, either Patricia or Harold Penrose would be able to call the aircraft in if required. In its rear compartment would be a small drum of aviation fuel: they were still unsure of the duration of the experimental machine, specifically its fuel capacity, and it seemed a worthwhile option. Alternatively, they had planned that if the experimental machine had been damaged during the landing, or could not be flown off for some other reason, the Lizzie would land subject to an exchange of prearranged light signals and take both Harold and Patricia home after photographing then destroying the experimental machine by setting fire to its fuel.

The briefing for the small Resistance team involved took some time. At the end, after questions, they were all fully aware of how very risky the plan was. No one made any comment about how it was to be done but they all knew they would have only one chance only to pull it off. A second attempt would be impossible. But as Claude remarked, they would have the advantage of total surprise, and if they actually managed to pull it off it may help prevent renewed and advantageous German activity on Europe's battlefields. A full-size machine with the flying capabilities observed by Harold and Patricia would present a serious threat to Allied armies everywhere and to the civil population in Great Britain.

Already the threat of Germany's V1 retaliation weapon, or buzz-bomb, attacks on London and other major population centres were arousing increasing concern within the War Cabinet. The interpreters at Danesfield had found odd-looking objects in reconnaissance photographs collected from an area around

Abbeville, hidden in woods, after a report via SOE from an agent in France. The agent had no idea what the new construction sites were for but he had located no less than eight of them. Interestingly, and significantly, he made the point that there were no rail connections to the sites but seemed to be firmly convinced that they were something to do with a rumoured new secret weapon. Sarah noted that all of the sites were very similar as though a template had been used for their construction; nine standard buildings, one or two of which were of an unusual shape. The Prime Minister was thought to have expressed the view that everything possible must be done to stop the Germans developing another weapon that might aid their fight against the Allies; an invasion of England could still not be entirely ruled out. As it was, unknown to most, his mind was obsessed with details of the forthcoming invasion of Europe.

❖ ❖ ❖

Ceci quickly scanned the ops room's deliveries-and-collections board, then glanced out of the window. It was touch-and-go whether there would be much flying activity today. The lowering clouds spelt out a depressing message curtailing any meaningful reduction in the growing list of aircraft awaiting movement from factory to squadron and vice versa. Yet she knew that there were a large number of Priority One collections and deliveries to be made from nearby Supermarine shadow factories at Chattis Hill, near Salisbury, producing Spitfires. The aircraft were desperately needed in Scotland to be shipped on board the United States aircraft carrier Wasp. The carrier was intended to transport the aircraft south across the hazardous Bay of Biscay and into the Mediterranean through the narrow Straits of Gibraltar, then eastwards to a small island currently fighting for its life. It was no secret; Ceci and the girls waiting about in the ops room had all read the newspapers. The plucky Maltese were facing continuing and overwhelming series of German and Italian attacks from the air. The Royal Air Force were desperately short of fighter aircraft; a point had been reached where, if new help in the form of fighters enabling them to strike back did not arrive very soon, Malta would be broken and a strategic Allied asset lost to the Axis.

With the Americans finally in the war, Churchill had persuaded Roosevelt to allow the USS Wasp to transport the desperately needed Spitfires to Malta. The problem was that Wasp lay ready to receive the machines in the River Clyde to the west of Glasgow; but the majority of the Spitfires lay scattered around the British Isles at shadow factories, maintenance units and at some operational squadrons.

The aircraft were to be flown first to Prestwick then onto Abbotsinch, a small grass airfield conveniently located near to where the Wasp was moored, in the Clyde. Everyone knew what had to be done, but the weather was far from favourable. Fog was sitting liberally over most of southern England. Harriet was under intense pressure to start moving machines from the south. Late in the morning, two of the more experienced girls volunteered to try despite the poor visibility. Their engines could be heard but the aircraft were not seen as they rushed across the field and into the air. Within a few minutes one had returned; as its brunette and pale-faced pilot staggered back into the ops room it was too apparent that she had had a nasty experience. Sitting, cradling a cup of tea in shaking hands and with girls standing and sitting around her, she told how, climbing away from the field, she had very quickly lost all sight of the ground. Everyone agreed that the Spitfire was always a difficult machine for observing downwards; its cockpit position in relation to its wings made viewing below difficult, even on a day with good visibility. She believed that if she maintained a steady climb on instruments, she would eventually come out on top of the fog, then be able to head north towards Prestwick.

She gulped a mouthful of tea.

"Got to about fifteen hundred feet when one of Southampton's bloody barrage balloons flashed past my starboard wing. I jiggled left a bit, hoping to stay within the normal barrage departure lane when another flashed past the port wing. Frightened silly, I pushed the throttle fully forward, maximum boost and pulled the stick back and climbed like hell. I had no real idea where I was, only looking for some safe height." Most of the girls nodded in agreement. She went on.

"At three thousand I began a rate one, turning back towards the field above the balloons, or so I hoped. As I completed the turn, I just happened to glance back for some reason and, lo and behold, just behind the trailing edge the murk had momentarily cleared and there lay the airfield. I can tell you, I did the hairiest split-arse turn ever and dived for the fast-disappearing patch of grass. Not the most elegant arrival but at least I got it down. Any news of Wendy? Hasn't she returned?"

"Not heard anything of her yet. I hope she made it out OK," said Ceci. There was an agreeing murmur from everyone and they turned their eyes to the windows. Forty-five minutes later, Harriet came out of her office, smiling.

"Wendy got as far as Colerne and decided that she would like to stay alive and has landed safely there in visibility not much better than here. She did sound a bit shocked, although she didn't see any barrage balloons, but she was only too aware that they were there, somewhere. OK, we'll just have to be ready for when this mess clears up," she said, nodding towards the opaque greyness outside. The knitting, games of cards, dress-making, reading and letter-writing continued until, at half past two, a pale shadow formed on the floor of the ops room. The sun had decided to make a late appearance. They managed just seven short deliveries in the remaining two and a half hours of daylight. There was some talk of the more experienced girls doing one or two night deliveries but Harriet firmly knocked that idea on the head in view of the trigger-happy anti-aircraft crews surrounding many airfields and factories.

◆ ◆ ◆

The news was splashed over most of the day's newspapers. Mussolini had been dismissed, his responsibilities being taken over by Italy's king. The deflated dictator had left the king's Villa Savoia late that July afternoon to be immediately arrested. Unlike Germans, most Italians realised that the war was going to be lost by the Axis; Mussolini's removal from office by the near-defunct Fascist Council was the first step in a major change in Italy's wartime fortunes and allegiances. The British and Americans were making progress northwards through Italy. Helen read every newspaper she could find, absorbing the black columns of words like a sponge. Her mind racing, she wondered and worried about her father; was he still incarcerated in a prison cell in Milan, or was it worse? Borrowing change from some of the girls in the flight office, she ran to the nearest telephone box just outside the camp gates. The ubiquitous red box was empty; lifting the heavy Bakelite handset, she dialled '0' for the operator and asked for a London number. Clicks and crackles escaped from the earpiece as Helen waited, biting her lip, then eventually the operator asked her to put money into the slot in the front of the machine. She heard the coins echoing as they fell down through the machine's mechanism, and dialled the number. The phone at the other end began to ring.

"Good morning, the Red Cross. Can I help?" Helen spoke hesitantly, asking to be put through to the woman who had helped her during her first contact with the organisation when she was desperate for information about her father. The operator answered.

"Hold the line please. I'll try to connect you." It rang. Helen listened to the repetitive purring in her ear; nobody was answering. 'Come on, come on.' Her mind was racing as she waited. After nearly two minutes someone picked up the phone.

"Pronto, Giorgio Mo speaking." The voice was heavily accented. Helen paused.

"I'd like to speak with Signora Pinetta, please." At the other end there was an outrush of breath.

"Oh ... er ... momento ... I'll a fetch ...." The voice went away. Suddenly the operator's voice came on the line.

"Caller, you'll need to put another two pence into the box if you want to continue with this call." Helen pushed more coins into the slot; some fell onto the floor in her haste. A new voice came onto the line.

"You are asking for Mrs Pinetta, I think?" Helen said yes. The voice then asked a number of questions, interrupted again by the operator asking for more money.

"I'm so sorry, Miss Lorenzo, but Mrs Pinetta is no longer with us."

Helen, conscious that she had used the last of her change, responded more sharply.

"Can you please give me her new phone number then, or where I can get in touch with her?" She struggled in her bag for a pen and an old envelope. The voice trembled.

"I'm so sorry ... Mrs Pinetta was killed last weekend," then came what sounded like a sigh and a gulp, "in a hit-and-run bombing raid while out shopping. Perhaps I can help ... I am Signor Pinetta." The pips were going. Helen slammed the phone down. She stayed, leaning in the phone box swallowing mouthfuls of air, tears forming, quietly remembering the kind, bespectacled and slim Italian woman who had comforted her when she had asked for help and information about her father. On her desk she'd noticed a framed photograph of a young boy with dark eyes and a wicked smile.

That overcast day, over tea, Mrs Pinetta had told Helen how she had left Italy in late 1938 with her husband and five-year-old son, afraid of where Mussolini was leading them. After a short period of investigation and internment by the British authorities after the outbreak of war, the couple had finally been released and had been working tirelessly at the Red Cross helping innocent Italians and others caught up in their country's steep descent into turmoil after Mussolini's ill-judged alliance with Hitler.

Two weeks later, Helen caught a crowded, slow train to London from Southampton. She met Signor Pinetta, a grey-haired man, tall and slim, like his wife, carefully and smartly dressed despite wartime shortages and rationing. His small, narrow office on the third floor had a single window looking out to the west; late-afternoon sun caught the sparkle of dust fragments as disturbed air from the opening door made them dance in its reddening beams. His desk, like the numerous shelves around the room, was crowded with buff-coloured files, some with contents spilling.

Listening to Helen's request, he recalled hearing something of her father's situation from his wife after Helen's first visit all those months ago. Sitting, holding a cup of weak tea on her lap, Helen felt pangs of guilt about asking this gentle man to help her when it was he who was probably in need of help, with the loss of his wife, only a few weeks ago, and the need to bring up a young boy in a foreign country in time of war.

"Do not worry, Miss Lorenzo. Soon the war will be over, I hope. In the meantime I will try to continue my wife's investigations on your behalf. We are having a little more success in our contacts with my country since Mussolini's removal. I will be in touch. At the moment all we know is that German Commandos have rescued Mussolini from imprisonment in a hotel somewhere in the Abruzzi mountains and asked him to set up what can only be described as a puppet Fascist government in the north of my stricken country, at a place called Salo. I don't know how much support he will get but, as you know from the papers, the Allies are making real progress north. For the moment, my dear lady, do not worry. I know it's difficult but I'm sure things will turn out alright for your father." She looked at him and nodded gratefully.

"Ciao." Standing, Helen shook the man's hand, looking into

his gently smiling face, touched by his dignity.

❖ ❖ ❖

Continuing her avid reading of every daily paper, Helen knew that the atmosphere was changing daily; there was increasing optimism. The Salerno and Anzio landings in Italy were accomplished, with much loss of life at Anzio, and the Eighth Army with the Americans were past Rome despite the strategic blunder caused by the American General Mark Clark's ego. Finally, reported in newspapers some time later was the fact that Mussolini had been captured by Italian communist partisans at a roadblock in the north of the country trying to escape with his mistress and loyal members of his Fascist party, hidden within a fleeing German military column making for Innsbruck in Austria. Taking the law into their own hands, the dictator and his unfortunate and besotted mistress Claretta Petacci were eventually shot dead. A day later the newspapers reported that their bodies suffered the final indignity, hung upside down in Milan's Piazza Loreto. The newspaper pictures were horribly explicit, thought Helen. Encouraged by the news, she made regular phone calls to Signor Pinetta, who was finally able to tell her that he had firm news about her father. He had been rescued from prison in Milan, emaciated but alive and taken somewhere safe; however, he was still stuck behind retreating German lines and information was difficult to come by in the chaos.

❖ ❖ ❖

Neither Patricia nor Harold slept that night. In their separate rooms at the Charon farm they both lay awake thinking of the plan for tomorrow. Claude sat downstairs in the kitchen, a mountain of cigarette stubs growing in his cold dinner plate as he slumped in a chair watched by the cat through slit eyes. The kitchen clock ticked ponderously; by two-thirty they were all still awake with their concerns over the operation and their own private fears.

Two hours later, thin curtains left undrawn allowed the first glimmer of dawn to penetrate the small east-facing windows into the room where Patricia lay staring at the slowly emerging pieces of furniture crammed against its picture studded walls. She sat up slowly then swung her legs over the edge of the narrow bed; standing, she walked to the window, the floor creaking softly. Looking at her watch she noted four forty-five. There was a loom of soft light emerging from somewhere below the horizon; the new sun was on the move. Below, in the yard at one side of the house, a few cows stood aimlessly about as though waiting for something to happen. The sound of chattering birds caught her ears as she looked about outside, a shiver running uncontrolled through her.

There was a gentle knock. She turned, slightly startled. An unshaven face appeared around the door. It was Harold.

"Bonjour, Mademoiselle. I'm sorry, I couldn't sleep; looks like you couldn't either." She nodded and, shivering again, got back into bed pulling the covers up to her neck. He moved towards her and sat cautiously on the end of the bed looking towards the window.

"Are you scared?" he asked quietly. She nodded. Moving to one side, she pulled the covers back, gently patting the bed next to her with her free hand. Waiting for just a moment, unsure, he slid into the bed and lay next to her under the covers. She was cold; turning on his side he placed his arm around her and slept.

The noise of the Charon boys leaving for school woke them both. Opening the door slightly he looked out onto the landing; no one there. He stepped silently back to his room as Claude emerged from the bathroom, coughing.

Slowly the hours passed, each of them quiet with their thoughts, mentally running over the broad plan and their detailed part in its crucial implementation. Maxime arrived on foot at half past three. As they stood for a moment in the yard the noise of an aircraft reached them from afar. Harold knew the sound by heart, identifying it as the remaining test machine. In one of the yard's surrounding outbuildings they gathered as the herd of Friesians were milked by the two young boys under the supervision of their mother, the noise of chewing and the occasional lowing echoing gently around the lofty roof. In one of the empty stalls Claude carefully pulled away some bricks below the hay basket to reveal a large, dark cavity. Reaching in, grunting with the effort, his arm finally emerged; wound around his hand were two slings attached to Sten guns. Passing them to Maxime, he reached in again, withdrawing two more, then a pistol, a German sniper rifle and a small canvas sack with some ammunition. Carefully covered with sacking, the weapons and ammunition were hidden under the rear seat of the Citroën along with Patricia's American walkie-talkies. Ten minutes later, the four of them climbed into the car with Claude driving.

Moving carefully through narrow lanes sunk deep between hedges and trees, and when absolutely unavoidable, along main roads, they headed towards the three barns airfield. The sun was sinking fast as they made their way to the point where Maxime had first been dropped by the farmer's tractor on his earlier twenty-four-hour reconnaissance of the airfield. Patricia opened the car door, pushing at the undergrowth that clung to the very edges of the rough track. With difficulty she managed to extricate her radios; before closing the door she turned and leaned back into the car.

"Bonne chance, 'Arold." Then she kissed him on the cheek and left, disappearing into the dense greenery and was lost from sight within a few feet.

"I 'ope she can find ze uzzers OK. Eet's very easy to get lost among all zis green," Claude said, waving his hands around at the deep vegetation. He pushed at the idiosyncratic gear lever, letting in the clutch, and the Citroën moved off slowly along the damp track; now and again the route ahead was completely obscured by the rich, young growth spilling from either side into their path, brushing along the top and sides of the car.

Maxime glanced down at his watch; it was nearly seven-thirty and dusk was well established over the countryside but they were still a little early. It would not be fully dark for another thirty to forty minutes or so, he knew. He mentioned this and Claude stopped the car in a small overhung clearing to one side of the track. Turning, Maxime motioned Harold out of the rear, then lifting the seat he removed the weapons from their hiding place handing half the load to Englishman. Claude walked slowly around the clearing looking for something, with a cigarette dangling from his mouth.

"Voila!" he muttered quietly to himself. Two minutes later he was carefully manoeuvring the car backwards into the soft greenery, which sprung back as he disappeared behind its curtain. Emerging, he whispered.

"'Arold, we are about two to three kilometres from the airfield here, I sink. The Boche doesn't patrol up here, zay stay down near ze edge of ze airfield. I sink zay are frightened to come into ze woods." Maxime said something Penrose didn't understand, then pointed. At one side of the clearing was something akin to a small natural window in the vegetation, which gave a distant view of part of the darkening airfield spread below them. He could make out that between them and the airstrip lay some rough pasture then the only field with a growing crop. It looked like peas or beans to Harold in the failing light. Thankfully it was quite well grown; some four feet, he estimated from a distance. Claude lit another Gauloise and leaned comfortably against a sapling. Harold sat on a piece of fallen timber doodling in the soft earth with a stick while Maxime hummed an annoyingly repetitive little tune gazing out at the airfield from within the tree line.

"OK, we should move. I sink zat it's dark enough now and Patricia's bombers will be over soon." Claude picked up two of the Sten guns, slinging one onto his back, and the bag of ammunition; from his pocket he pulled out a small pair of binoculars and hung them around his neck. Harold took another Sten and the pistol proffered by Claude from the ammunition bag. Maxime slung the sniper rifle on his back and carried the last of the Stens in the crook of his arm, cocked, his finger alongside the trigger. Each then picked up a small bag containing some bread, cheese and a bottle of water; it would be all the sustenance they would have until the operation was completed.

Edging one at a time out of the clearing and down the side of a thin hedge that bordered the pasture, all three made it to the maturing pea crop without problems. Maxime heard it first; a dull undulating roar gradually growing louder from the north-west. Within minutes the roar from four hundred and twenty mixed aero engines at low level engulfed them, subjugating all their senses. Now and again they could just make out the shadows of large aircraft turning and heading just south of west towards Brest, with its docks and submarine pens. Claude, leading, turned and mouthed something indecipherable above the penetrating din. Weapons ready, they plunged in single file into the crop, trying in the dark to stay within the rows, so as not to leave a tell-tale trail of where they had entered and progressed down the gentle slope towards the airfield. As they proceeded in an uncomfortable mixture of crouching and crawling, the ground became damp, then wet, and finally, as the slope bottomed out, puddled and muddy. The bellowing aircraft continued streaming overhead. Now and again a distant flash lit the night sky; the leading bombers had reached their target. The passing aircraft met with no resistance from the airfield's flak batteries, lying part concealed in woodland on the other side of the airstrip.

Maxime carefully raised his head above the surface of the plants. Barely visible, about fifty feet away, lay the edge of their field and a low wire fence bordering the grass airfield. In the darkness he could see no patrolling guards; in fact he could see very little but he knew it didn't mean there were none there. Squatting together, they discussed the situation in whispers. The bombers arranged by Patricia had provided an invaluable distraction and cover for their movements, helping them to penetrate the field to within a few yards of the airfield boundary. If they stayed this close they would be well placed to intercept a landing aircraft, thought

Harold, but Claude was worried about any sentries patrolling the airfield boundary seeing or possibly hearing them. His biggest worry was the German shepherd dogs, with their acute sense of smell, that sometimes accompanied the guards. They had been seen by Maxime. Compromising, they turned and retraced their steps back up the field a little before doing their best to settle down for the remainder of the night and the following long day. The wet ground had not been anticipated and they all sat or lay, wet, trying to sleep.

The surviving bombers would be nearing their home bases now, thought Harold, four hours later, still wide awake, the adrenaline refusing to ebb. Maxime lay on his side, legs curled up tight, his arms cradling one weapon close. He was snoring very gently but the sound was easily lost in the rustling of plants blowing in a soft breeze that had sprung up in the past hour. Claude sat on the bag of ammunition, which gave him some protection from the wet soil, his knees drawn up, arms folded across with his head resting on them. The thought of a cigarette was torturing him but the pungent aroma of a Gauloise in a pea field would be sure to alert the olfactory senses of even the dullest guard and his dog.

Morning light finally penetrated down to where they lay on the earth, damp, cold and not much looking forward to the afternoon's events. Penrose ate some of his bread and cheese in an effort to stop his stomach rumbling. After a few minutes of watching, Maxime took breakfast, his taste buds awoken by watching Harold munching, machine-like. Claude sat morose, dying for a cigarette. Maxime stopped mid-chew as a gentle clinking sound came to them over the tops of the protective screen of plants. Watching each other, eyes wide, all three sat stock-still, Claude with his finger placed firmly over his mouth at the other two. The sound grew closer. Maxime reached out slowly for his Sten, then changed his mind and opened the buttons of his jacket. Moving with infinite care, his right hand pulled out a large-calibre pistol onto the barrel of which he silently screwed a long, black cylindrical silencer drawn from a pocket.

The regular clinking, they were sure, was made by a guard moving along his allotted section of airfield boundary. Hopefully he would remain oblivious to the three men sitting uncomfortably among the peas. Claude timed the intervals throughout the day; they never varied by more than a few minutes or so. As the clinking moved away on a later occasion during the late morning, Harold gingerly raised his head above the surface of the crop. A weak sun caught his face as he watched the soldier moving away from him. He was smoking. Harold decided not to mention this fact to Claude.

Across the airfield he was able to briefly take in the scene. One hangar door was wide open and the small test machine was sat half-in and half-out of the building with a number of white-and-blue coated men gathered around it. A tractor was slowly backing up to the machine. Glancing around to look at the guard again, he estimated that he must be somewhere near his turning point, ready to clink back towards them with his leashed dog. Penrose whispered his observations to the other two before the guard was within hearing distance. It was now just gone ten and they had at least another six to eight hours to wait, noted Harold. Ridiculous as it may have seemed to the others, he wished he'd brought a book to while some of the hours away. It also struck him that the test machine might not actually be flying later today. Were they really going to stay put for another twenty-four hours if that proved to be the case, he pondered.

With Claude remaining alert, Maxime and Harold tried again to catch some sleep, lying curled up on the drying earth. Maxime appeared to be able to sleep almost anywhere and was soon snoring gently again. Harold watched the cloud formations pass through his narrow field of view as he lay looking straight up through the parallel stems.

He awoke with a start. The noise was very close, a sort of high-pitched whirring, and it was moving away from them. Harold knew within the next second or so that it was the noise of the small test aircraft. He listened as it moved slowly, distancing itself from their hiding place, wishing but not daring to take a chance look above the level of the plants. His watch said it was just before twelve; he'd been asleep for less than an hour. The noise of the taxiing aircraft faded until it was just a hum in the middle distance. As they listened, the hum changed to a deeper note and they were aware of it approaching rapidly again. Within a few seconds it was passing their hiding place, airborne, climbing steadily into a pale, rainwashed sky, occasional bundles of white cumulus wafting past.

The noise quickly moved out of earshot. Crouching awkwardly, Harold tried to see it, sighting up between the narrow rows of plants, but to no avail. Forty-five minutes later, the noise returned as the test machine flew overhead the airfield. Pushing some of the plants very carefully aside, helped by Maxime and Claude, Harold raised his head slightly, hoping to watch the approaching aircraft; it would help him to understand any particular quirks of landing it. But they could hear movement nearby and, once or twice, some guttural comment.

"I think there is a sentry with a dog coming this way," whispered Penrose. He'd caught a glimpse of the top of a steel-grey helmet just above the rows of peas, bobbing slowly in their direction. The regular schedule had changed. They let the cluster of plants they had been pushing clear move slowly back into their natural position. The sound from the landing aircraft masked any other noise nearby and the three of them sat, frustrated and tense.

Harold sat, eyes closed, listening to the engine noise of the approaching aircraft. He tried to picture the scene of the aircraft lined up with the runway and to see the picture from its pilot's perspective. A constant rate of descent, then over the runway threshold, flaring the machine, flying parallel to the ground for a few seconds with the throttle closed, then, as the aircraft slowed, pulling back gently on the stick, allowing its wheels to make gentle contact with the ground. He heard the engine noise dwindle as the throttle was shut and imagined it floating just above the grass as its energy declined, then touching down, braking slowly to a halt. There was a muffled rumbling noise as the aircraft ran along the bumpy grass surface. The engine was idling.

For a moment they sensed that the aircraft had stopped almost level with their hiding place. It was confirmed a few seconds later, the engine noise increasing as the pilot turned and taxied back across the grass towards the farthest of the barn hangars. The place they had chosen to hide had proved almost ideal; it was at the end of the aircraft's landing run. Harold patted Claude on the arm, smiling at their good fortune; it would make their approach to intercepting the aircraft on the ground much easier later in the day. Taking a last swig from his water bottle, Harold sat back and thought about what he had heard. An hour later, judging the moment, Claude raised himself slowly to look across the airfield towards the hangars. It took only a few seconds but he was able to see that the aircraft was nowhere in sight and all the hangar doors were now firmly closed.

"I 'ope I am wrong, 'Arold, but ze aircraft is put away in ze 'angar. Eet is not zer. Perhaps zey will not fly it again later, I don't know." He gave a huge Gallic shrug, looking disappointed.

"Bugger," Harold whispered softly. It was a severe blow to them all. Perhaps there was a snag with the machine after the last flight; one that they could not fix quickly and the aircraft had been put in the hangar to be worked upon.

❖ ❖ ❖

The specialist interrogation centre was located on Ham Common, near Richmond, in south-west London. A large, ugly Victorian house, it sat looking out over the common. From the outside it looked like any of the other solidly built red-brick detached properties except for one or two armed guards standing about outside. Inside, Guy van der Beek sat alone in a cell, secure in the property's extensive basement area. The area was brightly lit and he could hear the coming and going of personnel as he waited for another round of talks with the air force squadron leader and army major. Their first chat had been quite civilised; they wanted to know something about his past history, school, parents, where they'd lived in Holland, where he'd learnt to fly and how had he managed to make his way to England. He'd given all this detail to the authorities when he'd first arrived eighteen months ago, having escaped across the North Sea in a stolen aircraft. He knew that they wanted to check again that his story tallied with his original tale.

The next session would be more focused; why he was where he was when captured and what exactly was his relationship with the two German officers captured with him, one now deceased? He had no watch and had little idea what time of day it was; he thought it was Saturday but could not be sure. Considering wartime rationing, he'd been well fed and allowed to take a bath the previous evening. Boredom was his major problem. He had nothing to read, nothing to momentarily take his mind off his predicament. Quite deliberate, he knew. They intended him to think seriously about his situation; the penalty for spying was hanging. Depending on how things developed, he might have to tell them something.

Led upstairs and into a sun-filled room, he was invited to take a seat in a large chintz-covered armchair set in the middle of the room. Opposite was a long, ample sofa in front of which was a sizeable coffee table on which sat a pile of thick files. Around the walls, other pieces of good-quality furniture stood interspersed with pictures, mainly reproductions, of horseracing scenes. The armed guard remained for a few moments then the air force and army officers arrived, clutching more files under their arms. They sat at either end of the sofa after greeting van der Beek in an almost friendly manner, asking after his health and requesting tea for three from the departing guard. Ten minutes later a matronly woman wearing a flowery housecoat knocked the door and came in. She was carrying a large tray on which sat a large teapot, three cups and saucers together with a milk jug and spoons. Setting the tray down carefully on a space cleared of files on the table, she asked if there was anything else they needed, and left. The Major poured the tea, offering one steaming cup to van der Beek.

Sitting back comfortably into the sofa, the Major looked across at van der Beek. Quietly he spoke, looking directly into van der Beek's eyes.

"OK, let's get on, shall we? We need to understand just what you were doing consorting with two enemy officers on a field in occupied France while on a special operation, in command of one of His Majesty's aircraft? " The approach was no-nonsense. He didn't mince words, the Dutchman noted.

He tried the story about his compass being faulty and a problem with the Lysander's engine requiring a precautionary landing but this was abruptly countered by the squadron leader: the aircraft had been successfully flown back to England by another officer that night and there appeared to have been no problem with either the compass or the engine. And was it just coincidence that two German officers happened to be present in the middle of the night on the field he had chosen to land? The two Englishmen sat back in silence waiting for the Dutchman to speak, sipping their tea in a most genteel manner, occasionally staring across at him. He sat looking into his empty cup, avoiding their gaze for a full five minutes.

"I'm afraid I am not able to help you further, gentlemen." He looked up at them.

"I hope you will reconsider, van der Beek. A full explanation may help to save your life. When you were caught, the circumstances were, to say the very least, compromising; you must agree?" The squadron leader got up and walked towards the window, staring out at the beautiful day developing.

"I imagine you are aware of what happens to spies in these

circumstances. I have unfortunately recently attended one of these awful events. Getting up at half past four, in the cold, to witness some fellow with a misplaced sense of duty led shivering and blindfolded to the gallows is not something I want to repeat. When the trap opens and the rope suddenly tautens, it creeks, you know. There is something horribly final about it. Sometimes you actually hear the neck snap. I do hope we can avoid such a fate for you." He turned, "Why don't we meet finally tomorrow morning to see if you are able to co-operate more fully with our inquiries? After that, I'm afraid circumstances will lead in a very different, and I'm sorry to say, inevitable direction. I do hope I make myself clear, van der Beek?"

The guard was summoned and the Dutchman was led back down the narrow stairs to his cell in the basement. The verbal skirmishing was over. He knew that from now on only full revelation would save his life.

❖ ❖ ❖

There was nothing they could do right now. Even if the machine was unserviceable and did not fly again today, they would still have to wait until dark before making any attempt to escape from their precarious position concealed in the pea field. Alternatively they could wait a further twenty-four hours hoping for another chance. The patrolling guard continued to pass now at irregular intervals, on occasions accompanied by the large German shepherd dog. Fortunately, for the moment they lay hidden downwind of the animal's nose. Claude's concern was for the other arrangements made to facilitate the safe escape of the captured machine with Penrose in control. He hoped that Patricia would also note that the machine was put away and that arrangements for the squadron of Typhoons to strafe the airfield may have to be rescinded. It would be a waste of effort and not without risk. She had the radio and hopefully would warn them of a possible change of plans in good time.

By late in the afternoon all three men had eaten their rations. Hidden within the close stems of the pea plants they lay, uncomfortable and disappointed. The day had been uncharacteristically warm, encouraging a penetrating humidity within their earthy hiding place. Maxime slithered away through the stems looking for somewhere private to relieve himself. This accomplished, he began to move back through the greenery, stopping for a few minutes at one point, with baited breath, to allow the guard to pass their location.

Something struck him as he carefully negotiated the route back to Claude and Harold. The wind had changed direction. Before he had slept again that morning, he was conscious of the light breeze penetrating through the crop onto his back. Now, it seemed as though it was brushing the side of his face. He whispered this to the other two. They sat up, alert, sensing, and found it was true, the breeze had moved; it had veered from south-west to nearly north. For Harold the point that struck him forcibly was the possibility that if the machine did fly again today, it may well use an approach and landing in the opposite direction to the one they had anticipated. That would mean that they were poorly placed to capture the landing machine as it slowed at the end of its landing run. Based on this morning's activity, it would stop almost half a kilometre away from their hiding position at the other end of the runway; they would be exposed for some minutes as they attempted to run after it.

Claude's concerns were more immediate. If one of the guards brought the customary dog on the next shift of patrols, there was a reasonable chance that the animal's under-utilised olfactory senses would detect their presence hidden in the peas; they would now be almost upwind of the animal. It would be a disaster and would almost certainly lead to either their capture or their death, probably both, and a complete waste of resources and an opportunity to significantly help the Allied war effort.

"Merde," he muttered quietly to himself, "Merde, merde, merde!"

Harold looked across their little patch, quizzically. The dog and the landing run prompted a whispered discussion for the next twenty minutes. The outcome was an agreement to do nothing. Maxime argued that if they lay flat on the damp but slowly drying earth, where there was virtually no wind, it was possible that their scent might not be carried through the plants to the guard's dog.

"Anyway," Maxime had argued, "the guards did not always have one of the big German shepherds with them."

Harold, after some thought, wondered if the wind's veering would actually make a lot of difference to matters. If the machine was brought out to fly again today they may well decide to continue to use the landing and take-off direction used during the morning. The breeze was very light, and in any event it was not blowing directly down the runway from the opposite direction, either, and he thought that the pilot would be happy to accept a slight crosswind from the aircraft's port quarter.

They all lay down, thinking their own thoughts. Every fifteen or twenty minutes, they heard the soldier patrolling past their location. It would be at least another ninety minutes before it would be dark enough for them to make a move and to attempt an escape back up the field and away after a futile wait.

Watching a beetle climbing steadily up one of the pea stalks, Harold jumped as the noise of an aero engine pierced the early evening's tranquillity. Sitting, he looked down the row of plants, hoping to see something across the airfield. He whispered loudly.

"The buggers are flying again, Claude."

With that he very gingerly rose to his knees, pushing the heads of the plants to one side. The hangars were now in shadow alongside the dark trees bordering the far side of the field but bright light streamed out from one with open doors. Sitting on the grass outside was the unpainted test aircraft, the high-pitched noise of its engine pulsing across the airfield. Off to his right about a hundred metres stood the guard; the noise had attracted his attention and he had turned to watch, his back still towards Harold, a large dog sniffing around the man's feet. The sun was beginning to slip down beyond the horizon.

"They must be a little desperate to complete some tests, flying so late in the day," said Penrose pointedly to the other two. "They have less than an hour or so before it will be completely dark." Claude nodded in agreement.

"OK, we have to be ready for anysing. I 'ope zey will not be long, it will be difficult for you, 'Arold, if you 'ave to fly it in ze dark, n'est pas?" Harold thought about it. If it was dark and he managed to get airborne safely, he may have trouble finding the emergency field, should it prove necessary. Even if he could locate it, making a safe landing from which he could take off again might prove a problem. He made a mental plan: if he felt it necessary to land temporarily at the secret field he would make one attempt to find it. If he was unable to immediately locate it, he would turn north by the machine's compass and keep flying until he reached England's southern coast somewhere, and try to land. Even if he wrecked it in the landing, they would at least have its remains to investigate, assuming it didn't catch fire. Then it struck him: did the machine have lit instruments for night flying?

It was climbing steadily under full power; a few minutes later they heard the pilot throttle back as the machine set off westwards towards its usual manoeuvring area, not far from the Charon farm. Maxime was quietly and systematically checking over their weapons. Every now and then they caught the sound of the aircraft as it moved around the sky. After barely twenty minutes the noise no longer faded; it returned, increasing in volume. Looking up, Penrose caught sight of it for an instant as the pilot positioned himself for a landing that would end not far from their concealment. Sitting waiting, they all wondered if this was to be the final landing for the day or if the pilot would taxi back to the far-end threshold and make another take-off.

Slowing, it approached their position. They had moved, ready, towards the edge of the pea crop, only a few yards from the wire strand fence that delineated the peas from the airfield. Claude was concerned. Where was the guard at this precise moment? While they had been moving forward they had lost sight of his position. Claude muttered something in Maxime's ear. Nodding, he pulled the pistol from his jacket and again screwed the large silencer onto the barrel. On his belly, and very slowly, he edged towards the last line of pea plants, listening, alert. Daring to put his head beyond the plant line, he looked left and right. A grey figure was walking away from him in the growing dusk, the dog trotting quietly at the soldier's heel. As he watched, he saw the aircraft approaching slowly, the guard turning at the end of his patrol line. The unique aircraft taxied slowly past, its pilot head-down some of the time watching its instruments.

Waiting for the precise moment, Maxime shouted.

"Allez!" Up off his knees, he dropped the pistol next to Claude and was running, feet pounding after the slowly taxiing aircraft, half-bent, Sten gun at the ready. Harold too was out of the crop barely a second behind him, rushing after the machine and Maxime. Claude lay on the ground, his Sten pointing towards the guard and his dog. Neither appeared to have seen the two armed men chasing the aircraft.

Then the guard saw them. Possibly a little confused, he stood for a moment, perhaps wondering if they were engineers, perhaps wanting to make some adjustments to the test machine. The pfennig dropped as he saw the two chasing men attempting to climb up onto the trailing edge of the wings either side of the cockpit, their weapons clearly silhouetted against vestiges of crimson glowing in the western sky.

Odd, he thought. Raising his machine pistol, he broke into a trot down the field, still holding onto the dog's leash. Glancing across the airfield, Claude could see no action; they were obviously unaware that an attempt was being made to capture the machine. Opening fire on the running guard with a noisy Sten gun would certainly attract attention from everyone around the airfield. Still lying part-concealed, Claude reached across to where Maxime had dropped the pistol with its silencer. Now the guard was shouting something in his native German. He's making too much noise, thought Claude, and raised the pistol, sighting the approaching guard along its extended barrel. He was now within a few yards; the guard saw the movement at the edge of the crop and turned the barrel of his weapon towards Claude.

Squeezing the trigger carefully, the round flew near-silently from the silencer's muzzle, the few yards, impacting just below the soldier's left shoulder. As it tore into him it pulled fibres from the fabric of his grey tunic jacket and vest into his chest cavity before ripping easily through soft tissue, exiting at the back of the neck.

It was a reaction, a tightening of the hand and fingers in response to the surprise of being hit forcibly by Claude's well-targeted round. The short spray of machine-pistol fire drew a line of soil spouts across the well-trodden patrol path before finally hitting Claude across his left leg and right hip. Despite his own immediate trauma the Frenchman watched as the soldier fell just feet from him and lay writhing for a few moments, rasping noises coming from him as he endured the pain from the single but ultimately fatal wound.

Claude looked down at his legs and saw there was a lot of blood; dark growing patches on his clothes, but no real pain at the moment. He knew enough to realise that he was quite helpless, unable to move by himself. He glanced over at the dying German, whose head was turned towards him. He looked incredibly young, little more than a boy. He was still breathing, just, but quickly and was obviously unconscious, eyes closed.

Entering Claude's consciousness, and from some distance away, were sounds of shouting; something was now happening on the other side of the airfield. Rolling over slightly, despite growing and intense pain, he saw the first mortar explosion. A huge cloud of soil rose into the air. Patricia had better improve her team's aim if she was intending to have any effect. Why hadn't she waited until Harold was airborne, as agreed? He lay back, feeling slightly odd, light-headed, and unable to focus on anything but his legs and lower abdomen hurting badly – and it was getting worse. The dog lay near his dead master, its head cocked to one side, panting, at a loss.

Penrose was first to gain a position on the machine's starboard wing, much to the surprise of the pilot. There was not much space between the rotating vanes mounted in the wing and the fuselage side. Whatever happened, he must not damage the vanes: that had been firmly implanted in his mind. Holding onto the cockpit side with one hand, he managed to level his Sten at the pilot with the other. The unsuspecting aviator let his mouth drop open for a moment, then his left hand moved rapidly towards the throttle lever. His intention was instantly clear to Penrose. As the engine noise rose rapidly he was losing his balance. Harold felt himself slipping off the wing, sliding down its curved top surface. There was nothing to grip onto as the rotating vanes became a dangerous blur to his side.

Penrose looked up at the German test pilot, whose head seemed to disintegrate before his eyes as he continued to slide further down the convex slope of the wing's top surface. The German's face suddenly detached disgustingly from the head as he watched. The white linen helmet turned instantly red as Maxime's Sten took a toll on the unfortunate pilot's skull. Being stockier, Maxime had not been sufficiently athletic to gain a worthwhile hold on the port wing and to climb aboard to support Harold's efforts. Seeing, then hearing the danger from the rising engine note, he stopped, and standing still took aim at the only part of the pilot he could see. He had guessed something was awry. He couldn't see Harold now, attempting to stay on board the machine on the opposite wing. Even with a clumsy weapon like the Sten, Maxime proved devastatingly accurate, firing only single shots, not a damaging, spreading burst from its short barrel. The effect was devastating, immediate and gruesome.

Somehow avoiding the worst of the dripping remains of the skull, Penrose clawed his way over the side of the cockpit coaming. Leaning across the slumped dead pilot, he closed the throttle. The machine came to a halt. Like an automaton, mind blank, he reached down close to the remains of the pilot, locating the pin, releasing the blood-soaked canvas harness holding the shattered man to his seat. Opposite, Maxime had finally been able to clamber up onto the port wing. Each reaching under the arms of the corpse, they lifted him clear and allowed him to slide ungracefully off the wing onto the grass. Pulling the harness out of the way, Penrose sank into the seat. The interior of the cockpit was covered in blood. Wiping it off with his bare hands from the instruments and throttle lever, Penrose became aware of Maxime's agitation; the Frenchman was pointing and shouting. Looking to his right, Penrose could see running men, firing at them as they approached from the far side of the airfield.

Maxime jumped down. Lying near-flat on the turf, he began sending bursts of covering fire towards a group of approaching troops spraying dangerously from their waving machine pistols. Harold opened the throttle and the flying machine began to move. For a moment the approaching firing stopped. He briefly wondered if they were unsure who was piloting it; if they thought it was their pilot they may be cautious about hitting him. He turned the aircraft around so that it was pointing back up the airfield.

"Now or never," he muttered as he pulled the throttle all the way open. Not bothering to watch the few basic instruments in front of him, he concentrated on trying to keep it straight and on a diverging course with the approaching soldiers, scattered in the dusk. Despite his lack of familiarity with the aircraft, he sensed it quickly becoming light, ready to fly.

He caught its brilliant birth out of the corner of his eye. Within a split-second there was an enormous explosion off to his left; the following blast wave covered the short distance to him in no time. Lifted violently sideways off the ground, the aircraft turned instantly onto its side. He fought to right her as, despite the engine at full pelt, she began to fall from thirty or forty feet towards the ground. He realised then; in his rush to get away he had not had time to strap himself into the tiny cockpit.

The mortar team were elated. Their young girl spotter ran back with the news they all wanted; after two wasted shots, they had finally hit the fuel dump, and a huge gout of yellow-and-orange flame had erupted, throwing burning debris high above the airfield and momentarily lighting up the area with a brilliant flash. Glancing down at her map, Patricia then moved the tubular barrel a few degrees to the right, raising the weapon's elevation fractionally. The last precious round was brought to its still-smoking mouth. Placing its fins in the blackened hole, she let it drop. Covering their ears, they felt the compression as it fired, trusting it would find a worthy target somewhere among the hangars. Plunging earthwards, it landed close to a truck loaded with timber – additional prefabricated parts for the new, larger hangars. The truck's enormous diesel tank, punctured by shrapnel fragments, exploded with a dull crump, igniting its cargo of timber and setting the nearest small wooden hangar alight at one end.

The young woman burst through the trees again with the news of the last firing. She was excited, describing a truck catching fire and the bedlam in the camp as the fuel dump, truck and hangar fires caught firm hold. It seemed, she said, that troops were rushing about in panic trying to contain each blaze with one small fire truck. Keeping calm, the mortar team checked around, making sure nothing remained that could identify the area as the place from where the attack had been launched. The mortar was strapped onto the back of one of the two young men, who left the scene alone knowing exactly where he was to hide the weapon.

Quickly bidding farewell to the others, Patricia picked up her bag, made her way through the trees and the clinging, almost impenetrable shrubbery towards the east and the emergency airfield. The others melted away silently into the woods in different directions. She suddenly wondered about Harold and the aircraft. The team's spotter had not reported anything of him and the test machine before they had dispersed. How had she managed to overlook the whole reason for their action, she wondered. She needed to call in the RAF once she knew he was clear of the field, but at that moment she hadn't a clue where he was.

❖ ❖ ❖

"Christ!" the word shot from his lips as he found the aircraft falling sideways and himself falling from the cockpit. Slamming the stick over, he attempted to right the aircraft before it hit the ground, but fell back into the seat as his did so. He'd seen the machine's incredible flying characteristics from his earlier observations on the ground, and now he was about to experience them. As he moved the stick rapidly across the cockpit the aircraft immediately levelled off. The response to the controls was outside his experience: instant and quite remarkable. But the aircraft's downward momentum could not be halted in the little height available. Penrose braced himself, realising that they were going to hit the ground heavily. It struck very firmly, first with the starboard undercarriage leg, then bounced onto the left before careering back into the air again. Distinctly, above the sound of the revving engine, he had heard, but more crucially felt, two solid cracks: the sound of major damage to the undercarriage. Opening the throttle full again he tried pulling back on the stick. He had to keep it airborne. He suspected in that moment that it would not land again conventionally. To his left, soldiers were getting up off the ground, no doubt blown over by the force of the blast. One grey-coated figure, quite close, was firing steadily at him; it could only be a matter of seconds before he was hit.

❖ ❖ ❖

Pushing as best she could through the dark, grasping vegetation, Patricia reached the edge of the woodland and peered down at the airfield. Various fires had taken a steady hold and illuminated the whole of the barns area on one side of the airfield. Looking hard, she tried to see beyond the fire's glow: where was the aircraft? Had it escaped, or was it still down there? She was able to pick out occasional flickering gunfire from soldiers, bright-yellow streams arcing in the growing dusk. Then, behind the gunfire, she saw it: flying very slowly, barely gaining height was the test machine. Above the cacophony of noise, she could hear its high-pitched screaming as it moved, almost ponderously, across the airfield clawing for altitude away from the murderous fire aimed at it. As it passed quite close to her hidden position she watched it. There was something odd about it though, and she wasn't quite sure what it was.

❖ ❖ ❖

Harold Penrose huddled down into the small cockpit out of a misplaced sense of self-preservation from winging bullets and because he had no goggles and the increasing air stream was making it difficult to see where he was headed. It was only then he noticed that only a few shards of the small windscreen in front of him remained intact. Some bullets had come very close. Peering through half-closed eyes, he turned the machine left so that the woods rising behind the field would help screen him from further ground fire as he crawled away into the darkening sky.

Then he was clear. He'd actually made it out of the field. Surprisingly he was alive and the aircraft appeared to be behaving itself. His mind turned to the probability that the undercarriage was seriously damaged after his bouncy, unscripted heavy landing. If he made his way to their emergency field and attempted a landing it might well prove final. The machine would crash and be unable to fly on to England. He knew the decision was made for him. He would have to make a direct flight across the Channel and hope that there was sufficient fuel on board. Glancing back into the cockpit, he quickly scanned the instruments, with their unfamiliar calibrations. Speed was just under one hundred kilometres an hour; height now four hundred metres and still slowly climbing; his heading was ... ? He looked carefully for a full five seconds at the small, poorly lit instrument panel.

"My God, there's no bloody compass!" he shouted out aloud. How was he to find his way home without a compass? His training took control. The loom of the disappeared sun still glowed red and orange below the western horizon; keeping the last rays of light on his left would ensure that for as long as they lasted he would be heading roughly north. Turning slightly right, still climbing the machine, he tried to sink yet further into the confines of the tiny bloodstained cockpit.

❖ ❖ ❖

It disappeared from Patricia's sight into the near-darkness behind the trees. Pulling the bag off her shoulder, she groped around inside it, sitting on the damp grass. Switching on the heavy walkie-talkie set, she waited a moment for it to warm up, hoping that the attacking aircraft were within range.

"Laycock Red Leader, this is Curlew." Static filled her ear as she held the cumbersome handset against her head.

"Laycock Red Leader, come in, this is Curlew."

"Receiving you, Curlew, loud and clear," came a clear, metallic response. "Do you have trade for us? Over."

She gulped. Somewhere out there was a flight of Hawker Typhoons, ideally suited to ground attack and armed with both cannons and rockets. Patricia squeezed the switch.

"Laycock Red Leader, Azzaro is clear, fulfil your obligations. Over." There was a pause of a few seconds, then from somewhere out of the ether,

"Roger, Curlew. Good luck, out."

Switching off, she pushed the heavy radio back into her bag and, without waiting to see the outcome, headed back into the trees. A few moments later she became aware of a growing noise in the darkness above her, like a swarm of violent, very angry, deep-throated bees.

Maxime had the briefest of moments to watch Harold's escape in the experimental aircraft. For an instant he and the machine were silhouetted black against the blast of the exploding fuel dump as Maxime crawled back towards the pea field, and what he hoped would be sanctuary for a few moments while he regained his breath and gathered his thoughts.

Where was Claude? Maxime was too conscious that there had been a lack of supporting fire from Claude during the last few critical minutes. With the aircraft making its escape the troops rushing across the airfield had turned and were running back to the burning chaos around the barns. But where were the guards who had been patrolling the edge of the field – were they still about? Looking carefully for movement, he allowed his eyes to slowly scan the edge of the airfield. Far off to his right he could just make out what seemed to be a soldier, apparently moving away from him, still mechanically carrying out his patrol despite the chaos on the other side of the field. But where was the guard who should be patrolling the length of wire that divided the airfield from the pea crop? He could see nothing moving. His eyes flicked back again. There was something there: a low, elongated mound, something not quite natural. Lying still, he kept watching. As his eyes eventually penetrated the dusk, he could see that the long mound was actually made up of three distinct objects. One was moving about from time to time.

His Sten resting on his right arm, out ahead, he crawled slowly and carefully towards the objects. Thirty yards closer he was able to make it out: a dog. It was, he could now see, a German shepherd guard dog. Every few seconds it got up, walked about with its tail down, then sat again, close to one of the objects. Neither of the two other objects moved during the next ten minutes as he watched, all the while listening to the sounds of panic and mayhem behind him. He began to crawl again towards the fence line, which was now almost invisible in the dark. Suddenly he was aware that the dog was running towards him, making a low whining sound. His finger fell to the trigger, ready to fire if necessary. The animal appeared lost, unsure, its ears flat and its tail wagging slowly, low down. Maxime looked carefully around then rose and ran swiftly, half-bent towards the two inert masses near the fence line, the dog cowering, uncertain, behind.

The young soldier was dead. Taking his fingers from the side of the man's neck and getting up from his knees after checking for a pulse, Maxime became aware that his right hand was sticky. Only later, in the light of early morning would he be aware that the wetness soaking his trousers was not evening dew, but blood. Moving a few yards on, he came across Claude, still breathing and semi-conscious. Fearful of using a light, he gently felt the man all over, locating the ripped skin and smashed bone on Claude's right hip, and the deep flesh wounds to his upper left leg. He moaned.

"Maxime, c'est vous?" Putting his weapon down, Maxime removed his jacket and, folding it, placed it under the wounded man's head.

"Oui, Claude, c'est moi. Je suis venu pour vous ramener à la maison." But Maxime wondered how he was going to manage to get the seriously injured man home alive.

From where they lay, close together, the approaching noise became suddenly deafening. Aircraft were swooping in the darkness firing into the inferno on the far side of the airfield. Lying, cradling Claude's head against his chest, Maxime watched the final destruction of the hangars and vehicles. The dog lay on its belly close to them, quietly whining, ears still held flat along its head, tail between it legs. At some point a flak barrage opened up briefly from somewhere behind the burning hangars, the noise increasing to almost unbearable levels. In the brilliantly flickering light from the mass of orange-and-yellow flames he could see men running about as the swooping aircraft continued to wreak havoc on the site. Now and again one of the machines flashed across the airfield firing rockets, their streaming tails of flame pouring into the conflagration. Twice there were huge explosions from within the burning buildings, sending masses of burning debris high into the night sky.

It was suddenly over. The attacking aircraft left as quickly as they had arrived, their occasional black shapes merging with the night sky as they climbed away swiftly towards the coast, the drone of their powerful Napier engines slowly diminishing. As he watched the inferno, Maxime saw something oddly new, as men rushed about trying to quell the mass of flame that was engulfing the hangars and now being driven on by a gentle breeze. From somewhere off to the right he could make out a mass of silhouetted figures moving towards the core of destruction, reinforcements in the fire-fight, he imagined. Looking up from adjusting a crudely applied bandage on Claude's hip, he saw something unusual. As the mass of figures approached the fire-fighters he saw individuals detach, appearing to attack them. With a growing pall of smoke blowing across the field it was difficult to see exactly what was happening but it seemed from his low position, lying with Claude, that attempts to control the blaze by the Germans were being thwarted by others.

"Mon Dieu, c'est les prisonniers!" he mouthed quietly. The realisation struck him: the Russian prisoners had somehow managed to escape during the attack and were now taking revenge on their tormentors during the intense chaos of its aftermath. Suddenly worried about the possibility of any patrolling guards, Maxime decided that he and Claude needed to conceal themselves and if possible get away from the airfield altogether. Slinging the two Sten guns over his shoulder, he bent to lift the unconscious Claude, levering him over his right shoulder. Although strong – a lifetime's work on the land had developed his frame and fitness naturally – he staggered under the weight of Claude's helpless body. Lurching the few yards to the fence, he managed to climb over it without dropping either Claude or the weapons. Now and again Claude made short gasping sounds as pain broke through his unconsciousness. Maxime muttered words of encouragement.

Once through the fence, Maxime continued to stagger up the field along the rows of pea plants, intent on using his momentum to get as far as he could before needing to rest. Finally, he had to lower the injured man to the ground, slumping down beside him, out of breath and drained of energy. It occurred to him that they had eaten very little that day. The dog had been following, a few respectful metres behind, and lay watching them. Claude moved, trying to raise his head.

"Maxime, mon vieil ami," he croaked, "laissez-moi ici, il faut vous sauver !" Maxime took the man's head in his arms and, talking softly, made clear that he had no intention of leaving his friend alone; he was going to get him to a doctor – somehow. They lay next to one another on the damp earth, Maxime raising himself on his elbows every so often to look over at his colleague. He thought about the best course of action. If he managed to carry Claude the two kilometres or so back to the woods, he could leave him safely there while he went to recover the old Citroën from where Claude had hidden it. In Dinant he knew of a doctor who would take care of the injured man without asking questions.

Time was against them. Claude's condition needed urgent and professional attention. Despite Maxime's attempts at binding the wounds with pieces of his own torn clothing, the man was losing a lot of blood and was obviously in deep shock. If Maxime was going to move he would have to start before very long; early streaks of dawn light would soon be pushing the night aside. Now and again he could hear bursts of gunfire coming from across the airfield. Crouching, he raised his head above the pea crop and looked across at the brightly burning scene. Bringing his gaze nearer, he looked for guards along the airfield border. He could see no movement in the darkness and decided to take the risk.

◆ ◆ ◆

The sun's final glimmering had gone. It was now dark. Penrose's temporary use of its diminishing rays as a compass had expired. Below and ahead, foaming crests breaking on the black shoreline confirmed his position and general direction: he was leaving the French coast somewhere, he wasn't sure where. Ahead, the English Channel stretched uninvitingly, regular rows of waves showing occasional pale-white gashes in its black surface. It was those breaking waves, in particular their direction, that would give him some guidance as he progressed northwards. He was aware that maintaining a constant angle of flight against the direction of the white breakers would ensure that he held a constant course and that eventually he would end up somewhere off England's south coast. His main concerns were fuel, would he make it, and the cold that was penetrating his body up here, a thousand feet above the sea.

❖ ❖ ❖

It took some time and lots of effort to get Claude back up onto his shoulders again. Maxime could feel his crudely applied, blood-soaked bandages seeping against his chest as he trudged slowly and steadily up the field's incline in darkness, breathing deeply and trying not to trip against the sturdy stems of the peas. Recalling that night later, he told how he had somehow managed to ignore his body's protestations, just concentrating on putting one foot in front of the other until eventually, some hours later, they reached shelter within the trees. How long it had taken he had no real idea. If it had been much further his strength would have failed him, he knew. Straining and holding his breath, he laid Claude down gently. The man felt very cold. On checking his pulse in the growing dawn light, there was still a flicker of life. It had taken the best part of seven hours. The dog stood watching nearby as he collected leaf-filled stems from around them and placed them carefully over Claude in an attempt to preserve any heat he still possessed. He left his jacket over all.

Leaning over, he whispered into the wounded man's ear. He would return shortly with help. From somewhere deep within he drew new strength and pushed his way into the dense vegetation, not quite sure in which direction their original point of departure lay within the woods. The dog arose, appearing to want to accompany Maxime, then it turned, trotting back to Claude's body, lying down beside him, very close. He knew he had to find the Citroën quickly; the Germans would have the ground covered with troops after this attack if only to recapture escaped Russian prisoners. It took nearly forty minutes before he finally stumbled, angry and frustrated, into the clearing where they had pulled off the track nearly thirty-six hours earlier. He finally found the car, carefully secreted by Claude behind the curtain of vegetation.

He got in and pushed the starter button. The engine throbbed gently and he engaged a gear. Following the track for half a kilometre, he stopped, estimating that this was probably as near as he was going to get to where Claude now lay. It was a risk leaving the car on the track but he had few alternatives; the saving grace was that the narrow, overgrown route was rarely used these days and unlikely to attract any farm traffic at this early hour of the morning. Plunging into the undergrowth and relying only on instinct, he pushed his way towards where he believed he'd left Claude.

There was a noise. His heart pounded; his stomach a void. He ducked down quickly; there was definitely somebody moving nearby, off to his left. Hidden in a mass of dark shadow-filled greenery he tried to contain his noisy breathing, peering through the thick undergrowth. It moved again, about twenty metres away, from the same direction. A German patrol was out there; they had moved fast. Tense and sitting absolutely still, he strained his ears and eyes in the dimness. His Sten was hooked over his shoulder; moving it would rustle the vegetation resting against him and probably alert the troops to his position. His heart was in his mouth. Whoever was there had moved nearer, taking little care of the noise he made.

It was the tail that caused him to let out an unrestrained sigh of relief. Wagging its large tail to and fro against the close vegetation, the dog made itself known, its grey-green eyes luminous in the developing light. Unsure, Maxime watched the animal, conscious that it was actually a trained and normally vicious guard dog belonging to a regime that had little respect for non-Aryans. The creature, still wagging, slowly walked towards him. There was nothing menacing in its approach. It stood for a moment looking up, alert, then turned and walked deliberately away. When Maxime made no attempt to move, it turned again and slowly padded back, looking up, its mouth open, panting, then it let out a sharp single bark. Maxime jumped; it was unexpected. Was it trying to tell him something? He recalled hearing tales of animals communicating as best they could in an effort to help humans in some dire endeavour. The animal turned again and walked away, looking around every few steps. Maxime followed cautiously, pushing aside young trees and vegetation.

In less than fifteen minutes, and despite getting separated from the dog at one point, Maxime came across Claude's prone shape beneath his natural blanket of branches. He knelt down over him.

"Claude, ça va?" The wounded man's eyes flickered open; he tried to turn his head, mouthing almost inaudibly.

"Oui ... Maxime." It was clear that he was not OK, but in considerable pain, and it was essential that he had urgent professional treatment for his terrible wounds. Gathering strength for a moment, Maxime removed the leafy insulation covering Claude. Pushing his arm around his shoulder he managed to pull him up to a sitting position. Claude let out a hiss of pain as his posture changed and more weight was forced onto his shattered hip.

"Oh putain! J'suis vraiment désolé, Claude."

The helpless man nodded slightly in response, understanding Maxime's difficulty.

Kneeling astride Claude's bloodied legs, leaning forward, Maxime pulled him, grunting with the intense pain, up onto his left shoulder. Raising himself from this position with Claude securely held proved nigh impossible. His leg muscles strained to lift the load, but he couldn't manage it. It took four straining attempts before finally, and gasping, he stood upright. The dog watched. Then he noticed he'd left his weapon on the ground. It would be impossible to bend down to retrieve it again. Motioning to the dog while meaningfully kicking at the Sten's canvas sling, he hoped to make it understand. The dog now sat, ears cocked, head to one side, watching Maxime's odd antics. After a few minutes of Maxime's struggling, trying to communicate his wishes to the animal, it stood and walked towards the weapon. Picking up the sling in its mouth, it dragged the gun across the ground. It lifted its big head and the sling touched Maxime's hand. Bending his knees very slightly, he managed to take the weapon from the animal's dribbling muzzle and set off heavily along the broken path created by their arrival, back to the car.

Laying Claude across the rear seat, he managed to cover him with a dirty torn blanket he'd found in the car's boot. The seat was not quite wide enough, so Claude was propped up slightly against the seat back, diagonally into one corner, his damaged legs straight out, his head leaning back, mouth open, and breath rasping. Closing the Citroën's rear doors gently after making sure his passenger was settled securely, Maxime made to get into the driver's seat. The dog sat on the track in front of the driver's door. Reaching out, Maxime stroked the coarse fur on its head, hoping it would move. It remained, sitting, looking up at him, its mouth open in a sort of canine smile, anticipating. Maxime pulled the door partially open. The dog got up, sidled round it and jumped through the opening up and into the car.

"Alors, comme ça, tu veux v'nir aussi, toii?!" It was clear that the animal had no intention of being left alone in the wood.

As Maxime drove slowly down the rough track, the dog sat alongside him, watching, alert, through the windscreen, tongue lolling. They arrived at a minor road, stopping a few metres short. Maxime glanced at his watch; it was now gone five in the morning. The rural curfew had just ended but regardless the road was filled with military vehicles streaming in both directions. Last night's events had clearly opened up a hornets' nest. There were few options open in this situation. Letting in the clutch, he took advantage of a rare gap in the traffic, entering the road between a pair of heavy grey military trucks. The vehicle ahead of him was packed with grey-uniformed troops; after an initial look at the Citroën they took little notice of the muddy black car sandwiched between them and their Wehrmacht colleagues behind.

Then it struck him. The Boche would have roadblocks

everywhere now; sooner or later he would be stopped at one. Any benefits of being part of a German convoy would soon prove worthless; he had to get off this road, and do it without creating suspicion. Born and bred in the area, he knew the land and its roads and tracks and general geography like the back of his hand. Making it to Dinant without being stopped at some point was unlikely and he began to consider other options as he watched the heavy tyres on the truck ahead pounding the tarmac, emitting their characteristic low buzz.

He knew there was a crossroads about five kilometres ahead. If the Germans were going to have a roadblock anywhere it would be there, he surmised; it was an obvious place, at the junction of four important roads connecting Dinant with a variety of outlying villages around the compass. He had to get off the road before then. Littering the countryside was a series of lanes and tracks that had developed in an ad hoc fashion over hundreds of years, giving farmers and smallholders access to their fields. He knew there were a number of suitable rural tracks that crossed the road along which they were travelling. The convoy had speeded up for some reason. He found his mind working harder to choose a route that would give him a chance to escape from their current predicament. Still roaring along ahead of him, the truck did not slow even as they approached a series of bends that he knew they would be negotiating in a few minutes. At the second bend, off to the right was a narrow lane, just wide enough for a tractor or horse with cart. It led by a very roundabout route to Terenez, not too far from the Charon farm. Taking a risk, he deliberately slowed the car ready to pull off. The truck behind came close to his rear bumper, intimidating the Citroën to keep up with the rest of the fast-moving column. The horn blasted behind him, full of menace. Putting his left hand out of the window, he waved it up and down, trying to indicate to the German driver that he was going to turn off. The truck edged back slightly, again blowing its horn. In his mirror Maxime could see the German driver and his mate glowering at his back.

They were approaching the lane; he pulled well over to the right, giving the German truck driver every opportunity to overtake as he slowed further. A further horn blast from the truck made him jump, breaking his concentration on leaving the convoy with as little disruption and fuss as possible. They were on it. The entrance to the lane appeared with little warning as they rounded the apex of the second bend. Pulling the wheel hard down, he swerved off the main road, the Citroën's wheels sliding dangerously on the muddy surface. The rear of the car slid out to the left carried by the momentum of their rapid right lurch off the main road. He braked; even as his feet hit the pedal he knew it was a stupid thing to do. The rear wheels stopped instantly and the tail of the car spun, making a game attempt to catch up with its front. There was a resounding 'Crump!' The rear quarter hit a tree, causing the Citroën to lurch back across in the opposite direction. Releasing the brakes, he pushed the accelerator a touch. The car straightened, rushing between the high banks either side of the narrow route. With the car pointing in the correct direction Maxime slowed carefully and stopped, accompanied by a wild howling noise. The dog seemed unperturbed; it sat, eyes and ears alert. Glancing around, he looked into the back of the car. Claude was not there. Stretching around, he raised himself in the driver's seat and looked down and behind him.

The injured man lay in a heap, still covered by the dirty blanket in the rear foot wells, moaning barely audibly. Maxime quickly leaned over, pulling the cover from the man, noticing as he did so that the back seat was covered in a wide, dark stain. Rushing around, he pulled open the rear passenger door. Claude was unconscious, lying awkwardly, in a sort of heap. It proved difficult to raise the man from the narrow depths of the foot wells, back and up onto the back seat again. The dog remained in the front passenger seat still watching all around. The crude bandages had become dislodged and had to be repositioned although they appeared to be serving little purpose. Eventually, Maxime was as satisfied as he was going to be for the moment. Closing the rear doors, he restarted the car. As they moved away the loud screeching came alive again. He stopped, jumping out, worried. The Citroën's rear quarter had been bent and was rubbing on the rear tyre. Gripping the edge of the metalwork, he braced as he tried to tug the offending bodywork off the rubber. It gave a little but still caught in places. Searching quickly around, he found a thick, heavy stick; forcing it between the wheel and body he managed to dislodge the metal sufficiently to clear the tyre. They set off again, quietly.

❖ ❖ ❖

Striding along through more open areas of the woods and managing to avoid most of the fallen and rotting timber, Patricia hoped that Marcel, Claude's eldest son, had left the bicycle hidden as agreed. Unsure of what action Harold would take once airborne, she had to make her way to their emergency airfield in case he opted to land there. It was nearly four kilometres to where, two days before, Marcel had been ordered to conceal a heavy bicycle behind an old stone bridge parapet. Breathing heavily and tired, she reached the spot, and with her torch searched both banks of the dried-up stream, which was now active only in very wet winters.

It was not there, anywhere. Leaning against the parapet, she stopped to think calmly. She was worried; had Marcel been caught? Had she misunderstood the location arrangements? 'Merde! Where is the bloody thing?' she wondered. Then it occurred to her that the occasional stream meandered around the countryside. In the course of its meanderings it had required a number of small bridges to be built in times past. Perhaps it wasn't this bridge; in that case, which bridge was it? She had no idea how many there were.

Her decision was whether to go back to the previous bridge or to continue to the next one. She decided that she would go on to the next one. Rationalising, she considered the fact that Marcel and his father lived in that direction; she thought it more likely that the young man would have delivered the cycle to a location nearer his home, rather than further from it, particularly as he would then have had to walk home. Tired but determined, she strode on again, her torch lighting the way on occasions; at least it was easier to walk along the narrow track than through the woods.

Twenty frustrating minutes later she reached the next bridge. It was a much grander construction than the previous one, made entirely from local stone. Putting her bag down, she searched on either side of the bridge, the yellow beam flicking to and fro. Nothing. Now worried, Patricia leaned over the thick parapet, staring down at the dry bed of the stream's course. It was almost three in the morning and the tension of the last few hours had drained her. She wondered how far it was to the next bridge. If she was caught out during curfew, particularly after the attack on the three barns airfield, she knew she would be in serious trouble. But there were few alternatives, she was too aware. If Harold had landed at the emergency field he may require help of some sort; she would have to go on regardless, walking if necessary. It was in the plan, and anyway, in her bag was the bulky walkie-talkie set with which she could summon in a Lysander, with its small cask of aviation fuel, to offer them both a method of getting home if all else failed.

Sitting quietly for a few minutes, she summoned up the courage to get up and carry on. As she got up, the torch slipped from her hand. Striking the ground, it switched itself on. A beam of pale yellow light pierced the surrounding trees and shrubbery. The beam struck the wheel rims of the cycle, reflecting them weakly back. Carefully concealed about five metres from the left parapet was a heavy black bike with what had once been chrome wheels, now mostly corroded save for one or two patches of brightness. It was impossible to see it from the bridge and it would have been difficult to see even in daylight. The chance dropping of her torch had provided a clue. Patricia gave a silent thanks to St Antoine and struggled to pull the elderly machine from the encompassing shrubbery up onto the track. Collecting her bags, she mounted and set off.

The night was cool; clear skies had allowed the past day's warmth to escape into the atmosphere but as she rode hard she felt her temperature rising as she careered along the narrow track.

Hanging limbs and creepers struck her face from time to time in the gathering dawn greyness. After a few near misses with bends and trees she finally made it to the field. Concealing the cycle again, she crept through a thin stand of trees until she could see the outline of the field fully. There was nothing there; the large field was completely empty. Either Harold had decided to fly straight back to England or something had gone wrong. Both relieved and disappointed, she found a sheltered and comfortable spot and sat back against a tree, watching the moon begin its late descent from the heavens, thinking.

❖ ❖ ❖

Seeing Claude lying there, Madame Charon burst into tears. He was alive – Maxime checked. There was a flickering pulse but they could get no response from the unconscious Claude. Lifting him carefully once again, he carried the limp, bloody body into the house, struggling and panting up the narrow stairs. Imposing self-control over her concerns for the man, Madame rushed about, preparing hot water and clean bandages. Maxime drove to Dinant to collect the doctor, but not before cleaning off the bloodstains in the rear of the car, and making an attempt to further straighten the damaged bodywork on the Citroën. The two factors could arouse suspicion if he was stopped by the Boche.

By late morning the doctor was carefully inspecting Claude's wounds. By all reasonable and prudent standards the man should be in a hospital receiving expert treatment from an orthopaedic surgeon able to assemble the smashed hip-bones, muscle and tendons. Two and a half hours later the doctor emerged from the bedroom, his face lined with foreboding. With Madame

Charon assisting, he had used his considerable medical skills to undertake impromptu surgery, somehow rebuilding the remains of the smashed hip and suturing the wounds on his left leg, fully aware that Claude, if he survived, would never walk properly again – if at all. Sitting and supping a small glass of Calvados, the doctor lit a cigarette.

"And what about you, Maxime? How are you feeling? You must have enormous strength and will to do what you have done. Poor Claude has you to thank for his life, I think – if he survives." The dog lay exhausted and asleep in front of the range cooker as Maxime looked up wearily from his chair in the kitchen, sipping the last dregs of a black ersatz coffee. The cat watched everything.

"Perhaps, doctor, but if matters had been reversed he would have done the same for me, I think." The doctor nodded, then stood and kissed Madame Charon on both cheeks. Taking his bag, he climbed wearily again into the Citroën, his body tired, his face grey with exhaustion and worry. Maxime slammed the driver's door shut and turned the car to face the yard gate.

"Don't worry, Madame, I will try to return in two or three days to see how things are going," called the doctor from the open window. "Let him sleep and check the dressings every twelve hours." He closed the window and Maxime drove away with the doctor slumped back alongside him. On the road to Dinant the doctor managed to successfully negotiate three checkpoints; the Germans were out with a vengeance.

❖ ❖ ❖

Patricia must have nodded off for a few moments. Something had woken her. She sat listening to the night around her. Somewhere, ahead, she could see occasional flickers of light coming from where the emergency landing field sloped gently away to the south. She watched, unsure. Then, more noises: guttural shouting and dogs barking. The Boche were searching, that much was evident; she wondered, 'Why right here? How did they know'?

Standing, she waited for a moment, trying to see if there were others on the same task approaching from other directions. Picking up her bags and the radio case, she returned to her bicycle. Strapping the radio set onto the rear carrier, she slung the heavy bag with the walkie-talkie set around her neck and began pushing through the young trees towards a path that ran alongside the stream. Reaching it after a few minutes, she was pedalling firmly along the soft surface of the overhung path. The noises behind her had faded; now they could only occasionally be heard. After twenty minutes or so she joined a more substantial track leading north. Setting off along it, riding carefully, stopping every now and then to listen, she made good progress northwards away from the three barns field. The track was wider here and she managed to increase speed, putting valuable distance between her and any pursuers.

The light was improving and she could just see across fields and well up ahead where the track ran straight. Rounding a sharp bend, she almost ran into him. The field-grey uniform provided excellent camouflage in the early half-light. His weapon was aimed at her chest as she skidded to a halt. As she stopped, just managing to stay upright, three other Wehrmacht troops joined their colleague from where they had been relieving themselves in the hedgerow. A bright beam of light bored into her eyes as the four soldiers studied her. One of them, a sergeant, barked something at her in German. She raised her hands and the bicycle fell with a clatter onto the stony path; the brown attaché case containing the radio set broke free from its rack. Grunting, one of them bent and picked up the small leather case, opening it as he did so. He uttered something in astonishment and the others moved to where he stood; the lamp shone onto the open case with its wires, headset and Morse key.

It would have to be now. Adrenalin flooded her. She sprinted straight ahead. It was ten yards to where the trees grew, with their enveloping shadows. Patricia had almost made it when a short burst of machine-pistol fire ripped into the branches around her. Fragments of wood hit her in the face, some entering her left eye. Running almost blindly, crashing through young trees, bouncing off mature ones, she tried to pull the heavy bag from around her neck; it was an impediment. As she did so she remembered the old grenade that had lain there for weeks; would it work now? She couldn't open her left eye and she was aware that it was bleeding heavily, the warm blood running down her cheek and neck.

The soldiers were bellowing and firing indiscriminately through the woodland, hoping, no doubt, for a lucky shot, but so far she was not seriously hurt. Here the trees were mature and grew more widely apart. Trying to restrain the bag from bouncing around her waist, she ran on, her left eye firmly closed, but she knew she could not keep it up for long. Panting desperately, she could see in the shadowy light that not far ahead the trees stopped and open fields lay just beyond. They seemed to have lost ground to her but were not far away. Ducking around a substantial beech tree, she threw herself onto the ground, pulling the bag from her neck. As she upended it, the walkie-talkie radio, some personal possessions and all sorts of paraphernalia fell around the tree's thick base, including the battered grenade. Grasping, Patricia peered at it. The pin was secure. Looping her fine fingers around its ring, she pulled. It slid out easily as she held the trigger handle firmly down. They were blundering towards her; their firing had stopped and there appeared to be only three of them. As she estimated their closing distance, she stood back from the tree, exposed, and swung her arm as she'd been taught. As it flew she threw herself to the ground, covering her head with her arms.

Despite the soldiers being fairly well dispersed, the weapon exploded neatly among them in a small clearing. Two fell silently as the noise echoed away. The third, the farthest from her, lay screaming. Searching among the debris from her bag, her hand clutched at the loaded pistol. Standing again and treading with care, she approached the fallen group. The nearest two appeared to be dead; one, she could see, appeared to have pieces missing. The third man lay a few yards beyond, still writhing and now muttering softly through a stream of blood emerging from his mouth. He looked at her as she fired point-blank.

"That's from Christian," she mouthed, as the whiff of cordite smoke cleared from the muzzle of the weapon. The pain in her left eye was growing and she searched among her belongings, still scattered around the base of the tree, for her small mirror. It lay in two pieces. Picking up the larger piece, she recalled a saying she'd once heard jokingly said in England: breaking a mirror would bring seven years' bad luck. Squinting in the grey light through her right eye, she could see that the left was inflamed and very bloodshot, and cut badly at its outer corner. Carefully spreading the upper and lower lids with one hand, she thought she could see what appeared to be bits of debris and spots of damage on the surface of the eye. It was too dark to make out anything clearly. With the corner of a handkerchief she gingerly tried picking off the loose bits, still holding her eyelids open, the mirror fragment now jammed into a convenient crack in the tree's rough bark.

The shouting was close. It was worried and German. The fourth member of the German patrol was now somewhere in the vicinity, no doubt drawn by the noise of the grenade explosion and her single shot to the head of the dying trooper. Stupidly, she realised, she had forgotten all about the fourth soldier. To make the situation worse she had ignored the three Schmeisser machine pistols where the three men had fallen. Forgetting her painful eye momentarily, Patricia sank down behind the solidity of a mature beech trunk, trying to gauge exactly where the last blundering soldier was. Now and again she could hear him crashing through the trees, occasionally shouting something.

His voice had a high pitch and while she knew little German and did not understand his cry it was obvious from its tone that he was becoming increasingly worried, on the verge of panic. Moving slightly sideways, she edged to her right, keeping low. Where was he? A few metres away lay the scattered group of three dead soldiers; easy to see from where she lay was one of their dull-grey weapons as it had fallen from the hands of the nearest man.

She would risk it. Sooner or later he was likely to come across the carnage she had sown on the wood's damp leafy floor. The pistol, now back in her bag, would barely counter the rapid stream of lead from the approaching soldier's machine-gun. Crawling rapidly and near-silently across the leaf-strewn surface, one eye closed, she reached the weapon in a few worrying seconds, pulling it towards her by its sling. She turned for cover.

The exclamation was loud from behind her; he had reached the bodies. Glancing back, she saw a pale face shadowed by an oversized helmet, the young soldier staring in startled disbelief at his three newly deceased colleagues lying in grotesque but relaxed heaps. Patricia rolled over to face him, bringing her weapon up to bear and pulling the trigger as she did so; there was no report. Seeing her movement, he jerked and instinctively fired, holding the gun out awkwardly in front of him. Invisible, the lead spurted across the earth and into the trunk of a tree, one round passing though Patricia's abdomen as it did so. She'd been hit, she was well aware, the impact had slammed her backwards but for the moment there was no pain. Working overtime and fuelled by a further powerful boost of adrenaline, her brain instinctively commanded a check of the weapon. The safety catch? Glancing down with her right eye she saw that it was down. 'Off?' she realised instantly. Just within her lower field of view she could see a dark stain spreading across her clothes. No pain, just an odd numbness. Holding the weapon with one hand, she pushed the catch up with her finger and squeezed the trigger again. It surprised her, the Schmeisser nearly jumping from her hand. Another short burst in her direction saw him stumbling forward towards her. More lead hit her, running up her chest, the last bullet smashing into the side of her neck; she rolled over from the impact.

Patricia's own brief and wildly aimed burst had delivered only a single bullet of value to her target. It struck the soldier hard to the left of his breastbone. He fell, dying quickly as he did so. She lay for a few moments as her body automatically carried out escalating and automatic shutdown of her vital organs. In her final few seconds of life her barely conscious mind confirmed it was her end; a small tear began to form in her right eye.

Much later that day, in the early evening, all five bodies were finally discovered. They were taken to a nearby barracks. The remains of the men were removed from the back of the truck with dignity and carried into the unit's sick quarters.

Patricia's near-naked, shattered and bloodied remains were thrown like a side of slaughtered meat onto the damp stone blockwork of the square outside the Commandant's HQ. The contents of her bag and case were inspected at length by the SS and Abwehr intelligence officers. It yielded some interesting information. A local undertaker was summoned to remove her violated body three days later from a rubbish pit behind the local Gestapo HQ.

❖ ❖ ❖

Michael Kelly been airborne for nearly three hours, circulating low over the ocean to the north-west of Ushant's thrusting headland, in the dark, waiting since eight-thirty. There had been no call from Curlew, no request for pick-up. He'd checked that he'd set the correct radio frequency on more than one occasion but there had been only intermittent bursts of static. He banked the Lysander around for the last time and headed north-east for England and their base in Sussex. Disappointed, he desperately wanted to help her home if possible. He mulled over thoughts as he flew low over parallel rows of white horses rushing headlong in the dark, the engine turning regularly and noisily in front of him. Hopefully, the novel prototype aircraft they had set out to steal had made it back to England in the hands of young Penrose, and Patricia and her small band of courageous French colleagues had escaped the wrath of the Germans.

He landed just after two-thirty; barely morning, he thought. After debriefing he made his way to the mess. Aside from one or two yawning pilots it was almost deserted; only a few lights were on in the dining room and the place reeked of tobacco smoke. Most of the squadron's drop-offs and pick-ups had been completed earlier that night; just one orderly was on duty ready to bring a very early breakfast to Kelly.

"Will you be having bacon and eggs, Sir?" the white-coated man said quietly as he approached the tired pilot slumped in front of a table and leaning sideways against the wall.

"Just bring me some tea and a bit of toast, please, Clarkson. I don't think I can cope with a cooked breakfast just at the moment." The clock on the far side of the room read three-fifteen; sipping the tea, he wondered what had happened. There should be some answers by mid-morning, he suspected. Leaving the toast untouched, he rose exhausted from the table and moved to the ante-room and slouched in a tall chair holding the half-empty cup while glancing at yesterday's newspaper. The arrival of squadron pilots for breakfast at seven awoke him.

❖ ❖ ❖

Endlessly the waves passed beneath Harold in the almost pitch-blackness. He still held a course that ran at a constant angle to the white, surging seas, hoping they would eventually lead him to the south coast, somewhere in Devon or possibly Cornwall. It was cold, the broken windscreen providing little protection from the rushing, damp air. Ahead there was nothing. It was not difficult to fly, provided his tiring brain reminded him that some controls and instruments operated in the opposite sense to English machines. The engine droned on comfortably.

He had just two immediate worries: how much fuel did he have left, and what damage had been inflicted on the underside of the machine, particularly the undercarriage, as he had left the three barns airfield? His mind wandered briefly to Claude and Maxime; what a courageous pair. He'd been comfortable in their company under the circumstances. Then there was Patricia, young, attractive, with heart of a lioness. They'd made love, quietly, gently and with no complications on that warm, sunny day in the sheltered meadow. Was she safe? He'd experienced the results of her work, just as he'd got airborne; it was wild shooting with the mortar.

There was something there, he was sure. He stared ahead. No. He'd been mistaken, wishful thinking. Turning, he looked about him in the darkness, then stared deliberately ahead again. Yes. Some distance ahead, just to the right of the aircraft's nose lay a thin, pale line. Studying it, he was convinced that it could only be breakers on a shoreline. Where, he wondered? Buoyed up, he watched as the pale line slowly grew in definition. He was nearly home. Just one problem remained – getting the machine down in one piece.

There were two coughs followed by a brief series of elongated splutters. The engine stopped. The fuel had finally gone. Pushing the stick forward, he encouraged the machine to glide. The wind whistled eerily over the vanes in the wings. Otherwise all was silent as he contemplated the unbroken rows of white horses below. The wind had got up, he realised. The few luminous cockpit instruments, now deprived of power, glowed feebly; he was able to make out the altimeter; it registered just under three hundred metres – barely a thousand feet.

The machine proved easy to fly with no engine to drive the long vanes in the wings. However, he could see that he wasn't going to make the shore; he guessed it was half a mile or so beyond him. Fortunately, the wind was helping to carry him towards it, and the rate of descent of the unusual aircraft seemed to be very gentle. The glowing altimeter showed that he had lost less than one hundred metres over the past few minutes. Despite the dark he was low enough now and could easily see individual waves as they rolled towards the distant beach.

"Bugger! No bloody Mae West," he muttered as he entered lower, more turbulent air. He then became aware that he was still not strapped into the machine, and swore loudly again. Although a good swimmer, he knew too well from past dinghy drills during summer days the difficulty of swimming in clothes, both with and without an inflatable lifejacket. It would be cold, too, he thought. Now down to a height where it was obvious that impact would be only a few seconds away, he gently banked the quietly gliding machine into the wind.

He was closer to the waves than he thought. Perhaps he'd lost more height than he'd meant to in the turn. He had barely levelled off again before he was into the sea. He misjudged it in the dark; the waves were much larger than he had anticipated from above. Pulling back the stick, he tried to jump the machine over the first roller. It gave a solid slap to the belly of the aircraft, tossing it back into the air. Uncontrolled, and without any appreciable airspeed, the aircraft fell off sideways into the path of the next one. Because he was unstrapped, the impact threw him from the cockpit. He landed into the wall of the following sea, plunging deep into its rolling, foaming core.

It was dark as he was bowled over and over by the wave. Making it finally to the surface, he had time to gasp once before the next moving mass was on him and he was thrust under its boiling surface amid thousands of briny bubbles. It occurred to him that he might actually drown.

EIGHT

Southern England had become an armed camp since the early spring. As they flew on collections and deliveries, Hamble's ATA pilots were able to see huge columns of trucks and tanks parked silent on narrow country roads beneath newly leafed trees, or moving slowly through villages heading towards the south coast and ports. Everyone knew the purpose; it was a question of time and place. In Hamble, almost next to the Yacht Club, the Americans had arrived and were building a new jetty and slip facilities to cope with invasion landing-craft and their machines and equipment destined at some point for somewhere in France. As the girls flew along the south coast and across the Solent they became increasingly amazed at the sheer volume of shipping of one sort or another crammed in there.

The evening of 5th June saw Ceci returned from the RAF airfield at Hullavington with other pilots. There, as at so many airfields they had delivered to, hundreds of aircraft and troop-carrying gliders sat waiting. Signing off for the day, they made their way down to their billets in Hamble village. The late-evening sun, after a gale-ridden day, was setting, gloriously golden, on the river as it ebbed quietly into the Solent.

But this evening it was different; the laughing and occasional repartee with American soldiers and sailors that had been so easily exchanged on previous evenings was gone. Walking down the narrow, curving high street approaching the river, they could see why. Slowly, heavily loaded boats and landing-craft were moving off down river to join the growing assembly of craft in the crowded Solent. Not one of the girls spoke. Standing quietly near the jetty, they watched the men watching them as the water opened up between them.

No one from Hamble ATA went to the Bugle that evening. Some sat watching into the dusk as the final remnants of what would later prove to be the world's largest-ever invasion armada left for duty. In Hamble, as elsewhere in the free world, thousands of silent prayers winged heavenwards from soldiers, airmen and naval crews hoping for the best – hoping to survive. Finally sleep arrived. The following day, Churchill announced to the Commons news of the successful landings; the BBC Home Service broke the story in Alvar Liddell's inimitable newsreading style. Allied forces had successfully made it ashore between Cherbourg and Caen; reports of further gains punctuated transmissions throughout the following days.

Later, in mid-July, there was a panic to cope with. Just one week after the Normandy landings the Germans sent their first Vergeltungwaffe, or V1 retaliation weapon, to England. Harriet gathered all available pilots together and explained the problem, sitting on the edge of the desk in the ops room. Attacks by V1s, or 'Doodlebugs', as they had been christened by one newspaper, were becoming an increasing menace. A key ATA invasion support airfield at Redhill had contrived to be directly under the route of many of the sinister unmanned weapons as, launched from sites in the Pas-de-Calais region, they buzzed across England's rolling southern countryside heading for London. The reason for the hastily called meeting soon became clear to Ceci and a half dozen other girls who stood around with cups of tea and an occasional jam tart. Harriet spoke up.

"Some of you already know that Redhill was designated a Support Unit for the invasion and some of you have been delivering aircraft there over the last month or so." She looked across at Ceci and smiled slightly.

"Well, in response to the V1s, the army has had to move a large number of its AA batteries down towards the south coast to try to shoot the buggers down before they reach London." She drew heavily on a cigarette. "Unfortunately our fighter boys have been hard-pushed, chasing these bloody things from the Channel and south coast, and have increasingly been straying across London's anti-aircraft sites with the risk of being shot down themselves. Where they have had their successes in downing the V1s, it has been too far inland from the coast and some have been landing on populated areas."

Catherine spoke up, "My sister lives near Redhill and told me that there have been a number of near misses from V1s. She's going to move back with our Mum near Hertford until it's sorted out." Harriet nodded agreement and breathed in deeply.

"Sorry, girls. Cancel any arrangements you've made for this weekend." There was a collective sigh. "We've got to help reposition the Redhill facilities to Bognor; we are responsible, along with White Waltham, for moving all of the 2nd Tactical Air Force's aircraft out of harm's way."

It started immediately; within twenty minutes the taxi Anson was waddling out to the grass runway with six fully kitted ferry pilots prepared to fly aircraft from Redhill to Bognor and other safer locations. Ceci and two more of the experienced pilots were given some of the twins to fly. As there were only a few machines in this category they were soon cleared and the focus of all pilots was on the single-engine fighters: Spitfires, Mustangs and Typhoons.

The Typhoon had gained a bit of a reputation with its innovative Sabre engine. There had been a number of engine failures and instances of complete tails coming off in dives, and girls allocated to their delivery kept very alert to any possible sign of trouble. Even as they waited for aircraft to become available, four V1s crossed the skies within a few miles of the airfield at Redhill.

Jacqueline, a tall, tough American girl, who'd gained her experience in the States flying at some stage in the 'Powder Puff Air Races', spoke of her fiancé, who was a pilot in No 11 Group, Fighter Command. His squadron had managed, after some fairly hairy experiments, to develop a dangerous new technique for despatching the evil buzz bombs. As the girls watched and listened she recounted how, after an attack by one of the new Meteor jets, they would make a dive on the pilotless V1, enabling them to reach its speed of about four hundred miles per hour. Then, approaching with care, they would manoeuvre their aircraft's wing until it was just ahead of the stubby wing that protruded from either side of the V1's rotund body. The turbulent airflow from their own wing would then upset the stability of the V1 and, as often as not, it would dive into the ground away from built-up areas.

"It sounds as if you've got to be very brave to get that close to one of those things at that speed," said one of the girls, gazing across the airfield at a Spitfire beginning its take-off run. The others nodded in agreement and began walking over to the ops room.

On the second afternoon Ceci and two other girls were ordered to take three Typhoons over to Holmsley South, near Bournemouth. They were needed across the Channel in the morning to help clear tanks from the path of the invading Allied armies. She had never failed to be amazed at the size of this particular aircraft, and knew what it was capable of doing. Sitting atop the huge machine, she began her cockpit checks, the other girls doing likewise scattered across the dispersal area. Everything appeared to be in order. She pumped the Kigass plungers to prime the engine and carburettor with neat fuel. Signalling to the ground crew, she pushed the button. The Sabre engine roared into life amid a cloud of delicate blue smoke. With pressures and temperatures reading OK she gave the thumbs-up to her two colleagues and began to taxi towards the runway. Ahead of her, below the instruments in the large panel, sat a bright-red handle, which would activate the emergency exit from the Typhoon. She recalled her pilot's notes saying it needed to be pulled hard.

A 'green' from the chequered caravan off to one side of the runway allowed her to move forward and line up with the sward of flattened green stretching away ahead, looking south-west. She made her final checks, her hands moving swiftly and expertly around the cockpit: blower to medium; boost plus seven; mixture rich; elevator trim three quarters forward; rudder trim full left. No need to use flaps on this long runway. As she opened the throttle slowly to 3,700 rpm, her right leg pushed firmly on the rudder to counter the enormous torque from the roaring engine ahead of her.

The Typhoon moved noisily down the runway and was quickly airborne, climbing at over 200 mph. In her headphones she

429

could hear the local controller giving instructions to an inbound aircraft. The radio was a novelty in some respects; past ATA flights were often conducted without radio but the number of aircraft operating post-invasion around the south coast made it essential for safety. Gaining height quickly, she throttled back to just over 2,600 rpm and at three thousand feet her speed steadied at 280 mph. It was only a short hop to Bournemouth over the South Downs and she was beginning to enjoy the trip.

As Redhill faded behind her tail, she was approaching Horsham and alerted by terse comments coming through her headphones advising all aircraft to danger. It became clear that a number of V1s were swooping in across the coast passing just to the west of Brighton as reported by the Observer Corps. Estimated height was three thousand feet. She glanced south, knowing that they were approaching her immediate area at high speed. Listening, she heard the local controller pass further information.

"Now south of Horsham speed estimated four hundred. Angels four, vector three five five."

They were very close and she looked carefully around the southern horizon hoping to see the evil pilotless bombs bent on destruction, possibly falling on some innocent school or shops. Visibility was hazy, providing no evidence of their approach. In any event her experience told her that closing at 400 mph would give her very little time to see them and act. Throttle fully forward, she climbed the aircraft steeply, hoping to avoid them by flying above their reported altitude of four thousand feet. Still climbing through five thousand feet, she glanced down; below, a lone Spitfire was streaking across the countryside in pursuit of a sinister grey shape. Ahead of them were small towns and villages dotted around the southern fringes of Greater London. Watching, willing the Spitfire to shoot it down in time, her eye suddenly caught sight of another V1 heading in roughly the same direction possibly one or two miles behind the Spitfire. It was alone, unremitting in its pursuit of destruction when its fuel finally ran out.

She made a decision. Pushing the stick hard over left and forward Ceci banged the boost control through the gate, urging the throttle beyond its limit. The Typhoon plunged earthwards, its speed building rapidly, the airspeed indicator showing over four hundred and increasing. Quick! Back on the boost, throttle slightly closed, still in a shallow dive, she could see her prey in plan form against the green fields and ancient woodland. Should she tell the controller what she was doing? No time for that, she thought. Ceci was making ground on it; the thing was now only five hundred yards away, rock-steady, still heading north. Pushing open the throttle again, she carefully closed on the weapon, wondering how she was actually going to deal with it. She wondered about Jacqueline's story about her fiancé: was it plausible? Could she tip it over with just the turbulence from her wing, or would she need to actually push its stubby wing upwards? Now at the same level and just behind, she realised she was losing it. She set boost again to maximum, urging the engine to give all its horses. She was alongside. It was barely fifty feet off to her right.

Co-ordinating stick and rudder, her heart in her mouth, she edged gently across towards it. On its side she could make out black-painted German markings; it was evil personified. It had picked up speed somehow and was pulling away. Ceci carefully opened the throttle again. 'OK, Jacqueline. Let's see if it works.' Level again, with it just off to her right, she edged gingerly across, manoeuvring just ahead of the V1's path with her starboard wing. The air had become more turbulent as they crossed the Downs and Ceci was having difficulty positioning her machine. Ahead the small dormitory towns were giving way to the fringes of South London. She needed to do something within the next few seconds.

A combination of concentrated, skilful flying and turbulence causing a slight change of course by the V1 meant that she suddenly found herself ideally positioned just to its left and very slightly ahead of it. Handling the throttle and boost control with extreme care, she allowed her starboard wing to fall back as her speed very slightly decreased. The V1 wobbled in the wake of her wing's disturbed airflow.

Suddenly it flipped. It was so quick that for an instant she didn't realise where it had gone. Banking slightly right, she watched as the grey shape plunged, still under power and out of control, straight into a small lake in an empty valley. There was a huge explosion. After twenty seconds or so, as she circled, still watching, the landscape settled again. The lake was a muddy brown; halfway up the valley side lay a large piece of something she was unable to identify from her height.

Levelling the Typhoon and heading again towards Bournemouth, now barely fifty miles south-west, she became aware that everything was not quite as it should be. The problem was that she could not quite identify what it was that seemed odd. Lifting her leather helmet and headphone off her left ear, she listened carefully. The rhythmic roar of the engine had a slightly sour note. Ceci glanced at the oil-pressure and temperature gauges; no sign of trouble there. Without warning the engine began an unsynchronised series of stutters and roars. She looked at the two magneto switches; they were both on. Pushing the stick forward to maintain airspeed, she thought about the problem. Perhaps one magneto had failed? Rapidly switching first one then the other Magneto switches on and off produced no change in the engine's health; in fact, she realised that it seemed to be in terminal decline; it was now running very roughly.

Before leaving Redhill she'd glanced at the separate notice that had accompanied her small book of ferry pilot's notes: it succinctly covered pilot handling for almost all the types she was likely to fly. The notice warned pilots of the problems that could result from running the Typhoon's Sabre engine at maximum power for prolonged periods. Chasing the V1 had stretched the engine and her, but it had only been for a few minutes. Closing the throttle, allowing the aircraft to glide at its best speed of just under 125 mph, she recalled the detail of the notice. Plug failure: the all-important spark to ignite the volatile air-and-fuel mixture within the engine's cylinders was provided by the banks of spark plugs, and they had been known to fail regularly under continuous high pressure.

A forced landing was her only option without power. Selecting some flap down, she glanced around the landscape below and thought she recognised the small town of Cranleigh off to her right. If it was, then Dunsfold airfield lay just to the west of its small tight community. Peering through the haze, she recognised the field, with its grass strip and clutch of hangars and Nissen huts lying nearby. Now with less than a thousand feet to play with, she kept the engine idling. It popped and banged away, expressing its unhappiness with matters, but she decided not to shut it down altogether. With little height to play with, she thought it might just have to play a part in getting her to the runway threshold regardless of its declining health. Ceci was conscious that the Typhoon was not an aircraft with which to try a belly landing; its huge cooling radiators were fed air by an enormous intake neatly faired into the underside of the engine cowlings. They were ideally placed to trip the aircraft up if an attempt was made to land with the undercarriage retracted. Operating instructions recommended baling out of an aircraft where the undercarriage could not be lowered.

Now lined up with the distant grass runway, she realised that she was going to need some help to reach its length; she was now far too low. She would also need to lower the undercarriage. But that would increase drag and slow the machine still further. As she gently pushed the throttle lever forward the Sabre responded with misfiring and heavy vibration but its propeller was delivering some erratic but welcome thrust. Now she was too low, the idea of baling out had been wiped from her mental options list. She would have to land it – ideally on its wheels. Watching the slowly growing airstrip ahead, she glanced down at the airspeed indicator. It read 95 mph. Stall speed, she'd recalled was seventy with flaps and undercarriage down. Reaching for the undercarriage lever, Ceci made carefully controlled movements with the stick and rudder, keeping the sick aircraft aligned with the widening grass strip. Down went the lever. There was a noise from somewhere in the aircraft below her.

Two red lights changed quickly to green and she breathed out.

The wheels had locked down safely. Clearing the hedge by a few feet, the Typhoon touched down at the very beginning of the welcoming grass. As it completed its landing roll she pulled the idle cut-off lever, depriving the engine of fuel. It stopped. She put the two magneto switches in the 'off' position and with the last of its forward energy she ruddered the machine clear of the runway onto mown grass to its left. As Ceci opened the hood and pulled her mask from her face the smell of cut grass flooded into the cockpit. Undoing her straps, she looked for a second at the red emergency lever at the bottom of the instrument panel. She hadn't had to resort to that, she was pleased to think. As she stood on the wing, looking about, another aircraft was on approach to land; it was another Typhoon. As it taxied past, she recognised the pilot; it was Priscilla Cornwall waving excitedly. The young, recently arrived New Zealand girl had seen the whole episode; she'd taken the second Typhoon from Redhill and had landed at Dunsfold to see if Ceci was OK.

Clomping through the grass across to the ops room in their heavy flying boots, the two of them chattered and manoeuvred their hands wildly, discussing recent events, excited. Dunsfold's station commander arrived as they were booking in and requesting transport for Ceci back to Redhill. Her Typhoon would not be going any further today. The Wing Commander heard the story from Priscilla; as it unfolded Ceci grew increasingly embarrassed and worried. What she had done was strictly against ATA orders and could have ended in complete disaster for her – and her actions could have resulted in the V1 landing in a town or village. The Wingco's comments were encouraging. He had no jurisdiction over Ceci as an ATA pilot, but expressed admiration for her courageous actions, tempered with some concerns over her lack of experience in knocking down V1s.

She needn't have worried. Her seniors all agreed that, while her actions had been impulsive and potentially dangerous, they had resulted in the destruction of a weapon capable of dumping almost two thousand pounds of explosive over London had it been allowed to exhaust its fuel supply. Ceci and her colleagues spent the remainder of the weekend collecting aircraft from Redhill, delivering them to Bognor. By late on Sunday evening they had managed to complete the task, most of them having collected and delivered six or seven machines each.

❖ ❖ ❖

It had been four days. Van der Beek had had a lot of time to think, about his situation in particular. He had been taken from his cell after breakfast. The same two officers: one army, one air force, met him in a small room in an annexe to the main house. The window was barred, and standing mute outside the door was an army private with a rifle. Van der Beek was greeted pleasantly enough and asked if he would like tea, then they sat opposite him over a small table.

"When we last met, van der Beek, I suggested that you think carefully about your situation," started the Major, smiling slightly. "I hope you've taken advantage of the past few days and are now prepared to tell us all about your relationships with the German military, in particular the two officers with whom you were consorting on the airfield in France when you were captured?"

He looked down at the table, saying nothing. Despite the time, he had still not managed to think matters through to a conclusion. He was torn between saving his life and divulging key information. There was a knock on the door. "Enter!" shouted the Major, some annoyance in his tone. With a loud clicking and clatter the door was noisily unlocked and an army private placed a plain metal tray with three cups of steaming tea in the sunlight on the table between them. As the door was relocked, the air force officer, taking his tea carefully from the tray, looked across at the Dutchman.

"Oh, come on, van der Beek! We have shown great restraint so far but we cannot let this situation continue much longer. I can always arrange for the Provost Marshall to charge you with spying, effectively treason, for which you will certainly hang."

Putting his cup down, van der Beek looked across at the two men.

"Very well, I will make a statement. What I have to say will surprise you. At the moment I cannot support my statement with any proof but everything I will tell you is true – at least, as far as I can discover."

The two British officers relaxed slightly, sitting back into the upright wooden chairs, one with pen and paper ready. Guy van der Beek took a sip from his tea and began.

"When the Germans invaded my country they had a list of people they wanted to capture. My father was on the list; he was a senior official in local government in Delft and a director of a porcelain factory just outside the town; my father's side of the family was also Jewish, his great grandparents, but we were not practising Jews. He was taken from his office one day in early 1941 by the SS. Despite my mother's pleas for information, and to be able to visit wherever he had been incarcerated; the bloody Boche would only say that he was alive and would stay that way providing my brother and I gave ourselves up."

"I was serving in our air force at the time, stationed at an airfield near Amsterdam when they overran the country. My brother I have not seen since early 1941. I don't know if he escaped the Germans or what. In the interests of my father and mother I gave myself up to the Germans wearing the remains of my Dutch air force uniform. Somehow they had known I was a pilot and over a few days interrogated me then explained a plan whereby I was to 'escape' to England and provide them with key intelligence information. I was to find a posting as a pilot with the English air force and pass information back to them via some Mosleyites who had escaped detection by the British authorities at the outbreak of war. In return, my father was to be kept alive in prison and my mother left in peace at home. If I did not co-operate they and other members of my extended family would be sent east to labour camps."

The Major pulled out a packet of Capstan cigarettes, offering one and a light to Guy and his air force colleague. The room was soon wreathed in smoke.

"Please go on."

Exhaling, he took up the story again.

"My family also has a strong French connection; one of my aunts married a man in the Haute Savoie, near Geneva, and I used to spend long summer holidays in the mountains there – it made a real change from flat Holland, I can tell you," he smiled slightly. "In the winter we sometimes spent Christmas in the mountains, skiing. As a result I became almost fluent in French; the Germans clearly saw this as a key asset and as became later apparent, a plan was forming in their minds. For a week I was taken into Germany, somewhere in Bavaria, I think, and taught to fly a special aircraft, you will know of it, no doubt: a Fieseler Storch." The two Englishmen nodded.

"In some respects it is similar in characteristics to the Lysander; but much lighter, short take-off and landing, very manoeuvrable, ideal for battlefield communications or clandestine activity. The Germans told me that if I wanted to see my father alive again and if I wanted my mother to remain free, I should have to co-operate fully with their scheme. Your own records show that I arrived in England at the end of 1941 by boat from Norway. The Germans knew of the clandestine fishing-boat traffic that was being undertaken from Norwegian fiords across to Scotland and arranged for me to be left at the railway station in Oslo. I was picked up by a local Quisling who, I believe, was operating within the Norwegian Resistance, and taken north beyond Bodo and found myself accepted by a local Resistance group as an escaped Dutch pilot looking for a way to England."

"The German plan worked perfectly. I was in Scotland within a few days after a terrible crossing in a barely seaworthy trawler, and was taken to London by overnight train, interrogated over a few days and my prepared story was believed. Eventually, after some time, when I suppose my story was being checked out, I was sent to a flying training school somewhere near Salisbury for assessment, where, I think, I was able to demonstrate my flying skills, and then I requested a posting to a Lysander unit. You should understand that the Boche are increasingly concerned at the activities of the Resistance in France and were looking for ways to capture and liquidate their sabotage and intelligence-gathering operations, which were heavily reliant on the support and training of agents in England. A posting to a Lysander unit was finally arranged – it was surprisingly easy – which turned out to be a special operations squadron, not an army co-operation unit; the fact that I spoke fluent French probably had some influence on matters."

He stopped speaking and looked across at the two officers; one was avidly writing notes trying to keep up.

"Please carry on, van der Beek. This is all most interesting, but, I suspect, not the whole story?" The air force officer looked quizzically across at him as he swallowed the dregs of his now-lukewarm tea; the army officer continued to write furiously, his tongue just protruding from his tight lips. Putting his cup down with a clatter onto the saucer, van der Beek mentally prepared to continue.

"I am not sure how much you know about SOE's operations. As a pilot in a special operations squadron I have some idea of the problems they face. Also, I know that while I was in Holland under German control they had managed to infiltrate most of the local Dutch Resistance units; many of the agents dropped into Holland were picked up as they landed or shortly afterwards. After interrogation, usually under torture, they were either shot or sent to labour camps. The Germans had developed matters to a point where they could transmit using captured agents' own radios using their identity codes and verification words, giving a completely false impression of an active agent – although I know that within the Dutch section of SOE there were doubts about the style of transmissions. The Germans could not quite reproduce the 'fist', the unique characteristics of an individual agent's keying, unless of course the agent was being forced to transmit under some duress. I am sure the Dutch section of SOE has real worries about this." He stopped, licking his dry lips. "I wonder if I may have some water? All this talking is making me rather dry."

The air force officer walked to the door and banged on it. Rattling keys announced its opening. He spoke to the guard outside.

"Can you get some water for the prisoner?" Nodding, the soldier closed the door and locked it, his footsteps disappearing down the long concrete hallway outside. The three of them took a break and van der Beek was allowed to walk about the room. He looked out of the barred window at the normality of the scene outside. The warm sun struck his face and he wondered at the chain of events that had brought him to this place.

◆ ◆ ◆

Thrashing in near-panic, Penrose swam upwards, kicking frantically, his face occasionally breaking the surface as each new wave rolled over him. He was tiring and had taken in a lot of water, coughing and choking as he reached the surface in the troughs of the relentless waves. Which way was the shore? He could see little during his brief spells at the surface. The next wave was approaching and he gasped a lungful of air in preparation for submerging again. In the half-light he could see that there was something rolling off the top of the crest and heading directly at him. He prayed it was a boat, out to rescue him.

The crest broke and its white surge enveloped him. As he struggled upwards his hand struck something solid and was somehow caught. As the thing rolled on, it pulled him along with it, still under the surface. Past, he surfaced again in the trough of the receding wave and looked about him, coughing and spluttering. His left hand was hurting; whatever had caught him was tightening, cutting into the flesh. Then as they rose together up the face of the approaching wave he saw what it was: one of the aircraft's wings floating, now securely and painfully attached to him by wires or cables, he couldn't see exactly what. Pulling with his left hand, he managed to get alongside it just as the new wave broke. The wing surged away, jerking him along by the hand in its wake. Again he pulled it towards him, the pain now excruciating; he knew that he was going to drown if he did not somehow get onto, and stay on, the detached wing. Raising his left hand from the surface for a moment, he saw that it was caught in a web of electrical wires and control cables, some cutting deeply into his flesh.

The water surged boisterously around him until he found himself momentarily alongside the broken wing, its rotating vanes offering an opportunity to catch hold of it securely. Awkwardly, lifting his leg, he jammed his foot in between the lightly constructed vanes, giving him some leverage with which to climb aboard. It took five more waves before hand and foot were securely jammed into gaps in the vanes. Finally he lay prone on the wing's surface totally exhausted and now very cold.

His frozen hand claw-like around the vanes, he tried raising his head. The wing lurched over as it was thrust forward on each successive crest. Fearful that the thing would turn turtle, he lay still, trying to spread his weight evenly as it gyrated through the surging breakers. The light was improving; he could make out the detail of each humping wave as it surged over and under him. He estimated he had been in the water about half an hour; the freezing cold was taking its toll. He could not feel his hands and was shivering uncontrollably. Atop a crest he chanced to lift his head, glancing in the direction of travel. Less than a hundred yards away lay the shore, rollers bursting heavily on sand and rocks. Even in the precursor to a grey dawn he could see a fine mist over the area.

❖ ❖ ❖

The chairs scraped the painted concrete floor as they resumed their positions either side of the small oak table with its dented and marked top; it reminded van der Beek a little of a desk he'd had in his bedroom at the top of his parent's house in Delft, before the Germans came. The sun had disappeared and the room took on an altogether different personality; quite grey and depressing, he thought. Across the table the two English officers looked at him expectantly.

"Let's carry on, shall we?" The Major spoke, relaxed in his chair, the air force officer sat, pen poised. Taking a breath, van der Beek prepared himself.

"After joining the special operations squadron, and after some additional training, I undertook a number of sorties dropping and collecting agents from western France. On my third sortie, to a field near Callac, I was handed a note by the head of the reception committee. The message, in code, told me that the Germans had infiltrated the local Resistance group and wanted me to leave information concerning future operations involving agents at a dead letter drop near to our forward airfield in Sussex." The air force officer sat up sharply.

"Where exactly is this letter drop?" Sipping the water momentarily, van der Beek answered.

"It was in a small hole in a stone wall that borders the road outside the Hare and Hounds pub in Petersfield. A telegraph pole sits in front of the hole; it's difficult to see but by casually leaning against the pole, which also serves as a bus stop, it is possible to place or take messages quite easily without raising suspicion." The air force officer wrote the information onto a separate piece of paper, then, summoning the guard, passed it to him for action elsewhere. Van der Beek watched.

"The drop's not been used for some time; I don't think you're going to find anything there now."

"So, you were asked to pass information about planned agent drops and collections to the Germans so that they could intercept agents and Resistance reception committees?" The Major spoke aggressively.

"That is correct," he looked at both men intensely, "but I never actually passed any useful information to the Germans." The two officers opposite looked at him slightly askance. "How could I pass information in time? The dead letter box was some way from our airfield and usually we did not get much prior notice of SOE sorties. It would not be possible for me to pass information to help the Germans. After some months they began threatening me, saying that they had invested a lot in me and that if I was unable to provide suitable information they may have to reconsider our agreement concerning my parents and extended family." The air force officer looked at his papers.

"Are you saying that you had nothing to do with the loss of the Hudson piloted by your squadron colleague Flight Lieutenant Ben Kendle or the Norwegian pilot Per Lindquist, together with their agents a few nights later and, indeed, any other squadron losses over the months since you joined the special operations unit?"

Van der Beek swallowed hard. "None of these unfortunate events had anything to do with me!" He was getting angry. The Major went on.

"But you must admit, it looks odd; you managed to gain admission to a squadron that specialises in clandestine operations and by your own admission you are briefed, under threat, by the Germans to provide information that will help them to capture our agents and crews? Do you know how many have been incarcerated, tortured and probably died as a result of your activities?" He stood suddenly, the chair falling backwards, his face twisted in frustration and anger.

"Let me make it quite clear to you two gentlemen," he spoke the last word with sarcasm, "I had not the opportunity to pass information to anybody. The interceptions you speak off were not as a result of my involvement! You have a mole operating within SOE somewhere."

"Fine, van der Beek. Sit down and keep calm. We're not going to get very far if you can't control yourself, are we?" Neither of the two Englishmen seemed perturbed at his outburst; numerous past interrogations had led them to expect this sort of reaction at some stage. They both knew that it was either a sign of real frustration, that their suspect was really quite innocent but unable to substantiate it. More often it was a verbal smokescreen to cover guilt and its approaching exposure.

"OK, van der Beek, can you explain what you were doing consorting with two German officers, on the ground, with one of His Majesty's aeroplanes in occupied France?"

Sarah sat waiting for news with Ceci. Bad weather had yet again delayed or curtailed aircraft deliveries.

"What an awful summer this has been, and I don't just mean the war; it seems it's been lousy weather for weeks now," grumbled Ceci. She'd got permission from Harriet to leave Hamble for the rest of the day. The two women sat over a tepid teapot on the table in Sarah's kitchen, wind and rain beating against the windows. Mr Homburg had been in touch with Daphne at Danesfield and indicated that the operation to steal the German aircraft had been undertaken the previous night. News was limited at this stage but Homburg believed that the experimental aircraft did get away and there had been a great deal of destruction at the airfield. A PR sortie had been requested to Benson, and they were waiting for the aircraft to return with its results. Daphne had passed the information to Sarah in her office immediately; Sarah felt something between joy and a sense of foreboding.

Taking a day's well-earned leave, she'd been on duty for seventeen days non-stop, working on average twelve or thirteen hours a day, almost without a break since the invasion. Often being forced to sleep in the basic accommodation at Danesfield, she'd returned home to an empty house. Michael was heavily involved in delivering agents and supplies to Resistance units helping to frustrate German attempts to counter the US Army's progress inland in western Normandy.

Work at Danesfield had been more than hectic. The invasion and then the need to keep a check on the enemy's retreat had meant so many late nights, some evolving into all night, sitting over endless photographs. The V1 threat and searches for their launch sites was also proving particularly difficult; the Germans were now using mobile launchers ahead of the Allied advance. Spotting them either in transit or actually set up for firing required a certain amount of luck.

❖ ❖ ❖

The cold had numbed Penrose's hands and arms to a point where he couldn't feel them at all; they were quite useless in helping him to stay aboard his impromptu life-raft. His body was increasingly convulsed in shivering, the cold Channel seas soaking him over and over again. As he approached the shelving shoreline the waves had become much steeper. Staring through salt-gummed eyes, he could barely make out steep land rising out of the sea. Trying to raise himself on the broken wing's slippery surface for a better view, he slithered off to one side. The entangled wires still caught around his hand dragged him painfully after the wing as, relieved of his weight, it began to surf down the face of each steepening wave.

Atop one large crest he looked shoreward, gasping and coughing. Now he was a few yards from a rocky beach that was enshrouded in mist and spray. Seconds later the tension around his hand slackened; ahead of him, as he rose upwards on the face of a plunging wave, he made out the wing ahead and below him, caught in the rocks. He prepared himself; it was going to hurt like hell. He was thrown forward over the wing by the crest and his hand was nearly torn from his arm until, suddenly, he was free with a terrific burst of pain, his shoulder aching, his arm useless. The next wave plucked him clear of the first set of smooth rocks, carrying him into the shore in a mass of foam and roaring. His knees hit something hard: more rocks. He pushed his legs out, hoping to resist further damage as he was thrust forwards. He tried to stand. There was solid land beneath his feet. He managed a few steps in the surf's undertow before collapsing again into the dragging water. Three times he stood, made a few staggering steps, then fell, all energy depleted and near to unconsciousness.

He could hear the shouting but was unable to comprehend, or see what was in store. The two Americans splashed gamely through the surf and rock pools, calling to each other until they were able to catch hold of his body as it slid to and fro in the foam. He was lifted, it seemed, all too easily, and wrapped in something that cut the wind's attack on his cooled body. They were talking all the time, strong voices, encouraging and swearing. Finally, when they laid him on the hard floor of a truck, he came to, staring up into the face of a young man wearing a foreign uniform and smiling down at him.

"Well, buddy, I guess we just got to you in time!" Penrose, looking up, tried to smile. It was feeble and he drifted back into welcome oblivion. The floor where he lay vibrated slightly as the truck moved off. One of the Americans held his head in his lap, the salt water soaking his uniform.

❖ ❖ ❖

The phone rang. Sarah jumped and the empty teapot rocked slightly on the table. Scraping her chair back across the tiled floor, she stood and ran into the hall where the black vibrating instrument rang on the hall-stand.

"Hello, Sarah Kelly speaking." Her husband's voice came mechanically through the heavy Bakelite earpiece.

"Darling, is Ceci with you? I've been in touch with Hamble and they say she's not there this afternoon." Sarah waved to attract Ceci's attention in the kitchen.

"Do you want to speak to her, Michael?" He coughed.

"No, no, it's just that I've picked up a bit of gen that might give her some hope, but be careful how you tell her. One of my pilots landed at Dunkeswell, near Exeter, early this morning; he was short of fuel, been a long way south, if you know what I mean. Well, while he was there having some breakfast, there was a bit of a flap; apparently someone had reported seeing pieces of wreckage in the sea as it was getting light, and what appeared to be a person hanging on to one bit. By the time they had got an aircraft up and flown to where the sighting had been reported, the wreckage and, presumably, the person, were already on the foreshore near Branscombe. The Americans have some army units there and are trying to reach the wreckage and person. The report said that the person, a pilot, appears to be alive." Sarah sat down suddenly.

"Do you think its Harold they've found?"

"It could be, Darling; I understand from our man there that there are no reports of any other aircraft in trouble or ditching in that area yesterday or overnight. And it would be the sort of area Harold would be likely to end up in if he'd left France heading north looking for the shortest sea crossing." Sarah, relieved, cautiously repeated Michael's side of the conversation for Ceci, worried at her possible response.

* * *

Van der Beek had not slept well. Throughout the night there had been noisy comings and goings as prisoners arrived or left the small, secure cellar below the suburban house at Ham;

doors were clanging, boots and voices ringing loudly in the narrow corridor outside. As he lay under a blanket, the sound of birdsong penetrated his cell through the small barred window in the ceiling, matched in intensity by the growing daylight. With no watch he guessed the time was around five or possibly a bit later. So much had happened over the past three years, much of it unfair to him, he thought. Today he was to be moved; he didn't know where. The interrogations had finally not gone well and he wondered if in fact he had a misplaced sense of loyalty to the others. He hoped at some point they would untangle the secure web that bound him.

He looked across at the door as the keys jangled in the lock and it swung open; a soldier with a rifle stood behind the RAF officer.

"Come, van der Beek; let's have one last chat before you are on your way; I've organised some breakfast for you and we can talk afterwards." Funny lot, the English, he thought. 'A chat,' as a euphemism for interrogation. Still, he'd been lucky. So far he'd not been beaten or tortured.

Upstairs the early sun filled the room where he had first met the two officers. On the large coffee table in front of the sofas sat a meal the like of which he had not seen since 1938. Bacon and eggs – two, he noted – and coffee, toast, a small pot of marmalade and a clean white napkin, all on a large tray with gilt handles; he blinked uncomprehendingly. The two military officers sat opposite him as he gazed at the spread before him.

"Please carry on, we've eaten already. Thought you might need a good breakfast before your journey. When you've finished you can have a shave and shower, and some clean clothes."

They're softening me up for something, he thought, as he broke open the yolk of the eggs, allowing bright yellow to flood over the bacon. As he ate, the army Major talked.

"We've been looking at the documents you attempted to pass on to the two German officers before you were intercepted. They make interesting reading once deciphered. What we've not been able to fathom is why you were passing, among other things, information on how to make a bomb. It does seem to be a rather special bomb. But the Germans are quite good at making bombs, I've always thought." Wiping his mouth with the snow-white napkin, van der Beek looked up from his plate.

"At the moment, Gentlemen, I cannot tell you. I don't know what was in the envelope. If, as you say, it required deciphering, how would I know what it said?" The air force officer put his pen down.

"I imagine that you have some idea of the content; there appear to be code names for quite a large group of people." He was writing again.

The Major took up the reins.

"We have been talking to the Luftwaffe officer brought back with you from France. It appears he was acting in some sort of liaison role with the Wehrmacht, also working directly with Karl-Heinrich von Stülpnagel, the Military Governor of France. That's a pretty senior post to have connections with, either directly or indirectly, you would surely agree?" Munching noisily on toast, van der Beek made no comment but raised his eyebrows in surprise. There was a mole in SOE, he was sure. If he or she got wind of his involvement – and they were likely to at some stage because of his direct links through the special operations

451

squadron – and the facts about Operation Valkyrie, the Germans would use all their efforts to catch the conspirators through their infiltration of various Resistance circuits. When he had finished his toast, he sensed that the two men opposite were reaching the limit of their patience. Thinking all the while, he reconsidered matters.

"Gentlemen, since joining special operations I have been working with not only the Germans and SOE but also a special section within SIS. I am actually a double agent – but surely you must already know this? When I arrived for interrogation in London from Norway, I was preceded by a message, unknown to me, from a member of the German Military Intelligence at Wilhelm Canaris's HQ; as you must be aware Canaris is head of German Military Intelligence. It was sent as a coded message to some fictitious German unit in the knowledge that it would be picked up by the British monitoring services at Bletchley Park. The message, I understand, was eventually deciphered at Bletchley Park and the content passed to SIS. During interrogation they allowed me to tell my story and gave the impression of believing it. A couple of days later I was called in for what I thought was to be a farewell meeting when I was confronted with the German signal and the facts." He stood and walked around the room, the eyes of the two Englishmen watching him closely.

"With my family under threat from the Germans unless I delivered, I was caught. What could I do? Despite what I said the other day; I was given information by SIS to pass to the Germans via the dead letter drop. I passed three messages only, well, actually, I did not deliver them and I am unaware of their contents; an SIS agent delivered them." There was a loud knock on the door. The air force officer tutted and, rising from his comfortable chair, walked across the room and opened the door.

"Mornin', Sir. We've come for the prisoner van der Beek. I understand he's wiv you?" A huge military policeman stood outside accompanied by two more burly white-hatted individuals. The door was pulled to, the air force man tugging it closed from outside. Van der Beek sat again, his face white, his breathing slightly faster.

"Don't worry, old man, your story is too intriguing to let you go at this stage." The Major smiled with his mouth across at van der Beek; his eyes were cold. After a few minutes the squadron leader came in again, closing the door.

"Seems they're keen to take you away, van der Beek. I've managed to put them off for a couple of hours. With luck, after that they won't need to take you away. Please go on."

Now for the first time he had a firm deadline on his future.

"Well, the SIS man told me a few things I did not know; for example, they had long suspected that there was a plot to kill Hitler and thus bring this bloody war to an end. There was, he said, a theory in British Intelligence circles that the plot had originated in German Military Intelligence, headed by Admiral Canaris. They think the blind signal sent about me probably came from there. The SIS agent also explained that there had, they think, been a number of plots to kill Hitler. One plot for which they had some first-hand intelligence involved Major-General Helmuth Stieff. Apparently Stieff was a frequent visitor to Hitler's Wolf's Lair at Rastenberg in East Prussia. Two bombs were fitted into two large brandy bottles and sent to Stieff by Baron von Tresckow, another plotter. The intention was they could be positioned near to where Hitler spent time, and exploded, killing him. Apparently they failed to go off. SIS also mentioned that there was some evidence of other failed plots, both by the military and civilians. It was becoming increasingly difficult to kill Hitler because his security was closely guarded."

The dam had burst; he'd told them enough now to continue with the full story. It took four and a half hours and at the end the two Englishmen knew it all.

As their final report made clear, suspicion and fear had made plotting and making suitable bombs to kill Hitler a potentially lethal pastime. As a double agent, van der Beek was keeping to his side of the bargain by providing, through a third party, some information to the Germans. Some was real, maintaining his credibility; some was pure, but plausible, imagination. SIS set about sending messages through the ether that would eventually, they hoped, connect with the party that had sent van der Beek's introductory message. After some weeks there was a short response.

Over a weekend pass Guy van der Beek had earlier spent some time in a small house in Kent with a group of SIS people. In the course of a normal delivery of Joes, he was to include a brief touchdown at an agreed site to collect or deliver intelligence, in particular a set of codes to be used by SIS and the German plotters in future communications. It transpired, halfway through the lengthy report, that the German conspirators wanted the English to manufacture a special type of bomb that could be included somewhere in one of Hitler's cars. It was to be made in such a way that it would be detonated remotely by short-wave radio. Over a number of seemingly innocent special-operations sorties, van der Beek had made contact with a Luftwaffe officer, landing at the formerly secret site not far from Rouen collecting and delivering ideas for suitable bombs. On the fateful night when he'd been caught by the Resistance and Paul Mossman, the Luftwaffe officer who was also captured was his prime contact. The Gestapo officer had somehow got wind of a proposed enemy agent drop and invited himself along with the Luftwaffe officer, intending to capture the agents and their Resistance reception committee.

The latter had no real choice other than to allow the Gestapo man to accompany him and to hope that he could bluff out the situation. As he had said under interrogation after being brought to England, he would have killed the Gestapo Major if there had been a problem and, with luck, would have escaped in the Lysander with van der Beek to England. The unanticipated involvement of the Resistance had thrown his plans awry, resulting in the death of the Gestapo Major, the capture of the Luftwaffe officer, and forcible repatriation of Guy van der Beek under highly suspicious circumstances. However, the issue of the bomb remained.

❖ ❖ ❖

Boffins at the National Physical Laboratory at Teddington in south-west London had managed to perfect a suitably shaped charge that could be incorporated into the bodywork of Hitler's favourite Mercedes; into the door panel, next to where he normally sat. It appeared that this was not crucial; the power of the special explosive would have left very little of the Mercedes or its occupants when it went off. The report concluded that with the Luftwaffe officer now in England, bringing the bomb's introduction to fruition would be difficult. Finally, the Luftwaffe officer volunteered to go back to France with the bomb, try to make contact with other conspirators and place the weapon in Hitler's Mercedes. Initially SIS thought this a bad idea but with the Allies still some way from conquering Germany the matter was reconsidered; it might save many lives. The whole plan was kept secret from SOE for fear of a suspected mole.

Not waiting for a moonlit night, both in the interests of killing Hitler sooner and not giving fifth columnists any time to act, the Luftwaffe officer was returned to France by parachute near to where he'd been captured. Accompanying him was a small container with the bomb and the radio detonating device. No one would be there to meet him. Again they had considered contacting the Resistance for help. They'd dropped the idea once problems surrounding the possibility of a mole inside the French section of SOE or the local Resistance circuit were fully considered.

Dressed again in his Luftwaffe uniform, under a protective jump-suit, he was helped into the Stirling bomber. The bomb, simply disguised as a gift parcel tied up with string, was attached on a lanyard to his parachute harness. They would leave the aircraft together.

The engines were run up and the large black bomber turned carefully onto the runway. Only half a dozen smoking goose-neck flares lit the full extent of its six thousand feet. The throttles were opened and the machine lumbered down the tarmac. In the near-darkness witnesses saw its tail rise until eventually it was clawing up into the night sky, engines growling. Turning over the airfield, its opaque black shape could occasionally be seen against the paler night canopy as it gained height, heading south.

It was a brilliant eruption: white and red, as one observer described it. Climbing momentarily and glowing instantly brilliant in the night sky, it hovered for a moment then plunged; a split second later a secondary explosion lit the countryside brilliantly. From the airfield, large fragments of the stricken bomber could be seen gaining speed as they hurtled earthwards. Somewhere, a couple of miles away, another huge explosion launched boiling flame and smoke into the blackness. They stood, stunned, unbelieving; what on earth had happened? A German night fighter making a lucky strike? No, as they stood quietly absorbing the instant tragedy there was no sound of any other aircraft making a hasty retreat from the area. Back in the operations room few words were spoken as they stood about white-faced sipping tea. Kelly spoke.

"I don't understand it." He looked across at the Flight Sergeant responsible for preparing the aircraft.

"Was she carrying any bombs, Chiefy?" His voice was husky.

"None, Sir; only ammunition for the guns."

"What on earth could have caused it?" Kelly muttered, to no one in particular.

"She was unladen, Sir, only delivering the Joe and his parcel. Ammunition wouldn't have caused two such massive explosions." The Flight Sergeant sat down, spilling his tea as he did so. He looked across at Kelly, mopping tea off the desk.

"The only thing on board we had nothing to do with, Sir, was the ... er... Joe's bloody parcel."

Michael Kelly's eyes widened in disbelief.

❖ ❖ ❖

Ceci had borrowed Hamble's Magister and flown it down to Dunkeswell. Visibility was not brilliant. A young navigator from the Coastal Command squadron based there gave her a lift to the hospital in Exeter. Nervous, not knowing what to expect, she followed the matron into a darkened private room. A figure lay sleeping, gently snoring in one of two beds there. His hands lay composed on the neatly turned-down sheets pulled tight across his chest; the left was heavily bandaged, his right in plaster up his forearm. Here and there on his face small plasters were stuck. Smiling, the matron pointed to a chair and then quietly left, closing the door. Ceci looked at Harold fast asleep, his hair smelling of brine as she hovered over his face, placing a kiss on his forehead.

He licked his lips and smiled slightly.

"What are you doing attacking a helpless man?"

Looking up at her, he saw Ceci on the verge of tears.

"Come on, Darling, I need smiles, not tears; its all OK. The Doc says I'll be out of here tomorrow and ready for a spot of leave. Only some damage to my hands and wrists; everything else works." She laughed through her tears, looking down at him.

"You'd better be keeping your mind on getting better, not on other activities!" Despite that, she couldn't wait to hold him again, lying together, loving.

❖ ❖ ❖

The German retreat across northern France, the Allied break-out from around Caen and the subsequent murderous slaughter of escaping German armour and troops by RAF Typhoons through the tightening Falaise Gap meant that the special operations squadron had to fly further and further afield to accomplish anything worthwhile. Michael had been up to the Air Ministry in London to discuss the squadron's possible detachment to the Far East as part of an effort to cause greater behind-the-lines disruption to Japanese forces.

It transpired that during the course of discussions that he and his squadron were selected partly on the basis of his pre-war experience of flying in the region with Empress Airways operating the large 'C' Class flying boats. Although the Germans were moving further east towards the Rhine, Michael thought that there was still some useful work that his squadron could do in Europe. The AOC thought otherwise and intimated that they may find themselves heading east in the spring. Michael was unimpressed.

◆ ◆ ◆

By the spring of 1945 the ATA had long been delivering aircraft onto the continent. At Hamble, Harriet had few problems in finding volunteers to take machines to various airfields around Paris and Brussels; one of the biggest problems, however, was avoiding the Customs authorities when they got back to England with their contraband perfume, stockings and food. Ceci flew a Maryland bomber over to a US unit supporting the advance and was staggered to see the damage in the wake of the German retreat. Caen from the air reminded her of black-and-white pictures she'd seen of the Great War battlefields; total devastation with only bits of buildings standing amid roads deep in rubble and smashed trees.

Harold recovered from his injuries and returned to Benson and his PR squadron after two weeks' leave, some spent with Ceci. There was a lot of work still to be done taking pictures of the depleted German war machine moving inexorably eastwards, still able to give its pursuers a bloody nose from time to time. After the December Ardennes offensive – Hitler's surprise Christmas gift to the Americans – Harold, like the rest of the country, saw only defeat for the Wehrmacht . His photos were interpreted and brought the Typhoons from their base at Holmsley South into attack on long columns of trucks and tanks that quickly became shorter as the days wore on. He and his fellow PR pilots had also spent time capturing images of the proposed Rhine crossing points and the disposition of defenders. It was on one of these missions that he caught a fleeting glance of the new German jet fighter; the Me 262. Despite its superior speed, he had an overwhelming advantage of height on that occasion and managed to escape; his encounter a few years earlier with the Fw 190s was still fresh in his memory as he pushed the throttle to the firewall, turning north-west. During March he was gazetted as having been awarded the DFC and promoted to Flight Lieutenant with acting rank of Squadron Leader. The whole squadron celebrated, but not in the wild fashion seen in the early days of the war. However, there were a number of sore heads the next morning in offices and at aircraft dispersals.

By April the Russians were in the eastern and southern suburbs of Berlin; the newspapers were anticipating the end with pictures of troops marching through broken towns and villages, boy-like Hitler youth soldiers standing forlorn and thin in large barbed-wire cages, most with tearstains down pale, dusty faces. For Michael Kelly the European war was as good as over; their special operations sorties were few and far between now; their only role now seemed to be to carry senior officers to meetings in free

Europe. Only a week before, Sarah had broken the news to him over a quiet weekend with the children at home in Hampshire. She was expecting a child, her third, his first with Sarah. They joked about the miracle; the past four years had proved both tiring and stressful, poor conditions for lovemaking and babies. The only stain on their immediate future was the Japanese war; still taking lives, with the possibility that Michael's squadron would be posted east, entrusted with providing a service to the Allied intelligence services banging on the doors of the Japanese homeland.

For Hamble the news came suddenly: the ATA was to be wound up. The number of highly trained but now under-utilised pilots in the RAF and Fleet Air Arm meant that they could now undertake the job of collecting and delivering aircraft from factories scattered throughout England to squadrons still engaging the enemy. There were tears and a number of parties at Hamble, White Waltham and at all of the other ATA units scattered cross the country.

'Hitler Dead,' screamed the headlines in bold, large-point capitals. It was almost over but not quite. In northern Germany, in the town of Flensberg, the remnants of Hitler's senior acolytes tried to maintain an illusion of a continuation of the Third Reich. The farce was ended as they were captured by British troops and incarcerated until the Allies decided how they were to be dealt with in a democratic fashion.

Two days before the war in Europe was ended on 8th May, acting Squadron Leader Harold Penrose reported to the Ministry of War. Little was said in the signal sent to his station commander at Benson; just that this officer was to report at 10.00 hours. In the months after his involvement with the small German experimental machine, and his crucial part in its capture and regrettable loss, he had heard virtually nothing from the authorities. Now he suspected he might be about to learn something.

A cool spring day with patchy sunshine flooding the busy streets of London saw him turn into the large, still part-sandbagged doorway. He was met by an elderly civil servant, who swiftly accompanied him up three flights of stairs and along a series of long, wide corridors with occasional bright stripes of sunlight escaping from the part-open doors of adjacent rooms. Finally, the elderly man stopped and gently knocked on a large oak door at the very end of a corridor. There was a sharp "Enter!" above a hubbub of sound. The man turned the knurled brass handle opening the door and standing back, allowed Penrose to enter. The room was bathed in mid-morning sunlight and he had some difficulty seeing. A long table at the far end of a very large room was surrounded by a group of uniformed and civilian men and a single uniformed woman.

"Good morning, Squadron Leader Penrose. Thank you so much for coming. Can I arrange for some tea or coffee?" Taking off his hat, he moved towards a vacant upright chair between two civilians, who stood, smiling, facilitating his sitting between them.

"Thank you, Sir. Coffee would be fine." He looked about him. One or two faces he recognised from his meetings with SOE and SIS months ago. As he looked around the table he found Daphne grinning across encouragingly at him. She had a softer look about her: tired, but there was something new about her. The voice addressed him again.

"Well, as you can see, we've gathered a few people together, some you've met before; we think that perhaps we owe you an explanation after all of your efforts!"

He looked down the table to where a senior RAF officer with lots of 'scrambled egg' on the peaked hat in front of him was addressing him. He nodded, acknowledging the smiling Group Captain Hawkins.

"I imagine you are referring to the experimental German aircraft, Sir?" The officer stood, he was actually an Air Commodore.

"You are absolutely correct, Squadron Leader. I know you have received promotion and decoration for your brave... should I say, heroic capture of the aircraft, but I bet you are interested to learn what has happened since you were dragged, wet and cold, from the Channel by those two Yanks?" Harold nodded appreciatively.

As if on cue a thin man, dressed untidily, stood up. Harold recognised him as one of the boffins from his visit to the government's research facilities at Teddington during his brief visit before returning to France.

"Well, Squadron Leader, Despite your unfortunate and, if I may say so, untimely, ditching in the sea we managed to recover most of the machine and have spent the past months repairing and reassembling it at Boscombe Down." Harold knew of the place, in Wiltshire, and its reputation for testing and research of new aircraft. "But so far nobody has flown the reconstructed machine, although we have spent a great deal of time calculating its probable performance. You are the only one on this side of the Channel who has actually flown it and we should first of all like you to confirm our theoretical calculations from your experiences. Secondly," there was a pause, "we should like you to fly the machine again; to test and demonstrate it." The cup hit the saucer noisily. He looked around the table warily.

"But I thought that Boscombe had a number of test pilots who surely are better qualified to undertake this work?" The Air Commodore interrupted.

"It's true, Penrose, but you have had first-hand experience of flying the machine under very difficult conditions; also we want to keep this particular evaluation close to our chests. There are others who would be very interested in the unique capabilities of this aircraft, should its performance be confirmed. As Allied troops have moved forward into Germany they have been followed by specialists looking for secret and advanced German technology in a wide variety of fields: electronics, radio, rocketry and, of course, jet engines and aircraft. But nothing has surfaced so far that mentions this unique aircraft. The aircraft you managed to abscond with so brilliantly has huge military and post-war commercial potential. For the moment we should like to keep it to ourselves; I'm sure you understand." The tone of the last statement, he knew, gave him no other choice.

The remainder of the day was spent discussing the findings of the research boffins and looking at large photographs of the repaired and reconstructed machine. After a delicious lunch somewhere in the bowels of the building, the discussion resumed. Daphne gave an intelligence appraisal with someone from SIS. It appeared that no trace of the aircraft, or possible successors, had been found at any other site in Germany so far. It was too early to say that the secret site near Callac in north-western France was the only development location but it was looking increasingly likely. Daphne showed aerial pictures of the site after the attack by Typhoons and the small Resistance group. The pictures had been taken from relatively low level, two days later, and showed clearly that very little remained. All three of the original barns hangars were destroyed utterly. Here and there burnt-out vehicles lay scattered, along with a particular site of devastation: the fuel dump, pointed out Daphne.

Wrapping things up late in the afternoon, the Air Commodore assumed a more sombre tone.

"Our friends in the Resistance have, since the liberation of France, been able to fill in lots of detail about operations such as Azzaro. Regrettably there is some bad news. Penrose ... some of the people who were instrumental in aiding your escape have regrettably not survived the war. The man known to you as Claude unfortunately succumbed eventually to terrible injuries sustained while at the airfield, despite the care and attention of Madame Charon and a very brave doctor from Dinant. The young lady responsible for organising the show and code-named 'Curlew', and I believe known to you as Patricia, also lost her life. The circumstances of her death are unclear but we have reason to believe that she was evading capture and went down fighting; a truly remarkable young woman." A large lump formed in Harold's throat. "But there is some good news: the man Maxime escaped German detection and gave inestimable help to Allied forces after the invasion last year. He has, I believe, been suitably honoured by General de Gaulle and we will do likewise."

The meeting broke up and Harold left, having agreed to report to Boscombe Down on the Monday of the following week. He left the building with Daphne, walking out into the dusk of a dying

April day. They spoke little as they walked until eventually they found themselves on a park bench in St James's Park. Harold sat for a moment with his head in his hands. Daphne noticed he was shaking. When she turned towards him it was evident he was actually crying. Putting her hand on his arm, she tried to comfort him, to understand.

"Daphne, sorry, please ... leave me." Her hand remained. The stress and strain of war had been capped by his learning of the loss of Claude and the beautiful, wonderful Patricia. Standing slowly, he walked, head down, towards a clump of trees, out of sight of any passers-by. It would not do for an RAF officer to be seen sobbing in public. She followed at a distance, biting her lip, guarding, as he finally broke down in silence and out of sight. She hoped it would be therapeutic.

The following Monday he arrived at Boscombe Down with his kit, ready to begin testing. The RAF policeman asked him to wait in a small waiting room in the guard room. Twenty minutes went by, then suddenly a young man whom he recognised one of the scientists he'd met previously, entered the room, wide eyed and out of breath.

"Squadron Leader, I'm so sorry to keep you waiting. There has been an unfortunate disaster." Penrose, instantly worried, looked at the pale face with spectacles. Leaving his kit in the care of the guard room, he walked quickly with the young man through the administrative area towards the airfield and hangars. The smell assailed his nostrils, pungent and acrid. As he turned around the corner of one large camouflaged hangar the source was evident. In front lay the remains of a substantial building, pieces of its steel frame sticking up here and there. In the centre of the smoking mass lay piles of flaky grey ash and large lumps of blackened metal that he knew to be aircraft engines. Around one side of the destruction, a group of civilian and RAF men stood looking bleakly at the hot mess. He saluted as the Air Commodore approached, his shoes and trousers covered with fine ash.

"Bloody disaster, Penrose, as you can see. Don't know how it started yet. Everything has gone; the Azzaro aircraft and others, drawings, photos, calculations, the whole dammed shebang; brought here ready for the testing programme. Nothing left! All that effort and risk for nought."

It transpired that the hangar had been well ablaze inside when discovered at just after two o'clock that morning. The RAF fire service did their best but with the blaze well established it was all they could do to prevent it causing further outbreaks elsewhere. Later in the day, Harold walked down to the remains of the hangar again. Standing in the warm mass were some of the scientists poking about looking for anything that might be salvageable. From talking to one of them Harold established that there was nothing worth having. The offices in the hangar had disappeared. Inside them had been the valuable notes of studies of the aircraft, along with other priceless documentation. They'd been foolish: assembling all the information in one place with no copies lodged somewhere else, as was the norm. It seemed that the Azzaro project had ceased to exist.

"We were in such a bloody hurry ... failed to take proper precautions." The Air Commodore turned on his heel and left, shocked and disappointed.

Leaving Boscombe the following morning, intending to drive

down to Hamble, he thought he recognised a bearded figure, a part-familiar face, walking across the road from station HQ towards the airfield. As he drove off, he pondered who he had seen; the man was vaguely familiar.

Hamble airfield was deserted except for two training aircraft sitting abandoned and a little forlorn on the grass outside the operations room. Inside, the retiring CO, Harriet, was clearing up paperwork with two orderlies. Ceci was nowhere to be seen. After a quick cup of tea and a chat he left and drove down into the village to the house Ceci had shared with Wendy and another girl. They were sitting outside on a wall watching the river; Ceci squealed as he came into view. They enjoyed a fairly liquid lunch at the Bugle, and as they were leaving, the penny dropped. Harold thought it must be that Dutch pilot, van der Something, he'd met at a do at Michael's squadron. Couldn't be, though, he reasoned; he knew that the man had been arrested after being captured in France over some doubtful dealings with the Germans. It was forgotten as they walked together down to the river.

As the celebrations of VE Day dwindled into history, people looked forward to building a life without strife despite the fact that rationing still affected most things. Michael Kelly's squadron was preparing to ship out to the Far East, their final destination not yet disclosed. Paul Mossman also was not enamoured of the idea of going to fight another war on the other side of the world, and was considering resigning his commission and returning to Canada with Daphne. Matters were taken out of their hands. The two atomic-bomb explosions over Nagasaki and Hiroshima brought the war to a conclusion. The posting east was cancelled.

Early September saw a double wedding at the small thirteenth-century church in Longparish. Both brides were dressed in mountains of white, while their husbands looked elegant in their RAF best blues with all medals and regalia. Michael Kelly acted as Best Man for Harold Penrose, and David Rawlinson acted for Paul Mossman. The brides, Cecilia Miriam Grosvenor-Ffoulkes and Daphne Elizabeth Maltravers were given away by their respective fathers, who despite terrible privations had survived as prisoners of war, one a guest in Changi jail, Singapore, one as a guest of the Germans in various Stalags. Helen, soon to be reunited with her father, acted as Matron of Honour, with young Alistair as a rather wayward pageboy. Other girls from Ceci's now-disbanded ATA group acted as bridesmaids; they were stunning but none more so than Beth, Sarah's daughter.

The redoubtable housekeeper and nanny, Pauline, had scrounged a mountain of food and alcohol with the help of George Hudson. Dozens of friends and relations attended a wonderful informal reception at the Kellys' home, scattered throughout the house and garden.

Towards late evening Michael, Sarah, Ceci, with her new husband Harold, together with Daphne and Paul Mossman were all gathered in the garden watching a fiery red sun slowly decline into a deep pink haze; it had been a beautiful autumn day, flocks of midges still swarming under the trees. Looking around, Michael thought back over the last few intense years. He had survived, unlike too many, but what were they all going to do now, he wondered.

Emerging from the house with his arm around Helen, George Hudson read his mind.

"What now, Michael?" He remarked pointedly. Kelly was

tempted to be flippant and respond how he would sleep for six weeks, but he didn't.

"I think there's going to be a lot of opportunities in air transport now this lot is over."

"Yes, I think you're probably right," someone murmured.

The last limb of the sun finally sank.

Azzaro's Innovative Aircraft

As far as anyone knows, Azzaro, the 16th century student of Leonardo da Vinci is fictional. His detailed drawings of an aircraft akin to modern day machines unearthed during refurbishment of an ancient building in the walled Italian city of Lucca must also be fiction. However, the novel propulsion and aerofoil lift concept outlined in the story is not a fiction.

Experiments have and are being undertaken using ideas for a horizontal fan embedded along the leading edge of wings in both scale and full size aircraft.

The rotating fan, driven by an engine positioned somewhere within the aircraft fuselage, sucks in air along the wing's leading edge then pushes it up and over the top of the wing.

Importantly, in doing so, it greatly increases the lift generated by the wing by keeping the airflow attached to the wing's top surface – essential if maximum lift is to be generated. Some of the experiments undertaken demonstrate the effectiveness of the fan wing in being able to produce very high coefficients of lift at very slow forward speeds, with no fear of stalling resulting from a loss of lift. Such an arrangement has the potential to enable very short take offs and landings with heavy loads in full size aircraft.

It's important to understand that most fan wing experimental aircraft have no other form of propulsion such as a propeller to pull, or jet to push it through the air. They rely entirely for the aircraft's forward movement upon the rotating fan in the wing.

As the fictional Azzaro story suggests, the Nazis were keen to develop the fan wing concept using small, single seat models for testing the concept, as observed by Harold Penrose - and subsequently captured by him. British Intelligence were fearful that once satisfactory trials of the concept were completed, the machine would be further developed through to a full size aircraft capable of delivering many troops and materiel to the battle front, or, in an invasion scenario, into city parks and playing fields or other open spaces within important urban environments.

Fortunately, in real life, the Germans were not aware of the fan wing's potential in this respect; although they were very innovative in some areas of aeronautics.

But, the biggest problem for Azzaro and his design would have been the total lack of a reciprocating or jet engine of any sort to power the fan - nor suitable materials from which to build an engine for his aircraft.

More recently much research work has been undertaken by NASA scientists and notably, an American: Patrick Peebles – building and testing scale models working with Imperial College in London. His practical research clearly demonstrates the functionality and feasibility of the FanWing concept in scale form.

If you have an enquiring mind: try entering 'FanWing' on an internet search engine for further information.

If you have enjoyed Azzaro you may like to continue following the lives of some of its key characters through the challenges and dangers they face in resurrecting the pre-war Empress Airways in post-war England in Part Three of the Trilogy:

'Dividend'

By way of an 'appetiser' Chapter One follows.

ONE

Late January 1946, barely eight months since a relieved and exhausted Britain had celebrated victory in Europe. Squadron Leader Michael Kelly champed at the bit. Most of his colleagues had readily embraced demob and moved on to civilian life. Some were gainfully employed, others gently idling after six years of boredom interspersed with adrenaline rushes and bursts of bowel-loosening fear.

He read the letter in front of him for the umpteenth time. Dated just over a month ago, it lay creased and lightly tea-ringed between the butter dish and a crumb-strewn plate on the well-scrubbed kitchen table. It was headed with the familiar crest of a department within the Air Ministry and announced forthcoming aircraft sales.

Facing austerity, the Royal Air Force had begun an enforced equipment diet following necessary gluttony during the recent world conflict. The extensive list of aircraft made interesting reading: large four-engine transports including war-weary Avro Lancaster bombers and a clutch of Lancastrians, their civilianised sisters, alongside elderly Halifax bombers, a mixed bunch of twin-engine machines including Avro Ansons and American Hudsons: all for sale at ludicrous prices. It was to be hoped, he thought, that Great Britain's taxpayers were not party to the ridiculous deals completed at government aircraft disposals. On some of the aircraft listed he had gained worthwhile experience during highly risky transatlantic deliveries in 1940 and later when commanding a special duties squadron clandestinely flying agents, known as

'Joes', and their vital supplies into and out of occupied France. Standing behind him, Sarah squeezed his shoulder.

"Don't worry, darling. You're bound to be listed before long – most of the others have gone." He glanced up, smiling grimly at Sarah his wife as she nimbly picked up the breakfast debris from around him.

"Yes, I know," there was frustration in his tone, "but in the meantime all these damn aircraft are being snapped up at bargain prices by chaps like me aiming to make a living out of flying. It's my final dividend, after the war. Meanwhile, I'm stuck, looking after a virtually non-operational unit trying to look busy. Haven't flown now for nearly five weeks; going to lose my flying pay if I don't do some soon!"

Frustrated, he banged his hand hard on the table as she reached down and carefully pecked him on the cheek, slipping her arm around his shoulder. Outside, the weather was grey, damp and bone-chillingly cold. As he rose from his chair to do his wife's bidding – collecting logs from the shed – his prosthetic lower right leg bumped noisily against the table leg. Logs delivered, he prepared to leave their comfortable redbrick farmhouse home in Hampshire to motor north beyond Bicester, in Oxfordshire, to a bleak airfield that, for the moment at least, was his place of work and responsibility. It was not a pleasant journey in the tired, rag-topped, American jeep he had managed to acquire after their recent allies had left for home and, no doubt, warmer climes.

The airfield was shrouded in freezing fog. It was an English winter cliché with little prospect of a change over the remaining few days of January. Since the disbandment of the Air Transport Auxiliary – ATA, in Service jargon – he and a few other RAF pilots had now taken responsibility for ferrying aircraft around RAF stations and civilian maintenance units in the UK and near continent. Apart from one or two lifers they were all awaiting demobilisation and shared, to a greater or lesser extent, his frustration at the state of limbo they were in.

Occasional aircraft delivery trips brightened their bored existence; a pre-Christmas trip flying low over a Germany covered in deep snow showed the scale of recent destruction inflicted on its cities: stark, dark, almost gothic shapes, standing erect against dirty whiteness under lifeless leaden skies. He felt a brief pang of sympathy for the innocents living there, hungry, cold and unsure of their future; their erstwhile nation and its capital divided uneasily between four victorious but quarrelling allies. Stories continued to reach the newspapers of ongoing Russian atrocities and the hardships being suffered by Germany's defeated refugee population.

He had more than once pondered returning to his native Perth in Western Australia but eventually dismissed the idea: Sarah would find herself a fish out of water in the relatively unsophisticated life there. And it was also a long way from anywhere, despite growing air-transport links. They'd heard only the week before from Paul Mossman and his new bride, Daphne, since returning to Canada's western coast, way north of Vancouver. He was apparently flying again, well into the swing of being a bush pilot operating over Canada's beautiful raw muskeg and lake-strewn landscapes. Reading between the lines, however, Sarah thought Daphne was probably at a loose end after the hectic times she had spent working as a WAAF with the RAF photographic interpretation unit at what had become the legendary Danesfield House, in deepest Buckinghamshire. Their unexpected letter had brought back past feelings of unspoken comradeship and the trust that Michael and Paul had shared during their time in 1940, ferrying much-needed aircraft from frantic American aircraft factories across the wild winter Atlantic to needy British Bomber and Coastal Command squadrons – taking the war to the Nazis in the only way possible in those early desperate years after Dunkirk.

Eyes glazed, peering out of the frost-patterned office window, he recalled stories of Paul's later photo-reconnaissance trips; one in particular, a skilful low-level sortie over Brittany, in north-western France, capturing images that would lead eventually to the stealing by Harold Penrose of a top secret German aircraft, aided by the local Resistance. It had also led, regrettably, to the death of their ex-nanny Patricia, latterly a Resistance leader. The mission had ultimately proved of no avail.

Sarah, Michael's wife and the mother of three children, remained irregularly in touch with her friends Helen and Cecilia. Helen had left the Air Transport Auxiliary and her piloting activities when the ATA had been disbanded in early 1945. Later, she had made the long and difficult trip to Bologna in northern Italy across shattered, refugee-strewn Europe to look after her ageing father after his release from prison.

He had immediately returned to academic life and his continuing research and lecturing on Leonardo da Vinci's work, as a professor at the city's university. His time in captivity in a Milan jail had been the result of outspoken and poorly timed anti-fascist sentiments and had taken a heavy toll on his frail health. At 64 he was barely able to cope with the desperate treatment handed out by his perverted captors in cold and damp conditions

– with food fit only for his few pigs – they no doubt stolen by now by black marketeers during his incarceration. Helen spent most of her time ensuring that he ate as well as possible, and generally looked after him and his rambling, ancient house. She had hoped to continue her flying in some capacity after her wide and valuable experience in the ATA but her father took precedence – and just about all of her time.

Cecilia Penrose, or Ceci, as she was always known to friends and colleagues alike, also craved the challenge and excitement of flying again after the ATA's disbandment; her attempts to obtain work as a professional pilot were rebuffed by the growing number of new airline employers. It seemed that her extensive wartime aircraft delivery experience on something like twenty different types of machines from fast and manoeuvrable single-engine fighters through to heavy four-engine bombers counted for naught in a market now flooded with similarly craving ex-service male pilots.

But she had at least managed to fly a few ad hoc charters, operating an elderly and oil-streaked ex-air-force troop-carrying Douglas Dakota, the American DC3. It still carried the fading black and white stripes and vestiges of a glider hook from its involvement in the historic D-Day landings; now it was lifting food, medicines and other essentials to various airfields scattered across and around the fringes of Europe. Her return trips were usually at the limit of the sturdy machine's capability, loaded to capacity with all sorts of hard-to-obtain luxury goods that were only ever dreamed of in monochrome, rationed Britain. Where it had all been procured in a devastated Europe she never discovered – and felt it best that she didn't know.

On a few occasions she benefited from her almost clandestine flights; occasional gifts of wine, perfume, aromatic cheeses, nylons and silk underwear, much to the envy of her girl friends; cigarettes and cigars too, and, on one occasion, a beautiful dark fur stole. In the back of her mind she suspected that some of these trips were only a cover for black-market operations undertaken by men and women who were aptly described by a deprived British post-war populace as spivs. But landing the heavily, sometimes overly, laden twin-engine machine at night on poorly lit and frequently rough grass airfields led to her reconsidering her involvement. Her pilot husband, Harold Penrose, still serving as an RAF officer, would be horrified if he knew what she was actually undertaking in her determination to continue flying – through legally dubious sorties.

❖ ❖ ❖

Given the option, and based on his past record, Harold had decided to remain in the service after VE day; he was now learning to fly the RAF's new twin-jet fighter, the latest marque of Gloster Meteor, at a jet conversion unit in the West Country. Now a substantive Flight Lieutenant, a step backwards from his wartime rank of acting Squadron Leader, he was enjoying life in the peacetime air force, especially since being selected to join one of the early courses to convert to the new aviation paradigm. The only cloud on his horizon was the likelihood of his new squadron eventually being posted to Germany as part of the RAF's Second Tactical Air Force: Churchill's oft-quoted 'Iron Curtain' had now descended in the East; behind it lay a totalitarian regime, a future threat to Allied democracy.

Only now, since the peace had been declared, some eight

months earlier, had he been permitted by his CO to fly at the weekend to a small airfield near to where he had spent time with the French Resistance after a bale-out from his wrecked PR Spitfire, and the location of his later crucial involvement in stealing a new and unique German aircraft in a SOE-sponsored operation code-named 'Azzaro'.

Very early on that winter weekend morning, across a slumbering English Channel, Harold landed, chilled and stiff, at a field that had seen heavy but brief service as one of many advanced landing grounds after the Allies' D-Day invasion of Normandy. Now, apart from a couple of wrecks, it was empty of aircraft. Just two or three French military personnel stood around, smoking, drinking endless cups of very strong coffee and occasionally rough red wine direct from large unlabelled green bottles.

Beside the temporary landing strip a farmer was ploughing frozen soil making ready for sowing in the coming spring. Two dark and leaning horses moved determinedly parallel to earlier furrows, gouts of warm vapour pouring from flared nostrils as they dragged the silver blades powerfully through dark brittle earth. Walking from his draughty light aircraft, a borrowed Auster communications machine, he made his way towards a clutch of wooden buildings on the far side of the field; to Harold it felt a little unreal. Back on French soil, there was for him a strong sense of déjà vu.

Something, an odd, almost uncomfortable feeling, descended on him. He was increasingly reminded that some of his Resistance carers and helpers had not survived the recent conflict, including brave Patricia and the stalwart middle-aged man known only as Claude. Harold was strongly aware that he needed, as his CO had said, to lay ghosts from the past, to give some meaning to what had happened – and to pay his heartfelt respects to those he had admired and loved, now gone. It was for him an essential, cathartic exercise.

The French soldiers eventually arranged for a local taxi to give him a lift to the small town of Callac, pressing Calvados and more and more of the strong, bitter coffee on him while he waited – then, finally, saluting, laughing and smoking as the car stuttered away trailing clouds of blue fumes in the still, freezing air.

In RAF uniform, he walked Callac's cold, narrow streets, recognising some of the shops and houses, dropping eventually into a small estaminet for warmth and sustenance. Following a welcome cognac he decided that, as the weather was dry and getting brighter, he would walk the few kilometres beyond the town to the field that they had used for many of their dark, clandestine landings.

◆ ◆ ◆

The local boulanger picked him up as he strode purposefully out of town, giving him a ride some of the way in an ancient, rattling van; its rear doors secured closed with string. The old man, lean and unshaven, chattered away with shrugs and nods, the rich smell of newly baked baguettes and clouds of Gaulloise-smoke filling Harold's nostrils.

As the van drew noisily away he looked slowly and deliberately about; it was still, quiet, just a few birds chirping excitedly in bare hedgerows. Although it had sometimes been easy to recognise on a moonlit night from 800 feet, he experienced a few moments' difficulty in locating their impromptu landing strip from ground level. Then instantly the puzzle clicked into place. He knew where he was – the road, river and single rail track ran parallel for a short distance heading roughly south-south-west; ideal landmarks viewed from above but less obvious from his current earthly perspective.

Climbing awkwardly over the remains of a rusted wire fence and moving carefully over undulating ground alongside a wide, naked hedge running towards what he believed was his field, he was full of a strange anticipation. Now and again rays of weak sunshine shone fitfully between clouds across the brittle, frost-embalmed grass; he sensed his feet getting wetter as he walked towards the far hedge.

There it was. Stark. Empty. He had only ever seen it in pale moonlight or near-darkness, tense and alert, the engine of his Lysander turning, ready. He stood quietly, amazed, looking across the hedge at the narrow, almost flat strip of frozen grass where he and colleagues had delivered and collected Joes on those desperate nights. Walking farther beside the hedgerow, he saw inquisitive small birds flitting in and out of its sparse cover, clearly surprised at human invasion. He came eventually to a wooden gate sagging half-open, green moss well established on its top rail. Cold wet feet forgotten, he stepped into the field.

Yes, this was it. He relaxed slightly. This was where it had all taken place.

Something took him. Closing his eyes he sent up an impromptu prayer for those involved in his survival, and for those who did not finally see France's relief from the cruelty and depravity of German occupation. Walking the length of the hard frosty ground, he pondered again those adrenalin-filled moments, wondering how he had ever found the courage to do what he, squadron colleagues and heroic Joes had undertaken. Could he, would he, do it again, he wondered? He sincerely hoped that he would never be presented with an opportunity to find out.

When he emerged, some twenty minutes later, boots soaked, back onto the narrow road, a chill wind had sprung up from the north-east as he made his way, a little uncomfortably, back towards the town.

It passed him at some speed. Fifty metres on, it screeched suddenly to a halt then reversed dangerously fast towards him in a series of violent, seemingly uncontrolled swerves. In a moment of self-preservation he stepped back quickly off the road onto the raised unkempt verge, pressing back into the sharp naked bushes, half expecting to be run down by the black Citroën.

The returning sense of déjà-vu was almost palpable – a black Citroën – an identical model: Traction Avant? It flashed illogically across his mind; could it possibly be Maxime, or even Claude? Bending, he looked across to the driver seated on the left. A young man sat grinning across at him; the ubiquitous black beret perched jauntily above a smiling, unshaven face completed with a black moustache, cigarette dangling lazily from the corner of his mouth.

"M'sieur, bonjour...où allez-vous?" It wasn't Maxime or Claude. He knew too well that the latter was dead – and quite possibly the former.

"À Callac, s'il vous plait," his raw French emerging from a momentarily distracted mind. Perhaps it was his uniform, but they were soon sharing wartime experiences in broken Franglais, and moving far too fast for safety along the thin road's broken surface towards Callac.

484

Later, he managed to reach Madame Charon at her small farm, north, near the Baie de Morlaix at Terenez, using an ancient, wildly clicking telephone on a café bar – its bored customers feigning indifference at his shouted conversation in a mangled version of their language of diplomats. She almost broke down as he announced himself, and the fact that he was in France, hoping to see her that very day.

Forty minutes later he was collected by her still-emaciated, unshaven brother, then lurching dangerously fast over deeply rutted roads towards the coast in a battered Renault with a cracked windscreen; there was a hole in the floor through which the torn surface metalling could be seen whipping past. His driver, François Charon, had been forcibly taken by the Germans in 1943 and sent to Germany on a labour program with the Todt Organisation. Surviving, unlike so many of his compatriots, he had made his way finally through the chaos and confusion of post-war Europe, back to western France, walking, occasionally getting a lift on trucks or clinging, hidden and frozen, to any train heading generally in the right direction. Madame Charon's husband, Noel, had not returned but they had not given up hope yet.

The tall, wide kitchen with its large window occupying almost one wall was just as he had remembered from that tense afternoon when he had left with Claude, Maxime and Patricia, prepared to steal a secret prototype aircraft from under the very eyes of the damn Boche, who were believed at the time to be actively preparing for its large-scale development. It was to be a vital new weapon, potentially able to turn the tables on the invading Allies when they came. Crackling noisily in the huge grate, a log fire burned invitingly, radiating its yellow-and-red heat right across a room composed mainly of shades of brown and cream; behind him the old clock still clung to the wall, ticking loudly. Piled at one end of the dark, heavy table lay an untidy mound of old newspapers and discarded opened envelopes – just as they had always been. The resident tabby lay across the pile, paws in the air, eyes firmly shut, emitting a just-audible purr of contentment.

Madame Charon, unsure which emotion took precedence, stood smiling and crying, her large arms around him. He patted her ample back affectionately, emotion welling up in him, but he retained control. Her two boys, still boisterous, fell through the door, unprepared to see the RAF officer smothered by their mother. As recognition dawned, their faces broke into broad smiles that were followed by a stream of laughter and high-pitched French chatter. The table was soon full of Calvados, red wine, cheese, fresh bread, shellfish from the Baie de Morlaix and other local delicacies quickly assembled from the cool, cavernous pantry.

Barely half an hour later Maxime arrived, with a roar and screeching of near-naked tyres and well-worn brakes, having been alerted earlier by Madame Charon to Harold's surprise visit. As they stood facing each other there were moistened eyes from the true pleasure and relief of meeting again. As the small company enjoyed each other uninhibited by the fearful constraints of the past, an image was burned indelibly onto Harold's memory: happy faces, laughter and relief. By mid-afternoon, with the pale light beginning to fail, they stood silently in the small churchyard where Patricia and Claude now lay, finally. Beside each other: two heroes who had given their ultimate gift.

It was here that Harold finally lost control. Standing by the gate, the others turned away as he walked alone beyond the naked frost-stricken trees to grieve, shoulders hunched, sobbing silently, intense physical pain in his breast and throat. Alone, hidden, he made no effort to contain his emotions. The cathartic tears ran fast. It was near dusk before they finally got back to the now-empty airfield, soldiers long gone, wisps of blue wood smoke drifting gently from the embers of their fire.

Airborne, banking gently and looking down, he could see the five of them, faces upturned, a single handkerchief waving. Waggling its small wings, setting course northwards, he headed the draughty Auster out across the Channel, still calm, its dark stillness broken occasionally by the splaying wake of a vessel, luminous white in the growing gloom. It had been a day like very few others he had experienced; full of emotion, harsh, sometimes tearing – physically painful in his chest and throat, and at his heart. There were welling tears as he peered ahead through the light aircraft's dirty windscreen; the flash of St Catherine's, perched exposed on the southernmost point of Wight pointing his way home.

❖ ❖ ❖

By the next weekend the weather had changed; the high-pressure ridge that had sponsored the grey blanket above and penetrating fog below had finally skulked off to the continent, allowing a resumption of fresh low-pressure weather cells to rush ragged and pell-mell across Britain. Broken sun and rain resumed with a welcome slight rise in temperature.

Michael Kelly stood sheltering with his delivery crew of two under the wings of the Lancaster bomber while a new curtain of rain swept over the exposed airfield. They hadn't completed their external checks. The rain poured off the trailing edges of the aircraft's span in a near-constant glassy sheet. It eased finally and they walked purposefully around the puddled dispersal checking, pulling and touching key elements of the machine's structure and controls.

Clattering up the short metal ladder, all three boarded and the door swung shut with a tinny slam and was locked. Kelly had always enjoyed the smell of an aeroplane. The pungent odour of high-octane fuel, the unique smell of metal richly tainted with hydraulic oil and, no doubt, the sweat of past, sometimes-fearful crews was to him so evocative of aviation, past and present. Sitting in its left-hand seat, he looked about him. This was a worn machine, and one that had seen service on many occasions over the Reich, that was for sure. How many of the young pilots and crews she had safely carried on those fearful nights had finally survived to reach Churchill's promised 'sunlit uplands', he wondered.

Out of his mental meanderings, he whirled a finger at the ground crew; he and his flight engineer started each of the Merlins in order from port inner to starboard outer. Each start brought a brief cloud of thick white smoke before the engine settled down to a regular beat. Oil pressures and temps: OK; flying controls free and operating in the correct sense; waving chocks away, he released the brakes. Exiting the circular concrete dispersal, the tired Lancaster trundled slowly forward and around to the left, a burst of throttle on the right side aiding the old girl's arthritic response to sharp movement.

Encased in its huge wheels, brakes squealed in anguish at

each application as they followed the taxiway around the field to where the tarmac runway sat, solid and straight for nearly six thousand feet – struck black across faded winter green. Lumbering, it almost seemed that she didn't want to go, perhaps somehow knowing her fate. It was going to be her final trip in her real element. Having been sold for scrap, she was scheduled for uncaring dismemberment at a maintenance unit in South Wales – to be cut to pieces with an acetylene torch, saw and axe by men who would know little and care less of those nights lit with fire and fear.

Completing his vital actions – magnetos, trim and flying control checks – Kelly lined up with tail wheel straight, waiting for a green. It flashed.

"OK, boys, ready? Here we go."

As he edged the throttles forward the four Rolls-Royce Merlins spoke the unmistakably powerful language of almost eight thousand rampant horses; adjusting the throttles, Michael applied right rudder to counter the enormous torque from their grabbing propellers as she slowly gathered pace down the damp black tarmac. Empty, and finally at 90 miles per hour, she lifted surprisingly easily, as her mood changed, pleased to be climbing into a cloud-speckled sky. At nine thousand feet he levelled her off, allowing their speed to settle at one hundred and forty. Michael synchronised the four engines, and despite her obvious age, the Lancaster flew comfortably and sedately across the countryside, her crew chatting occasionally over the intercom while watching scattered towns and villages speed past below.

"Hope we get fed when we get there. I missed breakfast," flight engineer Tom Goodge's metallic voice came through their headphones as he checked the rows of fuel and engine-oil temperature and pressure gauges on his panel set behind the sometime co-pilot's position. The others responded with unsubtle and expletive-riddled comments, the general gist being about laziness and getting up early. As the flight progressed, desultory conversation turned to past experiences over a brew of stewed, lukewarm tea from their Thermos flasks, as they stood gathered around the pilot. Tom had served two and a half operational tours – nearly seventy-five trips – on Lancasters; the last stint with a crack Pathfinder squadron; he was full of lurid tales at the briefest of prompting.

"On one trip to the Big City – Berlin – we had problems gaining height even at full power: ice. Our skipper, he's gone now, God bless 'im – lost somewhere over the Ruhr, Bochum, I think – used a technique where part-lowering the flaps 15 or 20 degrees, quickly, while in the cruise, could lift you a couple of hundred feet. He tried it and it worked, and after two or three goes we finally managed to get above a freezing layer of cloud, just by that simple technique. Saved our skins!"

Michael, now a little bored with trundling sedately over England, thought it might be valuable to gain some experience in the technique; it could come in useful at some time.

"Yeah, heard about that, Tom – never actually tried it though. Let's give it a go!"

Looking about the sky, he automatically checked the aircraft trim and engine instruments, his hand moving across the instrument panel towards the flap lever. As he flipped it part-down, the wide, powerful flaps emerged symmetrically from the trailing edge of each huge wing. They all felt the upsurge through their backsides as the Lancaster responded, seeming to lift them vertically. Laughing to himself, he selected flaps 'UP' and the aircraft settled back into level flight about a hundred feet or so higher.

"Again, chaps?"

Laughing acknowledgment came from the other two through his headphones. The flap lever was flipped down again. She began to lift as before, they felt her rising pressure through their seats.

She lurched sickeningly over to her left, side-slipping violently earthwards.

Kelly was taken totally by surprise.

Applying full right aileron, he tried countering the leftward roll.

It continued, regardless.

Almost inverted, he was struggling.

Time was running out

The nose pointing earthwards.

Still with opposite aileron applied, the big machine was gyrating.

Throttles were at idle.

His mind racing.

Why was she not responding to his control inputs?

Built for punishment, Lancasters had had to perform desperate corkscrew manoeuvres instigated by skilled young pilots, motivated by survival: the need to avoid a focused German night fighter. But this machine was in danger of taking a final and catastrophic liberty with her elderly airframe.

Michael suddenly became aware of heavy and frustrated

breathing through his headphones; one of them was trying to speak through the plunging, rotating chaos.

Now, she was pointing beyond the vertical, still rolling around, rushing headlong towards lush farmland on either side the River Severn barely a mile below.

He later laughingly recalled that his life did not pass instantly before him as he struggled to effect some measure of control over the stricken aircraft. But the Lancaster continued mindlessly, no matter what obvious action he took, their height evaporating in parts of a second.

They'd have to abandon her. The altimeter was unwinding with horrifying rapidity, the numbers a blur; now through four thousand feet. As he opened his mouth to give the order, rasping words burst through his earphones.

"Flaaaapsupp...eeeechhhhh."

Later it emerged that Tom Goodge had managed to utter those two crucial sounds while trying to hold on to some part of the aircraft's interior aiming to stop himself being thrown about – he had not been strapped in but standing at Kelly's right shoulder in the cockpit. Something had parted company in the starboard wing's flap system. The huge landing flaps on that side of the plunging machine had suddenly slammed up, closed. Still fully extended on the aircraft's port side, they were acting as an enormous airbrake causing the machine to roll uncontrollably leftwards. No opposite application of the machine's smaller ailerons could counter the grand turning moment it induced. In just a split-second he reached out; difficult against combined, powerful g-forces created by the machine's increasing rotation rate, pitched downwards.

Holding his breath with the effort, the panel-mounted black metal lever slipped up as his fingertips managed to touch its end. Suddenly he felt a measure of control; the ailerons were reacting and the complaining Lancaster responded. There were audible crunching noises from somewhere behind him. They were still plummeting earthwards, but now the right way up, emerging, part-controlled, out of their near-vertical dive. Years of experience prevented him from pulling back rapidly on the column in an effort to kill its headlong momentum. Had he been tempted, the huge wings and their engines would probably have parted company with the rest of the machine as they found themselves unable to cope with massive aerodynamic forces.

His voice came over the intercom half an octave higher.

"Power!"

Tom Goodge was back on his feet behind him, the left side of his face covered in blood. Reaching, he pushed all four levers smoothly forward as his pilot centred the control column. The Merlins, resuscitated with fuel, roared. They flew. Kelly glanced – the altimeter read less than five hundred feet. Glancing down through the transparent panel to his left for a second, he saw a small hamlet. In the cluster of rooftops, narrow, wet roads and gardens, one or two faces were upturned, watching, frozen. A dog sat scratching, unconcerned.

Climbing up over the undulating Welsh borderlands, they took stock. At four thousand feet Michael Kelly allowed himself a breath. Looking round behind him briefly, he saw radio operator George Kerry applying a bandage to Tom's badly cut head; he had been thrown bodily about the tumbling aircraft when she had taken her first plunging turn.

With no flaps to assist in retarding them, their landing was faster than normal; she floated endlessly on a cushion of air above the runway without the benefit of their slowing effect until he managed to get her down and to stop before St Athan's long, rubber-scarred runway petered out. Walking around afterwards, they and the RAF station's engineering officer looked at the distorted and torn remains of her flaps, hanging buckled and disjointed beneath the starboard wing, their utility destroyed. Their nearness to disintegrating oblivion was spelt out vividly by the rippled and twisted skin on the upper wing surfaces, and by dozens of missing rivets in the Lancaster's rear fuselage. Standing behind her, looking forward, there was a pronounced twist along the Lancaster's long, sturdy body; other ripples were clearly evident down her flanks.

"I think she was not happy about us messing with her, Skipper, particularly as she probably knew this was her last trip. Lack of respect for an elderly lady."

The other two crewmembers glanced up from squinting along the machine's long, inclined spine at the radio operator, ruefully nodding agreement, then relieved smiles on their faces. They were given a lift home later in the day, after a brief incident inquiry, in a venerable Anson twin flying just a few hundred feet above quickly darkening countryside. Kelly silently thanked God that they had not been at this altitude when he had started messing about so disrespectfully; he recalled the old adage drummed in to him by his instructors years earlier: 'There are old pilots and there are bold pilots, but there are no old, bold pilots.' There would have been no time to react at this height, he was well aware. They would have plunged into the earth in seconds for no apparent reason. A black, smoking hole in the earth, scattered around with torn bits of aircraft – and their body parts. He shivered. How would Sarah and the children have received the news?